TO CLAIM A MATE

POPPY IRELAND

Alexei

Magic rippled through the air where the portal once was. A scream tore through my throat as I reached out with shaky fingers, praying that somehow my eyes were deceiving me. That my fated mate wasn't just ripped away from earth and dragged into another dimension. My worry for Nicole and the agony I felt drowned out the sound of fighting in the distance. Growling wolves and snarling vampires battled all around the forest, but I was too stunned to move.

What happened to her? Why was she so out of it? I had so many questions and didn't even know where to begin. Obviously, it wasn't safe to stay here, but how would Juniper and Cammie possibly think that Faerie was the best option? I knew that was where they went; there was no mistaking the shimmery green signature a portal to Faerie gave off. Many cautionary tales had been told to shifter children everywhere, warning them to stay away from the allure of one. Sure, Cammie was fae royalty and all, but practically every creature in that realm had bloodlust. Even the plants were out to kill.

"Alexei!" Corbin yelled. His voice was like an echo, and I had to weed through my fears to hear him. "We have to leave!"

He tugged on my arm and I snarled at him, not wanting to be dragged away out of some misplaced hope that Nicole would return.

I reached for the clearing again, watching my mate disappear before my eyes on a loop.

"Alexei!" Corbin yanked harder. "FUCK!"

The anguish in his tone knocked me out of my daze. As I turned toward my best friend, the panic was clear in his expression. Understandable, considering we were under attack, but when he lunged forward and started shifting in midair, I knew something else was going on. I looked up and saw what had made Corbin so terrified. General Minifred was on the ground in his human form, fighting off a giant gray wolf. He was naked and covered in dirt, so I assumed he had shifted at some point. What I didn't understand was why he wasn't still in his wolf form. The only thing that made sense was that he was hurt badly enough that he needed to accelerate his healing. The only way a shifter could do that was in their human shell.

The wolf's claws tore into the general's left eye and ripped it out of its socket. With a scream that made his attacker's ears go flat, General Minifred turned his face toward the sky as his wound gaped open and spewed blood. The eyeball went rolling across the ground, the attached nerves and muscles reminding me of a comet streaking through the sky. The wolf howled victoriously, tearing at his victim's body with sharp teeth, ripping away chunks of flesh with wild abandon, filling the air with snarls and the coppery smell of fresh blood. I glanced quickly in the direction Nicole had disappeared before sprinting toward the battle. I pushed myself to run faster, heaving for breath with every step.

Corbin rushed to the wolf attacking his mate's father as I bounded toward another one coming from the side. I composed myself, called my animal to the surface, and lunged at the second attacker with bared teeth. My rage was deep-seated as I bit into the wolf without hesitation. The metallic taste of its blood trickled down my throat and increased my passion for destruction.

A yelp echoed in my ears, and I turned away from the now dying shifter to follow the sound. My beta had wounds along his body that appeared to hinder his breathing, and he was pinned by his attacker. I thundered toward my target, plowing into his abdomen with precision and tearing out its entrails in the process. In a pool of blood, his mangled body slumped to the side, no longer posing a problem for us.

My best friend barked, warning me of an oncoming attack. I barely blinked before a crazed wolf with a white coat almost identical to my own slammed into my flank, causing us both to roll, grappling for the advantage. My fangs made contact with his shoulder, staining his fur a deep shade of red as my jaws snapped. Out of the corner of my eye, I could see a new disturbance in the air, signaling an incoming magical being. Was Nicole returning? Or was this battle about to get much bigger? The distraction cost me as my assailant bit into my back leg, causing me to howl.

I could feel the fibers of my muscles ripping apart as the wolf started shaking his head back and forth. His jaws were clenched tight and pulling hard; every muscle in his body was straining as he shook.

The sharp points of his fang dug into my bone, and I felt a tearing sensation as the cartilage in my knee splintered. I twisted my body so that I could snap at the closest thing within reach. My grip was not steady, but I somehow tore off a large piece of his ear.

After a moment, my attacker decided that the leg simply wasn't enough, so he released me and dove for my throat. But he underestimated the depth of my survival instincts. I had a mate that needed finding, and her loved ones needed my protection. There was nothing and no one that would get in the way of that.

We wrestled for a lingering moment before I clamped my sharp teeth along the back of his neck and snapped the bone with no hesitation whatsoever.

"Help!" Bee yelled as she sprinted toward us, her bare feet pounding against the hard ground. Tears streamed down her face, fogging the lenses of her glasses. She paused by Corbin's side, scanning his wounds with a critical eye before dropping to her knees next to her father.

"No, no, no," she said repeatedly while running her shaky hands through his closely cropped hair. "Dad. Stay with me. Please stay with me."

Corbin whimpered as he felt his mate's distress,

and I didn't blame him one bit. The general was in terrible shape and unconscious. The dark skin of his chest was shredded open from his collarbone down to his navel. His limbs had multiple bite wounds; his right arm looked like it had been through a meat grinder. The left half of his face was coated in blood from his now-empty eye socket.

"Why are you just sitting there?!" Bee screamed. "Help him!"

Corbin instantly shifted back into his human form, carefully scooping the general into his arms, despite having his own injuries. "Alexei! We need to get out of here."

"Over here!" Juniper's mother was waving frantically from beside a purple-tinged portal.

My mangled leg dragged as I followed Corbin and Bee toward the high priestess.

"Hurry," Eve Hale prompted. "We need to get out of here. I already transported the others and I'm growing weak. You won't survive if we don't leave now. I've seen the outcome."

I could sense the truth in her statement. Even so, I hesitated. A low whine poured from my wolf's mouth, and it had nothing to do with my injury. Leaving here felt wrong.

The high priestess's gray eyes clouded as she fell to her knees. "Alexei... the window is closing. Nicole is going to be okay. I'll explain everything once we get to safety. We must go now."

I nudged her offered hand with my snout, and in the next moment, we were being sucked through the magical transit system. I usually handled the transition from one place to the next with ease, but I'd lost a lot of blood in battle, so when we arrived at our destination, my body fell to the floor with a thud. My bones cracked and muscles stretched as the shift back into my human form came on. I lay there limply as my white fur became tanned skin mottled with bruises, and my claws stretched into fingers. I groaned once the transition was complete, my entire body and soul aching from what we'd just endured.

I rolled onto my back, not giving a damn about my nudity, blinking at the harsh overhead lighting. "Where are we?"

"Witch Headquarters," she explained. "Your friend's father needs immediate medical attention. This is the surgery wing."

Well, that explained the sterile white walls and flooring.

Eve snapped her fingers, and in the next moment, a team of scrub-wearing witches popped into existence before disappearing again with the general, Corbin, and Bee.

Under normal circumstances, I would be

shocked. The witches were very private about their headquarters and never allowed outsider access, from what I understood. But at that moment, I was too distracted with worries about my pack, my father, and Nicole to give it much thought.

I flipped onto my stomach, breathing harshly as I pressed up on my forearms. "You have to find me a member of the fae court."

The wound on my leg was still closing up, and I was dripping a puddle of blood on their pristine marble floors.

She shook her head. "Right now, you need to worry about healing. What happened out there?"

Her question gnawed away at my thinning sanity. I gulped as raw emotion caused my eyes to water. I couldn't even remember the last time I had cried, but the hopelessness of our situation with my father and my concern for my mate made everything much more difficult to navigate.

"Nicole is gone." There was a lethal calmness in my tone, as if I couldn't quite believe it.

"What happened?" she asked. "Did your father abduct her?"

The urgency in her tone was warranted. If my father had gotten his hands on Nicole, she would certainly be dead. The only relief I had right now was knowing that June was with Nicole. I had grown to trust that witch over these last few weeks, and I had faith that she would do everything in her power to keep my mate safe.

"You mean you don't already know?" I challenged. "Why would you tell me Nicole would be okay if you didn't know that for certain? Aren't seers bound by a certain moral code? You'd think lying would be against the rules."

The fates supposedly only gifted the most ethical witches with the power of sight. But then again, if they gave someone like Mara Sullivan the power of influence, maybe their morality gauges were skewed.

Maybe these witches weren't so trustworthy after all.

"I know you're concerned for your mate, so I will forgive your offensive accusation." Eve's eyes were sharp and assessing. "To answer your question, I saw the attack on your camp. I saw my daughter crossing through a portal to Faerie with your mate and the fae princess, but my gift for premonition is never concrete."

My fists clenched as a burning rage tore through me. "You knew we would be attacked? Why didn't you warn us? And what happened to your assurances that the cloaking spell would protect us from being found?"

She flinched at the anger in my tone but stood her ground. "No cloaking spell is foolproof! As for the warning, I didn't get it in time. I think I was given the vision for the sole purpose of getting you and your friends out of there."

I shook my head as I stood, taking care not to put too much weight on my bad leg. "What are you talking about?" Witches always spoke in riddles, and it was infuriating trying to decipher it all.

She looked down at my leg, her lips pressed into a line. "Why don't we get you settled in a bed and we can talk? You're bleeding all over my floor, and someone might need to reset your leg so it doesn't heal wrong."

I didn't care about my leg. I didn't care about anything. I wanted answers, and I wanted them now. But I was wise enough to recognize the power this woman held, and I knew my cooperation would get me a lot further than my impatience would.

"Fine," I growled. She guided me over to the twin-size bed with white linens, where I begrudgingly sat down, covering my lower half with the sheet. I kept a careful eye on Eve as she pulled out a drawer full of potions and medical tools.

"My visions rarely tell me what I want to hear." Her voice was somber as she fiddled with a bottle of amber liquid. "I got my first one when I was eight years old, just moments before my grandmother was in a car accident."

I didn't exactly want to go down memory lane with this woman, but I forced myself to be polite so she would keep talking.

"What does that have to do with what's currently happening?" I winced as she turned to grab another vial and jostled the bed. "And where is everyone?"

Eve briefly closed her lids, her eyes moving fast beneath the thin skin before she opened them again. "The girl's father is being treated by our best healers. Your beta and his mate are standing guard, if that eases your mind."

I frowned. "How do you know?"

Her yellow curls bounced as she shook her head. "I can communicate telepathically with other witches. It's one of my gifts."

I tried not to show my surprise, but I didn't think I was succeeding. This woman was a high priestess. It made sense she would be extraordinarily gifted. But I had never heard of any witch having more than one special power bestowed upon them before. I supposed Corbin wasn't exaggerating that day when he was boasting about how formidable Juniper's coven was.

"Can you speak to Juniper?" I asked excitedly.

If Eve could communicate with her daughter, I could get confirmation Nicole was safe.

She shook her head. "Telepathy can't cross dimensions. But I can assure you Juniper is alive and well, so I'm sure Nicole is, too."

"How can you be so certain? The fae aren't exactly known for their kindness to outsiders. Hell, they're not even all that civil to each other, from what I've heard."

"I know the fae can be a rather... savage species. But there are exceptions, the princess being one of them. As a member of the light court, Cammie would have the authority to keep Nicole and Juniper safe."

"Theoretically," I argued. "It hardly justifies any assurances that they are safe."

"My assurance does not stem from *theory*," she huffed, setting the vial down and crossing her arms over her chest. "Our family's magic is linked through our blood. Think of it like a well. I can sense when that well is drained, as it would be through injury, death, or distress. Right now, our coven's well is *fully* stocked, which means my daughter is not hurt, dead, *or* under duress. Do you honestly think June would be unbothered if something bad happened to your mate?"

I scrubbed a hand over my face. I didn't know

what to think anymore. "You saw nothing else in your vision? You have no idea why they went to Faerie?"

"I get the sense Nicole is on an important journey. Perhaps the fates designated Juniper and Cammie as her guides."

Fuck the journey. My mate needed to be here with me, not on some fucking spiritual mission. I didn't give a damn what fate had in store.

All of this was pointless and a waste of time. The seer obviously would not help me find my mate. "I need to leave."

"And go where? Your father is infiltrating every faction of the supernatural community. You're safer here than anywhere else. Our wards are impenetrable."

"How do you know my father is responsible for this?"

She gave me a look as if I had asked the stupidest question in existence. Sure, I suspected my father was behind this, especially after Mara's warning while she was under a truth spell. But if I'd learned nothing else recently, it was to not assume things were as they appeared on the surface.

"I've *seen* the war he's waging, Alexei. My visions... they're sporadic, and they usually create more questions than answers, but the one thing they all have in common lately? *Your father.* He's evil, arrogant, and powerful, which is never a good combination."

"What are you saying?"

The high priestess sighed. "I'm saying that the best thing you can do is stay here where it's safe and think about this critically. This is an interfactional issue, Alexei. We're in this fight together. The good news is my coven got everyone from your training camp back here safely. Miraculously, they all survived, though some were not without injury. Those who need healing are currently being treated as well. The others are resting, anxiously waiting for some direction."

"Not everyone. My mate isn't here. *Your daughter* isn't here."

"Do you honestly think I want Juniper in Faerie?" Her smoky eyes narrowed. "Even Antonio fled once the fighting began. He's with his boyfriend in Italy at our compound there. I want everyone to be safe, and if I could summon my baby girl home, I would. But I have to have faith she's okay and focus on the facts. I have connections in the fae community. I'll reach out to some of them and see if we can gain access to a portal. You know as well as I do how fickle they can be. You can't just storm up to some random fae and demand they take you there. In the meantime, you should focus on leading this little makeshift pack you've formed. It doesn't matter if most of them aren't shifters. They joined this fight of yours, and they need a leader, Alexei. With the general... *indisposed*... you're their only option. You're *the best* option. You've been preparing for this role your whole life."

Once again, I was caught between my duty and protecting my mate. It seemed like I was always coming back to this problem. Being an alpha was constantly stealing me away from her, and it felt like I was torn between the two all over again. In the beginning, I picked my role as alpha over Nicole, and I promised both of us I would never do that again. How could I go against my word and live with myself?

"I know what you're thinking," she whispered.

"Can you read minds, too?"

She offered me a small smile. "I don't need to read your mind to know what's running through your thoughts. There's no reason you can't be both. You can be a powerful alpha *and* a loyal mate. We will find my daughter and Nicole, but it won't happen in a day. And while we wait, you do your best to strategize and heal."

As frustrated as I was, logically, I knew what Eve was suggesting was the best course of action. My inner wolf was protesting adamantly, but I shoved the instinct to get to Nicole aside. I just had to hope taking this path wouldn't come back to haunt me later.

Because as far as I was concerned, if Nicole didn't make it safely back into my arms, going against my word was the last thing I'd care about. There was no life without my mate.

CHAPTER

TWO

Nicole

MY HEAD POUNDED and a roaring heat traveled through my veins. Everything felt wrong, *so fucking wrong*. I was levitating in the air, magic dancing across my skin like ethereal flames as Juniper and Dr. Viden walked by my side.

I tried to speak, but my words were mumbled, as if my tongue was too heavy to form anything coherent.

What the hell was wrong with me?

Through my hazy vision, I looked up at an other-worldly sky, astonished at what I beheld. Instead of the azure blue, the sky was adorned with faint pastels and mysterious mists, combining to create a remarkable display of glittering clouds.

"Wh-ere arrre wee?" I moaned, not even sure if I made any sense.

Dr. Viden looked back at me. "Keep your strength, Nicole. We're almost there."

A peculiar birdsong filled the air, unlike any I had heard before. The sweet yet disconsolate chirping seemed to tingle in my soul, promising wonders unseen and secrets untold. A symphony from a far-off land, exotic and beautiful in a way that was inconceivable to most.

I wasn't on earth, that was certain. Even though I could barely make out what Juniper and Dr. Viden were saying when they opened the portal, I remembered them mentioning Faerie.

Had I truly gone to another realm?
Why?

A searing pain swirled in my gut, growing bigger and bigger with every passing moment. It stretched to my limbs with prickling precision, targeting each nerve ending, making me feel claustrophobic in my own skin.

A pain-filled moan gurgled up my throat, and no matter how much I contorted on the magical gurney Juniper conjured to carry me, nothing eased my suffering.

"Shh, Nicole." My witchy friend smoothed her hand against my damp brow. "We're getting you help."

"He-lp for wh… what? What's… happening… to… me?"

Juniper frowned, looking away with worry written in her features. My eyes fluttered closed as she and Cammie spoke in hushed tones. I was so disoriented most of what they were saying was lost on me, but the few words I heard caused my anxiety to spike.

"Are you sure she's going to be okay?" That came from Juniper.

"Her power is burning her from the inside out. She needs help to balance it," Cammie answered. "Luckily, I know someone who can help."

They were walking up a grassy hill with me floating beside them. The floral notes on the breeze were pure ambrosia. A faint chime echoed in the distance. I swore I could hear the laughter of children, like they had been summoned from the heavens to play in this magical paradise. But it was also possible I was completely delusional and none of this was happening.

"Almo… st where?" I croaked.

One of the women by my side began to say

something, but the next thing I knew, everything went black.

MY LASHES STUCK TOGETHER as I came to. I blinked furiously, trying to clear the fog. When my eyes came into focus, I startled as I saw the man sitting next to me, perched on what looked like a literal cloud.

"Nicole." He offered me a warm smile. "We finally meet in person."

My brows drew together as I tried to make sense of everything. Where was I? Who was this dude? He looked familiar, though I couldn't place him.

I gasped as I recalled the attack on our training camp right before Cammie opened a portal. "Where's Alexei?! Corbin and Bee? Cammie and June?"

"Your mate and friends are fine," the man assured me. "Camelia and Juniper are nearby. The others were safely extracted from the battle by the high priestess."

I breathed a sigh of relief.

"Who are *you*?" I asked, my voice hoarse.

My eyes swam around the majestic chamber as I awaited his reply. This place looked like it had been plucked straight from a fairy tale. The walls were made of shimmering white marble, with tall spires of golden stone that stood like sentries on either side of an archway. The marbled surfaces gleamed in the sunlight, shining like beacons into the depths of the chamber. Lush vines snaked up toward the heavens, soft pink flowers blooming in abundance, coating the air in a sweet fragrance.

On a platform, gilded statues of pegasi stood tall, their emerald eyes catching the light as if they were keeping watch on us. The glowing jewels etched into their wings glittered in the sun. I gasped when my gaze reached the ceiling. It arched high above us, rays of light filtering through the stained glass dome, casting rainbows across the walls and floor.

"Stunning, isn't it?"

I nodded as I sunk into the fluffy cotton mattress, absentmindedly stroking the velvet duvet on top of me. The stranger and I were the only people in the room, though I could feel a mysterious presence. Both factors should've been disconcerting, but I was surprisingly at ease.

Wait a minute...

"Did you drug me?" I asked.

The man's dark blond brows drew together as he frowned. "Why would you ask me something like that?" His tone was haughty, as if he couldn't believe I had the audacity to ask such a thing.

"Something was wrong with me…" I waved my hand around. "I was in agony. Delirious. Next thing I know, I'm sitting in the middle of some Greek legend, suspiciously pain and worry free. Drugs are the only reasonable explanation."

His shoulders slumped a bit, as if he were disappointed, and for some reason that made me sad, though I couldn't figure out why.

"I didn't *drug you*," he insisted. "But I gave you *an elixir* that helped balance the distribution of your newly awakened powers. If you had been better prepared, we could've prevented your suffering entirely."

I didn't feel like I was being burned alive anymore, so that was good, but did he really think I was going to trust someone I just met? What if he just poisoned me and my relief was only temporary?

"Why would you care whether I suffered?"

"Because you are my kin. I've thought of you almost every day for over nineteen years, Nicole. I wish I could have spoiled you with presents. Taught you about our magic. I truly wanted to be a doting uncle, but I never had the chance. I'm hoping you'll allow me to rectify that."

My mind stuttered at his words. "Uncle?"

My dad was an only child. Same with my mom. Or so I thought.

He lifted his hand, as if he wanted to grab mine, but stopped himself. "Your mother was my sister. In earthly terms, I suppose you could say we were twins. Gods are not born in a traditional sense, but Celena and I were brought into existence as two halves of a whole. We spent many summers playing in the fields outside this very castle you are in now. She would cheat at every game, though. That girl hated to lose."

I frowned. "You knew my mother?"

He nodded but still had that look of uncertainty on his face. "I'm so sorry, Nicole. I wanted to know you. Protect you. I sent Macey when you were ready, but—"

"*You* sent Macey to me?" I felt a pang in my chest, missing my dear familiar.

"Yes, one of my powers is to create familiar bonds between wild animals and supernatural beings. He nodded excitedly. "She's sweet, right? Fiercely protective. Though I was dismayed that she wasn't at your side when your powers awakened. I trained her to help with your transition until you and I could meet."

"*Powers?* I'm sorry, I just... Can you start at the beginning?" This was a lot to take in. I wasn't even sure how to process it all.

He clapped his hands together. "Of course. Though... there isn't really a delicate way to say this."

I held up my palm, waiting anxiously for my mental encyclopedia to enlighten me. Even though I hated the damn thing when it first kicked in, it certainly made understanding the supernatural world much easier to digest.

"What are we waiting for, exactly?" he asked.

I closed my eyes, waiting for the magic to kick in. "For my reveal spell to tell me what you are. It'll speed things along."

He chuckled. "That spell comes in handy, but I can assure you, it won't recognize me."

Well, damn, there went that plan.

"Why not?"

"Perhaps we should begin with formal introductions." He lifted his chin and puffed his chest out. "I am Cyrus."

I stared blankly, waiting for him to continue, but he simply stared right back as if he were waiting for me to recognize the name.

"Cool name, bro," I said. "And you are a *what,* exactly? You're clearly not human."

"Thank goodness," Cyrus scoffed. "No offense."

I gave him a wry look. "Can we cut through the bullshit, please? Tell me what you are, and then tell me exactly where my friends are."

If I wasn't mistaken, my prickly attitude amused him. "You certainly are your mother's daughter."

"Yes, I am my mother *and* father's daughter. *And you are a...*" I made a hurry-up motion with my hand.

"A sun god," he blurted out.

"A what?!"

"A god of the sun. I've had a few names over the years, but I always preferred that one. For years, your mother and I worked in tandem. Her domain was night, and mine was day."

"What does that mean?"

"Your mother—*my sister*—was a goddess. More specially, a lunar goddess. Which makes you a—"

My eyes widened when I realized what he was telling me.

"I'm a goddess?!" I shrieked. "*That's* what I am?!"

Cyrus shrugged. "Technically, a *demi*goddess. You're half human, so... you don't get the immortality perk, but you have goddess powers, a much longer than average lifespan, and you're really hard to kill."

"I'm a lunar demigoddess," I repeated slowly, seeing if it became easier to accept if I said it out loud. I wasn't even going to touch the whole long-life-goddess-power thing he just mentioned. "And, uh, why didn't I know about this before now?"

"Demigods—*or demigoddesses*—do not magically mature until the nineteenth anniversary of their birth. It's a protective mechanism of sorts. Human bodies are disturbingly fragile. Reaching developmental milestones takes a lot of energy and brain power. Your godly powers needed to lie dormant until your human half had done most of the work. Now that it has, there's room for an influx of power. Typically, the elixir would've been administered the moment you started showing signs of your awakening, which happens up to a few months prior, but considering you were on earth and completely unaware of what you are, that didn't happen."

"You think?" I muttered.

"Is the snark really necessary?" he chastised. "I'm simply trying to explain."

I smacked my forehead when a memory hit me, wincing from the sting. "You're the man from my vision! The one Macey showed me."

His white teeth practically shone as he smiled.

"Yes. I am. I was wondering if the vision came through when you didn't recognize me upon waking."

Jeez.

Excuse me for not being on top of it while I was recovering from an attack and some crazy power surge.

I didn't want to continue this conversation in a prone position, so after some considerable effort, I sat up. The mental fog had lifted, allowing me to absorb everything he'd told me so far.

"Where are we?"

"In Faerie," Cyrus—I couldn't get on board with calling him Uncle yet—replied matter-of-factly.

I frowned in confusion. "If you're a god, why are we in fae territory? And what about my friends?"

"Camelia and Juniper will join us soon. As for your other question, before I answer that, I need to ensure you understand the importance of keeping this information a secret. It's imperative other supernatural factions never know about our alliance."

"*What* alliance?" I pressed.

"Do I have your word you'll protect our secret?"

I thought about his question for a moment, recalling how frustrating it was for Hannah and Jade as they tried to work around the secrecy vow they had made with my mom. "Wait. There are some people in my life who I trust without fail. And I don't like the idea of not being able to share everything I know with them. They're my family. I don't want to vow to keep something from them that could help our cause. I especially don't like the idea of keeping information from my mate. May I tell them?" At the mention of Alexei, I suddenly realized he was probably freaking the fuck out about where I was. I knew I would be if the situation were reversed.

"Yes, you may, but only so they can better protect you," Cyrus replied. "But if you do not trust them with your life—*if you do not want to risk their lives*—you should not trust them with this secret. I will know the moment the vow is broken with malicious intent, and I am not afraid to take *whatever action is necessary* to protect the sanctity of this alliance. Do you understand what I'm saying?"

"I understand." I nodded solemnly, the conviction in his tone making my stomach churn. My uncle may have looked like a golden boy supermodel, but at that moment, I could sense the violence he was capable of, and I never wanted to be on the wrong end of it. "And I promise not to share what I'm about to learn with anyone outside of my trusted circle. So where should we start? Is the beginning good for you?"

I was finally ready to learn about my mother and

how it affected me. Cyrus could give me a whole new perspective on her life. I'd always been curious, and despite the circumstances, I was excited.

"Your mother and I grew up here in Faerie. *All* gods and goddesses did, actually."

I frowned in confusion as my mental database called bullshit. "What about Elysian Point? The plane where gods are supposed to be?"

He brushed me off. "That's a myth."

My jaw dropped. "I'm sorry, what?!"

"Perhaps I should rephrase..." Cyrus began. "Elysian Point exists, but it's not a separate realm. It's a mountain range here in Faerie. Have you ever heard the saying, *there's always some truth in rumor*? Well... the name of the mountain range we live on *is* that truth. The rest is mostly legend. In reality, gods and fae have lived in harmony in Faerie since the beginning of time. Yes, we are two different races, but we are a unified, peaceful civilization."

Again, my mind called bullshit. "That makes no sense. Everything in my supernatural encyclopedia says the fae are a selfish, tricky, brutal race. They have an especially nasty rep where humans are concerned. An enormous appetite for hunting, torturing, and raping humans *for sport*. What's so *peaceful* about that?"

He was silent for a moment as he considered my

question. "Simply put, every unsavory thing you think you know about the fae was a fabricated story to protect our realm. The fae are actually some of the kindest, most loving, and magnanimous people you will ever meet."

I rubbed my temples. "I'm gonna need more of an explanation than that."

Cyrus took a deep breath. "Gods are powerful beings, Nicole. And if that power fell into the wrong hands, it could be detrimental to *every being in existence.*"

"Collectors," I whispered, thinking about the vision Macey showed me of my mother.

He nodded. "Yes. I've eliminated most of the avid collectors over the last couple of decades, but there are some still out there. We can never be too careful."

"I still don't understand why you'd go through all the trouble of maintaining some elaborate story."

"Because if people fear the fae, they're less likely to go looking for portals into this realm. We are *very* selective when inviting anyone to Faerie."

"Okay, now I'm really confused," I told him. "During rush week at Redwood U, the fae sorority hosted an open portal night. It was a big thing, all loosey-goosey-like. They wanted *any prospective pledges* to come hang out in Faerie with them."

"If any of those prospective pledges weren't fae, they wouldn't have made it past the first level of the portal. Instead, they would've been deposited into the stasis region of the otherworld where some fantastical illusion would've been waiting for them."

The otherworld was the realm for dead supernaturals. It was broken into three different sections—the equivalent of Heaven, Hell, and Purgatory all rolled into one. Where you ended up in the afterlife depended on the fates.

"Portals have levels?" I asked. "Why isn't this in my database?"

"Layering portals is a talent exclusive only to the fae," Cyrus explained. "And since we control the narrative on all things fae, we conveniently left that ability out. Every eternal portal will have that layer of protection. Only temporary portals, like the one you traveled through to get here today, don't."

I gasped when I thought about the only other humans at Redwood who were immune to the concealment spell. "I met these two people in my Supernatural Laws and Regs class who fell through a portal that was placed in some kind of Druid circle thingy. They were *really freaking traumatized* from whatever they experienced. If the fae are so kind and loving, why would they cast such a horrifying illusion?"

He winced. "I'm terribly sorry for their distress, but the fae aren't actually responsible for what happened to them."

"Why not?"

"If they fell through Druid stones, they would've been stuck in *a very unpleasant part* of the other-world. No fae or god in their right mind would go near a portal on Druid soil these days. The stones contain remnants of power from some very dark and ancient magic, which tainted those portals. The same applies to any portal located on old burial grounds. Your classmates were lucky to make it out alive. Few do."

God, I thought my reveal spell had given me an insane amount of information, but I was thinking there was still *so much* I had to learn.

"I still don't understand why the smoke screen is necessary. If portals have these protective layers that keep all the non-fae baddies out, why bother trying to paint the fae as these scary, atrocious beings?"

Cyrus thought about it for a moment. "Because if anyone located an eternal portal, they *could* make it to Faerie if they maintained physical contact with a fae while crossing dimensions. In theory, anyone with nefarious intent could stake out a portal, wait for some unfortunate fae to drop by to use said portal, then force them to be their guide."

"That's a lot of hypotheticals," I said.

"We cannot be too careful," he countered. "We must consider all possibilities if we want to preserve our peace and safety. If a collector crossed into Faerie, the consequences would be dire. *Never* underestimate a collector, Nicole. They are some of the most evil beings I've ever met. It's why gods and goddesses rarely leave our homeland."

"But my mom lived on earth for years," I argued. "Why would she do that if the risk was so high?"

"Because her gifts were directly linked to shifters. If she went too long without exposure to pack life, she would become hopelessly depressed. She needed the pack's love just as much as they needed her."

"What do you mean her gifts were connected to the shifters?"

"As are yours. Specifically *wolf* shifters since their faction is tied to the moon. The lunar goddess blesses fated mate bonds. It was no coincidence that when you came into your powers, many fated pairs emerged. But that's not all. The lunar goddess is a direct conduit to the wolf spirit. She can ask the mother wolf to make more shifters."

I blinked. "*Make* more shifters? But... that would mean..."

"*You* have the power to make shifters, Nicole.

You could help those born with a missing wolf, or you could transform a human into a shifter. I'm sure you can imagine how dangerous that could be if a collector or someone like Alpha Jones got a hold of you, considering the war he's waging. Collectors don't just want prized supernaturals to put on their shelf. There are always buyers wanting to use our gifts. You have to be careful."

I nodded in understanding. "What happened to the collector that tried to take my mother? Did you know about that? I saw it in a vision."

"I killed him." Cyrus's answer was direct and lethal. "And I'd do it again if anyone tried hurting you. I'd kill that bastard Alpha Jones, too, but your mate has to do it if he wants to take over the pack. Damn shifter politics."

"How do you know about my mate? Or Alpha Jones and the trouble he's stirring?"

"I've been keeping tabs on you through Macey."

I blushed, really hoping he didn't mean that he was literally watching me through her eyes. That was all kinds of creepy and invasive. I definitely would not open that can of worms right now though.

"And I have... *contacts* in the mortal world," he added. "Which will all be explained in due time."

"Why haven't we met before now?" If he was as

protective and doting as he claimed to be, then why wait until now to introduce himself?

"My presence would have just put you more in danger. Your mother wanted you to have a normal childhood. Staying away allowed you to be safe and under the radar. I hated that I wasn't a part of your childhood, Nicole. But I hope you'll allow me to get to know you now. I can help you learn about your powers and guide you."

"My powers of solidifying mate bonds and creating shifters," I clarified.

"Correct." Cyrus nodded.

I thought about that for a moment. "Please don't take this the wrong way, but why should I trust you?"

His golden hair fell over his eyes as he tilted his head, assessing me. "We are bound by blood. You saw it in your vision."

"Technically, that's not true," I argued. "I saw you talking to my mother. Not once did you discuss your relationship with one another. For all I know, you're some childhood friend of hers who's been playing both sides this whole time."

His full lips curved into a smirk. "You're definitely Celena's offspring."

"What's that supposed to mean?"

"Your mother was as obstinate as they come. She

was also constantly challenging the status quo, always looking for adventure or ways to defy the odds. When I learned she was pregnant... I was devastated, but... unsurprised."

"Why would you be devastated to learn she was pregnant? Shouldn't you have been happy for her if that's what she wanted?"

Cyrus released a harsh breath, looking off in the distance for a moment. "Forgive me. I forget you're so uninformed. It's common knowledge among our people, but it wouldn't be listed in any supernatural database."

"*What's* common knowledge? I feel like I'm missing some key information here."

He gave me a sad smile. "Nicole... Celena knew she shouldn't conceive. But as I've learned, she intentionally forwent contraception so she could become pregnant. She knew the consequence, but I believe she thought her brilliant mind could find a solution before it was too late. She loved your father deeply and wanted nothing more than to start a family with him."

"*What* consequence? What are you talking about?"

"You see, despite their divine origins, gods and goddesses *are* biologically capable of producing offspring."

"Obviously," I muttered. "But you said she knew she *shouldn't* conceive. Why not?"

Cyrus sighed. "A moon goddess is tied to one of the most influential celestial bodies *and* one of the most powerful spiritual beings. She is one of the few deities who are linked to two power sources, which makes her nearly impossible to kill. But one surefire way to end her life without fail is to upset the balance. The fates do not allow it."

"Okay... and?"

I felt like this guy was talking in riddles.

"And..." Cyrus continued. "Now that you've reached magical maturity... you must take steps to ensure you *never* conceive. The same consequence applies to lunar demigoddesses."

I held a hand up. "I'm sorry, but you've lost me. Can you please dumb it down a little? I grew up in the mortal world, remember?"

He nodded. "Simply put, a lunar goddess *or demigoddess* cannot reproduce. Only one lunar deity can exist at a time. The moment her offspring breathes outside of the womb, the goddess's life ends. It's impossible to overcome. Which means you can *never* produce offspring. If you do, you will forfeit your life."

Well... fuck.

CHAPTER

THREE

Nicole

I'D NEEDED some time to process what Cyrus had told me. It wasn't every day a girl found out she was a demigoddess or that she couldn't have biological children without dying. As strange as it may have seemed, I think I was more shocked by the latter. As someone who knew firsthand what it was like to grow up without a mother, I didn't know if I could ever pass that on to my child. My childhood was wonderful, but survivor's guilt was still deeply ingrained into my psyche. It wasn't like I was in any hurry to have babies, but knowing I didn't have the option really stung.

What would Alexei think?

Would he still want to be with me, knowing I could never give him heirs? I knew shifters were big on carrying on the bloodlines, especially with their alphas. The reality of my situation hit me like a ton of bricks. Alexei and I had been in a good place before I came here, but now I was scared. Doubt crept in and I wasn't sure if our relationship could survive the truth.

A gentle rapping at my chamber door interrupted my musings. The dress an attendant brought to me after I bathed was made from the most luxurious material that had ever graced my skin. Evidently, it was moon spider silk, harvested and delicately woven by the most skilled artisans in Faerie. I desperately wanted to gather every bit and sew some fabulous pieces, but the attendant told me gathering enough silk to make one gown took years. I supposed if you were immortal, you could afford to have that kind of patience.

"Hello," I greeted Cyrus while opening the door.

I'd been too preoccupied earlier to notice his apparel, but the button-up shirt he wore seemed to be made from the same material as my dress. Combined with his deep gold linen pants and matching sandals, he looked like a high-class hipster on a meditation retreat.

"Ready to see your friends? We've got a surprise for you."

I swallowed. There was no telling what Juniper had been up to since we arrived. I felt sorry for any fae she was trying to steal snot or pubes from. "Yeah, I'm ready."

Cyrus eyed me for a moment. "Wow. I can't get over how much you resemble Celena."

The shimmer in his eyes softened my heart toward him for a moment. Even though I didn't know him that well, it was still healing for me to meet someone who was close to my mom.

I tucked a strand of hair behind my ear, weirded out by how soft it felt. I had thick, healthy hair, but I could swear my dark strands were now as lush as the gown I wore.

"I'd love to hear more about her."

He smiled. "Of course. I'd love to tell you about her. But it'll have to wait a bit. Time moves much faster here on Faerie, so we need to make haste."

I blanched, thinking about the unlucky pair I'd met from Scotland who'd been sucked into the stones. By the time they'd returned to earth, over twenty years had passed, but to them, it seemed like only days. But then again, according to my uncle, they were actually in the otherworld, not Faerie. I made a mental note to study the difference in how time passes between the two realms.

"How long have I been here? I mean... in earth time."

"Not long." Cyrus waved his hand breezily. "You needn't worry about that, Nicole. I'm being very mindful. This is more important. You're not safe there without knowing some pertinent information."

"*What* pertinent information?"

"For starters, there's been a leak in your training camp."

I looked up, startled by the newcomer's musical voice. Cammie was walking through the arched doorway, wearing the most beautiful gown I'd ever seen. It was made of white silk like mine, but had golden embroidery throughout the entire thing, even its long train. Her blonde hair was piled on top of her head in soft curls, complete with a shiny bejeweled tiara. I was momentarily stunned as I absorbed her ethereal beauty. She looked like a literal princess.

"That's because I am. Remember?" Cammie smiled.

Her words made me realize I must've said that last part out loud.

"Oh. Uh... right." My cheeks flushed with embarrassment.

"Your uncle told me he gave you the lowdown on fae fact versus fiction, but my royal title is legitimate. Although, there isn't a light court and a dark court, because there are no dark fae. Officially, I'm known as Princess Camelia from the House of Viden, but you can stick with Cammie." She winked.

"Um... okay." I gulped. "What's this about a leak?"

"Let's get comfortable and we can explain everything." Cyrus offered his arm, guiding the princess-turned-professor into the room.

There was a small lounge area overlooking a garden, so we took a moment to choose a seat before speaking.

"Where's Juniper?"

Cammie chuckled while my uncle cleared his throat.

"She's safe," Cammie assured me. "She'll be here any moment, I'm sure. She's a bit... exuberant, shall we say? Running around collecting samples for potions."

"Oh, God. Is she plucking pubes again?" I scrunched my nose at the thought.

Cyrus made a choking sound.

Cammie grinned. "No. Much worse. Pegasus semen."

I blinked twice, not sure I heard that right. "Okay, yes, we can address that later. Much, *much* later."

Or, you know, *never*.

I crossed my legs as a willowy woman delivered us tea and cakes that were so vibrant and decorative that I didn't want to eat them.

"So about this leak," Cammie said. "Someone at your camp informed Alpha Jones where you were hiding. The good news is that we were able to suss him out. The bad news is—"

"Who was it?" I interrupted.

"One of the vampires," she replied.

"*Which* vampire?" Did Cristian betray me? My heart plummeted at the thought.

"A lower-level vamp named Pasqual," Cammie answered, filling me with relief. "Evidently, he had some gambling debts and was feeding Alpha Jones information in exchange for money. Don't worry, the traitor has been eliminated by the vampire prince himself. Pasqual's betrayal was considered a direct insult to the royal family since he was at the camp as one of the prince's guards."

I swallowed the sudden lump in my throat. "You started to say bad news. *What else* happened?"

"My cover was blown, so I had to take quick action." Cammie took a sip from her cup, moaning as she tasted the warm tea.

"Your *cover*?" I asked. "Why would you need a cover?"

"Alpha Jones has been obsessed with altering DNA much longer than most people know. Rumors of his experiments and the potential consequences if he succeeded warranted closer monitoring. Cyrus and I decided that I would be the best liaison since my proficiency in genetics and chemistry would secure my position at the lab. Plus, I promised your mother I would take care of you all."

I was incredibly thankful that Cammie was with my father while he was detained, but if she was here, then that meant... "But if your cover was blown, that means my father is all alone with Alpha Jones. This is bad, Cammie." I stood up, feeling frantic. "We need to get to him. Like, *now*."

"I'm okay, sweetheart."

My eyes snapped to the entrance of the room, where my father stood, wearing his own fae fashion and looking absolutely out of place. His cheeks were red, as if he was uncomfortable by our stares.

"Dad?" I whispered, shocked that he was here and safe. "Oh my God!"

I ran to him, arms outstretched, and when we

collided, he let out a little oof.

"It's really you!" I pulled back to look him over, making sure there wasn't a hair out of place. "Are you okay? Why are you here?"

Dad looked over my head at Cammie, and his blush deepened. "Cammie brought me."

I spun around. "You brought my dad to Faerie?"

She nodded. "Hello, David. I must say it's strange seeing you out of a lab coat."

I grabbed my father's hand and tugged him over to the sitting area. "Are you hungry? Thirsty? We have snacks. Come sit. Rest."

My dad pushed his glasses up the bridge of his nose. "Relax, honey. I'm fine. They've been taking great care of me here."

My father and I took a seat on a small couch.

"You brought him through a portal?" I asked Cammie.

"I did," she confirmed.

"Are you okay? With all this supernatural stuff?"

He smiled. "Sweetheart, I've known about the supernatural for a long time. I had my memories blocked since your mother passed, but they were restored the night Alpha Jones imprisoned me. Granted… I didn't know *everything* until recently." He gave Cyrus a pointed look, to which my uncle returned a frown.

What was that about?

"What do you mean?"

My father sighed. "I knew your mother was... special. But I didn't know exactly what made her special until I spoke with Cyrus upon my arrival. Your mom occasionally mentioned an estranged brother over the years, but I had assumed they parted on bad terms, because she cut off contact with him. Looking back, the few times she referenced Cyrus, there was nothing but fondness, and she was strategically vague. She gave me just enough information to satisfy my curiosity, but never enough that would force her to lie to me."

"It was for your own protection." Cyrus's blue eyes narrowed. "For *her* protection."

"I know that," my dad insisted, turning back to me. "Honey, your mom and I had... an understanding of sorts. I knew there were things she was hiding from me. But I also knew she had good reason for making that secrecy pact with Jade and Hannah. It didn't matter, though. I knew Celena's heart. Her brilliant mind. Nothing she could've possibly revealed about her heritage or her abilities would've scared me away. She was my soul mate." He smiled wistfully.

My eyes filled with tears, and looking up at Cammie, I could see hers were doing the same.

"If you've known Alpha Jones was up to something for a while now, why didn't you bring my father here the moment he showed up at Redwood?" I asked our resident princess. "You knew who he was married to, right? I know the fae are selective about who can gain access to their realm, but we're sitting in your family's castle right now, correct? Surely if anyone has pull, it'd be a member of the royal court."

Cammie looked uncomfortable for a moment, which seemed unnatural with her elegant posture and the tiara on her head. "We had to weigh the risks. I'd been undercover at Redwood for many years. My position at the university gave me an opportunity to gather intel as inconspicuously as possible. When Jones hired your father to find a cure for the missing wolf gene, we *knew* he had more sinister motives, but we couldn't prove it. Since David is such a brilliant scientist, we decided to let him do what he does best, and hope it flushed out Alpha Jones's true motive in the process."

My fists clenched. "So you *willingly put my father in danger* so you could use him?"

My dad placed a hand on my forearm. "No, honey. That's not what she's saying."

I threw my hands up. "That's *exactly* what she's saying!"

"Nicole, think about it for a second. Think of how jarring it was when that warlock slipped you the reveal spell. Think about how traumatized you were, learning the world was nothing like you'd known it to be," she said.

"And?" I blinked. "What's your point?"

"My *point was*, at least you had a wealth of knowledge at your disposal to help you cope. And you were still on earth, which was exactly the same as it'd been before you were spelled. *Those little comforts matter.* I couldn't just take your father—the most logical, pragmatic person I've ever met— through a portal to Faerie when he was immune to the reveal spell. Look at this place." Cammie held her toned arms out, gesturing to our surroundings. "Look how alien everything looks. I wasn't going to risk David's sanity by bringing him to a foreign realm that defied logic."

"Sweetheart, Cammie would never hurt me," my dad said. "I have no doubts about that. And you have to admit, her reasons make sense."

Dammit, they *did* make sense.

"I still don't like it." I crossed my arms over my chest to punctuate my statement.

"Look, if it makes you feel better, I knew it was only a matter of time before the block on your father's mind would be removed. Once that happened, we had more options. His safety was one of my highest priorities at all times."

I tensed. "*How* did you know it was only a matter of time?"

"Because I'm the one who suppressed his memories," she admitted.

"*You* put that block on his mind?"

She nodded. "Cyrus and I knew Celena wouldn't survive childbirth, so I was at the hospital on the day you were born to ensure protective measures were in place. Blocking David's memories of the supernatural world until your awakening was imperative in keeping you alive. Your dad wouldn't have raised you as a human if he knew you weren't *entirely* human. He would've spent the last nineteen years obsessively trying to identify your other half, which could've exposed you. You would've *both* been at risk. We had no other choice."

"But his block was removed before my birthday," I argued. "How do you explain that?"

"The spell was cast using a drop of your blood, creating a magical tether. Your goddess powers awakened gradually in the months *before* your nineteenth birthday, remember? There would've been little signs, but untrained, you may not have recognized them," Cyrus answered for her. "The spell was set to expire upon sensing the slightest rise in power. We'd planned to give you the elixir and tell you about your heritage once David's block was removed. Unfortunately, Alpha Jones witnessed the whole thing and abducted your dad, so we had to improvise for a bit. Camelia isn't the villain here, Nicole."

"He's right, honey," my dad agreed. "I would've done all those things they'd predicted, and would've inadvertently put our safety at risk. You know how single-minded I can get with my research."

I sat back in my chair with a sigh, once again overwhelmed with the information they were giving me, but knew they were right. "Thank you for getting him out of there, Cammie."

She smiled at my father. "Of course. David is a good man. I've grown very fond of him."

My dad wrung his hands together nervously and cleared his throat. "Uh... thank you. I've grown... fond of you as well."

I looked between the two of them, trying to make sense of the weird vibe they were giving off. I knew my dad found the fae professor attractive. How could he not? But was he actually developing feelings for her?

"Dad—"

"Hellloooooo!" a familiar voice called out, seconds before my purple-haired friend bounded into the room like that bouncy stuffed tiger on crack. "Oh my God, Nicole! This place is ah-mazing! The magical mojo in Faerie is unreal! There's so much power everywhere you look!" She patted the woven crossbody purse on her hip. "I can't wait to see what kind of potions I can make with the samples I've collected. Let me tell you, getting semen from a pegasus took *a lot* of effort, but I was committed."

I was sure I spoke for everyone else in the room when I asked, "Juniper, please do not tell me you *manually* extracted that sample?"

She laughed a little maniacally. "Don't be ridiculous. I may be adventurous, but I draw the line at humping while my partner is in animal form."

"Thank God," I mumbled.

"Luckily for me, Faerie has gobs of rainbows everywhere. There's a big field right outside the castle that even has these giant rainbow-infused flowers! That's where I found a whole herd of horny bastards."

I knew I'd probably regret asking, but my curiosity got the best of me. "Why do I feel like I'm missing some information?"

"Rainbows make pegasi randy," Juniper explained matter-of-factly as she flipped a curl over her shoulder. "Like, really, *really* randy. They were munching on the colorful flowers, which didn't seem like that big of a deal at first, but then all of a sudden, I was standing in the middle of a giant pegasi orgy. The studs kept rubbing their big horse dicks against one another. A bit of grunting and *a lot* of whinnying later, and the jizz started flying. Thank God I always keep a spare specimen jar in my bag. It was difficult to predict which direction they'd shoot their load in at first, and it got pretty messy, but I got the hang of it soon enough and caught *tons*. Besides, it's certainly not the first time I've been showered in wayward semen. It happens."

I was pretty sure I was turning green, thanks to the gross image the crazy witch put into my head.

"Could we please get back to the issue at hand?" Cyrus asked.

"When can I go back?" I asked, changing the subject. "I'm glad my dad is safe, but Alexei is probably worried sick and we need to take Alpha Jones down. Not to mention my poor aunts are—hey!" I changed directions mid-sentence because it suddenly occurred to me that Jade and Hannah were probably still searching for the magical horn, and Cyrus probably knew all about it. "What is this horn I saw in the vision? Seemed pretty important. Jade and Hannah have been trying to dig it up."

A wicked grin crossed Cyrus's expression. "Jade is truly inventive with her curse words. Last I popped in to spy on their progress, she said, 'Shit son-of-a-bitch motherfucker curse this horn to a lifetime of crabs and flaccid dicks.' She's quite entertaining."

I dropped my mouth open in shock. "You're purposefully fucking with them?"

Cyrus straightened in his seat. "All in good fun. The horn is fine; I dug it up ages ago. But I figured you wouldn't mind having them far away from Alpha Jones, preoccupied with finding it." He looked at the ground and chuckled to himself.

"Jade is going to kill you," I whispered.

"Is it wrong that I look forward to her ire?" Cyrus laughed again.

My father cleared his throat. "What is this horn?"

Cyrus sobered up some and responded. "The horn is what allows Nicole to create more shifters. It's a tool Celena used to call upon the wolf spirit."

June gasped. "Wicked!"

"And *you* have the horn?" I clarified. "Why have Mace show me the vision if you didn't want us to dig it up?"

"I *do* have it. The vision was a way for me to introduce myself. Give you clues until you were ready. Sending Jade on a wild goose chase was just a bonus."

I drummed my fingers on my chin. "I can't just stay here forever. Alexei needs me. The shifters need me. Bee and her father. I have to go back."

Cyrus leaned forward, propping his elbows on his knees. "Nicole, I understand your urgency. And I give you my word, we will return you to earth as soon as possible. But there are things you must learn first, for your safety and everyone else's. I will get word to your mate. They've been requesting an audience with the fae. But while you're here, I need you to focus on what I'm about to tell you. Teach you. Then, and only then, can you safely return."

Well, shit. It didn't seem like I had any other choice.

"I want to show you something," Cyrus said.

I swallowed. "I'm not sure I can handle much more right now. My head is buzzing."

Cyrus gave me a kind smile. "I know these powers are intimidating, Nicole, but they bring so much balance and peace to the world. Our existence is for the greater good. You have a huge responsibility on your shoulders, but it's also pretty... ah... what's the word the humans use now?"

I gave him a curious look and shrugged.

"Cool," he said, snapping his fingers. "It's very cool."

He rose from his seat and extended his arm,

offering me his hand. I accepted it, though with a hint of hesitation. He led me out to the balcony, where we looked out at the sprawling garden below us. "Close your eyes and listen," he told me.

I closed my eyes and took a deep breath. The garden was alive with the sounds of nature. There were birds chirping, crickets singing, and bees buzzing. I heard the soft rustle of leaves as the wind blew across them and the gentle trickle of water from a nearby fountain. The air was thick and fragrant with the scent of jasmine, lavender, and rosemary.

Cyrus squeezed my hand reassuringly as he verbally pointed out other small details in the garden—the sound the metal wind chimes made in sync with one another, the bubbling laughter from children playing nearby, and even an old man humming an ancient folk song as he tended his vegetable garden. It all came together to create this strange harmony that seemed to make everything stand still for just a moment. I had never felt such peace before.

I opened my eyes and looked at Cyrus, who was smiling proudly at me. "Do you feel them?"

I arched my brow. "Feel *who*?"

He nodded at the garden once more, and I

peered out, looking for... well... I wasn't sure what I was looking for.

Suddenly, hundreds of bright lights began to crawl across the garden toward me. "What is that?" I asked with a gasp.

"Fáel came to greet you," Cyrus said reverently.

"Fáel?"

I squinted at the glowing orbs and realized they were in the shape of wolves. They hovered just barely above the ground and shifted from a bluish to a yellow hue as they moved. The closer they got, the more vivid and distinct they became. I could see each limb, each claw, and each tooth as if they were tangible beings. Their eyes were a spectrum of hues that shimmered.

The ghostly creatures filled the garden. Hundreds of them, each shrouded in an ethereal light. A pup at the forefront stepped forward and peered up at me with eyes of mystery and more knowledge than I could possibly imagine. His gaze seemed to pierce right through me, as though he could read my every thought. The other spirits slowly stirred and moved toward him in unison, as if they obeyed some silent command. I had never seen anything so beautiful in my entire life.

I was in awe as, one by one, they bowed their heads, watching me with their glowing eyes.

"They're here to welcome you and show you their support," Cyrus said softly.

I swallowed hard and nodded, feeling a strange sense of belonging as they swarmed around the balcony like moths to a flame. I could feel the power emanating off of them, and I knew that this wasn't something that I could ever forget—the power of my ancestors and the responsibility I had been given.

"This is the mother wolf's pack," Cyrus explained. "As her direct conduit, they can give *you* the strength to do what is right." He took my hand and led me down some stairs into the garden. The spirits followed us closely with their unblinking eyes trained on me. "You have the power to lead them. To make decisions for them. To protect them. It is your duty to guide them. To comfort them. And if you find a human worthy of them, you can summon them to the human realm to create more shifters."

The spirits began to grow—some so close to me that I could have reached out and touched one if they were sentient beings. I felt the warmth of their love and wholehearted devotion. I was honored that these beautiful creatures trusted me to lead them.

"This is your purpose, Nicole," Cyrus said. "This is your legacy.

Alexei

"I'm sorry, Alexei. I'm trying, but you know how the fae can be," Eve said, her eyes full of disappointment.

Juniper's mother was doing the best she could, yet it still wasn't enough. I slammed my fist into the punching bag, sweat dripping down my face as I listened to excuses. A whole fucking week had passed, and we weren't any closer to getting Nicole back.

"Is there *anyone else* we could talk to?" I grunted before landing another punch.

My fists were bare, the skin ripped open from my

furious blows as rage coursed through me. I felt powerless, engulfed in a wave of anger.

"I have another contact but he's gone underground. With your father gaining power, many people are in hiding."

I punched again and again, imagining my father's face as I landed hit after hit, cursing his name and begging for an opportunity to end him.

"Atta boy!" Corbin exclaimed, entering the training room with General Minifred scowling by his side. Bee was following closely behind them, appearing lost in thought. I realized that, just like me, she was concerned for Nicole.

"It's important to be intentional with each punch. Anger is good, but if you don't strategize your punches, they will be less effective," Minifred explained as he took his seat to observe my training session.

"Here's your B12 vitamin," Corbin said before holding out his palm.

General Minifred slapped his hand, sending the pill flying. My best friend had been waiting on his mate's father hand and foot, and the old alpha was getting more and more annoyed.

Corbin huffed before setting his hands on his hips. "Vitamins are good for healing, Dad."

"Please fucking stop calling me Dad."

My beta pouted, and Eve giggled to herself. Bee looked like she wanted to throttle both of them.

I punched the bag, and the chain broke, sending it flying across the room. It slammed into the wall, sand spilling from its maw.

"That's the third one this week," Eve grumbled before waving her hands and fixing the mess with a simple move. Once it was secured to the ceiling again, I went back to punching.

"Hannah wants you to call her back," Bee told me.

"Is she having any luck?" I asked.

Since Hannah was half fae, she too, was trying to request an audience to find out what happened to Nicole. Unfortunately, the last time we spoke, she was hitting as many roadblocks as we were. As a half-breed, she couldn't conjure any portals.

Bee shrugged. "Not yet."

I slammed my fist into the heavy bag again.

"Hey!" Corbin griped, dodging the swinging bag. "Watch it, bro!"

The general barked out a laugh. "Too bad your aim wasn't a little more to the left."

My gaze sliced toward him. He was wearing a black patch over his eye where the socket beneath sat empty. Unfortunately for him, shifters couldn't regenerate any body parts that were completely severed from their body. The witches' healers and his accelerated shifter powers were able to repair the rest of his injuries, but he was now adjusting to life with one eye. He acted as if it were a non-issue, but I couldn't imagine that actually being true. I knew having limited vision would throw me off.

"I wasn't trying to hit Corbin," I deadpanned.

"Maybe I should take a stab at it." The general punched the air, narrowing his good eye on my beta.

Corbin whimpered under his breath. "Let's focus more on our game plan and less on filicide, shall we?"

"Who's focusing on filicide?" the general questioned. "Certainly not me. I'd *never* harm my daughter. And you're *sure as shit* not my son."

Bee groaned, rubbing her temples. "Dad. Please. Can you lay off Corbin for just a bit? He's right. We need to focus on what matters. And right now, that's figuring out what happened to Nicole and her dad."

The general nodded once. "My team still cannot locate her father. He seems to have gone off the grid entirely. The only thing we know for sure is that David disappeared around the same time as Nicole, Juniper, and the fae professor."

I lifted my shirt, wiping the sweat off my face. "I wouldn't be surprised if my father moved Dr. Fairweather to another location."

I felt sick, thinking of the possibilities. I knew my father had no qualms about torturing someone. While David's research was valuable to my father, I was pretty sure my father was past the point of acting rationally. If anything happened to my mate's dad, she'd never forgive me.

I moved over to sit on the ground, my legs bent as I cradled my head in my hands. I didn't have time for a full breakdown, but it was all adding up. Worrying about Nicole. Wondering what the hell my father was up to. Stressing about the future while feeling trapped at the damn witch head-quarters.

"Hannah is calling again," Bee mused with a sigh.

I didn't really have time to talk with her, but maybe she found us a lead.

I held out my hand for the cell phone, and Bee placed it in my palm. The moment I answered, Hannah's screeching voice boomed in my ears.

"Alexei? Do you have any news?"

I held the phone away from my face for a moment and sighed. "No. I was hoping you did."

She cursed. "I tried reaching out to my aunt, but she said there was no way in hell she'd help a shifter right now. Especially not Alpha Jones's son. It's such a mess. I hate that we can't get to her."

My heart felt like it was racing out of my chest. I fucking hated this. "How is Jade doing?"

"Not good," Jade answered for me. Hannah must have had me on speakerphone. "I'm worried about David and Nicole. And I'm still pissed we didn't find that damn horn. I feel that whoever was sending us those messages through Nicole's familiar wanted us to search for something that wasn't there."

"How is Macey?" I asked.

Jade cursed. "She's lounging as if she doesn't have a damn care in the world. I keep giving her treats and brushing her fur, hoping she'll give us another vision, but nope. Nothing. But she doesn't seem concerned, so that has to be a good sign, right?"

I had to admit, it was a relief to know Macey wasn't freaking out. As Nicole's familiar, she was attuned to her in a way no one else could ever be. If Nicole were truly in danger, she'd be tearing down the fucking world to get to her. It was the only thing that was keeping me sane. "Well, keep trying. That's all we can do."

"I hate this," Hannah murmured.

Yeah, I hated this too. But there wasn't much we could do. I'd daydreamed about kidnapping a fae and demanding that they open a portal, but I'd have to find a fae first, and Eve was right, all of them were underground, hesitant to be seen by anyone associated with my father. Even though I'd formally renounced my pack, I was still his blood.

"Let me know if anything changes," I grunted.

"Same," Hannah agreed.

When I hung up the phone, Bee reached out to take it. We exchanged a look, both of us consumed with worry.

"We'll find her, baby," Corbin said to her. I was glad he wanted to comfort his mate, but I was annoyed that he had been absent for me lately. I knew that there was a priority shift between us and he wanted to take care of her the same way I craved to be there for Nicole. But I was hurting too, and he was too busy taking care of General Minifred and Bee to step up for me.

I wouldn't normally be so petulant, but I just felt so fucking alone.

"I know everyone is frustrated," Eve said, "but I have some good news."

I perked up. "Yeah?"

Eve nodded. "My team of healers finished their project. They made you an eye, General."

As soon as the high priestess had finished talking, the entrance to the gym swung open, and in walked a lady in a white coat. She had a container in her grasp and a look of excitement on her face.

"It's perfect, ma'am! You're going to be so pleased."

"Who is this?" General Minifred asked while eyeing her cautiously.

"Senior Healer Karen Heart," she replied proudly, her yellow curls bouncing as she spoke. She was so excited she could barely stand still.

"And what's this about an eye?"

With shaky fingers, Karen opened the box and tilted it down for all of us to see, looking like a game show host showing off her prize. Propped on a bed of velvet was what appeared to be an incredibly realistic glass eye. I had a feeling it was much more than that though.

"It's wonderful, isn't it?" the healer asked. "We couldn't get the color to match your exact shade, but I added a few features I think you'll appreciate."

"What *kind* of features?" the general asked warily.

I didn't blame him for being skeptical. I knew I needed the witches' help right now, but that didn't mean I would blindly trust them. Too much was at stake for me to blindly trust anyone outside of my immediate circle.

Karen flashed a toothy smile as she approached the general. "It's better if I show you. Let's take off that patch and you'll see." She giggled. "Literally."

Bee's father looked to Eve, who was nodding her head. "You have nothing to worry about, August. You know me well enough by now to know I'd never allow anyone to hurt you."

What? Since when were they so well acquainted? First, my mother, and now this? Was there anyone in the supernatural world this man didn't know?

The general took the box from the healer and removed his eye patch. Bee and Corbin both looked away, as if it pained them to see the evidence of the man's injury. "What do I do?"

"Simply lift it to your eye socket, and it'll do the rest," Karen answered. "Don't worry, it's perfectly sanitary, too. It's spelled to resist bacteria."

"Well, that's reassuring," the general grumbled sarcastically.

He took a deep breath before lifting the eye from the box and aiming it toward his face. I think Corbin, Bee, and I all held our breath as we watched the eye do as Karen promised, levitating off the general's hand before fusing to his empty socket. The man blinked rapidly as it settled into place before looking around the room, his expression curious.

Damn.

Besides the obvious color difference between the left and right sides, you couldn't even tell he had suffered an injury. The general's magic eye moved in sync with the one he was born with.

"Why is everyone surrounded in different colors?" he asked.

"That's the best part!" Karen announced. "When you look at your daughter, what do you see?"

His gaze focused on Bee. "Light purple, and… a reddish purple, like a raisin."

"That makes sense," the witch healer proclaimed. "Light purple signifies love. The darker color would show worry. What do you see when you look at Alexei?"

I stood still as the general assessed me. "Black… a lot of it. And crimson."

She nodded. "Also makes sense, all things considered."

"What do you mean?" I asked. "Why is he seeing colors?"

"He's seeing *auras*," she corrected before looking toward the general. "Pretty neat, right?"

"Ooh!" Corbin raised his hand like an idiot. "Do me! What color am I?"

General Minifred looked at Corbin and sighed. "Purple again."

"Well, of course it's purple!" my beta said. "That's because I love your daughter so much."

"Yeah, well, you can knock that shit off anytime now," the general grumbled.

My best friend rolled his eyes. "Impossible, Dad. She's just so damn lovable."

"Quit calling me Dad!" General Minifred clenched his fist while Bee blushed. "I suppose this will come in handy. It could help me see people's motivations. Will take some getting used to, though."

"I was thinking it would be useful at the Summit!" Eve said excitedly.

I snapped my head to the witchy woman. "There's still going to be a Summit?" With every-thing going on, I wasn't expecting the supernatural council to hold their annual schmooze and snooze event.

Eve nodded. "Just got confirmation today for the twenty-eighth and twenty-ninth of this month. It'll be a great opportunity to show your father we're a united front and see what he's been up to, without risk of an attack. Plus, all council members are required to attend, so we'll have at least one fae present to petition for a portal."

A surge of hope filled me. She was right. This was good. *Really good.* I knew my father would be present; his ego wouldn't allow otherwise. Only the most powerful families were invited to Summit each year. He wouldn't dare risk not showing in fear that someone would assume he wasn't worthy. And this event was fiercely protected by an anti-violence spell. It was the only way so many powerful beings could safely gather.

"There's more," Eve added.

"What's that?" General Minifred asked.

"Since the council will already be gathered close by, we set a date for Alpha Jones's hearing immediately after the Summit presentations conclude. First, we'll perform a timeline spell to dispel any confusion on which supernatural faction has rights to Nicole and her father. After that's settled, we'll review the charges against your father regarding the recent massacre at the university."

"Have the council investigators finished gathering witness statements and evidence?" I asked.

"As much as possible," Eve confirmed. "You and the vampires will give your testimonies in person, but all other witnesses have submitted sworn statements."

I thought about the opportunity at hand. My father's hearing was the perfect place to challenge him. Mass murder and kidnapping were some serious charges, but my father had an excellent legal team. I couldn't afford to rely on a guilty verdict, but I *could* challenge his position as alpha right then and there. The council couldn't deny my right to challenge my father. The law required an immediate fight to the death or by submission, and the council headquarters had a chamber specifically for that in the lower level of the building. I would catch my father off guard, and we would fight in a controlled environment, which I wouldn't get anywhere else.

"It's the perfect location," I murmured, mostly to myself.

"For what?" Corbin asked.

I looked around the room, locking eyes with everyone as I came to terms with what I'd have to do. "I'm going to challenge my father at the hearing."

There was a moment of silence as my pronouncement landed like a boulder in a lake, the ripples spreading through everyone's expressions.

"Are you sure you're ready for that, son?" General Minifred asked.

Corbin whined. "Why do you call *him* son and not me?"

The general and I both ignored my beta's poorly timed question. "I guess I'm going to have to be." I slammed my fist into my palm. "Let's train."

FIVE

Nicole

"TRY AGAIN."

"I *am* trying," I whined.

My uncle was tutoring me in astral projection, but I was failing spectacularly. My father and Juniper were off somewhere in the palace so I wouldn't be distracted, but my focus was complete shit. There were so many thoughts running through my brain at once, it was pure chaos.

"Breathe, Nicole," Cammie suggested. "I know this is a lot, but you have the power inside of you. You just need to coax it to the surface."

"Easy for you to say," I grumbled. "You've known who you are—what you are—your entire life. I've had… what? A few hours to grasp the concept that I'm supposedly a demigoddess with actual magic inside of me?"

"There's no *supposedly* about it," Cyrus insisted. "You have these abilities."

"Are you positive about that?" I raised a brow in challenge. "I am half human, remember? I thought half-breeds didn't have special abilities."

My uncle scoffed. "I am *positive*. The fact that all those mating bonds were occurring on the day you fully reached magical maturity proves it. I think your lack of faith is inhibiting you from tapping your power. You need to believe you can do it, and you need to stop relating yourself to common supernatural factions. Gods are anything *but* common."

Sheesh. Superiority complex, anyone?

Cammie sighed. "Cyrus has a point, Nicole. You need to suspend disbelief."

"*Suspend disbelief?!*" I barked out a laugh. "Isn't that what I've been doing since the day I came to Redwood?"

"We're getting off track again." My uncle muttered something under his breath. "Focus, Nicole! Linking to your mate should be easy. You already share a bond. You just need to search him out in your mind and find him. See him. *Now, close your eyes and think of Alexei.*"

I let out a lengthy sigh, feeling defeated but knowing that I needed to succeed if I ever wanted to get out of this place. Spending time with my father and getting to know my uncle was great, but I was itching to get back to my mate. It was an overwhelming sensation, calling Alexei my mate, but I knew our connection ran far deeper than any surface emotion. Just a few weeks ago, I would have been petrified to commit to such a union, but now, my soul ached in his absence.

Closing my eyes, I thought of Alexei, his dark eyes burning with passion, the fresh outdoorsy smell that clung to his skin. My thoughts drifted to our tightly clasped hands, two puzzle pieces that fit together snugly, as if they were meant to be connected.

"I'm thinking of him," I whispered, longing in my chest.

God, I missed him. It seemed like every time we took a step forward in our relationship, something pulled one of us away, and I hated it.

I felt a tug in my chest, like a tiny string made of fishing line that connected us. "I think... I think I can feel our bond."

"Great!" my uncle said. "Grab hold of that bond."

I visualized touching the string. It seemed so

dainty and weak, and that really frustrated me. I wanted metal chains forged by the strongest steel to connect Alexei and me. I was even more determined to get back to him so we could work on being stronger together.

A sudden jolt in my chest made me inhale sharply.

"What?" Cammie asked. "What is it?"

My eyes moved rapidly as colors formed beneath my lids. "I think I'm getting something."

"Stay locked on it," Cyrus encouraged.

It took a moment for it to materialize, a lot like the visions my familiar had shown me. But once it did, it was as if I were standing in the same room with Alexei. He was sitting on an oversized couch, his hands plastered to his face, elbows balanced on his knees. My mate looked despondent and exhausted beyond belief. God, I could feel the lonesomeness in his soul as he released a harsh breath. It was identical to mine.

Corbin walked into the room, handing Alexei a glass filled with amber liquid. "Here, dude. Junie's mom said this should help."

Juniper's mom? They were with the witches? I looked around and didn't recognize a thing, so I knew they weren't at the Kappa Zeta house. The small, dimly lit den had dark paneling and several seating areas. Oil portraits hung from the walls, depicting different women through clearly different eras in time.

Alexei took the glass and sniffed. "Whiskey? How is that going to help me find Nicole?"

Corbin shrugged. "It won't. But it will help you chill. You've been training hard all day. You deserve this."

Training? Where were they? How long had I been gone in earth time?

"I'm so fucking restless," Alexei said. "I need to shift and run."

"Me too, bro. If we weren't in fucking New York City, I'd be sprinting and howling at the moon." Corbin sighed and stared at the door for a moment. "Bee is warming up to me, but her father keeps cockblocking me every time I get her alone. And it's not even like I'm trying to get in her pants. She's worried about Nicole and all this shit. I just want to comfort her, get inside her heart. Her father's like a fucking blood clot." He patted his chest, and I giggled to myself. I had a feeling that was about as poetic as Corbin would ever get.

"You just compared your future father-in-law to a blood clot," Alexei deadpanned.

"It's true, though. Also, can you try to be a little less amazing? I know you're training to take down your father at the hearing, but the general called you *son*, and I'm feeling a little jealous. Can you, like, do something that'll make him hate you but also puts me in a better light?"

Wait. Alexei was going to challenge his father at the hearing? Did the council finally set a date? My heart raced and images from the last time Alexei was up against his father hit me full force, making the vision turn hazy for a moment. I tried to focus so I didn't lose the connection, but my fear was making it difficult.

"I'm not going to do that," Alexei said before taking a sip. "I need him for training. Since General Minifred took me under his wing, I've gotten better at fighting. Once I've found Nicole and killed my father, I promise to make you look good, though."

Corbin whined. "I'm not sure I can wait that long. I'm getting blue balls of the soul, man."

I giggled again. Leave it to Corbin to make me feel better even from worlds away. I missed him. I missed Bee, too.

Alexei looked up from his glass, almost staring directly at me. "I get it," he whispered. "I hate I wasted so much time pushing Nicole away. And now that she's gone, it makes me sick. I can almost feel her in my chest, man."

"Listen to us," Corbin said with a sad smile.

"Pining over our women. Remember when we used to talk about normal things? Like threesomes and which butt plug worked best?"

Alexei cringed. "For the record, *I* never talked about any of that. *You* rambled about bedazzled butt plugs and threesomes with a raven—*speaking of*, has anyone told Juniper's mate that she's off in Faerie?"

Corbin sighed. "Eve helped me send him a magic letter. He's flying here right now. Apparently he got held up in Texas with some storm. He replied with a pile of bird shit in an envelope."

Alexei let out a loud, booming laugh. "I like him. Maybe he can help us, too."

"I wouldn't count on it. Ivan lets Juniper do her own thing. He loves her, but I think they work because he just trusts she'll always find a way back to him. Maybe that's what we need to do."

I smiled to myself. Ivan really was best for Juniper. I didn't even know the guy, but he seemed to let her shine on her own. As I grew into my goddess powers, I wasn't sure how Alexei would feel about that. I was going to be in more danger and have more responsibilities. How would that affect our dynamic?

"I know Nicole will come back," Alexei whispered. "Because I'll burn all of Faerie down to get to her if I have to."

"No!" I shouted as the vision faded. "Come back!"

I opened my tear-filled eyes as I lost the connection.

"What did you see?" My uncle was looking at me with great concern.

"Alexei..." I started. "Corbin... they were in New York City. Why would they be there? He mentioned Juniper's mom."

"The witches' headquarters are in the city," Cammie explained. "The high priestess lives there most of the year. They don't just let anyone in though. They're highly protective of that space, considering how many important magical beings reside there. Something must've caused them to be so accommodating."

"Like a full-scale attack in the woods?"

"Must be," Cammie agreed.

"Must be, what?" Juniper asked, walking into the room with my dad in tow. "How are the magic lessons going?"

"Nicole just successfully executed astral projection," my uncle announced, pride heavy in his voice. "She saw her mate at your faction's headquarters. Any idea on how they would've gotten there?"

June twirled a purple curl around her finger as she thought about it. "My mom probably had a premonition." She looked at me and smiled. "Well, that's a relief, right?"

I frowned in confusion. "What do you mean? I'm not connecting the dots."

She waved her hand. "Oops. Sorry, sometimes I forget you're so new to this world. My mom has these visions sometimes... warnings from the fates. She likely saw the attack at training camp and intervened. If Alexei and crew are back in the city with her, they probably rode with her on the Witchy Express."

My lips curved as Juniper used her preferred term for teleportation. "I have to go back. Alexei is going to challenge his father, and I need to be there to support him."

Cyrus shook his head. "You're not ready, Nicole. There is still a lot you have to learn. I haven't even taught you how to use the horn."

I rolled my shoulders back. "I have no choice. Look, I get that I need to learn about my powers, but this has to take priority. My mate is in trouble."

Cammie chewed on her lip. "She's right, Cyrus."

Cyrus spun around and glared at the fae princess. "We'd be literally tossing her to the wolves with no knowledge on how to protect herself. What if she's captured by a collector?"

I understood why he was worried, and if I was

being honest, I had my own reservations about these new gifts. But they would have to wait. My priority was Alexei, and I refused to let him challenge his father without me by his side. "Well, I guess you're going to have to find a way to teach me as much as you can in the next hour. Because I'm going back whether or not you like it."

I crossed my arms over my chest, leaving no room for discussion.

Cyrus looked conflicted, his eyes narrowing.

"Cyrus, it'll take years to teach her everything, and we don't have the time for that," Cammie added. "The mating bonds overwhelmed her when she first came into her power, but the elixir leveled that out. It's not like she can walk around accidentally creating shifters—not unless she has the horn. And she'll be at the witches' headquarters, the safest place in the world right now, aside from here of course."

"I suppose you're right," Cyrus relented. "But I still want her to study our ways and her gifts. There is so much to learn."

Juniper snorted. "It's not like there's a Demigoddess 101 class she could take. You're literally the most elusive supernatural faction there is. You made up an entire fake land of the gods just to evade us. Hell, my brother's reveal spell doesn't even recognize you, and that's a pretty powerful bit of magic."

Cammie smiled. "I have sacred texts here that aren't available to the public. I'd be happy to lend them to you, Nicole, so you can learn more about yourself."

I chewed on my lip. I wasn't sure how much time I'd have for studying once I got back, because we needed to deal with Alpha Jones, but I would try. "I appreciate that."

Cyrus scowled. "I don't like it, but... I'm willing to compromise. Perhaps I can come for a visit soon."

"Great. I'll go back and help my mate, and we can deal with all the demigoddess business later." I smiled triumphantly.

Cyrus narrowed his blue eyes. "It's not something you can put off, Nicole. It's in your blood—your soul. It's your purpose. I know you're overwhelmed, but you need to accept your role. You have an important job to do."

I slumped, feeling like a chastised child. "I know. It's just... a lot. I just want to help Alexei. One problem at a time, right?"

Juniper spoke up. "If I had some dragon snot, I could clone you. Just saying."

Cyrus rolled his eyes at my witchy friend before turning back to me. "For the record, I don't agree with this, but as you are my sister's daughter, I also know I have no chance of changing your mind."

"You're right." I nodded. "You don't. So let's do what we need to so I can get back to Alexei."

If I wasn't mistaken, my uncle actually seemed proud of me for standing my ground. Looking over at my father, I could see that he did, too. And when I thought about it... I was pretty proud of myself. I was done sitting on the sidelines and being a victim.

It was time I took matters into my own hands and claimed my mate.

Nicole

"Are you sure you're okay with this?" I frowned, not entirely comfortable with it myself, but deep down, I knew it was the safest option.

"I'm positive, honey," my dad assured me.

When my uncle had suggested leaving my dad behind with him in Faerie, my first instinct was to argue. I'd just gotten him back, and I didn't like the idea of my father being on an entirely different *dimension*. But then my dad pointed out that Alpha Jones wouldn't hesitate to use him as leverage again. He would have no qualms about torturing my father, or even ending his life. Alexei's dad was too unpredictable to place any value on my father's research at this point. The least likely place the psychotic shifter would find my dad was Faerie, so I agreed.

My dad looked at me, concern peppering his expression. "Besides, *I* should be worried about *you*. I don't like the idea of you going back there. Are you sure this is a good plan? You could stay here longer and—"

"*I can't*, Dad. You *know* I can't." I grabbed his hands and searched his eyes for a response. "Alpha Jones is doing terrible things, and I know it's hard for you to understand how I feel about Alexei, but I can't let him face this alone. But I also don't like the idea of leaving you. Who's going to take care of you?"

"Sweetheart, *I* can take care of myself." He took a step closer to me and placed a hand on my shoulder. "I know your first instinct is to care for me. You've always been so brave, so selfless. Always worried about everyone else instead of yourself. And for the record, I may be an old man, but I understand how you feel about Alexei. The first time I saw your mom, it felt like someone had taken a defibrillator to my heart. Every beat thereafter was solely for her until you came along."

I sniffed as my eyes filled with tears. "You're not *that* old, Old Man."

My dad chuckled. "Just be safe, okay? Please don't hesitate to come back here if things get too dangerous."

I had no intention of running, but I nodded to ease his worry. He embraced me fiercely, like he was trying to shield me from the oncoming danger. My throat tightened, knowing that this was the last time I would see him for a while. I had to be strong, even if it broke my heart a little, leaving him behind. But every second I was away from Alexei was *excruciating*, and nothing would stop me from being by his side as he challenged his father.

"Are we ready?" Juniper strutted inside the sitting room, her spelled trunks overflowing with random ingredients for potions and hovering in a single file line behind her. I didn't want to know how many magical beings she had to collect *specimens* from, but she was practically overflowing with giddy excitement as she assessed her collection earlier. "I have enough ingredients to make some killer defense spells. Alpha Jones won't know what hit him!"

My father laughed. I think part of the reason he was okay with me leaving was because I had Juniper with me. She was absolutely a talented witch, and he liked that she was on my side. She'd quickly won him over with her quirky attitude and love for potions. Dad kept calling her a chemist, which June thought was adorable.

Cammie's flowing gown trailed behind her as she crossed the room to stand next to my father. "I promise you have nothing to worry about, Nicole. I'll keep him safe."

"And you're sure the stasis thing will work?" I asked for the tenth time in as many minutes. I wasn't convinced that it was foolproof.

She nodded. "I'm positive. As long as David remains in Faerie, the tether between you two will remain intact. His timeline will mirror yours back on earth."

I inhaled deeply, blowing out through my mouth. That was one of my biggest worries. Time passed on Faerie so differently from earth. I didn't want potential decades to pass before I could see my dad again. I was already concerned about the amount of time I'd been away from Alexei. When I'd asked if Cammie could do that tether thing with us to make time pass slower, she'd informed me it didn't work that way. For a time-line tether, as she called it, to work, both people needed to be in Faerie when the magical link was forged.

I let out a shaky breath, feeling anxious but eager to get back to Alexei and share with him everything I'd learned.

"Nicole?" I turned toward the entryway and spotted my uncle walking inside, carrying a wooden box that seemed to have light bleeding through the cracks. He gave me a sheepish smile. "I think you're going to need this."

I took a step closer to him. "Is that?"

Cyrus nodded. "Your mother's horn."

Being so close to the magical tool made my blood sing.

I reached out my hand as Cyrus lifted the lid, gasping as the golden bejeweled horn came into sight. "Wow. It's stunning."

"The horn is very sacred. Guard it with your life, Nicole."

I nodded nervously. "Wouldn't it be better to keep it here?"

He looked at me, then back at the horn. "I think you're going to need it. And I trust the witches to keep it locked up."

He waited patiently as I ran my finger over the precious metal, tracing the designs that were intricately carved into the side. "Remember. The moment you return, you must secure the horn in the Crystal Vault at all times unless you need to summon the spirit. It would be disastrous if this fell into the wrong hands."

"No worries there." Juniper winked at him. "It'll be the first thing we do."

According to Juniper, the Crystal Vault was located at the witches' headquarters, and it was more secure than Fort Knox times a thousand. The thing was supposedly warded so heavily an unauthorized being wouldn't stand a chance of penetrating its defenses. Since we were already going there to join Alexei and the others, it worked out perfectly.

"Okay, then." My uncle nodded. "I suppose we're ready."

"Gentlemen, you might want to take a few steps back," Cammie warned as she began waving her hand in a counterclockwise motion. "We wouldn't want anyone to accidentally fall into a portal, now would we?" The fae princess turned toward Juniper. "Juniper? May I please have a strand of your hair? It'll ensure you don't have any issues getting past the wards."

"Sure thing," my friend said, plucking out a purple curl and handing it to Cammie.

I watched in awe as the shimmering light swirled in a large circular motion. The ground seemed to tremble beneath us as a bright flash that looked like green lightning cracked through the air. The portal appeared and fractured the space, creating a ripple of power that made my bones shake from the intensity of it.

"I love fae portals," Juniper said in awe. "They're way more exciting than the Witchy Express."

"Hurry. I can't hold it for long," Cammie said, spurring me forward. "The wards your mother has in place are incredibly strong."

I took one step and could see colors forming on the other side. Another step and the edges of my vision grew fuzzy. Pressure filled my ears. Something about portals and getting ripped through time and space made me nauseous. Juniper, annoyed with how slow I was going, rushed past me with a childlike giggle before sprinting through the portal, her train of trunks floating behind her. I glanced back at my father and gave him a shy smile before running after Juniper. The moment I stepped through, my entire being felt electric. Power boomed in my core as I jumped across the space and landed on a hard wooden floor.

My ankles wobbled with the landing, and I straightened my spine just as the portal closed at my back. My fingers tightened around the box safely tucked under my arm in its case as I waited for my vision to clear.

The moment it did, my eyes locked with a familiar brown gaze that shook me. There was so much determination, relief, and *love* in his eyes that my heart stalled. "Nicole?"

I smiled at my mate. "Hello, Alexei."

"Nicole! Oh-thank-fuck-you're-back-Alexei-has-been-an-absolute-nightmare-since-you've-been-gone!"

I barely had a chance to make sense of Corbin's lengthy string of words before he was tackling me in a fierce hug that took me to the ground.

"Ow!" The corner of the box I was holding was digging into my ribs.

"Get off her, you asshole," Alexei growled, pulling Corbin by the back of his shirt and flinging him to the side. In a much gentler tone, he added, "Are you okay?"

I took the hand he was offering to help me stand, adjusting the box in my arms. The tips of our fingers brushed as I rose, and my entire body flushed. My throat and lips were suddenly dry, and my pulse hammered a million miles a minute. It was exhilarating, like I had been diving off a cliff overlooking a clear blue sea.

"Yeah, I'm good." I shivered as tingles coursed through my veins. "I think."

Alexei drank me in, scanning every inch of me with obvious concern—and a healthy dose of lust.

"It's been twelve days, Nicole. Where have you been? What have you been doing?"

"In—"

Juniper approached us, gesturing to the wooden box. "Sorry to interrupt the caveman's interrogation, but we need to put that in a safe place."

I jumped when the air suddenly shimmered and Juniper's mom, Eve, popped into existence right in front of us.

"Darling!" She pulled June into a hug. "You're back! Did you have a pleasant time in Faerie?" Her gray eyes turned toward me. "Nicole, welcome to our home. May I take that for you? I *saw* how important it was, so we should secure it immediately."

I handed Eve the box, confident it was safe with her. My uncle wouldn't have suggested allowing her to store it in their vault if she wasn't trustworthy. "Thank you."

Eve carefully took the horn from my hands and said, "I'll be back shortly," before disappearing into thin air.

"Nicole!" Bee screamed. "Oh my God, you're back!"

My bestie attempted to tackle me much in the same way her mate just had, except she was considerably smaller, so the impact wasn't the same.

Thankfully, I had nothing in my hands this time. I leaned into her tight hug, thankful she was okay.

"Hey," I said to her.

Bee pulled back, pushing her wild hair out of her face and fixing the skewed frames perched on her nose. "I was so worried about you." She pulled on my hand, leading me to a nearby couch. "Sit down. Tell us everything."

"You first," I say. "Tell me how you got here."

Alexei was mumbling something under his breath, seemingly irritated about the interruption. The weight of his gaze was tangible as Bee went on and on about how June's mom had a vision and showed up to magically transport them back here. She rambled about how they'd known I was in Faerie—evidently a Fae portal couldn't be mistaken for anything else—but they had no way of reaching me, though not for lack of trying. The fine hairs at the back of my neck rose as my mate struggled with impatience, clearly unhappy about being on the sidelines of this conversation.

It was disorienting to know that twelve whole days had passed here while it had only been hours in Faerie.

Eventually, Alexei let out a huff of obvious frustration and stomped over to me. I was mid-sentence when he picked me up, sat down, and pulled me into his lap. Bee giggled as I melted into his embrace while his nose nuzzled my neck. And when he breathed me in, I practically panted.

Bee cleared her throat. "What happened? What's the deal with that box thingy Juniper's mom just took?"

I opened my mouth to answer her, but Alexei gripped my hips, stalling my thoughts. "I... came into my..."

He trailed his lips along my ear and whispered. "I missed you so fucking much." The way he spoke made my legs tremble.

"Powers," I finished, practically rasping out my words.

Bee gasped.

Juniper wiggled with excitement, but I couldn't tell if the witch was happy to show off her goods or something else. She eyed Alexei with a smirk.

"Seems Alexei *really* missed you, Nicole," the sneaky witch said. "I can practically taste the lust rolling off of him."

I wiggled on his lap a little, eager to release some of the tension coiling in my stomach. And when Alexei groaned, Bee let out a nervous laugh. I could feel his cock digging into my ass, and his grip on my hips tightened.

"Uh…" Bee's cheeks flushed. "Maybe we should continue this conversation later?"

"Excellent idea," Alexei said.

I yelped as he stood abruptly before maneuvering me around and tossing me over his shoulder. Bee and Corbin laughed knowingly, while Juniper offered a lewd gesture in my periphery.

"Alexei!" I shouted as my hair brushed the back of his legs, and blood rushed to my head. "Put me down!"

His arms banded tightly around my hamstrings as he speed-walked across the room. "Not happening until I get you somewhere private."

The promise of what was to come made me ache with anticipation.

He started kicking at doors, cursing loudly at every locked one, his tense shoulders flexing in frustration.

Finally, *finally* he found a room that was unlocked and strutted through it as quickly as possible. I could barely glance at the exquisite office before Alexei's lips crashed against mine with untamed ferocity, his tongue feverishly exploring my mouth. My fingers curled around his shirt, feeling the rapid rise and fall of his chest. My moans were quickly smothered by his sturdy grip, as I was swept away by the burning passion that blinded us both.

"I was so fucking worried about you. Thought I'd never see you again," he groaned while kissing my neck. "Is this real? Are you here?" He walked us back toward a mahogany desk, and when I hit it with the back of my legs, he lifted me up, perching me on the edge.

God, being with Alexei was something sinful.

My eyes rolled back as he tore at my clothes. "I'm back, Alexei. It's real."

"Don't ever disappear on me again," he said in a voice full of anguish. "I can survive anything as long as I have you. If I lost you..." Tears glistened in his eyes, and I quickly interrupted him.

"I won't go anywhere," I told him firmly. I ran my fingers along his jawline to soothe him. "I promise."

"Good." He nodded, seemingly satisfied with my answer, before his lips curved into a wicked grin. "Now, spread your legs and let me taste what's mine."

CHAPTER
SEVEN

Nicole

MY WHOLE BODY heated at his command, my skin burning. His alpha instincts were in full effect, everything about him so intense and dominant I had no choice but to obey. When I opened my legs, Alexei instantly dropped to his knees in front of me, ducking beneath the long material of my dress. My hand fluttered against my chest as his fingers lightly brushed my skin. Goose bumps scattered across my thighs as his fingers climbed higher and higher, but not quite high enough.

"Alexei," I whimpered. "Now is not the time for teasing."

He kissed my inner thigh as he moved my

panties to the side. "Don't worry, baby. I don't have patience for that either right now."

I closed my eyes as I felt the first swipe of his velvety tongue. A long moan escaped me as he buried his face and licked me greedily, the stubble lining his jaw scratching my skin. My mind went blank as pleasure took over, and I had to grip the edge of the desk to keep myself afloat. I leaned forward, giving him full access as he sucked my clit and used his tongue to stroke me into oblivion. I arched my back and gathered the silky material covering his head, bunching it around my hips so I could see his dark hair moving between my thighs. Alexei was relentless as he devoured my pussy, grunting as he made me feel so fucking good. I'd missed his mouth and his touch, his body and the way he took from me like he owned me.

It seemed like only a few seconds before I was shaking, crying out as I came. I fell back on my elbows, needing a moment to catch my breath. Alexei rose from the floor, towering over me when he got to his full height. As our eyes met, I was certain the hunger in his gaze matched mine. Our desire for one another was palpable, and I couldn't look away from him as he grabbed my hips and pulled me closer. I wound my arms around his neck, and he crushed his lips to mine.

"There's my girl," he said before he kissed me. He wrapped a hand around the back of my head and squeezed my hair as we kissed. "I've missed your sweet scent," he said against my lips. "Your taste. You're so fucking beautiful, you know that?" A sound escaped me as he nipped at my chin. "Tell me you missed this, baby. Tell me you missed me."

"I did," I whispered, kissing his neck, as a guttural sound came from deep in his throat. "So much."

"I need to be inside you," he rasped, lips trailing from my neck down my collarbone. I shivered with a burst of arousal as he bit the sensitive spot where my neck and shoulder met.

"I need that, too," I promised him. God, I needed that so badly. "But we should talk. I have important things to tell you."

"Whatever it is can wait until after I get inside of you," he demanded, pulling hastily at my gown. "Nicole, you need to get naked before I rip your pretty dress to shreds."

The white silken material was already askew, but with its built-in corset, it wasn't exactly the type of dress that could easily be removed. The fae-designed garment was definitely made more for style over function.

"It's too complicated," I panted. "Just leave it on for now."

"Fuck that." His lust slammed into me as he pulled back, his fingers going to the neckline of my gown, forcefully shoving it down.

"Alexei!" I cried, but he didn't stop until my breasts were revealed, my exposed nipples ready to cut glass.

His full lips sealed around one, licking and sucking me into a frenzy until I felt like I was about to come from that alone.

"Now repeat what you just said," he said in a dark tone.

My heart jumped into my throat as I stared at him in confusion.

"Repeat it," he demanded.

I blinked through the haze of lust. "Which part?"

Coarse stubble grazed my skin as he switched sides. "The part about how much you missed me."

"So much," I repeated breathlessly. "Being apart caused this... void inside of me I didn't know existed before then."

His eyes darkened as he reached up to cup my cheek. "Tell me."

"It felt like an essential part of me was missing," I said with no hesitation, and he kissed me roughly. "I couldn't stop thinking about you and wanting you. Despite how overwhelmed I was, you were always on my mind. I feel like I'll never get enough of your touch. Your mouth." He groaned. "Of you. I need you like I need air. You're truly the other half to my soul, Alexei. Before we met, I honestly didn't understand what the word soul mate meant, but now, I do."

He let out a low moan, his eyes blazing. "I love you so much it fucking hurts, woman."

I slid off the desk, offering him my back so he could unlace the corset. As he tugged on the ribbon, he kissed my spine with each section he untangled. I took a deep breath as the last tie was undone, kicking off my slippers and turning around to face him. Alexei's chocolate gaze drank me in as I pushed the dress over my hips and stepped out of my panties, completely bared to him.

When I started to reach for his shirt, he grabbed my wrists and pinned them behind my back. "I need to be inside you." He ran his nose up my neck, nipping at my jaw.

"Alexei," I panted. "Please let me touch you."

I wasted no time as he released my hands, reaching out to unfasten the button on his jeans. The sound of our panting and the zipper being undone reverberated around the room. Alexei moaned as I shoved his pants and boxer briefs over his hips, gripping his thick length. I glided my thumb over the sensitive tip, mouth watering as I imagined licking up the bead of clear liquid that was there.

Alexei reached behind his neck, pulling his shirt over his head. When he saw I had dropped to my knees while he was undressing, he groaned. "Damn, that's a beautiful sight."

I reached for him and pulled him closer, pressing a soft kiss against the head of his dick. "I want you in my mouth, and I don't want you to take it easy on me. I need to know I'm yours, that you're mine. Choke me with your cock, baby."

His eyes flared. "Fucking hell, woman. You keep talking like that, and I'll be coming before I even get inside your mouth."

I placed another chaste kiss on the tip before flattening my tongue and tracing the large vein on the underside of his shaft. "Mmm. That would be very disappointing, because I want it hard. Make me gag, Alexei."

He groaned as he slowly threaded himself into my mouth. "Fuck. Part of me wonders if I'm dreaming right now."

I sucked him in deep, making sure he knew how very real this was. When he still hesitated to take control like I needed him to, I dug my nails into his backside and pulled him closer. Saliva pooled in my mouth as Alexei triggered my gag reflex, but I was careful not to show any signs of distress. I relaxed my jaw even more, breathing through my nose as I sucked him in as deep as he would go.

"Goddamn, Nicole." He fisted my hair. "You really want it like this, huh?"

I peered up at him with watery eyes and growled my agreement.

"Fuck. Okay." His fingers tightened. "Hands behind your back. Don't move them until I say so."

I immediately complied, clasping my fingers together at the small of my back. The position thrust my cleavage forward, which Alexei seemed to appreciate. He pounded into my mouth quickly and fiercely, just as I'd wanted, and tears ran down my cheeks as he continued. Some may have thought he was being domineering, that he was trying to degrade me with his rough behavior, but I knew the truth. *I* was in control here. *I* was the one giving him pleasure, and *I alone* had the power to take it away whenever I chose.

Not that I would, because I was so damn aroused I could implode at any moment.

Alexei massaged my scalp, watching my lips stretch around him. "Such a good girl. Look at how well you suck my cock. I think you deserve a reward. Don't you?"

I hummed around his shaft, causing him to jerk inside my mouth.

"Fuck yeah, you do," he panted. "Touch yourself, baby. Flick that pretty clit of yours until you're nice and ready for me."

I was *already* ready for him, dripping with need, but I followed his instructions, whimpering as my fingers met my needy pussy. I pumped my finger in and out a few times, gathering my arousal before sliding it over my swollen nub in slow circles. Alexei continued fucking my face as I played with myself, the erotic soundtrack we made making the whole thing even hotter.

"God, it's so good," my mate praised. "So fucking good I will not last much longer like this, Nicole. I need you. Get up."

Before I even had the opportunity, Alexei was freeing himself from my lips and picking me up with his muscular arms. He kissed me with such passion that I barely had room to breathe. I could feel the depth of his love for me, and how much he needed me. I wrapped my legs around his waist as he carried me back over to the desk and pressed his cock against my entrance.

"Mine," he growled.

"Yours," I agreed.

The moment the word left my lips, Alexei entered me with one long stroke. I cried out as he filled me to the hilt, my nails digging into his shoulders. He was so thick I felt like I'd never get used to being stretched like this. He pulled all the way out and thrusted back in, burying himself inside my body, indelibly imprinting himself on my soul. I moaned and dropped my head back. Alexei leaned forward, kissing my neck while fisting my hair and forcing my head back at an awkward angle. The mild sting somehow intensified the pleasure he was giving me, though. My mate filled me completely, thrusting and plunging with the force of a roaring river current. He stopped and grabbed my gaze, demanding that I see the pleasure on his face as he moved within me. Fire danced across my skin, and I gasped as I flew higher and higher with each stroke. His intensity was overwhelming, and I silently begged him to never stop.

Alexei reached out, running the back of his fingers against my cheek. "Look at me. I want to watch the way I make you feel."

"Yes," I whispered.

"You're never fucking leaving me again, Nicole," he grunted, plunging deep, pushing my body across the desk until my head hit the back wall. "You fucking stay with me. I never want to worry like that again. Do you understand?"

"Always," I promised.

"Nothing will ever come between us again," he promised, pressing my knees back into my chest as he fucked me harder. "You're mine."

"I'm yours," I repeated. "Forever, Alexei."

"I'm going to come so deep inside of you," he grunted. "I'm going to fill you until you're dripping with it."

I moaned, feeling his cock thicken, my pussy tightening around him. I was close. As I came, I rubbed my clit and cried out, calling out his name. He grunted and held himself against me. I could feel him pulsing inside of me as he came. We were surrounded by the scent of sex and wanton desire, and I buried my face in his neck and held him as I rode out the last of my orgasm.

"I missed you so much," I whispered, brushing my lips against his neck.

"I can't do this without you. Nicole, I can't live without you. I'm sorry I ever made you think I could. I was a fucking arrogant fool."

"The past doesn't matter," I assured him. "Only the future. *Our* future."

He kissed me softly, and I could feel his cock still twitching inside of me. "I can't wait for you to get pregnant one day. Watch you growing with my child."

My heart clenched as I pulled back and met his eyes. "Alexei..." I placed my palms against his chest. "We need to talk."

His cock was thickening inside of me already, and his eyes darkened. "About what?"

"There's something I want to tell you. Something I *need* to tell you." I could see the confusion in his eyes as the guilt of never being able to bear his children ate at my soul. I frowned, but before I could think too much about it, Alexei was reaching between us and sliding his fingers over my clit. He rubbed me roughly, and I groaned, my body aching for more. He kissed me again and moved his hand down to my entrance, his fingers sliding inside of me, the fullness a foreign yet not unpleasant sensation.

I gasped. "Oh. That's new."

He smiled devilishly as he curled his finger upward and rocked his hips, the combination of the two making me writhe. "I'll always take care of you. You know that, right? Mind, body, and soul. You're safe with me, Nicole."

"I know." My heart squeezed at his words. "But—"

He placed a gentle kiss on my mouth. "Then the

only thing that matters right now is *this*. Everything else can wait."

I knew it was irresponsible given our circumstances. But I allowed myself a moment of selfishness to indulge in our reunion. Because no matter what happened in our future, we were fated to be together. There was no longer any doubt in my mind. If Alexei needed this physical escape to reassure himself, then that's what I was going to give him. And if I was being honest with myself, maybe I needed it, too.

CHAPTER

EIGHT

Nicole

I STROKED Alexei's chest as he held me. We were lying on the floor in the office, drunk with pleasure and feeling more connected than ever before. "Wow. That was…"

"There are no words for what *that* was," he said. "But at least I can check *banging a goddess* off my bucket list."

"*Demi*goddess." I giggled, playfully smacking him.

Somewhere in between our second and third round, I managed to at least tell him that part.

"My bad," Alexei laughed.

I lifted my chin to look at him. "It's weird, right? Of all the possibilities, I never would have imagined."

"I'd say it's more ironic than weird. I thought we couldn't be together because you were human, and to most shifters, humans are the lesser race. But the truth is, *I'm* not good enough for you."

I propped myself up on my elbows and looked into his dark eyes. There was no mistaking the insecurity in his tone. "You know that's not true, right? It doesn't matter what either of us are. We're fated to be together, regardless."

His lips curved into a soft smile as he brushed some sweaty hair away from my face. "Look at you, readily accepting the concept of fated mates. You've come so far."

I rolled my eyes and laughed. "Well... it's kinda hard not to when it's *my literal job* to bless mating bonds. Don't you think so?"

Alexei sat up, prompting me to do the same. "What do you mean?"

Oh, right. We didn't exactly get around to what *kind* of demigoddess I was. I was suddenly glad I had thrown his discarded T-shirt over my head after we finished making love. As comfortable as I was with Alexei, having such a serious discussion in the nude didn't seem right. Plus, there was the matter of all that skin being distracting. Like right now, as my hungry gaze drank in Alexei's muscular frame and the growing appendage between his legs.

"Uh... maybe we should get dressed first." I nodded to said appendage. "Your naked body is making me lose focus."

Alexei smirked the sexiest smirk there ever was as he leaned closer. "I'm okay with that."

I scrambled to my feet and took a few steps back. "Nuh-uh. Get dressed, mister. We need to talk. And I have a feeling whoever this office belongs to doesn't want to find us naked on their floor."

Alexei rolled his eyes but eventually agreed. "Fine. I suppose everyone needs to hear this."

"Finally!" Corbin said through the door. "It's been *hours* and I want to know what happened!"

I went still. "You don't think he was listening the *entire* time, do you?"

"No worries there, Nicole!" Juniper's voice piped in. "I put a sound block while you were doing the dirty in my mom's office. I legit just lifted it a few seconds ago to see if you guys were done yet."

Oh, my God.

Alexei frantically got dressed while I tossed my gown on. I couldn't believe they were out in the hall waiting for us.

When we opened the door, Juniper, Bee, and

Corbin were standing there with matching shit-eating grins.

"Not a word," Alexei growled.

"My man's got stamina," Corbin teased, ignoring his threat.

Bee giggled. "My dad and Juniper's mom are waiting in the conference room. They sent us to pull you away from your sex fest."

Corbin nodded. "I believe General Daddy's exact words were, 'Tell those idiots to stop humping like dogs in heat and get their asses in here so we can have a long overdue conversation.'"

Great. Now everyone knew we were getting it on, *and* I was being reprimanded by my bestie's dad.

"No need to look so embarrassed," June said. "We have a firm sex-po policy here at Witch Head-quarters. You should've seen the look on the gener-al's face when my mom told him he needed to release some built-up tension and invited him to an orgy."

My jaw dropped. "She did what?!"

"It was hilarious," Corbin snickered. "When he declined her invitation, she then had to explain why he should stay away from any rooms with a pineapple posted outside the door."

"Why would someone post a pineapple outside

of their door?" I asked, thoroughly confused why we were suddenly talking about fruit.

"Aw, Nicky, you're adorable." Corbin booped my nose. "I'll let your mate explain that one to you. Who knows? It might result in some fun."

Alexei pinched the bridge of his nose. "Enough! I don't want to hear another word about anyone's sex life, okay? Especially mine." He turned to me and lowered his voice. "I'll explain the pineapple thing later. And trust me when I say you will *never* have to worry about it because *I don't share*."

Corbin and the girls laughed as we headed toward a meeting room down at the end of the hall. I was sure that my cheeks were bright red from blushing as my mind finally filled in the blanks.

Corbin came to a dead stop mid-stride, causing us to nearly slam into him.

"What the hell?" Alexei groused.

"Sorry, dude," his beta whispered. "I just wanted to make sure you warned her about General Daddy's eye before she walks into that room. He won't admit it, but the guy's obviously pretty sensitive about it. He gets super pissed whenever I stare, so I wanted to make sure Nicky had a heads-up."

"A heads-up about *what*?" I whispered back. "What happened to his eye?"

Alexei scrubbed a hand down his face and sighed. "When we were under attack at the training camp, the general lost an eye."

I gasped. "Holy shit! Is he okay?"

"You know how he is," Bee answered. "He'd rather have his toenails ripped off than talk about mushy feelings. But... yeah, I think being in such a vulnerable position messed him up. He seems slightly better after the healer gave him a prosthetic, but I think he'll need a while to adjust. His new eye is a different color than his real eye, so every time he looks in a mirror, he's reminded of the day when he wasn't as invincible as he'd like to think he is."

"Oh, man."

I didn't really know what else to say. That *would* be tough for someone like the general who had a *mind over matter* disposition. I made a mental note to keep an eye on him, no pun intended.

"Yeah." Bee gave me a sad smile. "But knowing my dad, the first time the aura eye gives him a tactical advantage, he'll be glad things worked out the way they did."

Huh?

"What the hell is an aura eye?"

I knew auras were the layer of energy someone had around them, and that witches were gifted with the ability to see them, but my mental database had nothing about aura *eyes*.

"Ooh!" Juniper raised her hand. "I'll field this one. My mom told me all about it while you and Alexei were banging. So, the aura eye looks and acts just like a regular eyeball but *better*. General Hotpants now has a built-in color-coded aura detector. Each color has a specific emotion or intention assigned to it. Apparently, he was a little grumpy when she gave him the laminated study guide we hand out to the kiddos at witchling school, but he's obviously been using it, because he memorized the whole thing. Rumor has it, he's been practicing by cockblocking Corbin. Anytime Corbin shows a hint of horniness, the general gets all growly and starts spewing threats."

"Rumor, my ass," Corbin muttered. "The man's determined to ensure I never make sweet, sweet love again."

The apples of my bestie's cheeks flushed scarlet. "Corbin! Not the time."

Wait a second...

I peered closer, noticing how there was an intimacy between Bee and Corbin that wasn't there before I went to Faerie. Corbin's fingertips rested on the small of Bee's back. Her body was curled inward, subconsciously leaning into her mate's side. I felt the stirrings of something precious as Bee gazed up at him lovingly, despite the annoyance in her tone.

I gasped when it hit me. "Oh, my God!"

My best friend was straight-up dickmatized! I didn't know when... or how they got to that point, but I *knew* they had, in fact, done the dirty while I was gone. They had passed the point of no return in solidifying their mating bond.

"Later," my lifelong best friend mouthed, obviously knowing I was on to her.

"Stop bullshitting and get your asses in here!"

The five of us startled as General Minifred's voice boomed down the hallway.

Bee stroked Corbin's arm as he whimpered.

"Oopsie," June singsonged. "Looks like we're in trouble. Maybe if I'm lucky, he'll spank me."

"Gross." Bee made a gagging gesture.

Juniper shrugged. "Sorry, Bee, but your dad's a DILF."

"Jesus fucking Christ," Alexei growled, taking my hand and leading the way into the conference room. "Let's get in there before this conversation goes off the rails again."

The high priestess smiled brightly as we reached the threshold. "Did you two have a pleasant reunion? Orgasms are great for clearing the mind. I hope it helped."

The general scowled.

Okay, now my *entire body* was probably bright red. I knew there was nothing shameful about sex, but that didn't mean I wanted my *friends' parents* to know I was just getting dicked down. I certainly didn't want to *talk to them* about it, especially when one of those parents was like a second father to me.

"Uh..." I shifted awkwardly on my feet. "Fine. Can we please change the subject now?"

"Thank fuck," General Minifred muttered.

"Come in." Eve waved us in. "Have a seat."

The five of us selected chairs around the large conference table. Alexei's hand never left mine as we sat next to one another.

Bec's dad straightened his shoulders, going into general mode. "Okay, let's start by hearing from Nicole about her time in Faerie. In the interest of disseminating information as efficiently as possible, I think we should reserve any questions we may have until the end. Sound good?" He looked around the table as we all nodded. "Very well. Nicole, the floor is yours."

I sat up straight. "Okay. Well, as you all know, June, Dr. Viden, and I all stepped through a portal to Faerie." Murmured acknowledgments rang through the room. "And it's pretty obvious the professor... er, Cammie, didn't return with us." More murmurs. "That's because she stayed behind to watch over my father, who's also in Faerie."

"What?!" Alexei shouted. "When?! How?! Why didn't you tell me?!"

The general cut him a sharp look. "Alexei, no questions until the end. Remember?"

Alexei glowered, making it clear to everyone he didn't appreciate being scolded like a child, but he simply nodded for me to continue.

"Long story short, Cammie was spying on Alpha Jones and has been for a long time. Her cover was blown, so she grabbed my father and brought him to Faerie. My dad's safe for now, and that's what matters, right?"

"Why would the professor spy on my dad?" Alexei asked.

General Minifred glared at my mate for interrupting again, but then he motioned for me to continue.

"Because the fae are concerned about your dad's obsession with altering DNA. They're not buying his story that he's only trying to find a cure for the missing wolf gene to help shifters. They think he has some evil agenda that poses a risk to *all* supernaturals." I gave him a pointed look. "They're not exactly wrong, Alexei."

"Okay… that's fair." My mate frowned. "But speaking of agendas, what's *Cammie's* agenda? She's *fae*, Nicole. Are you sure we can trust her? I know she doesn't act like your typical fae, but their entire race is known for trickery. How do we know her kindness thus far isn't part of some elaborate ruse?"

Oh, it was an elaborate ruse alright, but not like he was thinking.

"I agree with Alexei, Nicole," the general said. "What assurances do we have for your father's safety right now? Fae-human relations are volatile at best. They may have outlawed the Wild Hunt, but that doesn't mean every fae is a law-abiding citizen."

I nibbled on my lower lip. "Yeah… about that. It turns out everything you think you know about the fae is wrong. Nearly every part was carefully culti-vated and hand-fed to all the other supernatural factions."

Eve's yellow curls bounced as she shook her head. "I don't understand."

"Cammie would be a much better person to explain this, but since she's not here, I'll do my best." My gaze swung toward General Minifred. "The fae made it all up. The trickery, the selfishness, their appetites for torturing humans... it's all fake. Everything all the other supernatural factions have been taught... all the legends... they were all stories fabricated by the fae. They wanted others to fear them, but not because they derived any sort of pleasure from it. They were just trying to protect themselves. Protect their land."

The general's newly heterochromic gaze bore into mine. "I can plainly *see* you believe all of that to be true, but there's no way that's possible. Do you understand how much time and effort it would take to craft and maintain such a large-scale deception? We're talking about *thousands of years* of history, Nicole. It's *impossible*."

Everyone but me and June were nodding furiously in agreement. They were all looking at me with pity, as if they thought I was some poor naive girl who was just duped into leaving her father behind for the nasty fae to torture and kill.

"Baby..." Alexei tugged on my hand. "I know you think—"

I yanked my hand out of Alexei's grip and stood up. "I don't *think* these things, you guys. I *know*! *With every fiber of my being*, I *know* it's true!" I jerked my head to Juniper. "Help me out here, would ya?"

"It's true," June told them. "Look. If I didn't see it myself, I would absolutely call bullshit. But I met quite a few people while I was in Faerie, and *every single one of them* had squeaky-clean auras. Not an ounce of deception or malice in sight."

"That proves nothing," Juniper's mom argued. "A few nice people do not speak for an entire species."

Juniper sighed. "Nicole, it'd probably make a lot more sense if you told them about the alliance. The spirit pack. If you explained *what* you are."

Shit.

Why didn't I think of that? If they knew about my heritage and the fae's alliance with the gods, then they would understand. Sure, I was skeptical at first, too, but after my experience with the mother wolf's pack, I was a devout convert. My connection to Fáel was just as real as my bond to Alexei. Neither were tangible, but both were unequivocally an essential part of my soul.

"Wait…" the general said. "You learned about your heritage while you were in Faerie? Why didn't you just start with that?! What *are* you?"

I resisted the urge to cry from the overwhelming emotion. Instead, I sunk into my chair and closed my eyes. Alexei scooted closer, nuzzling his face into my neck.

"I'm sorry," he murmured. "I wasn't trying to upset you."

I took a few deep breaths, grounding myself in the tranquility his presence gave me. "I know."

"Nicole?" Bee's dad prompted.

I inhaled one more time and then looked the general right in his magical eye. "I'm a demigoddess."

Alexei

THE STUNNED SILENCE after Nicole dropped the goddess bomb was deafening. Juniper and I'd had a little time to process it before now, so we were okay, but everyone else seemed to be in varying stages of shock.

Eve's gray eyes widened as she mouthed, "Wow."

"Holy shit," Bee blurted.

The general's jaw dropped open. "How…" A crease formed between his dark brows. "Where…" His broad shoulders straightened as he cleared his throat and tried again. "What…"

"Oh, my God," Corbin whisper-shouted. "Is General Daddy actually speechless?"

Bee whacked him with the back of her hand. "Shut up, Corbin!"

General Minifred glared at his daughter's mate. "Call me that one more time and see what happens."

Corbin held his hands up in surrender. "Hey! I was just making an observation. Don't shoot the messenger! I don't know what the big deal is, anyway. We've always known Nicky was special. I, for one, am not surprised one bit that she's a goddess. Now that I think about it, I kinda had an inkling. It makes total sense."

I snorted. "Yeah, right."

Corbin was a smart guy, but if *I* didn't see this coming, he sure as shit didn't.

"*Demi*goddess," Nicole corrected.

"Semantics." Corbin waved his hand dismissively.

Juniper giggled. "Uh... there are some pretty big differences between the two, Corbin."

My idiot best friend scoffed. "I guess it all depends on how you look at it."

"That makes no sense," I said.

"Sure it does," he insisted. "It's subject to interpretation."

"No, *it's not*." I gave him a wry look. "There are

gods and demigods. One is immortal, one is half human.”

Corbin shrugged. “Guess that’s in the eye of the beholder, bro.”

Juniper lifted a single brow. “You do realize you keep saying the same thing, right?”

He pointed at her. “Don’t get sassy with me, lady. You’re still high on my shit list for giving me an elephant peen.”

I groaned. “Not this again.”

His mouth gaped. “What do you mean, *not this again*?! I needed a goddamn holster for my Johnson, Alexei! Do you know how traumatizing that is? DO YOU?! If it’s *not that big of a deal* like you keep telling me, maybe she should give *you* a whale dick, too! *Then* we’ll see if you still think I’m being a big whiny baby!”

“I thought it was an elephant pecn,” Juniper gibed. “Which one was it, Corbin? Whale dick or elephant peen? You can’t have both.”

“Does it really matter?!” he shouted. “I looked like I was smuggling an anaconda in my pants!”

“Oh, *now* it’s an anaconda?” June rolled her eyes. “You sound terribly confused about the whole thing. That must’ve been awful.”

“Finally! Someone cares. Thank you!” Corbin

shouted, clearly not picking up on her sarcasm. "It was fucking awful."

Nicole smirked. "Eh, it wasn't *that* bad."

Bee laughed. "But it *was* funny as shit."

Juniper high-fived Bee.

"Babe!" Corbin whined. "Are you really gonna do me dirty like that by siding with the enemy?"

Bee pushed her glasses up her nose as she rolled her eyes. "Don't be so dramatic, Corbin. June is not the—"

"Enough!" her father yelled. "You're acting like a bunch of children! What is wrong with you? Have you forgotten the serious situation we're all in?"

Well, that effectively sobered us up.

Muttered variations of *sorry* echoed through the room.

"I don't need your apologies," General Minifred told us. "But I *do* need answers. So can we please get back to the subject of Nicole's lineage?" He waited for us all to agree. "I just have one thing to say first. Corbin?"

Corbin sat up straighter. "Yes, General Da... er, *sir*?"

The general waited until he had my beta's full attention. "If I *ever* hear you bitching about your giant magic penis again, you won't have *any* penis left to worry about. Are we clear?"

Ouch.

Corbin blanched. "Crystal, sir."

"Good." The general nodded. "Now, Nicole, please continue."

My mate cleared her throat. "Sure. Um... where was I?"

"You left off at demigoddess." I winked.

"Right." She smiled. "Maybe I should back up a little and tell you about my uncle."

"Uncle?" the general questioned. "I wasn't aware David had any siblings."

"He doesn't," she confirmed. "Cyrus is my mom's twin brother."

"Twin brother?"

She shrugged. "I mean, technically, they both were just willed into existence at the same time, but they had a whole yin and yang thing going on, so it's easier to call them twins. He lives in Faerie. Actually, he and my mom grew up there."

Everyone but June's brows rose as her words sunk in.

"How can that be?" Eve asked, assessing her carefully. "If you are a demigoddess, I would presume your mother was a goddess."

"She was," Nicole replied. "More specifically, the lunar goddess."

"What?!" I shouted. "Why didn't you tell me *that*?"

She gave me a pointed look as she whispered, "We were kinda busy with *other things*, remember?"

Fuck.

Now I was thinking about Nicole's pink-tipped breasts bouncing in my face as she rode me.

I discreetly adjusted myself. "Right. Sorry for interrupting."

Her pretty blue eyes lit up with amusement as she picked up on my ill-timed arousal. "Anyway, as I was saying, my mom was a lunar goddess."

Corbin's eyes met mine from across the conference table, and I could tell he was thinking the same thing I was. The lunar goddess had a direct line to the mother spirit. She was the only being in existence who could restore a shifter's missing wolf. But she stopped answering our prayers when I was just a pup. Nearly my whole damn life, my father had preached about how the goddess had abandoned us. How we needed to rely on *science*, not fate. How *he* was the man to restore what was so cruelly taken from us. Before I'd met Nicole, I had honestly questioned whether the goddess had ever existed. But now I knew she *did* exist, and she didn't *abandon* us. She *died* while giving birth to *my mate*.

What kind of crazy cosmic shit was that?

"Whoa," Corbin mouthed.

Whoa, indeed.

"So this uncle of yours…" Eve started. "He is the sun god, yes?"

"Yeah!" my mate replied. "How'd you know?"

"The old legends about gods are irritatingly vague, but there was a nursery rhyme I used to recite as a girl. How did it go?" She tapped her chin in contemplation for a moment. "Oh, yes! I think I've got it. Let's see…

A pair of gods born as one,
Sister of moon, brother of sun.
One rises with the day,
The other with night.
One painted in colors of dark,
The other in shades of light.
One rules the wild, unlike any other,
The other's rule is eternal until she becomes the mother."

She quirked her head to the side. "Some believed it was based on a prophecy, but I never bought into that theory. That last line doesn't really make sense though, does it? How odd."

My gaze sliced to Nicole as she stiffened. "Yeah… weird."

"You okay?" I asked.

She gulped. "Yep."

I knew that wasn't entirely true, but we could discuss it in private later.

"So, what does being a lunar demigoddess mean exactly?" Bee asked. "Do you have, like, really cool superpowers and shit?"

"Um... according to my uncle, I have the same goddess powers as my mom did, but that's a work in progress. I'm supposed to bless mate bonds for fated wolf shifters, and I can summon the mother wolf to create more shifters. And even though I have no clue how to do either of those things yet, something pretty amazing happened to me while I was in Faerie that proves everything my uncle and Cammie told me. *The mother spirit's pack came to me.*" Nicole paused for a moment to let the enormity of that sink in. "There's no way words can do it justice, but it was this unbelievably sacred experience. I *felt* my connection to them and the mother wolf in the deepest depths of my soul."

"That must've been incredible, Nicole." General Minifred smiled proudly. "I'm sorry for doubting you."

"Thank you," Nicole replied.

"Hold up." Corbin made a time-out gesture with his hands. "You can't, like, *revoke* mate bonds, can you? 'Cause no take-backs. Bee is mine."

"I don't think so?" Nicole answered. "Even if I could, I'd never do that to you guys."

Corbin slumped in relief, then subsequently stiffened once the general growled deep from within his chest.

I stifled a laugh.

"There's one more thing." Nicole worried her bottom lip. "Remember how I said my uncle and mom grew up in Faerie?"

"Yes…" Eve replied. "Which is quite peculiar. Why would two gods be raised in Faerie instead of their own realm?"

"Yeah… about that." Nicole shrugged. "The god realm? Elysian Point? That was made up, too. Elysian Point is actually a mountain range on Faerie, which is where *all* the gods were raised. Fae and gods all live on Faerie in one big, happy, peaceful colony. The whole reason the fae purposely trashed their reputation was to protect the gods. I guess you could say the fae are like god guardians or something."

What the fuck?

"What the fuck?!" Corbin shrieked, verbalizing my thoughts.

"You guys haven't even heard the best part yet!" Juniper said excitedly. Everyone turned to face her, wondering what the hell she was talking about.

"There's *more*?" General Minifred asked.

"Yep!" She beamed. "I got pegasus semen!"

"Uh... not what I was expecting, but okay," I grumbled.

June stuck her tongue out at me. "Anyway, the collection process was... sticky... but I got like a gallon of their jizz. Do you realize what this means?!"

Corbin laughed. Bee looked like she was going to be sick.

Eve clapped her hands in excitement. "Oh, my! Imagine the possibilities. Pegasus semen is a powerful accelerator."

"Exactly!" Juniper fist pumped the air. "I was thinking we could use it to do a locator spell. Find those poor kids that Alpha Jones kidnapped for his psycho boot camp!"

"That's amazing, Juniper!" my mate exclaimed.

"That *is* great," the general said. "Good job, Juniper. But please never tell me how you got your hands on the magic ingredient, okay?"

June laughed. "Deal."

"Oh!" Nicole grabbed my hands. "I thought of something else, but I swear, this is the last thing. I can astral project places. Not for long and it's really tricky, but I kinda sorta popped in on you while I was practicing."

"Can you see what Alpha Jones is doing right now?" General Minifred asked excitedly.

"*When* did you watch me?" I said over him.

"Oh, my God. You could project yourself to a sold out concert and get front row seats!" Corbin added.

"Uh..." Nicole frowned, probably wondering where the hell Corbin's random statement came from like I was. "I suppose I *could* do that? Maybe? But, I wouldn't feel right about going to any paid concert and not buying a ticket, so that won't be happening. I'm a firm believer in paying artists for their masterpieces, whatever form they come in."

"Nicole?" I tightened my grip on her hand. "*When* did you project to me? What did you see?"

"What's wrong, dude?" Corbin asked. "Afraid she caught you trying to wrestle your one-eyed snake?"

Juniper and Bee laughed while General Minifred rolled his eyes.

I gave my supposed best friend the bird. "Would you be serious for one goddamn minute, Corbin?"

Corbin pouted and crossed his arms over his chest. "I'm just trying to lighten the vibe a little, man."

"Be that as it may," the general replied, "there's a time and a place for your childish quips, and this is not it." He narrowed his eyes as Bee placed her hand on Corbin's forearm. "Are you seriously lusting after my daughter right now?!"

Corbin's hazel eyes rounded. "What?! Of course not! What kind of question is that?"

The general pointed to his left eye. "Magic eye, remember? I can *literally see* you have a one-track mind right now."

Corbin sank lower into his chair and grumbled, "Damn that thing."

"Can we please get back on track?" I begged. "Nicole. What exactly did you see when you projected to me?"

She shrugged. "Mostly just you and Corbin talking. I can tell you more about it later. It's nothing important."

"Can you use it to spy on Alpha Jones?" General Minifred repeated.

"I could *try*," Nicole offered. "But I think it would take some practice. It was really difficult for me to see Alexei, and the only reason I think I could accomplish that is because I followed our mating bond."

The general sighed. "Nicole, I don't need to tell you how beneficial being able to get information directly from the source could be for our cause, do I?"

"No." She shook my head. "I'll work on it. I promise."

"Good. I think we're done for today then." General Minifred looked around the room. "What the hell are you still doing here? Go!"

He didn't need to tell me twice. Nicole and I had twelve days of lost time to make up for, and I intended on being very thorough.

Nicole

I STOOD in the grand hallway to the witches' headquarters with a nervous smile on my face. Jade and Hannah had screamed a stream of obscenities at Alexei when he called to tell them I was here, and I was worried they'd still be angry we didn't reach out the exact moment I'd arrived.

I was *also* worried Corbin would let it slip that I was busy having life-changing sex with my mate in favor of letting them know I was safe.

"Why do you look nervous?" Alexei softly said at my side.

"You know how they can be." I could feel the blush rising to my cheeks.

"It's me they're angry with. I'm about to fight my father for control of the pack, but it's *Jade* that has me shaking in my boots."

A burst of laughter escaped me just as Eve appeared through the main portal with both my aunts and Macey in tow. The second I could see Hannah's Prada shoes and Jade's black turtleneck, they both started sprinting over to me, fierce expressions of concern on their faces.

"My sweet baby! Oh, my goodness, you poor thing!" Hannah crashed into me with a hug, ripping my hand out of Alexei's. She stroked my hair like I was a child afraid of the dark and gave me kisses on my cheek, leaving what I was sure was a line of lipstick smears along my skin in her signature shade of ruby red.

Once Hannah was done, it was Jade's turn, who was a little more aggressive about her hug. "Don't you ever leave me again, young lady!"

A bark drew my attention, and I had to force Jade to let me go so I could greet my familiar. I crouched low and held my arms out for the sweet wolf, smiling ear to ear when she got closer, allowing me to wrap my arms around her neck—which currently had a bedazzled bow around it. Hannah's doing, I was certain.

Mace barked happily, tail wagging as I nuzzled her neck. "I missed you, too, girl."

When Alexei joined us, Macey growled at him.

"Get over it," my mate grumbled. "I'm not going anywhere."

My familiar turned her nose up at him as if to say *whatever*, making me laugh. "I see nothing has changed between you two."

Juniper crouched beside me and my wolf, tickling Mace behind the ears as they had one of their silent conversations.

"Mace is just feeling a little possessive right now since she missed you so much," my witchy friend explained. Her lips twitched when Macey's black eyes narrowed and she released a yip. "Okay, *and* she's not exactly sold on Alexei."

"What the hell?" Alexei threw his arms up. "Why not? Surely she knows by now I'd never harm Nicole."

My familiar whimpered, nudging me into a sitting position so she could pretend she was a little lapdog. I let out an *oomph* as she curled her enormous body over my legs.

Juniper stood up with a shrug. "She does. But she's still pissed because you hurt Nicole in the past."

"Oh, sweet girl," I cooed. "You're just looking out for me, aren't you?"

Mace barked excitedly.

Alexei crossed his arms over his broad chest but said nothing. I could sense his underlying guilt, so I made a point to smile softly, reminding Alexei that *I'd* forgiven him for the past, even if my familiar wasn't quite on board yet.

Alexei smiled, receiving the message loud and clear.

"Well, this reunion has been lovely, but you have *a lot* of explaining to do," Jade said.

I winced.

Alexei cleared his throat before speaking up. "Why don't I let you all catch up? I need to meet General Minifred in the training arena in fifteen minutes."

"Hannah, it seems like Alexei is avoiding us." Jade's tone was snarky. "Don't you think so?"

Hannah breezed, "Yes. It does. It's almost like he knows he should have called *the second she arrived*."

Juniper choked on a laugh, and my cheeks flamed, easily predicting her next words. "He was a little preoccupied giving Nicole orgasms."

One of these days, I was really going to talk to her about boundaries.

Jade's eyes widened.

Hannah let out an awkward cough.

"Well," Alexei said, awkwardly staring a hole through the ground. "I think that's my cue to go anywhere but here."

He didn't even kiss me goodbye, sprinting away from us so quickly his body was a blur.

"If I could, I'd hex him," Jade growled.

Juniper giggled. "I'm an expert at hexes if you ever need a guide. Why don't I show you to the tearoom? You'll be much more comfortable there while you're grilling Nicole. Snacks make everything better."

"Thank you," Hannah and Jade said at once.

I was a big fan of baked goods, but not even cake would make this conversation any easier. As we followed Juniper's lead, I let out a shaky breath, sticking close to my familiar. I had a feeling I would need to lean on Mace to get me through this.

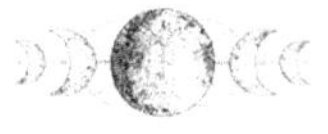

"THAT BASTARD!" Jade shouted. "I don't care if he's a god, I'll strangle him with my bare hands!" She was wringing a napkin in her lap and cursing to herself.

"He just *watched us*, laughing as we searched for the horn he *knew* wasn't there?"

Ugh. I probably should've broken that news to them a bit more delicately. They'd already known the truth about the gods and fae, so that part was shockingly uneventful. At least they were sufficiently wowed when I told them about my encounter with the spirit pack, I supposed.

I winced. "Um... sort of?"

"There's no *sort of* about it." Hannah rolled her eyes. "I'm with Jade. God or no god, that man will fear our wrath when we get a hold of him." She fanned out her fingers. "Look at my nails, Nicole. *Look at them!*"

"Mine, too!" Jade thrust her hand out next to Hannah's so I could examine her nails before turning it palm-side up. "And do you see those?" She pointed to a few rough patches of skin. "Calluses! Don't even get me started on how many days I had to go before I could slide my feet into my Louboutins again!"

Oh, boy.

These two took their nail care seriously. They'd always had the most perfectly manicured and polished nails. I appreciated a good mani-pedi as much as the next gal, but I wasn't obsessive about it like Jade and Hannah. They'd been known to cancel dates at the last minute if they chipped a nail.

I put my hands up in a universal *calm down* gesture. "I appreciate your... sacrifice, really. But can we please get back on topic? You said you sensed the secrecy spell lifting. How could that have happened? Why?"

Jade took a tiny bite of cake followed by a sip of chamomile. Evidently, the witches offered a formal afternoon tea every day without fail. Juniper said the tradition started about ten years ago after one member of their coven magically sealed another witch's mouth shut because she supposedly had *the world's most obnoxious laugh*. In reality, that witch was simply hungry because she'd been so busy working on potions all day she'd forgotten to eat. According to Juniper, there was nothing scarier than a hangry witch.

"It must have happened when you learned about your mother," Jade said with a shrug. "Since you discovered the secret, we didn't have to keep it anymore."

Hannah leaned back in her chair. "And boy does it feel good. I could shout from the rooftops."

"Don't be ridiculous, Han," Jade replied. "We still have to keep it a secret. Nicole is in just as much danger as her mother was, if not more because her mate's father is a psycho. In fact, I think she should have stayed in Faerie. We should look into a way to send you back. The protection charm can only do so much now that you're magically mature."

I thumbed the locket around my neck. "What do you mean?"

"It's not your typical protection spell. It's more of a... decoy. For obvious reasons, I couldn't tell the witch I had hired to make the charm that you are a demigoddess, but I *did* tell her I needed to hide your true nature. Gods and goddesses give off different vibes than any other supernatural being. Even before your full powers came to you, if anyone was paying close attention, they would've figured out you weren't quite human. The protection charm concealed your goddess half. But now that you have reached magical maturity, the best the charm can do is slightly mute that peculiar vibe you've got going on."

My shoulders slumped. "Great."

Hannah leaned forward. "Maybe going back to Faerie isn't such a bad idea after all."

Sure, it was daunting to think about the future ahead of me. I felt safe with Alexei by my side, but there was no telling what enemies we'd face if my heritage ever got out. But hiding wasn't an option. Leaving my mate wasn't an option.

"I'll be okay," I said, trying my best to sound convincing. "*I have to be.* I won't leave Alexei, and he can't run off to another dimension, because his father needs to be dealt with."

Hannah nodded. "Yeah... I thought you might say that. But I had to try."

Jade smiled softly. "Your mother was scared when we first met. She'd been running from collectors her entire life. She battled with the decision of going back to Faerie where it was safe versus staying near the shifters where she was happy, every day. But then she met your dad, and she no longer had a choice. *Nothing* would've convinced her to voluntarily leave his side."

I swallowed. The reminder that *I* was the reason she died made my stomach feel heavy with guilt. "Did you know? About... about the pregnancy and..." I couldn't even say it. "My uncle said I can't have any children." I looked down at my lap.

Jade placed her hand over mine. "Celena didn't tell us until a couple of days before you were born. She wanted to make sure we'd take care of you and your father."

"But one thing I can guarantee, Nicole, is that your mom didn't regret getting pregnant with you," Hannah added. "Not for one second. She loved you so much. She *knew* giving birth to you was her destiny. Even if she couldn't be here with you afterward."

Nodding, I forced myself to take a sip of tea while processing her words. "I never really thought about having kids before. It's a lot to think about. And a little scary."

"We don't need to have the sex talk again, do we? You're... protecting yourself?"

I nodded. "Always. I just... not having the option without forfeiting my life is kind of hard to wrap my head around. Alexei wants to have children. What if he doesn't want me because I can't give him that? I can learn to live with this reality. But what if he *can't?*"

"You haven't told him yet?" Jade's dark brows climbed up her forehead.

"I don't know how." I fought back the tears forming in my eyes. "Or... maybe I'm afraid this will be a deal breaker for him."

Both women gave me smiles full of pity, but it was Hannah who spoke up. "Nicole, we would *never* want to take your mother's place, but we've always felt like you were the daughter we chose. We never settled down. Had no kids of our own." Jade squeezed Hannah's hand. "Family isn't always blood. I know that's hard to hear, but Alexei is your mate. You both will figure out what your family looks like when the time comes. You're not without options."

I sighed. "I suppose you're right."

Hannah smiled. "I'm *always* right."

"Well, at least you're modest about it." I chuckled softly, trying to lighten my mindset, but it wasn't working so well.

"Man, these sugar plum scones could almost replace sex for me!" Juniper took a big bite out of the aforementioned scone as she walked into the room, plopping on the couch next to me. Through a mouthful of pastry, she added, "Mmm. So good." She looked around our little gathering as she finished chewing, frowning. "Why do you guys look so gloomy? You can't be gloomy around baked goods. It's, like, a rule or something."

Ugh.

I didn't want to lie to her, but I also didn't want to tell her about the whole *I can't give birth without dying* thing before I told Alexei. I hadn't even told Bee, and she'd been my best friend since kindergarten.

I swallowed the lump in my throat. "Just thinking about everything that we're facing."

"Yeah, it's all pretty heavy." June nodded in understanding. "You know what I think you need? More orgasms. You should ask Alexei to eat you out again. That always brightens my mood, and from the noises you were making before I put up that silencing spell, I can tell he's good at it."

"Juniper!" I groaned. "Could we save the detailed sex talk for when my aunts *aren't* sitting right next to us?"

Hannah and Jade laughed. "We were *just* talking about your sex life!"

"Not in *detail*," I pointed out. "I'm sorry, but like you pointed out earlier, you've been like moms to me my whole life. I have limits about what I *am* and what I am *not* willing to discuss with you about that part of my life."

Juniper snorted and pinched my cheek. "You're so cute."

"Ow!" I rubbed my sore cheek. "Could you not?"

Her golden eyes lit up with mirth. "Relax, Nicole. I was just saying the big O is always a dependable solution when you're stressed out or upset. It's science. I, for one, know Ivan and I are going to bang like bunnies the second he gets here." She looked at the time on her phone. "Oh! Speaking of, I need to head out to get him. He can't get into headquarters without taking a ride on the Witchy Express. I'll be back soon." June stood and held up her index finger. "On second thought, I'll probably ride his big, beautiful cock a few times first, so I might be a bit. Tootles!" With a finger wave, she flounced out of the room, leaving me blushing in her wake.

"I don't think I'll ever get used to her lack of filter."

"I think she's fun," Jade said.

"Same," Hannah agreed. "There's nothing wrong with a woman owning her sexuality."

"I know there's not," I assured them. "But... *for me*, I prefer to keep those things private."

"That's probably for the best." Jade reached across the coffee table to grab a mini cake. "Alexei gives off major jealous-possessive vibes. I can't imagine he'd be okay with sharing you or allowing another guy to see you in your birthday suit."

I cringed, thinking about the fact that the *entire campus* saw us both in our birthday suits, mid-bang.

"You can say that again," I muttered.

My aunts and I continued to talk, and I felt normal again—which was a tremendous relief considering how much upheaval there had been in my life. I enjoyed catching up, hearing about their antics, and reveling in the uplifting comfort their presence brought me.

"Nicole?" Jade said after a lull in the conversation. "You know we'll be with you every step of the way, right?"

My eyes shone with unshed tears. These two women were there for my mother.

And they'd be there for me.

We had a makeshift pack all of our own, and I knew I could conquer anything with them at my side.

CHAPTER
ELEVEN

Alexei

GENERAL MINIFRED SLAMMED me to the ground, and I could feel the bones in my back crack. He was a brutal fucker, but unlike my father, he taught me something new every time he landed a punch. He didn't attack me for pleasure. It was a lesson.

"You're too busy watching my fists when you need to watch my feet. Your father leads with his dominant foot."

I groaned and rolled over, forcing myself to stand back up even though everything ached. "I still don't understand why we aren't in our wolf forms." I wiped blood from the corner of my mouth.

"Because as I've told you, exposure therapy is a critical component of your training regime. With your father, your wolf's physical strength or fighting skills aren't the problem. You need to *mentally* toughen up to overcome the trauma from a lifetime of abuse."

"No shit," I agreed. "But how does taking a beating in my human shell help? The only way for an alpha to be acknowledged as a true victor is to overcome their challenge while in animal form."

"Because most of your father's abuse took place in your human form, even when you were just a pup, long before your wolf could beat his. And do you know why?"

My back cracked as I stretched. "Why?"

"Because your father is a cocky asshole who likes to hear himself speak. He's a master manipulator; that bastard knows how damaging words can be. When bruises and broken bones heal, it's easier to pretend the injury never occurred. But you don't have that luxury when physical abuse is coupled with emotional abuse. That vitriol digs and digs into your psyche, settling in for the long term, just waiting for the smallest trigger to let it loose. Hope and confidence can be incredibly valuable tools, Alexei. Your father is going to do whatever he can to squash both before the battle between your wolves ever begins."

I resisted the urge to shudder. It made me sick to my stomach to know the power he had over me. But General Minifred was right. The very sound of my father's voice was a trigger.

"Fine," I gritted.

I needed to work on this. Even if it hurt like a bitch.

"Attack me." General Minifred crouched low, his wild witchy eye scrutinizing.

I wondered if he could see my insecurities. My fear. My doubt.

When he narrowed his gaze on me, I had my answer.

Fuck this.

I couldn't let my father get to me. Logically, I knew I was capable. I just had to figure out how to overcome the psychological warfare my father inflicted while we were engaged in combat. I didn't know how I was going to accomplish that, but I knew that failure wasn't an option, childhood trauma be damned. Time was running out, and I needed to learn. The hearing was next week.

I broadened my stance, surreptitiously watching the general for any weaknesses. Of course, the man was extraordinarily well trained in combat, so he gave nothing away. I took a deep breath, exhaling as I strengthened my resolve.

"Stop overthinking it, Alexei," the general barked. "Just *do*. Your instincts are one of your greatest strengths. *Fucking use them!*"

He was right. My instincts were exceptional. The only time they'd ever failed me was when I was being a stubborn bastard and tried ignoring them. In the next breath, I did exactly what the general had demanded.

I lunged.

This time, I aimed lower, using his center of gravity against him. I'd been going for his chest, but he kept blocking it. When I collided with his legs, I knocked both of us down to the unforgiving ground, pinning him before landing a blow at his ribs. I didn't have to hold back with the general; he was strong enough to take my hits. And for the first time in my life, I unleashed everything I had.

He grunted in pain and rolled away from underneath me, throwing a punch to the side of my head in retaliation. My brain shook, my head was spinning, but I didn't let the fatigue or disorientation stop me. He tried to flee, but I leaped forward again, using a partial transformation to extend my claws and sharpen my teeth.

"Good!"

The ability to partially shift was rare; only a small percentage of alphas could do it. My father wasn't one of them, so when he found out I could, he completely lost it and punished me far worse than ever before.

I hovered my teeth over the general's neck, forcing him to submit.

"Impressive," General Minifred said. "I yield."

A thrill shot through me. I'd done it. I really took him down.

I relaxed on the mat and took in some deep breaths. As General Minifred struggled to stand, I almost felt a pang of guilt for pushing him too hard. But if I didn't train as if I were in an actual fight, it would be pointless.

"Do you think I can do this? Honestly?" I grabbed my water bottle, taking my time unscrewing the cap and gulping it down.

The general thought about his answer for a moment. "I think if you can fight the hold he has on your mind, you'll be unstoppable."

That was the problem, wasn't it? I was stronger and more capable than most, but my father had beaten me down—made me nothing more than a hollow shadow of the alpha I could be. At the time, I didn't realize he was doing it to make me less of a threat. He never wanted me to become the next alpha. He wanted to *punish* me for being better.

"I'm working on it," I muttered, my voice barely audible.

I felt like I was in a cage, unable to break free from the memories that kept swirling in my mind. Nicole had helped me last time, her presence providing me with the courage and strength to move on from the pain. But I couldn't depend on her, I knew that much. I had to find a way to heal my wounds on my own.

"Your father beat the shit out of you, kid," General Minifred said, surprising me with the blunt way he spoke. "It's not something you just get over. We need to come up with ways around your trauma, coping mechanisms to keep you focused on the task at hand. What helped you the most the last time you saw him?"

I swallowed, feeling embarrassed for admitting this. "Nicole. I knew I needed to survive for her. I had to be strong enough."

He nodded as if he understood. "Mates are mighty encouragers."

I shook my head. "I should be able to do this on my own."

"You're right, you should." He nodded again. "But knowing your strengths—using every single one to your advantage—is an invaluable resource. Thinking of Nicole, focusing on surviving whatever life throws at you so you can be there for her, is one of your greatest assets. You need to stop trying to be everything for everyone. This isn't just your fight."

I frowned. "What does that mean? *I'm* the one who needs to take my father down. *I'm* the one who literally has to end his life if I have any chance of protecting my mate. My pack." I raked a hand through my damp hair. "Fuck. If there's even a pack left after everything is said and done. Taking down my father is only the first step. What if I do that and find out they were all loyal to him? What if they won't accept me as their alpha?"

"So what if they won't?" General Minifred challenged. "Who the fuck cares?"

My fists clenched as my blood boiled. "What do you mean, *who the fuck cares?*" I stood up, slamming a fist into my chest. "I fucking care! This is what I was born to do!"

"Exactly!" The man got right in my face until our chests were practically touching. "So man the fuck up and do what needs to be done! But you don't have to do it alone! You're never going to succeed unless you can see the truth in that!"

I stumbled back, trying to decode his statement.

After a few moments of coming up with nothing, I said, "Explain."

General Minifred exhaled, cautiously taking a step forward so he could brace his hands on my shoulders. He waited until I gave him the direct eye contact he was looking for before speaking.

"You have many people depending on you, Alexei. Hell, if your father isn't stopped, the entire supernatural world could be affected. Alpha Jones is a formidable man, as much as I hate to admit that. And he has influence, people who want him in a position of power, likely because he's made a lot of empty promises to them. But nobody knows that crazy son of a bitch like you do. Nobody pushes his buttons like you do, which is a *great* weakness on his end."

"I know this. And no one has more to lose than me." I'd been processing Nicole's newfound power and thinking of all the ways my father would abuse it for his gain. I was fighting for my pack. Fighting for my mate.

But I was also fighting for *me*. The boy that got the shit beat out of him. The man that always lived in his shadow. The alpha that has always been too scared to rise for fear of failure.

But I didn't have the luxury of fear anymore.

"But as I was saying earlier, you *aren't* in this

alone, regardless of the fact that you'll be the one who actually challenges Alpha Jones for his title. You have your mate. Your beta. Me. But that's not all." General Minifred spread his arms out. "Look around, Alexei. We're at the witches' headquarters! You know how protective they are of this compound. They would *never* put themselves at risk if they didn't believe in you, if they weren't standing behind you. Offering us refuge was a formal state-ment to *every* witch *and the rest of the supernatural community*. They have faith in you. Hell, I wouldn't be surprised if High Priestess Hale actually *saw* your victory through a premonition. And let's not forget everything your mate brings to the table. With her newly discovered ancestry, the gods and goddesses will automatically back you because you are Nicole's mate. The vampire prince has publicly vowed to protect her and, by extension, you. All in all, you've got some pretty fucking powerful allies at your disposal."

Well, hell.

He was right. Why couldn't I see that before?

I frowned when I thought of another fucked-up variable in this shitty situation. "Can I ask you something?"

"Sure, kid."

I let out a nervous puff of air. "What about

Mara? I don't like her, I certainly don't trust her, but she's Corbin's sister, and if she's telling the truth, she's pregnant with... my... sibling." It was so strange to say. The entire situation was severely jacked.

General Minifred pondered my words for a moment. "I won't lie to you. It scares me that she's pregnant with an alpha that could have her compulsion abilities. But that child is innocent, which means I'll do everything in my power to protect them both."

I was surprised by the amount of relief I felt. Mara didn't deserve Nicole's or my forgiveness, but it was a complicated situation, and we needed time to sort through it all. If she really was pregnant with my half brother or sister, that gave me a vested interest in her safety. That baby deserved a chance to be born. To not be raised the same way I was—with an abusive father beating the shit out of them or controlling them for their own personal gain. He or she needed an advocate. They needed a pack leader that would care for them. Regardless of their parentage, the general was right. The child was innocent, and I, too, would protect them at all costs.

Yet another thing weighing heavily on me. There was so much to think about.

"Should we continue?" General Minifred asked.

I sucked in a deep breath and looked up at him, feeling invigorated and ready to fight once more. "Let's go."

I had to be the best. I had to fight.

Nicole was counting on me.

Everyone was counting on me.

And most of all, I was counting on myself.

Nicole

I GLANCED at the gown I had borrowed from Juniper. It was a witchy deep purple hue, simple yet soft to the touch. Its thin straps were perched on my shoulders, and the heart-shaped bodice glittered with Swarovski crystals hand-sewn into the fabric. It wasn't my regular aesthetic, but I still felt pretty.

As I strolled down the corridor toward Alexei, I kept my gaze trained on my mate. He was dressed to the nines in a tuxedo, plucking at his fingertips as if in deep contemplation. The sound of my stilettos echoing off the marble floor caused him to lift his espresso eyes.

"Wow…" His Adam's apple bobbed as he gulped. "You look… incredible, Nicole."

"Yeah, she does!" Bee fist pumped the air. "I feel so underdressed."

I looked over at my best friend, feeling Alexei's eyes following my every move. Bee was stylish as ever in an off-the-shoulder cashmere sweater, raw-hem distressed designer jeans, and leather booties. Her dark, wavy hair was piled on top of her head as usual, and her black-rimmed glasses were perched on her delicate nose.

"You look amazing as always, Bee." I wagged my brows. "I'm sure Corbin has already told you so at least a dozen times today."

My best friend blushed as Corbin grabbed her hand, placing a kiss on top. "Give me a little more credit than that, Nicky. It was twenty-three times, thank you very much. Some of them in *very explicit* detail. For example, Bee's pussy juice is like the finest—"

"For fuck's sake," Alexei muttered.

Bee snorted. "*Oh my god, Corbin!* You can't talk about my juices"—she gagged a little as she whispered that last word—"*or anything involving sexy times for that matter*, in front of people."

"Why not?" He shrugged. "You're my mate. I

don't care who knows I want to eat your beav for breakfast, lunch, and dinner every day for the rest of my life." Corbin's face scrunched up. "That said... maybe we should keep that on the DL in front of your pops? I think we'll both be much happier if he does *not* rip my dick off with his bare hands."

I giggled. "Probably a good idea."

God, these two. They were kinda adorbs. Despite her initial reservations, Bee was undoubtedly on board with Corbin being her mate now. After we were away from her father's preternatural ears, Bee confirmed my suspicion that they had begun solidifying their bond by sleeping together. Unsurprisingly, it was the best sex of her life. But unfortunately for her, the general was giving his new aura-seeing eye a workout. I'd lost count of how many times I'd seen him thwart my bestie's attempts to sneak off for a repeat romp over the last week. It was amusing as hell, but Bee's dad was bound to realize soon enough that it was a lost cause. As I had learned from personal experience, there was no going back after the process had been started. Like Alexei and me, all that was left for Bee and Corbin was to have a ceremony under a full moon, asking for the goddess's blessing.

I frowned as a thought occurred to me.

Of course, my mate picked up on my sudden change in mood. "What's wrong?"

"Nothing," I assured him, shaking my head. "I mean... nothing more perilous than what we're already facing. I just had a random thought."

"About what?" Corbin and Bee asked in unison, making my lips twitch in amusement.

"I was just wondering about the whole mating bond process. You know how there's two halves to it, right?"

Alexei, Corbin, and Bee nodded in acknowledgment.

"Well... if I'm the moon goddess, and shifters need my blessing to seal their bonds, whose blessing do *I* need?"

This goddess stuff was weird. I searched my mental database and came up empty-handed.

Macey barked, nudging the skirt of my gown with her nose. I placed my hand on her snout to soothe her, gasping as I was immediately smacked with a vision. Only... it wasn't anything like the visions she'd shown me in the past. I felt... closer to it, somehow. As if I were experiencing it firsthand. I was lying in a hospital bed, with my father at my side, wincing as I squeezed his hand.

"Okay, Celena, I think one more push will do it," the doctor at the end of the hospital bed said.

Celena? Push? What the hell?

I looked toward my father, noting how much younger he looked. Then a sharp pain tightened my abdomen, stealing my breath.

"We're almost there, Lena." My dad smiled warmly. "We're almost parents. Just one more push and our little girl will be here."

Oh my God. I was in my mother's head. This vision was her memory.

"Push, Celena!" the doctor instructed.

As my mom bore down, pushing with all her might, I felt every sensation. The pressure, the blinding pain, the anticipation, the dread, knowing what was about to happen. The undiluted love she had for me and my father.

Her eyes opened, and I felt a cord of power in her chest, linking to me. Tears streamed down her face as she whispered, "My gift to you, sweet girl. Your fated mate has already been chosen. When the time is right, know that you have my blessing."

The vision went black, and I gasped for air. I could feel Alexei's hand on my back as I bent over and tried to process everything. "Nicole? Are you okay?"

Holy shit, experiencing your own birth firsthand was a new level of weird.

When I stood up, Macey nudged me softly. "I

saw my mom," I said. "She... she blessed us. When I was born." I patted my chest just over my heart. "I could feel her power."

With shiny eyes, I looked up at Alexei. Knowing he was a gift from my mother made our bond feel that much more precious to me. Wait... if we already had the goddess's blessing, and we'd slept together, that meant our bond was *already* completed!

Maybe.

I had to look into the moonlit ceremony to see how critical that component was.

Alexei cupped my cheek with a warm smile, telling me he had the same realization. "I'm honored and thankful to be your mate, Nicole."

"Goddammit!" Corbin snapped his fingers. "How the hell am I supposed to top that? I was going to have ABBA play at our reception, but now I feel like I need to get a hundred doves to release at the mating ceremony."

Bee sighed in frustration. "I already told you, Corbin. I'm not on board with the dove idea. And ABBA? Seriously?!"

"Fireworks?" Corbin asked. "I could easily swing fireworks. Ooh! What about swans? Swans are even better than doves!"

My best friend shook her head. "For the

hundredth time, we have too many things to worry about right now. We can save the ceremony talks for *after*."

Corbin's face fell. "But—"

Bee pointed a stern finger at him. "None, Corbin!"

I swear to God, he whimpered before he muttered, "Fine."

I couldn't hold in my laughter anymore, and neither could Alexei.

"Sucks to be you, dude." Alexei patted his beta on the back.

Corbin glared at Alexei. "Screw you, man. I didn't give you shit when you had your tail tucked between your legs for screwing up with Nicky."

Alexei's dark brows rose. "Uh… yes, you did. *Many times.*"

"Okay, people, I'm here!" Juniper announced as she wandered into the hallway, her golden chiffon gown trailing behind her. Let's get this Summit shit-show over."

Her mother joined us, wearing a similar yet slightly more extravagant dress. "June, honey, remember not to actually call it that when we get there. The council tends to be a little stuffy about this event. It's very important."

"Yeah, yeah." Juniper waved her mom off. "It's the annual gathering to strengthen interfaction relations and form alliances. It's our duty as leaders of our coven to present our best selves."

Bee giggled and whispered into my ear, "It sounds like they've had this conversation more than once."

It sure did.

The high priestess looked around with her smoky eyes. "Is everyone ready?"

"I wish you could come with me," Corbin whispered softly to Bee. "But at the same time, I don't want you anywhere near these people. Especially if Alexei's dad shows up."

"I'll be fine, Corbin," she promised. "My dad can't attend either, remember? He'll be with me the whole time you're gone."

Alexei took a deep breath. I knew he was nervous about not having the general there, but as a lone wolf, he wouldn't have received an invitation. Even if he had, he wouldn't have been present. Alpha Jones couldn't know the general and Alexei knew one another. It would do nothing but raise suspicion, and that was the last thing we'd wanted. It was bad enough the general was now on Jones's radar because he was listed as a witness for Alpha Jones's hearing. The video evidence he'd collected during that impromptu culling at the university could be imperative to a conviction, though, so withholding it wasn't an option.

Unfortunately for us, the footage Cristian's second-in-command got wasn't nearly as clear as the general's. When I asked if the witches could simply place a cloaking spell over him like June had done for us back at Redwood, the high priestess had stated it would be too risky. With so many magical beings in attendance, someone was bound to sense cloaking magic in the air.

"Maybe you should stay, too, Nicole," Alexei said while eyeing me. "In case the anti-violence spell glitches or something."

I looked at the others for a moment, then reached for his wrist, dragging him toward a secluded hallway with a huff. "You're not going anywhere without me, Alexei," I said sternly. I would have stomped my foot for emphasis, but Juniper's heels were very uncomfortable.

He pressed his forehead against mine and breathed me in. "The thought of putting you in danger makes me sick."

I stroked his chest before grabbing the lapels of his jacket and looking up at him. "We are going to be okay. Have faith."

He leaned down and kissed me tenderly, making

the butterflies in my stomach roar in appreciation. "I'm going to succeed. For you. For us. For our future together." He wrapped his arms around me and held me close. "For our future family. I don't want to raise kids, worrying about my father targeting them."

His words were innocent and kind, but it made my muscles clench with tension. I knew I needed to tell Alexei about what my uncle told me, but now wasn't the right time. We were about to go to Summit, and I didn't want him to be distracted.

"You okay?" He pulled away to scan my face.

"Yeah," I choked out. "You just focus on what you need to do. I'll be okay. I promise."

I lifted to kiss him once more, feeling guilty that I was harboring a secret that might make him rethink a future with me.

"Are you ready?" Eve asked.

Macey whined, and I knelt down to scratch behind her ears. "I know you want to come, girl, but I'm not willing to risk the anti-violence spell. You tend to be unpredictable at times."

Macey barked, as if laughing at me. She was mischievous under the best of circumstances, and I didn't want her lunging for Alpha Jones's neck. "We'll be back soon, I promise," I told her before standing up.

I turned to face Eve, forcing a smile on. "We're ready."

Eve clapped her hands together. "Well, everyone. Let's go to Summit."

We made our way back to the portal entrance, and Eve started waving her hands. Bee had tears in her eyes when she blew Corbin a kiss.

"I'll be back, gorgeous," he promised.

I sucked in a deep breath as everyone walked through the portal. First Eve, then Juniper skipped through like this was a grand adventure. Alexei went next.

And when it was my turn, Corbin placed his hand on my shoulder. "Come on, Nicky-poo. Let's go support our boy."

I stepped through the portal and was instantly tackled by someone. It was disorienting and terrifying, but a familiar chuckle made me melt in relief.

"Nicole! I've been worried sick about you!!"

Alexei growled and ripped Cristian off of me. "Hands to yourself, vamp."

Cristian then turned to hug Alexei, which was… awkward and forced. My mate gave me an incredulous look while patting him on the back. "I have been so worried about both of you."

Alexei pulled out of his grip and arched his brow at the affectionate vampire. "That makes one of us."

Cristian playfully punched my mate in the arm. "I thought we were bonding back at camp. We're best friends now."

Corbin growled. "Alexei only has one best friend, and I'm a bit territorial."

Cristian rolled his eyes and slung his arm over Corbin's shoulder. "I missed you, too, Corbin. How are things with your mate and the general?"

Corbin softened. "Great. Bee is wonderful, and I'm very close to getting matching tattoos with my soon-to-be father-in-law."

"Oh," Cristian replied, stunned. "Well, that's great?"

"See, Alexei! Cristian thinks the tattoo is a great idea." Corbin's grin couldn't have possibly been any cockier.

Before Alexei could say anything, I spoke. "I didn't think you'd make it, Cristian. I heard a lot of vampires went underground."

Cristian gave me a forced smile. "We couldn't miss the Summit. We're hoping that all of us could come up with a solution for the Alpha Jones problem."

"I didn't realize I was a problem," a sinister voice said. Shivers traveled down my spine as I scanned the expansive hallway. When my eyes landed on

Alpha Jones, I could feel my stomach clenching at the sight of him. Alexei moved to my side, his harsh glare trained on his father.

Alpha Jones cracked a manic smile. "Hello, everyone. I am delighted to see all of you."

CHAPTER
THIRTEEN

Nicole

"You look absolutely beautiful, Nicole," Alpha Jones purred, making no attempt to disguise his leer. Alexei's grip on my hand tightened as his father lowered his voice and added, "Some might even say you're a goddess."

Every instinct inside of me was telling me to get the hell out of this crazy man's path, but I shoved them in the back of my mind, knowing the psychotic alpha would exploit any weaknesses he'd identified.

His shrewd gaze flicked to Alexei. "Alexei. I must say, your presence is... unexpected. Since when are lone wolves invited to these gatherings?"

Cristian puffed his chest out. "Alexei and Nicole are my esteemed guests for the evening."

The alpha's lips curved into a sinister smile. "Ah. How convenient. In any regard, it's lovely to see all of you here. It'll make things much easier for what I have planned later."

"What's that supposed to mean?" Alexei demanded.

Alpha Jones laughed mockingly. "Relax, Alexei. You know as well as I do there is a spell prohibiting any violence at Summit. You're safe. For now. Truly, it's a pleasure to have you here." His eyes roamed over the high priestess's ample curves. "Especially you, Eve. You're quite the vision. I'm not sure if you've heard, but my lovely wife seems to have gone missing. There's an empty seat at my table if you're interested in joining me."

Juniper's mom raised her brows in a *you can't possibly be serious* gesture but said nothing.

Alpha Jones turned his attention back to my mate. "You had heard that your mother suddenly disappeared, did you not? I don't suppose you have any idea where she ran off to, do you?"

Alexei's mouth curved into a knowing grin. "Can't say that I do. But it's about damn time she left you. You were never good enough for her."

Alpha Jones barked in laughter. "Well, look at

you, actually standing up for yourself for once. Good for you. A little too late, but I appreciate your gumption."

God, we'd been here for two minutes, and already, the tension was sky-high. Everyone in the vicinity could read between the lines here. When Alexei's nostrils flared in irritation, I knew it was time to intervene.

"I don't think there's any point to frivolous small talk, do you?" I asked cooly, raising my chin. "You've made your opinion of Alexei—*of all of us*—very clear. Why don't you move along and pretend we're not even here, since we'll be doing the same with you."

Holy shit! Where did that come from? I knew antagonizing this man was dangerous, but the words just seemed to slip out.

"Shots fired," Corbin muttered under his breath, disguising his laughter with a cough.

"It's interesting how confident you sound now that you've gotten a bit of power," Alpha Jones said.

He knew. I could feel the truth curdling in my gut.

"Whatever do you mean?" I blinked innocently.

My mate grabbed my hand and squeezed in warning.

Alpha Jones cocked his head to the side. "I hear whispers, Nicole." He took a step closer to me, making my hackles rise. The energy rolling off of him was vile. I could practically feel how evil he was. "I guess you aren't the helpless little human I thought you were."

Cristian gave me a tentative look, curiosity bleeding in the way he scanned me with his eyes, as if he were searching for power under my skin.

"I've *never* been helpless," I replied.

Eve stepped between Alpha Jones and me, plastering a political smile on her face. "We should get ready for the festivities. Tonight is very important, is it not?"

Alpha Jones straightened his tie. "Of course. After you." He held out his arm, but I didn't like the idea of having him at our back. It seemed I wasn't the only one feeling cautious, because no one moved a muscle. A knowing laugh escaped Alpha Jones. "Or not."

We all watched as he straightened his spine and strolled down the hall toward the banquet room, not a care in the world. He seemed cocky. Confident. He was up to something, and suddenly, our plan of coming here seemed futile.

"He knows," Alexei said while turning to me. "I don't know *how* he knows, but he *knows*, Nicole. We have to get out of here. It's not safe for you." He grabbed my wrist, as if he were going to drag me out of there. But I pulled out of his hold and wrapped him in a hug.

"We're going to be okay. I'm safe. He can't do anything to us here. Remember?"

"She'll be fine, Alexei," Juniper's mother assured him. "The spell prohibiting violence anywhere on Summit grounds is foolproof. Anyone who dares to defy it will instantly forfeit their life. You know that."

"Instantly?" I asked. "Like they're killed? How?"

"It's... unpleasant." Cristian winced.

"Unpleasant, how?" I didn't know why I was pushing this, but everyone's reluctance to speak about it made me morbidly fascinated. "How are they killed?"

"I've only seen it happen once. I believe I was thirteen... maybe fourteen at the time? So, about eight or nine years ago?" Cristian looked to my mate, who nodded in confirmation. "My father says it's only happened a few times over the last century, because anyone who witnesses the offending party's execution will never forget it. It's quite a powerful motivator to control your temper, no matter how badly you're being provoked."

"I'll say," Juniper added, looking nauseated. "I'll never forget the smell either."

"Ugh, the smell is the worst!" Corbin looked sick

now, too. "But I wouldn't expect anything less when you're skinned alive and incinerated from the inside out."

I choked back bile at the visual he'd just planted in my head. "Oh my God. That's... barbaric."

"Maybe." Corbin shrugged. "But it's *effective*. The whole thing takes thirty seconds max, but those thirty seconds are fucking horrifying."

I was really glad I'd skipped lunch now.

"Gore aside, the most terrible part is that some men and women had genuinely honorable intentions. Take the shifter involved in the last execution, for example." Eve sighed. "He was protecting his mate from another man who got a little too drunk and far too handsy. But one punch was all it took before he was swiftly killed. Such a shame."

My eyes widened, and suddenly, I was considering taking Alexei's suggestion of leaving. His father knew exactly how to provoke him, and the stunt Alpha Jones pulled a few minutes ago was proof he had no intention of playing fair. What if he antagonized Alexei into throwing a punch? My mate wasn't exactly the most even-tempered man when his alpha instincts took over.

I tugged on the sleeve to Alexei's tux coat. "Maybe we should get out of here. I wouldn't put it past your father to intentionally rile you until you attacked him."

Alexei's gaze focused on the ballroom entrance. "Neither would I, so I'm expecting it. I won't let him get to me, Nicole."

"What do you think he has planned?" Corbin asked.

"World domination?" Juniper offered. "Oh, wait. We already knew that."

"Whatever it is, it isn't good." Alexei inclined his head toward the ballroom. "We should get in there and take our seats. The council chairman's speech should begin any moment now."

"My father has saved us all seats," Cristian said.

"Lead the way," Alexei replied.

Cristian straightened his shoulders and led our motley crew into the ballroom, with an air of regalness befitting a prince. It was easy to forget he was legitimate royalty in our everyday lives, but the jeweled crown on his head tonight served as a glaring reminder. I could feel hundreds of eyes following our every move as we entered the gala, hushed whispers traveling through the air.

"Why is Alexei Koenig here? Didn't his father disown him?"

"Why is the human here?"

"Who cares about the human? Did you see how deli-

cious the prince looks in that tux? I'd let him bite me any day of the week."

"Maybe she's his blood bag."

Alexei stiffened at that last one, but when I pressed up on my toes to place a kiss on his cheek, he instantly relaxed. A collective gasp rang out as he turned his face into me so our mouths pressed together.

"Well, that's one way to grab everyone's attention," Corbin snickered.

My eyes widened as I realized we had just publicly outed ourselves. Back at Redwood, everyone already knew we were fated, but I didn't think that news had carried across the country yet. Then again, what did I know? My supernatural reference guide didn't supply any information about gossip mongers.

I licked my lips as I pulled away, looking at my mate in question.

He placed his hand on the small of my back and leaned into my ear. "We have nothing to hide, Nicole."

I shivered from the sudden wave of arousal. "Well, maybe a few things."

His lips lingered near my temple. "True. But not this. Not from anyone. You're mine. And when this dinner is over and I get you alone, I'll be happy to remind you."

"Whew!" Juniper fanned herself dramatically as we crossed the elegantly decorated space. "The desire coming off of you two is making my nipples hard. That's some potent stuff."

I practically choked on my saliva. "Juniper!"

"What?" She shrugged. "It's true."

Corbin laughed. "She's not lying. Except my problem is a little further south."

My cheeks flushed as my gaze roamed over to Cristian, whose fangs were on full display. "Oh my God, not you, too."

His icy blue eyes drilled into me as he licked his lips. "Sorry. Physical lust and bloodlust go hand in hand, remember? I don't suppose you're in the mood to donate, are you?"

"Watch it, vampire," Alexei warned.

Cristian chuckled as he held his palms up in surrender. "Can't blame a guy for trying."

"The fuck I can't," my mate muttered.

"Calm down, caveman," I joked. "Cristian and I can always do the donor thing tomorrow."

His chest rumbled as he leaned into my ear again. "I'm going to spank you for that later."

Great. Now *my* nipples were hard. I didn't know if

I'd ever get used to this feeling. You'd think the imminent danger we were facing would be a libido killer, but it seemed to have the opposite effect between us. With one word, or sometimes even just a look, Alexei had me practically panting, squeezing my thighs together as my body ached to be filled by his.

Cristian's father, also known as the vampire king, stood as we approached the table. I cleared my throat, hoping like hell that he, too, couldn't sense the lascivious vibes in the air. It was bad enough knowing Bee's father saw our auras lighting up with passion all the time. My only saving grace there was the fact that his attempts to keep Corbin away from his daughter kept him plenty occupied.

"Welcome. I'm glad to see everyone made it tonight." Vasile Luca fanned his arm out. "Please. Have a seat."

Alexei pulled out a chair for me, and I settled at the opulent table. Silver plates and more forks than I knew what to do with were lined up neatly in front of me. The tablecloth was a deep champagne color, and candles hovering by magic over the middle of the table illuminated each space.

The room was enormous, with three long tables side by side. Each table could fit at least a hundred people. Corbin took the seat directly across from me, Alexei sat on my right, and Cristian sat on my left, snagging the chair before Juniper could. Magical violins in a corner were playing classical music. And naturally, Alpha Jones sat at the head of our table. It was an obvious power move that made me bristle. And I hated that he could easily look down the long row directly at me.

I stared at the wineglass in front of me, and when it magically filled with something fizzy, I resisted the urge to gasp in surprise. I had seen plenty of magic these last few weeks, but it never stopped amazing me.

"Is it safe to drink?" I asked Alexei, for some reason feeling unsure that his father hadn't somehow tampered with the food.

Cristian lifted his own goblet and took a gulp, a bloody mustache left on his skin. "Not only is it safe, but it's delicious. All the food here will be your favorite. The plates are spelled to deliver the food and drink you like best."

Alexei mumbled something I couldn't understand, but he seemed annoyed that our vampire friend was talking to me.

Eve stood up and tapped a knife against her glass, the ringing gathering all of our attention. "I am so thrilled to be here with all of you today. The Summit has been a long-standing tradition between all the supernatural factions. Even when we face trials, we always come together as a community and stand firmly against anyone or anything trying to tear us apart." Her eyes sliced over to Alpha Jones. "I look forward to enjoying this dinner and the subsequent events with you all."

"We have so much to celebrate," Alpha Jones said while standing up. Eve bristled, annoyed that he was taking over the announcements for the evening. "The shifter community has made great strides recently, and I for one am very excited to share it with you all."

"I didn't realize killing your own people and kidnapping were reasons to celebrate," I murmured bitterly.

Alpha Jones sliced his eyes to me; I could feel the maliciousness in his gaze. "Did you have something you wanted to say, Nicole? After all, you are one reason the shifters have much to rejoice over."

I narrowed my eyes at him. "What do you mean?"

Alpha Jones waved his hands. "A few weeks ago, an astonishing amount of fated mates were discovered. My intelligence informs me you are to thank for that."

I looked around at our table. All eyes were on me, a mixture of curiosity and astonishment in their expressions. Some of the other tables were leaning out of their chairs so they could hear my response.

I scoffed. "I'm sorry to say, but your intelligence is wrong. How could I possibly be responsible for mating bonds?"

"How indeed," Alpha Jones challenged. "Makes me wonder if the legends are wrong… or…"

He wasn't seriously going to do this in front of every leader from North American supernatural factions? Was he?

I refused to take the bait. I knew what he was implying. Everyone in this ballroom probably knew, if their assessing looks were anything to go by. But I would not make this easy for him.

"Or maybe we have a goddess in our midst," he finished.

Some people gasped. Most looked amused.

Vasile Luca laughed boisterously. "What you're suggesting is ludicrous, Alpha Jones. I did not know you gave so much credit to children's bedtime stories, but everyone knows the gods haven't graced us with their presence in centuries. Hell, even collectors have practically given up on their search. Besides, my son—*the prince*—has fed from this girl. Don't you think he'd know if she were anything other than human? If he had tasted a goddess in our midst, he would've been required to report that to his king, and he's done no such thing. Have you, Cristian?"

Alexei growled at the reminder of Cristian feeding from me.

I could feel Cristian's curiosity as he stared at me. We both knew he sensed something different in my blood, but if he was obligated to report it, why didn't he? I silently implored him to play along, with the promise of an explanation later.

The vampire prince's lips curved upward. "No, Father, I haven't, because there was nothing extraordinary to report."

Vasile nodded toward his son. "Well, there you have it. You have the vow of the vampire prince."

Our enraptured audience nodded resolutely, as if that settled it.

Alpha Jones cocked his head to the side, narrowing his eyes. "We know that the moon goddess is responsible for mate bonds. She has a direct link to the mother spirit. They work in tandem. How else would you explain the sudden rush of fated pairs?"

The high priestess lifted her chin and looked him right in the eye. "Correct me if I'm wrong, but aren't you the man who'd insinuated that the moon goddess didn't even exist? That shifters needed to rely on the scientific advances your team of researchers have made in genetics?"

"I never said she didn't exist," he spat. "I said she'd *abandoned us*. Why is a *witch* so well versed in pack relations, anyway?"

Eve looked cool as a cucumber as she replied, "Because I am also a *council member*, and as such, it is my responsibility to stay informed on *all* factions and *all* packs. Especially those that are known to stir controversy."

His face reddened. "My pack is none of—"

"*Your pack*"—Eve's tone was filled with authority as she cut him off—"has been blessed with mate bonds, something we should all celebrate. If you ask me, this seems like a ploy to aid you in your dispute of who has a valid claim on the girl and her father, but let me assure you, baseless accusations or distractions will not stand up in council matters. We judge based on *facts*, which will be revealed using indisputable magical means. As for the gods, I'm sure they are watching over us from Elysian Point, as they have been for a long while. They would not risk themselves by coming to this dimension. Even if one did as you are suggesting, they could not possibly be mistaken for a human."

Alpha Jones puffed out his chest. "*Then she is a demigoddess!*"

More people laughed, making his face deepen to a purplish color.

Holy crap, was I thankful for the gods' elusive habits.

"What you're suggesting is insane," Alexei spat. "Nicole is human, as anyone in this room can plainly sense." My mate laughed mockingly, causing others to do the same.

I mindlessly rubbed the locket around my neck, thankful for its protection.

"Really, Jones," Eve added. "I know you enjoy hearing yourself talk, but I believe the floor belongs to the council. So if you'd be so kind, the other council members and I would appreciate your cooperation."

Damn.

I already knew Juniper's mom was something special, but watching her school Alpha Jones like that in front of hundreds of people was really impressive. This woman had balls made of brass, that was for sure.

Alpha Jones narrowed his eyes briefly before plastering a giant smile on his face. "Of course, of course. Please forgive me. I was simply excited to be in the same room with so many powerful families again." His gaze roamed around the room in a perfectly polished politician kind of way. "I look forward to this event each year. It's not every day we're surrounded by our equals, right?" He took his seat and added, "Please, High Priestess Hale, by all means, continue."

Eve rolled her shoulders back and tilted her chin up in a regal way that commanded everyone's attention. Her fierce eyes locked with Alpha Jones. "You are correct, Alpha Jones. We have much to celebrate. New alliances. Powerful magic. And the fierce devotion to good prevailing over evil. Many of us here are united. Together, we are stronger than ever. And together, we will take down anyone that threatens the careful balance we have achieved." Eve looked at her daughter. "And the next generation of leaders are full of power. They are driven, intelligent, and stronger than we've ever seen before. They work together and are a force to be reckoned with. I truly look forward to seeing all their accomplishments, and I am so thankful to have all of you here with me. We've worked hard to build a safe community, and I, for one, will continue to defend the unity we have cultivated."

Everyone started clapping, and Eve bowed slightly. Her words were powerful, but full of warning. She made it clear that we would all stand together against Alpha Jones. I surreptitiously glanced his way, and my stomach dropped. He had a manic grin on his face and lifted his glass to his lips, easily taking a sip.

I didn't know what he had up his sleeve, but it was dangerous.

Juniper muttered something under her breath before leaning over the table and nodding at me. "I need to steal a strand of Alpha Jones's hair."

My eyes widened. "What? We can't do anything at Summit. And should we really be discussing this right now?"

She gave me a small smile. "Don't worry. I just put a jumbling spell around us. Anyone listening will hear us making pleasant small talk. Now, as I was saying, I need a strand of his hair so I can finish the spell to find those lost kids. I put the pegasus essence in moon water last night. All we need is one strand so I can extract his knowledge about the missing kids. If we can do it tonight, then General Minifred can do the rescue mission while Alpha Jones is distracted at Summit.

Alexei grumbled. "And how do you expect to get that? He's on high alert, expecting one of us to try something. And I don't want Nicole anywhere near him. We need to figure out how he knows."

Juniper smirked. "I can extract that information, too. When I get his hair. I was hoping my favorite vampire could help me. Perhaps, use your super speed to pluck the strand?"

Cristian frowned. "Wouldn't that be against the spell forbidding us to do anything? Forgive me for sounding like a pussy, but that's not a risk I'm willing to take."

"In years past, Jones has been known to frequent the Den of Carnality after closing remarks," Eve offered. "Perhaps we can get some assistance from one of the ladies working the event tonight?"

"What's the Den of Carnality?" I asked.

It couldn't possibly be what its name suggested.

Alexei leaned into me. "It's a boys' club thing, so to speak. Very old-fashioned. Very well loved by men like my father. They offer it at Summit to temper all the animal instincts in the room to avoid any mishaps."

I quirked my head to the side. "And what exactly takes place in this den?"

Corbin shrugged. "Imagine a bunch of dudes lounging around bullshitting, while naked women cater to their every need and tell them what big dicks they have. Some of them ride or slobber over said dicks. It's essentially one giant ego stroke for old dudes with LDE."

Okay... so, I supposed it *was* what its name had suggested.

My jaw gaped. "But... there are families here! Wives and children!"

This event seemed so classy from what I'd seen so far, but what Corbin was describing was a veritable den of inequity.

"It's not held in the ballroom. It's on the lower level of the hotel." Vasile piped in. "As far as the wives are concerned, they're usually well aware of their spouse's extra-marital activities. A mated man would never even think of entering the den. Besides... many supernatural marriages are a matter of convenience, and they have open relationships. Mine included."

To each their own, I supposed, but it seemed rather sad to me if that was the *norm*. What was so bad about good old-fashioned monogamy?

"But the key factor is these naked women," Eve continued, "aren't just any women. They're powerful succubi. The overwhelming amount of lust in the room only bolsters their powers at an event like this, where a bunch of predators are forced to suppress their inner animals. The succubi love it. They hold a lottery every year to see who'll get the honor of working the event, since only a dozen or so positions are available. The moment a man walks into the den, he's pulled into their orbit. Think of it like a fever dream, so to speak. Their lust—and satisfying that need—is all they can think about. They're aware of their actions, but their one-track minds cloak anything else in a thick haze. It would be easy for one of the girls to pluck a strand of Alpha Jones's hair completely unnoticed."

"That's brilliant, Mom!" June said excitedly. "My friend Charisma is working the event tonight. She'd be perfect."

"Do you trust her?" Alexei asked.

"With my life," Juniper said solemnly.

I cringed. The thought of Alpha Jones being in some sex den was enough to make me sick to my stomach. But whatever got the job done. Once we got a hair, then we could safely extract the information and rescue those kids. We needed that information before Alexei formally challenged his father.

"I guess it's as good of an idea as any. I just worry..."

Alexei rubbed my back. "It'll be okay. We have to do this and find those children. We also need to figure out exactly what my father knows about you."

I nodded. "I know. He's just unpredictable. Are you sure he'll visit this den?"

Corbin snorted. "One predictable thing about Alpha Jones is that he's a horn dog. Pack Daddy will definitely go get his freak on tonight. He can't resist."

"Gross." Alexei shivered.

Eve nodded.

I supposed one thing we had in common was that all of us were disgusted by thinking of Alpha Jones's sex life.

"I'll go too," Cristian offered before clearing his throat. "To make sure Charisma doesn't get into any trouble. I'll be her back up."

Juniper rolled her eyes and giggled. "Of course you will. Last time you saw her, you literally drooled. Hoping you can get a second shot with the succubus, vampy?"

Cristian tugged at the collar of his shirt. "You know I have a weakness for pretty girls with blue eyes."

He eyed me, and Alexei growled.

"Yes," I laughed. "We all know."

"Maybe Charisma is the one who got away." Cristian pretended to swoon.

"I don't care who he likes as long as it's not Nicole," my mate grumbled to himself, making all of us laugh.

"Okay, it's settled then," Eve said. "We need to wrap this up before anyone notices my daughter's spell. Juniper, why don't you go talk to Charisma before the den opens? If anyone asks, I'll tell them you went to powder your nose."

"Works for me," June replied, subtly waving her hand around, presumably disbanding the jumble thingy. "I need to visit the ladies' room before the keynote speech begins. Will you all excuse me for a bit?"

The men in our group stood like the gentlemen they were as June got up and left the table. When Alexei sat back down, he wound his arm around the back of my chair, pulling me into his side.

"This will work, Nicole." He kissed my temple. "It has to."

"I hope so." I sighed, leaning into my mate's embrace.

I didn't know if we were going to pull this off, but one thing I knew for sure was that Alexei would be by my side. The uncertainty that drove a wedge between us before was nowhere in sight, and for that, I considered myself one lucky girl, despite everything else we were facing.

Alexei was mine, and I was his. No one, no matter how psychotic they were, would change that. When we took down Alpha Jones, it'd only be that much sweeter knowing what we'd overcome to be together.

CHAPTER

FOURTEEN

Cristian

THE AROMA of carnal pleasure hung in the air beyond the enormous doors, and my heart rate spiked. My cock swelled in anticipation as I bit down on my tongue, willing my fangs not to emerge. I hadn't even entered the den yet, but already, I had become mesmerized by the pulsating essence of a succubus. I loved an orgy as much as the next guy, but there was something intoxicating about the species as a whole. Especially a particularly fiery redhead that had stolen my attention. Succubi were literally designed to seduce, but there was something about Charisma Callahan that intrigued me beyond satisfying a physical need.

I thought Nicole and I could have been great, but I would not fight fate. She loved Alexei, and I'd mostly—begrudgingly—accepted that. Plus, her blood had a beguiling effect on me, making her a poor choice as a feeder. It wouldn't do for me to become inebriated every time I drank from her. It was impractical and not exactly conducive to maintaining a boner.

I adjusted my tie, reminding myself that I couldn't afford to get distracted. Alpha Jones had slipped into the den the moment the dinner was over, eager to get his rocks off. But if I proved to Charisma that I wasn't just a party-hard playboy like she accused me of being the first night we'd met, while at the same time helping Nicole and her mate, so be it.

"I'm not interested," she said with a giggle while looking me up and down.

"Not interested? And why not?"

She dragged a manicured nail down my chest, but I felt it right in my dick. "Because," she purred. "You're nothing but a privileged prince. A playboy. You're no better than the rest of the guys in the supernatural world." Her expression darkened. "You just want to use me for pleasure. And sometimes that can be fun, but I crave something real."

I shook away the memory and cleared my throat.

I could be real, dammit. I'd been really fucking helpful when I stepped up for Nicole. I'd gone against my father's wishes and befriended Alexei, too. I wasn't just the vampire prince. I really cared about the future of our world.

Even if I sometimes liked to have fun, too.

I nodded to the guards stationed outside the double doors leading into the den.

The one on the right—a lower-level vampire from a clan up in Ottawa—opened the door for me. "Enjoy indulging in your desires, Prince Cristian."

"Thank you." I stepped into the antechamber, breathing in the incense floating through the air.

It was a mixture of anise and cinnamon, with heavy notes of clove. The scent was heady, playing into the old world glamour they were trying to project. The walls were covered in maroon and gold damask wallpaper, with intricately woven golden sconces every five feet or so. A plush Persian rug lined the path to the second set of wooden doors.

I took a deep breath as I grasped the handle, preparing myself, before pushing the heavy door open and stepping into the den. The antechamber was soundproofed, so the immediate assault on my ears was disorienting at first. A thumping, sexy beat was being pumped through the state-of-the-art sound system, but the speakers were no match for the sounds of rapture being torn from dozens of bodies.

Limbs were tangled with passion, lots of skin on full display as magic swelled in the air.

Gods, I loved the den.

It was exactly the kind of place I enjoyed spending time in. Heady. Hot. Sensual.

"Why am I not surprised?" a raspy voice said to my left.

I swiveled my head and looked at the most intriguing woman I'd ever met in my life. Long, wavy red hair the color of blood. Ocean-blue eyes chilled with scrutiny. The temptress wore a delicate ensemble of jewels around her throat, and tight, lacy lingerie. It was the perfect blend of temptation with the infinite twinkle of a night sky.

"Charisma," I said softly. "Lovely to see you again."

She nearly took my breath away. Whenever I was around her, my lungs refused to work, which was downright infuriating considering she smelled divine.

"Juniper said you'd be visiting," she whispered before taking a step closer to me.

She moved like a cat, willowy and light. The sensual sway of her hips made my mouth water. Everything about her was a tempting treat.

"You don't look happy to see me," I noted.

"I don't need a babysitter. Why don't you go find one of my friends to spend the evening with so I can get to work?" She winked playfully at me, and I swear it felt like she was stroking my dick with her damn mind.

I groaned.

"I just want to make sure you're safe," I mumbled, trying not to sound like a pathetic idiot.

Her eyes widened, as if she was surprised anyone cared about her safety.

I didn't like that.

No, I didn't like that one bit.

Maybe I had a savior complex, but people in need were my weak spot. There was something about it that made me feel powerful. Necessary.

Okay, maybe there weren't any *maybes* about that complex. I was man enough to admit that. I enjoyed feeling wanted. I certainly wasn't the first person who did.

I covertly glanced around, searching for our target. Sure enough, Alpha Jones was stretched out on an oversized chaise lounge, being serviced by two beautiful succubi. I'd heard rumors that the alpha took sadism to a new level, but the succubi's magic would mute that impulse while he was under their spell. I knew firsthand that certain succubi were drawn into the BDSM lifestyle, but since the Den of Carnality was at Summit, everyone here was held just as accountable for peace as they were in the ballroom earlier. That was one good thing about this event being hosted at such a large facility. Whether you were attending presentations, mingling, or sleeping, as long as you remained within the perimeter of the Summit hotel's grounds, you were safe.

"See anything you like?" Charisma whispered into my ear.

I tried playing it cool, but as her round breasts pressed into my arm, I was having difficulties focusing on anything else.

I turned my face into hers until our lips were barely a hairsbreadth apart. "I'm looking at her."

Her red lips curved into a grin. "Always such a smooth talker."

"It wasn't a line," I assured her.

"Well, regardless, Prince Cristian, I have a job to do tonight, which affords me very little time to soak up your compliments." She nodded to the people in various stages of fucking. "Now, as I suggested earlier, why don't you allow one of my friends to take care of you, while I do my part?"

Her long hair swished back and forth as she approached a beautiful woman who appeared to be in her early twenties, but I knew looks could be deceiving with immortals. Succubi and incubi stopped aging physically at the age of twenty-one. Remaining young and beautiful for eternity was part of the package when you were a creature built to subsist off others' desires. I had never met one who wasn't extraordinarily beautiful. I just happened to think Charisma was exceptionally stunning. If someone asked me to confess my greatest fantasy, I would've given them her exact description, down to the slight scattering of freckles across the bridge of her nose, from her C-cup tits down to her ruby red-painted toes.

Charisma's friend, a brunette with curves in all the right places, looked my way as they spoke, sending me a flirty wink. In the next moment, she was striding toward me, while Charisma was heading in the opposite direction toward Alpha Jones. My fangs lengthened, but surprisingly, I didn't think it was because I was aroused. No... I was pissed at the thought of Charisma going anywhere near another man right now, which confused the shit out of me. She was a succubus, for fuck's sake. She dealt orgasms like cards in Vegas. But nevertheless, it didn't stop the overwhelming surge of possession I was feeling.

Okay, maybe I was a little aroused, but I wasn't

some prepubescent boy who couldn't control popping a fang boner. If my fangs were on display from lust, it was because I *wanted* them on display. Nicole was the only exception, as evidenced by my faux paus tonight, but I believed that was because I'd fed from her, and despite my earlier statement, her blood *was* indubitably unique. I'd never felt such power before, but I couldn't pinpoint the exact source of that power. Over a month later, I was still lured by the call of it. I didn't know why I never mentioned the incident to my father, but after that weird conversation with Alpha Jones, I was glad I hadn't. Nicole and I would definitely have a conversation about it later though. Something had obviously changed with her since I'd seen her last. She seemed more... confident. Aware. If she had new information, I needed to know what that was if I was going to be useful in this war we were facing.

"Hello, handsome. I'm Leia. Want to have some fun?" Charisma's friend ran her hands all over my chest. I forced myself not to push her away and kept my eyes trained on the fiery redhead that had me twisted up.

"How about this," I whispered while scanning the room. I found an open seat with a clear view of Alpha Jones and dragged the girl over to it. "Sit on my lap and watch. I'm more in the mood to see the action than take part tonight, sweetheart."

She playfully smiled as I sat down. "Of course. I love watching. And Charisma puts on quite the show."

I remained still as the brunette draped herself over my lap and looped her arms around my neck. She smelled nice but not as good as Charisma. I casually looked to where Alpha Jones was and forced myself to remain seated when Charisma sauntered over to him. He gave her a condescending look when she bent down to speak in his ear. I tuned my sensitive hearing to them and listened, hating every fucking second of it.

"Hello, Alpha Jones. Are you having fun?"

He shifted in his seat and grabbed her ass. "I prefer shifters, but the succubi are nice when I'm bored. It's like all your holes were made and primed to be fucked."

I wanted to rage at his words, but Charisma was a true professional. She didn't flinch or slap him like I wanted her to.

"I *like* to be used by powerful men like you, Alpha," she purred seductively. "And you're absolutely right. We succubi are *always* primed to fuck. There's *nothing* on earth I enjoy more."

That could be true, and the thought alone made

me hard as a rock, but as I'd learned over the years, a high libido didn't mean they weren't selective when choosing a sexual partner. A succubus could feed just as well from other people's pleasure as long as they were in close proximity. Their mere presence was an aphrodisiac, so lack of arousal wasn't a problem.

The brunette in my lap leaned back to whisper in my ear. "Watch how she curves her body. Those full breasts ready to burst from that sexy bra? Her tight ass in the air, just *begging* to be railed by some lucky guy's cock. She's stunning, isn't she?"

Charisma ran her hands over Alpha Jones's thighs, making him smirk. "That's right, you fucking worthless succubi, kneel before a proper king."

Fucking hell.

Evidently, a succubus's thrall was no match for Alpha Jones's douchebaggery. That motherfucker needed his tongue ripped out for speaking to her so disrespectfully.

"I think of Charisma every time I touch myself," the girl on my lap said in a voice barely above a whisper. "I imagine her lips wrapped around my nipples. Her fingers pumping inside of me as she fucks my face with her pretty pink pussy." She moaned, as if imagining that very thing right now, as she slid her fingers beneath the sheer panties she wore. "Have you ever experienced the sheer nirvana of Charisma's cunt? She tastes absolutely divine. I can feel your lust, handsome. Are you imagining she's the one sitting on your lap right now? It's okay if you are. I don't mind at all."

Leia's hand began moving faster, her breathy pants making her ample chest rise and fall. "In fact, I'm imagining the two of you together now. Charisma freeing that big, hard dick from your pants. Taking you in her mouth, sucking you deep, until you couldn't handle it anymore. Then, you'd bend her in half, commanding her to grab her ankles as you sunk inside of her. She'd scream in pleasure. Cry out your name in ecstasy as her tits bounced with every thrust. She's quite bendy, which comes in handy if you're feeling adventurous. Hmm... I wonder if you'd take her fast and hard... or soft and slow? You seem like the kind of guy who'd enjoy a little of both."

I *was* that kind of guy. And I was so fucking turned on as she made herself come, I was about to embarrass myself. I clenched my fists, resisting the temptation to whip my dick out as the images Leia fed me ran through my head. I definitely wasn't immune to what was happening on my lap, but I was also disgusted and oddly possessive watching Charisma tempt Alpha Jones.

It was very confusing.

Alpha Jones tilted his head back as Charisma leaned forward to kiss up and down his thigh, and just before landing those perfect, soft lips on his cock, she hovered just inches above him and worked her nimble fingers up his torso.

"What the fuck are you doing? Suck my dick, bitch. I'm here to get off, not to get toyed with."

Charisma stood up and placed her heeled foot on the arm of his chair, then dug her fingers through his hair, tugging back until his neck was exposed. As an alpha, Jones didn't appreciate the submissive position, and he bared his teeth to show her.

I was about two seconds from storming up to them and ripping her away from him.

"Kneeling is fun, Alpha Jones, but I prefer a man who lets me take charge. What do you say?"

"Fuck off," Alpha Jones growled before shoving her away. The other two women, who had paused their tag-team blowjob to watch his interaction with Charisma, stared up at him. "What the fuck are you waiting for?" He glared at the blonde on the right. "I want my dick in your throat." His furious gaze flicked to the brunette on the left. "Put my balls back in your mouth and rub my taint while you're at it. I came here to get off, so fucking make it happen."

God, this guy was a real prick. I'd already known

that, but I never understood a man who could talk down to a woman. Women should be worshiped, not degraded. Unless they were into that sort of thing.

The succubi got back to work, and it was only a matter of seconds before Jones was throwing his head back, roaring with his release, which he so graciously splattered all over the women's faces.

Leia scoffed, all previous displays of sensuality removed from her repulsion. "Normally, I'd be game for a sexy facial, but that was a jerk move. That was one hundred percent about trying to humiliate them. Why are men like that?"

"Not *all* men are like that," I whispered back.

My dick jerked when Charisma met my eye before she wandered out of the room.

Leia raised a sculpted brow. "Really, now? Then why is your dick currently poking me in the ass? That kind of thing clearly gets you off."

"No," I assured her. "It doesn't. Debasing women isn't really my thing."

Leia twisted her torso, leaning in closer. "Then what *is* your thing, Prince? Wanna show me?"

I wrapped my fingers around her wrists as she reached for my belt. "Thank you for the pleasure of your company, but it's time for me to go."

"So soon?" Her brown hair fell over her breast as

she quirked her head to the side. "Planning to chase after a certain redhead, perhaps?"

I smirked. "Perhaps."

I left out the part where I'd been chasing that particular redhead unsuccessfully for the last three years. But that was then, and this was now. I was done letting Charisma walk away from me. One way or the other, I was going to figure out how to convince her I wasn't the man she'd perceived me to be.

And when she saw me for who I truly was, leaving would be the last thing on her mind.

FIFTEEN

Nicole

"WHY ARE you always wearing these big-ass gowns?" Alexei complained as the zipper on the back of my borrowed dress got stuck. "I've been waiting to get you naked all night."

"Alexei, hold up!" I smacked his arm away playfully. "First of all, I rarely wear fancy dresses. And second, Juniper said this was one of her favorites. Ripping it is *not* an option."

I smiled as he pouted. My mate was far too masculine to be called adorable, but that was the only word that came to mind.

"Turn around." He motioned for me to twirl. "I promise I'll be careful."

He tugged on the zipper for a few seconds before getting it unstuck. I breathed a sigh of relief as the chiffon pooled at my feet. I was just as anxious as Alexei was to get undressed. After dealing with the stares from gossip mongers on top of the not-so-veiled threats from his father all night, I needed the comfort that being skin to skin with him provided.

We were staying at the Summit hotel with the anti-violence spell firmly in place, so we knew we were safe for the time being, a luxury that seemed in short supply lately, so I planned on taking advantage of that while we could. I could sense some big bad brewing in the air, but tonight, I was going to make love to my mate. The more often we were together physically, the stronger our bond seemed to become. And I had a feeling we would need to rely on that bond in the coming weeks, so fortifying it the best we could seemed like a good plan.

Plus, as High Priestess Hale so wisely said to me recently, orgasms really helped clear the mind.

Alexei's hands found their way to my waist, and he pulled me in close, his arms wrapping tightly around me. His eyes searched my face, and I shivered under the intensity of it. Would I ever become accustomed to the way he looked at me? It was like a flame that could ignite me in an instant.

"I love you," I whispered before his lips pressed against mine.

"I love you." He kissed me again, this time licking at the seam of my mouth, prompting me to open.

I released a throaty moan as his tongue invaded my mouth. His lips were like a heavenly fire, burning away my inhibitions and setting every nerve in my body alight with passion. I trembled with anticipation as his hands explored my body, my breath catching in my throat as a wave of pleasure washed over me.

"You're so fucking beautiful," he growled, scooping me up and carrying me to the four-poster bed.

I yelped in surprise, clutching the lapels of his suit jacket as he set me down on the edge of the mattress. I could already feel his hard cock pressing against the lace of my panties. I wanted to touch him, feel him skin on skin, but he remained annoyingly overdressed. Alexei stood, his fiery eyes roaming over my lilac push-up bra and matching thong.

"You wanna play a little game?"

My brows rose. "What *kind* of game?"

Alexei loosened the tie around his neck, running

the silky material through his fingers as he held it out. "The kind where I enhance some of your senses... by blocking others."

My eyes widened in excitement as I decoded his statement.

"You want to blindfold me?"

The look on his face was one hundred percent predatory, and I was undoubtedly his prey. "And tie you up."

"Oh," I breathed out. "Okay."

I had never tried any kind of bondage before, but I trusted Alexei with my life, so I knew he would make the experience immensely pleasurable.

He cocked his head to the side. "You sound unsure. We don't have to do this."

"No, I *want* to." I shook my head. "I just... I've never tried it before."

"I know." His lips curled up in a sexy smile. "But I promise I'll take good care of you. We can stop at any time. Just say the word."

"I trust you."

"Good girl." He grinned. "We'll start with the blindfold. Close your eyes."

I shut my eyes as he reached around to the back of my head. I gasped as he grabbed a handful of my hair, tugging my head backward and lifting the silky fabric to cover my eyes. As he tied it securely, I let out a small gasp.

"Feel okay?"

I nodded. "Yeah."

"Lay back, Nicole."

I could feel Alexei's need radiating from him in waves as my back met the bed. It was an amazing sensation, being desired by someone so intensely. My body responded, my pussy pulsing.

"Beautiful," he murmured, kissing my throat. He toyed with the front clasp of my bra for a moment before working it free.

I hissed as his mouth closed around my nipple, his tongue flicking over it to tease me. I squirmed, pressing my thighs together as my body ached for more.

"Easy," he whispered, biting down gently. "We've got all night."

"I'm so wet already, Alexei."

"Yeah?" my mate chuckled. "I don't know if I should take your word for it. Maybe I should check."

I sighed dramatically. "If you must, I *guess* that'd be okay."

"Oh, yeah?" I couldn't see him, but I could hear the smile in his voice.

Alexei's lips continued to tease my breasts,

flicking and sucking until I was a trembling mess. He slid the straps of my bra down my arms, pulling it away entirely before tossing it to the floor. Or at least, that's where I assumed it had gone. I let out a little gasp as his fingertips dipped into the waistband of my panties. He peeled the fabric away, leaving me in nothing but my heels. I could sense him admiring my body, hear his breathing slow down and become ragged as he inspected me.

His hand slid up the inside of my thigh. "God, you're fucking soaked."

"Please..." I whispered, my back arching off the mattress.

Alexei slid one finger into me, pumping it in and out as I moaned. His kisses continued up my body, back to my mouth. The only sounds filling the room were the pounding of our hearts and the wet sounds of him fingering me. A few moments later, he pulled away, leaving me shivering in his wake.

The bed creaked as he shifted his weight. I groaned as his hands gripped my shoulders. "Flip onto your stomach."

I rolled to my side, swinging my legs over the edge of the bed until my heels touched the plush carpeting. Alexei placed an open palm between my shoulder blades, encouraging me to keep my torso low. I was bent in half over the bed, my bare ass sticking up. I squirmed in excitement as I heard the telltale sounds of Alexei unbuckling his belt, sighing when my nipples rubbed against the cotton duvet.

Was he going to spank me? Was I into that kind of thing?

I thought maybe I was.

I gasped when he pulled my hands behind my back and fastened my wrists together with the leather strap.

"Spread your legs, baby."

I smiled as I did as I was told.

"Wider," he demanded.

I pulled my legs apart, the cool air of the room nipping at my wet pussy. I moaned as his fingers slid between my lips, testing my slickness.

"So fucking wet for me." He groaned as he pressed his body against mine, his hard cock nestling against my ass. "Let's see how dirty you're willing to get, shall we?"

I whimpered as his finger slid between my ass cheeks.

"Alexei..." I said as he pressed against the tight ring of muscle back there. "I've never..."

"Shh..." he murmured, trailing kisses down my spine. "I'll take care of you, Nicole."

I bit my lip as Alexei spoke quietly to me. I could hear the longing in his voice as he whispered sweet promises of passion, of pleasure and connection, of desire and delight. His words washed over me like hot honey, sending a tantalizing shiver through every inch of me.

"Alexei…"

His fingers traced the curve of my ass, goose bumps spreading over my skin as he shifted his weight to the side.

"What are you—"

"I promise it'll feel great, baby. Just trust me."

He spread my cheeks, and the next thing I knew, his warm, wet tongue was licking my tight hole. My entire body flushed with awareness, with arousal. Who knew there were so many wonderful nerve endings back there?

"Oh my God." I was pretty sure I had stretched that last word into at least four syllables.

"Do you like that, my beautiful girl?" Alexei murmured, his voice dark with desire.

I nodded as he continued to lick me. It felt so good, so different from anything I'd ever experienced before. I really liked this.

No, I *loved* it.

My mate groaned as he slid two fingers into my

pussy, pumping them in and out as his tongue wriggled against me. I screamed in pleasure, the sound muffled by the mattress as I struggled to remain still. I didn't want to risk moving away from the delicious torment of his tongue.

"That feels amazing," I panted. "Why does that feel so freaking good?"

Alexei chuckled against my skin, making me squeal from the vibration.

I'd never known that being tied up and blindfolded removed all your inhibitions. I felt confident, sexy and open. A deep sense of belonging, of trust, of unbelievable arousal.

My pussy clenched around Alexei's fingers. I wanted more; I wanted everything he had to give.

I wanted to submit. I wanted to please my mate.

I wanted to please *myself*.

I let out a little whine when Alexei removed his fingers and his tongue slid away from my ass.

"Don't worry," he said, chuckling. "I'll be back in a minute."

I whimpered impatiently as I felt him undressing behind me.

"Alexei…" I cried out. "I was *so* close."

"I know, baby," he assured me. "Don't worry, you'll be there again in no time."

He slid the head of his dick against my aching clit, making me whimper.

"Are you ready for my cock, baby?"

"Yes," I gasped. "Give it to me."

A split second later, the head of his dick pressed against my pussy. I gasped, arching my back as I pushed my hips backward, impaling myself on him. Alexei growled as he grabbed the belt that bound my hands together, using it for leverage.

"You are so fucking tight," he said with awe. "So wet, so warm. You feel fucking incredible."

I could only moan in response as I wriggled back against him, wanting to feel him deeper inside me. He answered my unspoken plea by sliding out, only to thrust forward again. A loud, pulsing slap rang through the room as his open palm collided with my ass at the same moment his hips slammed into my body. It was a jarring sensation, but in the best way possible.

"Do it again!" I pleaded, desperate to feel that delicious friction again.

Alexei gave me exactly what I wanted. He grunted as his hips pounded against my ass, his balls slapping against my cunt. He paused the spanking to slide his hand around the front of my body, fingertips making little circles over my clit. As he claimed me, he buried his face in the crook between my neck and shoulder.

My orgasm was quickly building as Alexei released the belt, hand sliding between my cheeks, fingertip exploring my tight hole.

"Oh, God," I groaned, barely able to form words as pleasure cascaded through my body in pulsing waves. "I'm going to come."

"That's the goal, baby." He pushed his finger into my ass, his cock still pounding against my pussy.

"Oh, fuck!" I screamed as my orgasm hit me, harder and more powerful than ever before.

My body bucked against his as I came, my pussy squeezing him tightly. Alexei's hips pounded against me, driving me forward as he groaned, his cock pulsing inside me as he followed seconds later.

Alexei slid his finger out of my ass, trailing kisses up my spine until his mouth was at my ear.

"I love you," he whispered. "You are *my every-thing*, Nicole."

He collapsed on top of me then, both of us completely spent. His heart was pounding against my back as our breathing slowed. I wiggled my hands, giggling when I realized they were still tied together.

Alexei chuckled, lifting his hips just enough to

untie me. He pulled my arms to the sides, rubbing the slight ache from my wrists. Then, he lifted the blindfold from my eyes.

As I stared into his loving gaze, I replied, "We're *each other's* everything."

A blinding smile stretched across his face. "Always."

SIXTEEN

Alexei

"Mmm, you're so comfy," Nicole mumbled sleepily. "Do we have to get out of bed?"

I tightened my arms around her and kissed the crown of her head. "As much as I'd love to stay here all day and have several repeats of last night, duty calls. I have to make it a point to attend each one of the presentations. Show everyone that I will not allow my father to intimidate me."

My mate's warm body wiggled out of my hold so she could look up at me with her beautiful blue eyes. "Remind me what the whole presentation thing is about again."

"Each year, one representative from each of the

four major supernatural factions showcases a new magic, product, idea… whatever. It's a show of alliance—an opportunity to forge business connections throughout the entire community." I smoothed some dark hair away from Nicole's forehead. "If I'm being brutally honest, it's mostly a bunch of posturing, but the presenters wouldn't have been voted in by their panels if they didn't have something valuable to offer, something that was guaranteed to benefit their faction financially. Anyone who wins the bid to present is required to pay taxes directly into the faction's pension fund."

"Each faction has *a pension fund*?" Nicole snorted. "How very… human."

"Not really." I shrugged. "That pool of money isn't spread out in a traditional sense. It's used to fund the extravagant lifestyles of the panel members themselves, which is why each panel is so small. The fewer panel members they have, the bigger the paycheck."

"So each supernatural species has their own panel?"

I nodded. "Yes. They vary in size, but they're mostly elders or more influential leaders. The shifter panel only has six men, and every one of them is an old-school elitist."

"Lovely." A crinkle formed between her brows.

"And this year, your father was voted to present, yes?"

"Unfortunately. I'd like to say I'm surprised, but…"

"You have no idea what he's presenting?" Nicole sat up in bed, pulling the sheets up to cover her bare breasts.

"Not a clue," I answered, frustration bleeding through my tone.

Whatever my father had up his sleeve, he'd been working on for quite a while and had been tight-lipped about it. He refused to share any information with me or even his beta as far as I knew. Corbin and I believed he'd been outsourcing.

"Whatever it is, your father is essentially speaking on the behalf of all shifters on this conti-nent, right? Wouldn't a democratic voting process make more sense?"

"You'd think," I told her. "But you need to remember supernatural communities don't govern themselves like most developed human societies. We have the council to rule over any interfaction disputes, but even then, that justice system is anti-quated. As for the shifter panel, those men are a lot like my father, and he knows how to schmooze. I'm sure it took little to win their votes. I wouldn't put it past him to *pay* for their vote or, more likely, resort to blackmail. I've learned over the years, when he has his mind set on something, he'll do whatever it takes to make that happen."

"But what about the charges against him?"

"Unless he's convicted by the council, those charges don't matter." I sat up as well and turned toward Nicole. "And considering the council hearing isn't until *after* the presentations, the floor is his."

"That's so messed up." Nicole blew out a breath. "What about the other presentations?"

I let out a puff of air. "I'm sure with my father's recent behaviors, the other factions will put on a show of strength."

"I'm kind of curious what the vampires and witches will do. I asked June, but she was really hush-hush about it."

I smiled a little. "Juniper has collected enough semen to create some massive spells. I have a feeling the witches will come out with the big guns on that."

My adorable mate wrinkled her nose. "I'm not drinking anything she gives me."

"Probably a good idea." I looked away as I got lost in a memory.

Being at Summit wasn't easy. When I was a young pup, my father would drag me here to show off how strong his offspring was. I used to love it because it was one of the few times in my life he couldn't beat me into submission. With the anti-violence spell in place, he wouldn't hurt a hair on my head, which meant these trips were some of the few happy memories I had with him.

But it always got worse when we left. He'd have all this pent up rage and would take it out on me. It made me sick to think about.

"Hey," Nicole whispered, stroking my cheek. "What are you thinking about?"

I let out a sigh. "My childhood. It was rough, you know? And I just don't want that for our future child." I held her hands as a flash of pain crossed her expression. I furrowed my brow as her lip quivered.

"Alexei... I... I don't know how to say this..."

I peered into her blue eyes. Something was definitely wrong, and my stomach dropped when I realized what had her worried. "Baby, are you scared I'll be like him?" I choked out, fear wrapping around my heart. "Because I promise I'll be a good father. I would never—"

"No, no!" She cut me off before biting her lip. "It's not that. I know you would never hurt our child. You're a good man, Alexei, but there is something I need to tell you."

I nodded, waiting for her to continue. This was

obviously weighing heavily on her, and I hated seeing her upset.

"I can't have children, Alexei. If I do, I'll die like my mother did." Her voice was raw with emotion as she spoke, and I pulled her tight against my chest as tears streamed down her cheeks. "My uncle told me. It's part of being a lunar goddess. I wanted to tell you sooner, but with everything going on—"

"Baby, you shouldn't have had to deal with this alone," I murmured as she pulled away to look up at me. Her eyelashes were wet from the tears, and I wiped away some drops that had collected on her lip. I took a minute to process everything she said, feeling guilty as hell that she was so upset.

"I just know you want to have kids one day. You're an alpha shifter and—"

"I want *you*, Nicole. You're all I want. We are a family. You are my greatest purpose in life. Is that why you're upset? You're worried about me? Do *you* want kids?"

She chewed on her lip. "One day. It's not something I really put too much thought into. I like the idea of being a mother—in the far future. It's not something I'm determined to do any time soon. And I'm happy with adopting, but I know you have to continue the alpha line for your pack."

I shook my head. "I don't care about any of that.

Nicole, if you want ten kids, I'll make it happen. If you want to enjoy life with just the two of us, I'd love that too. All I want more than anything is to build a life with you. I don't care about anything else."

A small smile curved her lips. "You mean that?"

I wrapped her up in my arms. "Of course. You're my mate, Nicole. My everything."

"You're not even a little disappointed?" she croaked.

I pondered her question for a moment. "Would I love to see your belly swollen with my child? Yes. Would I love to have a daughter that looks like you, or a son that has your eyes? Absolutely. But not at the expense of losing you, Nicole. And we don't have to discuss other options right now, but if we decide to have a family together, they'll still have your heart. My courage. Our love. We can pass down more than just genetics. We can give them two parents who love one another. That's what matters." I cleared my throat. "My father... he was consumed with continuing his line. He cared more about strength and our lineage. I *refuse* to be like him. He didn't teach me the importance of blood. He taught me that family and love can be born from unlikely places. I'm more loyal to you than I've *ever* been to him."

"Alexei..." she whispered as more tears streamed out of her icy eyes, but these were full of love and acceptance. "That's... the most beautiful thing anyone has ever said to me."

I held her for a long time, thinking about our future together.

"We should probably get going," she whispered.

"Are you okay?" I didn't care about the events of the day; I wanted to make sure she was all right. Nicole was my priority—now and always.

"I am now," she admitted. "It's a relief to tell you."

"You can always tell me anything, Nicole. I love you."

She smiled. "I love you, too."

I watched her get out of bed and slip on some pants and a button-up shirt. She looked classy and professional, and all I could think about was ripping those buttons off and spending the day in bed. I hated that we hadn't had many moments alone together lately. I wanted more time to reassure her, to show her how much she meant to me.

Under normal circumstances, new mates would need weeks and weeks of connecting, both physically and emotionally. I was ready for all of this shit with my father to be done so we could do that.

She pulled her hair up and then looked over her shoulder at me. "What are you looking at?"

I got off the bed and sauntered over to her, wrapping my arms around her waist and tugging her toward my chest. "You. You're stunning, you know that?" She leaned into me and let out a contented sigh that made me happy to hear. I loved that I comforted her. I loved that I could finally be a mate worthy of her.

"I'm nervous about today."

"I'll keep you safe. I promise," I said, and I meant every damn word. Nothing would hurt Nicole.

She spun around and looped her arms around my neck. I breathed in her sweet scent. "I suppose we should get going. Don't want to miss it."

"Just stay by me, okay?" I pushed a stray hair out of her face.

"Promise," she whispered.

NICOLE and I were leaning against the wall of the banquet hall, waiting for the first presentation to begin. Juniper slipped in through a side door and let out a huff as she started fiddling with her shoe.

"Targets have been located," she whispered out of the corner of her mouth.

I breathed a sigh of relief as the three of us started walking toward the rows of chairs set in front of the stage. "Did you send word to Minifred?"

She tucked a purple curl behind her ear. "He has the coordinates."

"And did you figure out what he knows about me?" Nicole asked softly.

Juniper looked around the room and lowered her voice even more. "I'll tell you later."

Nicole chewed on her lip, but we didn't have time to process Juniper's ominous statement because the room erupted in applause as Cristian's father took the stage and approached the mic right as we took our seats that Corbin had saved for us.

"Ladies and gentlemen, I am honored to be here today representing my clan. I believe what we offer not only benefits vampires worldwide, but any supernatural beings who rely on blood as a power source."

Hushed murmurs were all around, wondering what the vampire king could possibly allude to.

"As you know," Vasile continued, "until now, we've had to rely on human donors or blood banks for sustenance, both of which can be scarce, depending on how populated the area is in which you live. Both of which carry the risk of unnecessary exposure of our kind." He paused for effect as his gaze wandered the room. "But I'm happy to report, we now have a synthetic alternative!" The king nodded to someone offstage, and a moment later, a wiry man wearing a lab coat and black-framed glasses crossed the stage, carrying a bottle of red liquid. "I need a volunteer from the audience for this next part. Preferably a vampire. Do I have any takers?" Vasile flashed his megawatt smile, fangs fully extended as he took the bottle from the man beside him. "C'mon, now. Since when are vampires shy?"

Chuckles coursed through the audience.

A vamp off to the left climbed onto the stage. "Do I have your word that this substance is safe, Your Majesty?"

Vasile nodded. "On my life."

That seemed to be all the man needed before continuing his trek until he was standing before his king. A vampire's word didn't mean shit to a shifter, but there was a certain code among their kind where it carried significant weight.

I leaned closer, as did Nicole. We were both very curious about what the vampires had come up with.

"As you're aware," the king said while scanning the audience, "a vampire's greatest weakness is their need for blood, as we operate according to a strict code of conduct that prohibits us from drinking from someone without their consent. In times of war and unrest, vampires have suffered in search of food. But no more." Vasile handed the bottle to his volunteer. "Drink."

The man unscrewed the cap and sniffed it. "Smells normal," he commented, making the king smile.

"What do you think it's made of?" Nicole whispered to me.

I shrugged. Blood wasn't really my thing. I wasn't sure how they'd come up with a suitable alternative.

Vasile watched as his subject tipped the bottle back and gulped it down. A few gasps could be heard in the room as he happily drank it. And when he was done, the man wiped his lips with the back of his hand and exclaimed, "It tastes real. It's... good, actually. *Very* good." The volunteer then flexed his muscles. "I feel strong."

The king stood tall. "It's more potent than human blood, and we have various flavors based on your taste preferences. Our test subjects are stronger, faster, and can go longer between feeds thanks to this new formula."

I looked over at my father, who was sitting in the

front corner with a scowl on his face.

"Incredible!" some vampire lady yelled, clapping her hands.

"Bravo, Your Majesty!" another one called.

The king smiled at their praise. "It's also very cost-effective to manufacture. Cheaper than a drive-through at your local burger shop. And easily produced in mass quantities. I have a team working on distribution now. Soon, every vampire in the world will have the food they need, and they'll be stronger for it. We'll be an unstoppable force." The audience broke out in applause again, clearly impressed with the vampire's presentation.

Vasile stepped off the stage, taking the empty chair waiting for him next to Cristian. The pair spoke quietly while eyeing my father from the opposite end of the row. As an elder fae took the stage next, talking about some new advancement in communicating with animals, I studied my father. His square jaw was clenched in anger, but he sat there looking as polished as ever in a designer suit, with his dark brown hair slicked back. Corbin tensed from his seat beside me when his sister approached the alpha, her manicured hand gently placed on her stomach as she bent down to whisper in his ear. My father smiled at whatever she was saying—probably because her tits were spilling out of her too-tight dress and practically in his face—before turning to his assistant beside him and barking out a command. I couldn't hear what he was saying, but I could tell by his expression and how quickly the man vacated his chair that it wasn't pleasant.

As Mara strutted on her high heels toward the now empty seat, our eyes met. She frowned as she spotted Nicole, but then, her red lips curled into a sinister smile that mirrored my father's from a minute ago. Shocked murmurs rang through the crowd as Mara sat down and my father wound his arm around the back of her chair. Looks like she got her wish in the end. My father's pack rescued her from the training camp when we were ambushed. I just wished she knew that he didn't give a shit about her. He just wanted an heir.

"What the actual fuck was that?" Corbin whispered.

His parents, who were seated two rows ahead of us, seemed just as shocked as we were by my father's obvious claiming. The news that Mara was pregnant with the alpha's child had already spread far and wide, but frankly, no one was surprised by it. My father had so many fuck toys over the years, it was bound to happen, eventually. But this... a public showing where his wife was noticeably absent? This was a *statement*.

"I don't like this," Nicole added.

I grunted. "Me neither."

My father kissed Mara on the cheek, then stood up to do his presentation.

"Hello, everyone. I am thrilled to show you what my talented team of scientists has been working on this last year. But before I get to that, I'd like to update you on our progress in restoring the missing wolf genes. There will be a formal press release soon, but I assure you, we are *well* on our way to building our population up once more."

Shifters all around us clapped, and the asshole just stood there soaking it in.

I was nauseated as Nicole glanced at me, likely concerned for her father's well-being. I was relieved that Dr. Fairweather was in Faerie, but I was anxious that my father seemed to know about Nicole's heritage. He didn't seem fully certain, but that he even suspected she had lunar goddess blood running through her veins scared the shit out of me.

"Now that that's out of the way, how about we get to the real reason I'm on this stage?" My father chuckled, flashing a grin that could be perceived as charming if you didn't know what a psychotic asshole he was. "I believe you will find this invention of ours to be quite remarkable."

He clapped his hands twice, prompting a terri

fied-looking man to run onto the stage, holding a vial of liquid. The man bowed to my father as he handed him the clear container and backed away with his gaze trained submissively on the floor.

My father held up the vial, showing us the milky substance inside. "This is a powerful serum. An unprecedented tool for shifters everywhere. While looking for a cure for our missing wolf problem, we stumbled upon something *much* bigger." He looked at the crowd. "Any volunteers?" No one moved. Not a soul spoke up. Every hair on my body stood on edge. "No? None? Fine. Come back here, Frost."

The scurrying man reluctantly appeared on the stage once more. He was trembling so hard that I wondered if he would fall over from the force of his fear.

"Sir," he pleaded. "Please. I beg of you."

My father ignored him. "This man is an elemental. Banned from his community for misuse of power. Burned down an entire street."

A few people gasped. Nicole's eyes glazed over for a moment, and I knew her mental encyclopedia brain was giving her information.

My father continued. "He killed three innocent people and came to my pack looking for refuge. But I'm going to give him something so much better. I'm going to remove his greatest burden."

Frost bowed his head in shame, as my father continued. "This elemental is a danger to our society. He had no control over his powers, and I found a solution that will save him from himself and anyone around him. This will give you the peace you seek, Frost." The tone my father used in that last sentence sounded sinister and deadly, even though the words themselves were anything but.

The elemental took the vial and stared at my father, looking unsure.

"Drink," Alpha Jones commanded.

Frost's hands trembled as he looked around the room. I knew my father wouldn't risk the anti-violence spell and force him to take the serum, but I still was sitting at the edge of my seat, waiting for what would happen next.

"Don't make me remind you what's at stake, Frost," my father growled when the elemental hesitated once more. "I'm saving you from yourself. *You asked for this.* Now take it."

The elemental let out a shaky breath and pressed the vial to his lips. Tipping his head back, he downed it like a shot and fell to the floor with a gasp. We all watched with horrified expressions as he squirmed on the ground, screaming in agony as whatever was in that serum burned through his system. And after a few more seconds of piercing screams, he went silent.

"Well?" my father asked while looking down at the ground at his victim. "Did it work?"

With trembling legs, the elemental stood up and stared at the room. We watched with bated breath as he held his hands up and stared at them, as if they didn't belong to him. "My powers are gone," he said in awe, a dark melancholy in his tone.

My father's hazel eyes roamed the audience, reveling in their state of shock. "Frost is now no more powerful than a human. Witches, shifter, vampire, fae—it doesn't matter. This serum can remove the abilities you were born with. Anyone who doesn't want the burden of their power like Frost here, no longer has to suffer. More importantly, anyone who doesn't *deserve* that kind of power can be punished."

Looks of horror passed through the crowd as we processed his words. My head spun as I imagined the potential fallout. If that serum did what my father had claimed, that sadistic son of a bitch had accomplished the impossible. If he could remove our greatest strengths, that would make Jones Koenig the most powerful being among us.

And *that* was fucking terrifying.

CHAPTER
SEVENTEEN

Nicole

Tʚɪs was bad. Very, *very* bad.

The thought of a psycho like Alpha Jones having such a powerful weapon was terrifying. The destruction it could cause would be catastrophic.

After the initial chatter from the audience wore down, we all stood silently—at a cautious distance—to hear what he was going to say next.

Alexei's evil father nodded to someone offstage right before the two henchmen who took my father from me stepped out, hauling that poor neutered elemental away. I instantly tensed at the sight of them, which did not go unnoticed by my mate.

"What is it?" he whispered.

I shook my head. "I'll tell you later."

"Now that the demonstration is out of the way," Alpha Jones purred into the mic, "shall we go over the specifics?" He paused for a moment, daring anyone to object, but no one did. "As you can imagine... having a weapon like this could be a game changer. It does not come without great responsibility or expense. Manufacturing this serum takes time because it requires the utmost precision. And as any business owner knows, time is money. If you were hoping to procure my invention at a discount, unfortunately, that won't be possible. I've also decided I'll need to be *incredibly* selective in who I sell to. It'd be an awful shame to put this much power in the hands of one of my enemies, don't you think?" He chuckled darkly, making a point to look directly at me and Alexei.

A man off to the left raised his hand before asking, "How do we know it works? Do you expect us to take that elemental's word for it?"

I held my breath, hoping this was all a farce, but I highly doubted Alexei's father would look as confident as he did if it were.

Alpha Jones narrowed his eyes briefly before clearing his throat. "I absolutely understand your concern, Alpha Desmond. But let me assure you, if you pass through initial vetting, I'd be more than happy to allow you to bring along a test subject of your own when you come to pick up the serum. I am giving you *all* my word that, if the serum does not work on the spot, I will refund every penny paid."

Well, fuck. There went that hope.

He waited for the murmurs of approval to quiet down. "So, if you're interested in negotiating, contact my office, and my secretary will send you the necessary disclosures and application. If I feel you're worthy, I will be in contact with you to discuss pricing." His gaze roamed the room from left to right, a sinister smile blooming on his face when he saw the obvious terror from most and calculated interest from a few equally scary-looking individuals. "Thank you for your time. Now, if you'll excuse me, I have a meeting to get to."

You could hear a pin drop from a mile away as Alpha Jones walked away with his head held high.

Once he was completely out of sight, Alexei grabbed my hand and said, "We need to get you out of here."

"No way!" I argued. "Besides, the hearing is starting soon. We need to get over there."

"I don't want you anywhere near him." Alexei's chocolate stare was pleading, begging me to listen. "He's unhinged."

"I think we could all use some privacy to discuss

this new... problem," High Priestess Hale said as she joined us, with Cristian and his father at her side.

"Agreed." The vampire king frowned as his eyes darted rapidly throughout the room. "The hearing begins shortly, but we can spare a few moments. Eve, would you like to do the honors?"

Juniper's mom nodded. "Of course."

Before I had a chance to ask questions, our small group was being sucked into the Witchy Express, spitting us out in a lavish hotel room.

"Where are we?" Alexei asked, grabbing my arm to prevent me from toppling to the carpet.

"My suite," Eve answered. "It already has a silencing spell in place, so I felt this was the best spot to have this discussion. I don't trust Alpha Jones not to have spies near all the council members' suites."

"Good thinking," Corbin said. "Pack Daddy is one shady son of a bitch, that's for sure."

The vampire king raised a regal brow. "Pack Daddy? Are you referring to Alpha Jones?"

Corbin shrugged. "I called him that once and it stuck."

Alexei shivered. "I wish it would unstick."

I started pacing the room, thinking of what this meant for Alexei challenging his father. "If he takes your wolf away..."

"I'll be fighting without a weapon," Alexei finished for me, letting out a deep sigh as he did.

Eve stroked her chin. "But Nicole summons wolves." She snapped her inquisitive eyes to me. "Do you think you could summon Alexei's wolf back if the serum suppresses it?"

I shook my head. "I'm not sure. I haven't even tried that, and there is no telling what the suppressant serum actually does. What if he takes my powers from *me*?" I rubbed my arms anxiously. All of this was bad. Very bad. It made taking down Alpha Jones that much more terrifying.

The vampire king joined me in pacing. "He made this serum. Maybe there is some sort of antidote? And what do you mean Nicole can summon wolves?"

Eve sighed. "One problem at a time, Vasile. Let's focus on Alpha Jones, first."

I contemplated things for a moment before realizing we had a weapon in our arsenal, someone smart enough to find a cure. "I could ask my father. Alpha Jones said they stumbled upon this serum when searching for a cure to the missing wolf phenomenon. My father is probably already familiar with the compounds. And with Cammie's help..."

Eve and the vampire king exchanged a look. "What does he need?"

"A lab," I answered. "Time. We can't challenge Alpha Jones until we are protected. I'll need to talk to my father, and he probably needs some of the serum. Jones said it was very expensive, though."

The king waved his hand. "Money isn't a problem, but I doubt the alpha will sell it to me. We need someone able to convince Alpha Jones they are his ally."

All these politics were driving me insane. It felt impossible to navigate. "He's not going to sell it to anyone that isn't a shifter," Alexei said.

"What about General Minifred?" Juniper asked.

I looked at her. "The general is avoiding Alpha Jones. You know his alpha status makes him a target. Not to mention, General Minifred submitted the video evidence of the culling to the council. He's enemy number one."

Alexei shook his head. "We need someone my father would want to work with."

"A shifter pack he wants an alliance with or... already has an alliance with," Eve added.

I chewed on my lip. "What about the Greenwood pack? When I had a letter of recommendation from their luna, everyone started taking me seriously. Would one of them help us?"

Alexei nodded. "My father has lots of dealings

with them, but I don't think we can trust them to ask them to work with us."

Juniper held an index finger up. "We don't have to ask them anything. I can make another mask, and one of us can pose as someone from the Greenwood pack."

Corbin shook his head and held his hands up. "Not it. Last time you made a disguise, I had a cock the size of Mount Vesuvius."

Alexei waved his hands. "We can figure out the logistics later, but I think that could work. My father respects the Greenwood pack and would easily sell to them. He wouldn't want to risk closing future trade with them."

I looked at Eve. I trusted Alexei to know how his father's mind worked, but she was wise. "I think it's our best bet. Goddess knows he won't sell it to the witches."

"Great. Now that that's settled, we need to discuss the other problem at hand," Alexei said with a heavy sigh. "I can't challenge my father at the council meeting. And I'm not comfortable bringing Nicole there either."

I opened my mouth to protest, but Eve spoke before I could. "Nicole has to come. The meeting has two purposes. We're discussing who has rights to Nicole and her father as well as deciding the disciplinary action for the culling. Dr. Fairweather is currently considered missing, but if Nicole doesn't show up, she gives up her rights. There would be no need for a timeline spell, and she will automatically be handed over to Alpha Jones."

"Fuck," I cursed.

The vampire king straightened his collar. "Part of me hopes Jones doesn't show up so we can arrest him. His team of lawyers make me nervous. Slimy bastards will probably find some loophole out of it."

I scrunched my nose. "I still don't understand why we even need this meeting. We're mates, Alexei. We announced it and everything. I'm not even human anymore. The mate bond supersedes everything, doesn't it?"

"We will have to prove our bond at the council meeting," Alexei gritted.

Cristian cleared his throat. "Speaking of not being human, I'm going to need one of you to explain that to me. I'm assuming Alpha Jones wasn't completely wrong in his accusations last night? The high priestess just said 'Nicole can summon wolves.' What does that mean?"

The vampire king leaned in, seemingly curious about this as well. "I sensed we needed to divert the conversation last night," he added. "But I, too, am curious. If we have a goddess on our side, then it improves our odds significantly."

My chest constricted. I was still learning how to use my powers, and I wasn't even sure how much I could help. "Technically, I'm a *demi*goddess. Lunar to be exact."

Both vampires raised their brows.

June looped her arm through Cristian's. "We really need to get going. I'll give you all the deets along the way to rescue those kiddos. I promise."

"And I'll fill you in after the council meeting," Eve said to Vasile.

Alexei growled. "We're trusting you, vampires. You'd better not breathe a word of this to *anyone*."

Cristian looked at Alexei, then to me. "I won't tell a soul. We're allies, remember?"

The vampire king nodded in agreement. "Your secret is safe with us. I give my solemn vow that we shall not tell a soul, or be punished by death."

Alexei peered at both vampires before finally offering a single nod, wordlessly accepting their promises. Meanwhile, I felt like I was going to vomit.

Eve spoke to me. "Nicole, your father is still very important to Alpha Jones. Once a meeting is established, it cannot be undone. Even if it's clear he has no claim to you, the meeting must happen. It's magically binding once a session is agreed upon. We lucked out that your father is in another dimension. The binding can't reach Faerie, thank the gods. But you must be present for your and your father's sake."

"I just hate this," I murmured.

Alexei wrapped his arms around me, holding me close. "I know, baby. But now that I'm no longer challenging him, whatever happens will be over quickly. Council hearings are pretty cut and dry. My father has no claim to you. Everyone here knows it, but the timeline spell will prove it beyond any doubt."

"Let's get going. The faster we can get this done, the better," Vasile Luca said.

"Is everyone ready?" Alexei asked.

I let out a shaky breath. "Let's do this."

EIGHTEEN

Nicole

EVE PORTALED us to the judgment room at the council headquarters, away from Summit and away from the anti-violence spell. As soon as I stepped foot into the room, a searing wave of anxiousness swept through my veins. I was bombarded by a sense of dread as I surveyed the circle of ancient desks. The atmosphere was rife with an impending sense of doom, though that was unsurprising considering Alpha Jones's presentation.

The dozens of council members that crowded the large room were all dressed in formal attire, from white collared shirts to pressed slacks to delicate suits. Most of them had a look of concern on their faces, while others tried their best to appear stoic. Despite the formality in their outfit and demeanor, I could sense a hint of magic radiating off each of these men and women. Some looked like they had just strolled out of a medieval fairytale, with pointed ears and sharp facial features; others appeared more like humanoid foxes or raccoons with coats ranging from midnight black to auburn red; still others were adorned with strands of glimmering beads that seemed to reflect their inner light.

It was an odd mix, for sure. One guy held an ancient-looking staff, a couple of women clutched thick-spined books that gave off ethereal glows, and one person of indeterminate gender carried an exotic bird perched upon their shoulder as if they were part of the family. The sheer variety of creatures that were gathered here to discuss Alpha Jones's fate made me dizzy. Of course, Corbin and Alexei observed the room as if it were perfectly normal to see all these supes in one room.

"Every supernatural faction is represented on the council," Eve explained with a small smile. "Even the rarest of creatures." She nodded at a humanoid fox. "Shifters, vampires, witches, and fae might have the largest population, but we feel that everyone should have a voice on the council."

A man who had been sitting in the center of the

circle stood up. He was bald and had thick, hornlike growths protruding from his head. My mental resource book started flaring excitedly. He wore a flowing robe in dark purple that almost matched his skin.

I gasped when my mind flashed with what he was. "A goblin?" I hissed to Alexei.

My mate sighed. "Tricksters and problem makers. They make perfect lawyers."

The goblin walked up to us and bowed slightly. He had a wicked smirk on his face, and his green eyes glowed with malice. "Let me introduce myself." His voice was deep and gravelly, as if it were born from the depths of hell. "My name is Gaborok." He waved his hands around the room and grinned wickedly as if he were proud of something. "I have been hired by Alpha Jones to represent him in this case," he added with a sharp cackle. "I am here to ensure justice is served." His eyes twinkled playfully, as if he was enjoying himself immensely.

"I want to get this done as quickly as possible," a man with jet black hair and pointed ears said.

"That's the fae representative," Alexei murmured to me.

I wondered if he knew Cammie. We needed to talk to him about getting a message to my father.

The fae cleared his throat, gathering everyone's

attention. "The only reason I'm here is because my people want to see that psycho shifter locked up. It's clear Alpha Jones has no claim on a mated bond, and the evidence against him in the culling is damning. It should be a straightforward case. He has five minutes to show up, or we'll summon him by force."

Eve looked at Gaborok—what the hell kind of name was Gaborok anyway? "Where is your client?"

Gaborok waved his hand dismissively. "He will arrive soon enough." His words were spoken with an air of confidence, though I didn't trust him. He seemed to hold something back, something important. The meeting was scheduled to begin right now, yet Alpha Jones was nowhere to be seen. "Although, my client isn't the only key person who seems to be missing." He looked down at the tablet he was holding. "What about General August Minifred? I was quite looking forward to cross-examining him."

The high priestess's nostrils flared in annoyance. "General Minifred is on government assignment, unable to attend in person. He has a special pardon to join us via video call during the second half of the hearing. You should've received an updated agenda stating that."

The attorney smiled. "Oh, yes, I did. My apologies, High Priestess."

Vasile Luca narrowed his eyes in distrust.

"Let's all take our seats, shall we? Like Torvald said, if Jones Koenig does not arrive in the next three minutes, he'll forfeit his right to defend himself and we'll be forced to proceed with sentencing."

The vampire king and high priestess took the two empty chairs that circled the platform while Alexei guided me and Corbin to an empty bench against the wall, where several other people sat. The platform itself held a rectangular table and a podium, for the defendant, I was guessing, since that was where Alpha Jones's attorney stood waiting for his client.

The tension in the room was palpable. Gaborok seemed edgy, his eyes flicking around the chamber and his feet pounding against the ground. He would periodically break into an unfamiliar melody, further heightening the anxious vibes that filled the room.

"Mr. Koenig." A blonde woman approached our group excitedly, shoving a portable recording device in our faces. "Kyra Klaussen from the *Shifter Times*. What are your feelings on your father's hearing? Do you have any idea why he's not present? Do you even consider him your father since you formally renounced your claim on the pack and he announced his new heir?"

"No comment," Alexei growled, shoving the recorder out of the way.

Her blue eyes sliced to me. "Miss Fairweather, how does it feel to be a human mated to a shifter?"

My mate's chest rumbled, the threat clear in his tone as he repeated, "No comment. Find somewhere else to be."

High Priestess Hale banged an honest-to-God gavel. "Silence! There will be plenty of time for journalists to ask questions *after* the hearing. Is that understood, Ms. Klaussen?"

"Yes, ma'am." The blonde newswoman scampered away with her proverbial tail between her legs.

"Two more minutes," Vasile murmured, looking at his very expensive-looking watch.

"Where is your father?" I whispered to Alexei. "This isn't just about his claim on me and my dad. Isn't he on trial for what happened at the quad in Redwood, too? I thought you said they were addressing everything at once."

"I did," he whispered back, eyes darting across the room warily. "I don't like this at all. Maybe he's avoiding it all together. He knows he's guilty and thinks they won't have the balls to track him down."

"Do you think he got wind of the... camp thing?" Corbin posed, choosing his words carefully. "Maybe he went there to meet the parents as they picked up their kiddos?"

"It's possible," Alexei replied. "But we would have heard something if there was any trouble."

"Where is your client?" Eve asked again, making us all turn to look at her. She was glaring at the goblin lawyer. "It is customary for the defendant to be present at these hearings, especially considering the severity of the charges against him."

"My client should be here any moment, High Priestess," he assured her, taking a seat in the far right chair at the table. I knew he would be a problem, given what my magical thesaurus told me about his species' reputation. The air of mischief surrounding him—the way his eyes glistened with the promise of trouble—made the small hairs on the back of my neck stand on end. I took a deep breath and vowed to remain calm.

He huffed, then said, "Would you like me to call the alpha?"

"This is ridiculous." That fae guy—Tor-something—scoffed. "Blatant disrespect to this council. It would behoove your client not to incense the council before the hearing even began, don't you think?"

"Of course," the attorney agreed. "I'll just dial

his number and we can figure out what's causing the delay."

"I really fucking don't like this," Alexei repeated to me.

"Me neither." Corbin's knee was bouncing furiously.

I was making a conscious effort not to show my anxiety in such an obvious way, but the slight shaking of my hand was betraying me. I took a deep breath as Alexei clasped his fingers with mine, steadying me.

The goblin lawyer pulled out his cell phone and dialed the number. He put it on speakerphone and we all heard the ringing in the background. After a few moments, a gruff voice answered.

"Hello." He sounded bored, yet... somehow, also excited.

"Ah, Alpha Jones," the goblin said. "The council is quite eager to see you. Do make haste, for if you don't, there will be unfortunate repercussions. But, why listen to me? I'm sure you already know that. You're on speaker phone if you'd like to tell the council anything." He then chuckled wickedly, as if this was a game.

Alpha Jones's reply was loaded with disdain. "Hello, council, and thank you, Gaborok, for allowing me the pleasure of speaking to everyone." He cleared his throat. "Do you really think I'm so foolish as to come to this hearing? If I made an appearance, it would be a death sentence for me. You may have your fancy council and your rules, but they won't save you when I'm done with you. I am the law. I am the ruler. I am the strongest. *I am the only true alpha.* Don't think that just because you are all here in the safety of your little courtroom that I can't get to you whenever and wherever I please." He laughed menacingly before continuing, "You want me there? Then come find me, and bring an army if you must— but know that I will *never* submit willingly." His laughter echoed in our ears as he hung up the phone.

"Wha—"

Before I could finish my sentence, the room shook violently as a loud explosion sounded from somewhere beneath us. Everyone in the room glanced around in confusion until a louder, closer explosion rattled the room, and it sunk in what was happening.

"Get down!" Alexei yelled, shoving me down to the ground, shielding me with his body just as the stained glass windows shattered, raining shards of glass upon us.

"Fuck!" Corbin shouted before grunting in

obvious pain. "We're under attack! Bombs. I think they're bombs."

Just then, the goblin snapped his fingers, and a cloud of glittering purple magic filled the room. In an instant, he had vanished, leaving behind only the smell of smoke and fear in his wake. We were left to fend for ourselves against an enemy we couldn't see or even comprehend.

In a flurry of activity, some ran from the court-room to find refuge from the chaos. The area was filled with screams as panicked people pushed and shoved past one another, desperate to escape.

Chaos was breaking out all around us, but I couldn't do anything but lie there as my mate crushed me to the hard floor. Water from the over-head sprinklers rained down upon us, mixing with blood that I knew was coming from my mate.

"Alexei!" I yelled. "We have to get out of here."

He pulled on my arm and helped me up. "Stay low."

Another explosion rocked the room, chunks of marble from the walls flying. I used my free hand to block the rubble from falling on my head. My vision blurred as Alexei stumbled toward the door, tugging me behind him as we avoided smoke and flying debris. Shrill screams filled my ears as another body pressed into my side, holding me up as we moved.

Through the chaos, I realized it was Corbin and breathed a sigh of relief, though there was blood pouring down his face and he had a slight limp.

The smoke was too much, and I had to use my arm to shield my face. We pushed through the confusion, headed for the exit, but just before we made it to the door, another high-powered blast went off behind us, knocking us forward.

"Alexei!" I screamed.

"Oh, fuck," Alexei groaned.

I scooted closer to him, ignoring my pain as I tried to assess where he had been hit. There were no visible wounds, but his head was bleeding profusely. He groaned again, rolling to his side as he clutched at his skull. Corbin limped over to us, and I could see that his left arm was covered in cuts. His shirt was shredded and stained with blood, the leftover scraps barely holding him together. He dropped to the floor beside us, his breathing ragged as he surveyed the scene.

"We have to go," Corbin said weakly. "Now."

We both nodded in agreement before helping Alexei to his feet. We moved faster than we ever thought possible toward the exit, my heart in my throat as we darted through broken glass and wreckage to make it out alive. The smoke was so thick that it felt like a blanket on my skin, burning my eyes and filling my lungs with its toxic fumes. It got harder and harder to pull Alexei, who was barely conscious.

"Get out of here, Nicole."

My ears were ringing. I was pretty much reading lips at this point, but the message was clear.

"Not without you," I grunted.

Another blast went off as Corbin and I dragged Alexei out of the room. We made it out the door just as the ceiling collapsed.

Alexei groaned, his brows drawn together. "We have to get out of here."

"What about Cristian's dad? And Eve?" I shouted while looking behind us.

Tears welled up in my eyes as sparkling mist filled the air. A large beam shifted, and I saw a soot-covered Eve float out of the rubble toward us, looking like a fallen angel as tears and dirt fell down her cheeks.

"We have to go!" she yelled.

"What about Vasile?" My shrill voice echoed around the room. Or maybe it was in my ears.

Eve looked at me, the remorse heavy in her expression. "I put up a shield, but... it was too late." She looked back at the beam she'd moved to escape, and I could see the smoldering remains of Vasile's body, crushed beneath its weight. I fell to my knees and squeezed my eyes shut, trying to deny what had just happened. "Nicole, we have to go."

I could hear more explosions, but I couldn't move. My entire world was falling around me, and there was nothing I could do to stop it. Corbin pulled me to my feet, and I focused on Eve. "We have to get out of here," she repeated. "Your mate needs you to pull yourself together."

"We can still save the others!" I screamed.

"I couldn't save everyone, Nicole. We have to get to my healers." Eve cradled her arm to her chest, the bone bent at an awkward angle as tears filled her eyes.

"No. They can't be dead—"

"Everyone is gone!" Eve roared. "There are no magical signatures left in that room. We must go now!"

My heart raced and my breathing became erratic, my throat tightening in terror. More bombs went off, the sound of it piercing my ears like sirens, and the ground shook violently with each impact. My God, was this entire building wired with explosives? I stumbled as the floor threatened to give way beneath me. Desperation clawed at my chest. I looked around, frantic to help those in danger, to save them from the looming chaos. But the fear of more destruction kept me frozen in place.

Eve exchanged a look with Alexei, then all three of them crowded in a circle around me.

"We can't just leave them there," I croaked.

Alexei wrapped his arms around me. "If we stay, we're dead. This whole building is going to crumble at any moment."

"I'm running on fumes here," Eve exclaimed, her voice quaking. She was wrapped in a cocoon of golden light that sparkled with prismatic rainbows.

I clutched onto Alexei's back, my fingers dug into his tense muscles. Corbin glimpsed at the council room, his skin illuminated by the captivating sparks of magic. Fear crawled up my spine as I waited, unsure of what would come next. A ripple of vibrant enchantment glowed around us. And then... Eve transported us to the witches' headquarters, while I sobbed at the injustice of it all.

NINETEEN

Nicole

I HANDED a blanket to a young boy who had wide eyes and dirt smudged on his cheek.

"You don't have to help, you know," I whispered to Cristian as he was setting up a pallet on the floor for another child. "We can do this."

We'd turned the ballroom at the witches' headquarters into a makeshift shelter for all the children. This was one of the safest places for them.

For now.

Eventually, we'd have to figure out whether they had any family members who'd care for them, but that couldn't happen until Alpha Jones was taken down. There was no sense in drawing attention to the children's return only to allow them to be kidnapped again, or worse.

The newly appointed vampire king's lips pressed into a thin line. "I need to keep busy. Stewing over my grief in solitude won't do anyone any good."

It had been a rough twenty-four hours filled with both sorrow and relief. General Minifred and his team had saved all the children Alpha Jones had kidnapped, but we received confirmation that there were only a handful of survivors from the blast at the council building. Cristian had dark shadows under his eyes, and Alexei hadn't really spoken since the incident. I knew my mate was devastated over what his father had done, and the pressure to take him down weighed heavily on him. Forensics teams were still sorting through the wreckage, but the building wasn't very large, so according to Eve, they should be finished soon.

The official press release for human consumption blamed a gas leak, but we all knew it was only a matter of time before supernatural officials charged Alpha Jones with the crime. Evidently, the only part of the building wired with explosives was the judgment room, but there were *dozens* of freaking explosives. It was clearly a coordinated attack meant to take down the entire council—along with me and

Alexei—in one fell swoop. Who else had the motive to do such a thing?

"Thank you, sir," a little girl with bright blonde hair said before giving Cristian a big hug.

At first, he looked uncomfortable, but then his shoulders softened, and I could see the sadness in his eyes as he hugged her back. He murmured something to her in a soft voice before standing up and turning away.

"What did you say to her?" I asked him, walking over to wrap my arms around him.

He smiled sadly before gently pushing a few strands of hair away from my face. "I just told her it was going to be okay. That I know things are confusing right now, but she's safe, and eventually, everything will be alright again."

My heart ached for him, knowing the pain he was experiencing right now was more than any one person should have to bear. I wanted so desperately to shoulder it for him, but all I could do was offer him my friendship and support as we slowly worked toward getting our lives back on track again.

Cristian cleared his throat and started sorting through more supplies, making more tears well in my eyes. I could understand his need to feel busy, though. We all just wanted to feel like we were actually doing something productive.

"I come bearing clean clothes." My best friend blew a loose strand of hair away from her face as she walked into the large room with a pile of clothing in her hands. "Come and get it, kiddos!"

Corbin stepped into the room right behind Bee, with a large box. "I have shoes in all shapes and sizes." He set the box down with a huff as the children stormed past him to get to the goods.

It was bittersweet, seeing the excitement on their faces from something so simple. But I supposed when you were subjected to God-knows-what at a soldier-manufacturing fortress, being able to have the choice of your attire again would be a blessing.

Cristian joined me up against the wall while we watched the children sort through their options. "You know I can't let this slide, right? I can't let my father's murder go unpunished. I can't afford to show any mercy, or it'll be perceived as weakness."

"I know." I nodded solemnly, careful to keep my volume low. "But you don't have to do it alone, Cristian. We're all in this together, remember?"

He glanced down at me with a mixture of sadness and regret. "I know that, but this is something I need to do on my own. I always saw my father as a great man, and now he's gone. It kills me to think that his life was taken away because of some master plan concocted by a madman."

Tears spilled from my eyes, and I reached up to wipe them away with my thumb. Cristian looked away for a moment before turning back to me, his expression full of sorrow. "It's so hard not knowing if he felt any pain or suffered in the end. If I could've saved him somehow if I were there…"

My throat tightened as Cristian looked down at the floor with an unspoken grief etched into every line of his face. I wrapped my arms around him tightly. "Cristian, if you were there, you might not be *here* right now. I still don't know how *any* of us survived."

I truly didn't. It made no sense. Eve had suggested that a higher power had been looking out for us, but who could that be? Did my uncle have that kind of influence? The mother spirit? She said it was anyone's guess.

"I should have been there," he croaked. "But you're right, Nicole. I'm the heir, right?" He let out a bitter laugh.

I pulled away and looked up into his eyes. "Cristian, it's not your fault. There's nothing you could've done. Besides, what would have happened if you both died? The vampires would have no leader. Your father wouldn't have wanted that. I barely knew him, but I could tell how much he cared for your kingdom."

"I know," he whispered. "I just feel… so utterly unprepared."

"We'll get through this together, okay? We'll make sure that justice is served and Alpha Jones pays for what he's done. You don't have to do this alone." Cristian tensed for a moment before finally nodding in agreement.

"What are we talking about?" Corbin asked as he and Bee joined us.

"Revenge," Cristian replied.

"Uh… maybe we should table the *evenge-ray* talk for when there aren't tiny supernatural ears around, yeah?" Corbin suggested.

"Plus, I'm sure my dad and Alexei would like to be present for this conversation," Bee added.

"Where are they anyway?" Cristian asked. "I haven't seen either of them all morning."

"Probably doing some pseudo father-son bonding thing," Corbin pouted.

Bee smacked his arm with the back of her hand. "Quit being such a drama queen, Corbin. You know exactly what they're doing." She turned her gaze to Cristian. "Alexei is giving my dad pointers on his father's strengths, weaknesses, tells, and all that jazz so my dad can be as prepared as possible when he meets with Pack Daddy about buying the serum. Juniper is working on the mask potion now."

Corbin beamed as Bee used his preferred nickname for Alpha Jones.

"Not you, too," I griped. "Alexei hates that name."

Bee shrugged. "What? It's catchy."

Corbin kissed the top of her head. "I'm growing on her."

"Like a mold," I said with a playful roll of my eyes. "Surprised you want her calling anyone Daddy."

Corbin's face dropped. "Good point. No calling anyone Daddy. Only me. And your father. But no—that's weird. Let's not do the whole Daddy thing."

Bee tipped her head back and laughed. It was nice to see her smile in the middle of so much darkness. Corbin was definitely rubbing off on her in a good way. "Let's go find Alexei and General Minifred and talk about the game plan."

"Plan, plan, plan," Corbin said. "I normally love plans, but I'm ready to kick some Pack Daddy—Sir—asshole? Pack Asshole ass."

"Pack Asshole?" Bee asked.

"It's a work in progress, babe."

"Let's go," Cristian grunted, souring our mood, not that I could blame him.

We left some of the witches to watch over the kids and made our way to the training room, where Alexei was beating the shit out of a punching bag. His knuckles were bloody, and he had a furious look on his face. It seemed all of us had a lot of frustration to work through.

"Alexei?" My mate turned to face us. He and the general were both dripping with sweat, likely from a full morning of working.

My mate wiped a towel across his face. "Are the kids okay? I know staying here isn't ideal, but..."

"But they don't really have anywhere else to go," I replied.

Pain sliced across his expression. It was hurting him to know these kids were orphans and had suffered.

"We will do everything in our power to make sure they are safe," Alexei said. His voice was gravelly and firm with determination. "My father will regret the day he ever thought to kidnap them."

General Minifred nodded in agreement. "We will keep them safe, Alexei. And we will bring Alpha Jones to justice for all the suffering he has inflicted. I promise you that."

"They have clothes, right? Should we get them toys?" Alexei asked.

Bee cleared her throat. "We're making sure they

have everything they need. It'll take some time for them to adjust, but we've got it covered. The witches are brewing some dream spells, too. Giving them pleasant dreams before bed to help with the trauma."

Alexei nodded. "Good. God, I'm going to owe Eve a lot after this." He looked at Cristian, who was stroking the watch on his wrist tenderly. "Are you... How are you holding up?" Alexei winced at his question. There wasn't really a good way to ask how Cristian was doing. His father was just murdered.

"I'll feel better when I can go back to my people. I'm glad I was here to help the kids get settled, though. My father would be happy to know they're safe."

Alexei put a hand on Cristian's shoulder. "I know your father would be proud of you. He was a good man, and he didn't deserve what happened to him. We will make sure his death wasn't in vain."

I swallowed a lump in my throat at the sight of my mate putting aside his animosity toward Cristian.

Cristian nodded. "We need to solidify our plans to take down Alpha Jones and get our hands on that serum. Where are we at on that?"

"I've scheduled a meeting with Jones," General Minifred said. "Well, I should say *the Greenwood pack* has a meeting scheduled with Jones. I'm going to pose as their alpha—Juniper wasn't confident her masking spell could mute my alpha energy entirely, so I figured working around it would be best."

The vampire's dark brows rose. "You're not worried about Jones or one of his representatives communicating with this pack beforehand?"

General Minifred shook his head. "Not at all. Eve placed a magical rerouting spell on all communication devices between Ridgeview or Greenwood pack members. It's a lot like the containment spell that filters content from the university campus. Any other calls or messages will go through, so it shouldn't raise suspicion. I've been researching this other alpha's mannerisms and prior business dealings with Jones, so I'm confident I'll be fully prepared before we meet." He paused for a moment to guzzle half a bottle of water. "Besides, Jones is floundering right now. Getting sloppy. He knows all the kids were taken from his camp and the other supernatural factions are becoming allies. He's been impulsive, which means we can capitalize on that."

Alexei nodded. "You're sure you can close the deal? If my father—"

General Minifred smirked. "I can handle it, kid. I'm *very* skilled at negotiations."

"Speaking of fathers," I interjected. "How are we

going to get mine here to even work on the antidote?"

Cristian cleared his throat. "I believe I can help with that. My court secretary has a contact in the fae court. I'm sure he'll be able to get word to Professor Viden and, in turn, your father. I'm sure they'll be eager to assist, considering Jones killed their council representative."

I cleared my throat. "I was thinking about trying astral projection again. I should have been working on it sooner, maybe then we could have avoided..." My voice trailed off as my throat constricted. I couldn't help but feel like the bombs could have been prevented.

"Don't do that, Nicole," Alexei snapped. "You are *not* responsible for that bombing." He took a deep breath, cupping my face in his hands. "I agree the insight would be helpful, but I don't want you putting any more of a target on your back. Is there any danger in this?"

I shook my head. "No, it's not dangerous."

I didn't think so, anyway. Man, I really needed to take time to study those ancient books. "It just takes a lot of concentration. I can try it with people I know before testing the waters elsewhere."

General Minifred nodded in agreement. "It's a

good idea. The more information we have, the better chance we have of succeeding."

"You're amazing," Alexei mouthed before releasing me and stepping to the side so I could face the general.

"Antidote aside, I'm afraid we're still at a disadvantage numbers wise." He frowned. "My source's latest report was... troubling. Alpha Jones's army has grown exponentially since he revealed the serum the other day. Packs from all over North America are volunteering their strongest members to join his fight—luckily, Greenwood has been shying away from conflict, so we won't have to worry about them actually stepping forward and ruining our plans."

Well, at least there was some good news in all of that. "When will Juniper be done with the mask potion?"

"She said in the next day or two, which works out perfectly."

"Pack Daddy will actually be at this meeting you've scheduled?" Corbin asked.

The general nodded. "Yes, *Jones* will be there. His secretary specifically told me he was looking forward to seeing me. Obviously, that could change if he's formally charged for the council attack, but then again, it's possible his ego will override his common sense in that regard. There's some buzz starting about Jones claiming responsibility, citing that it's time for new leadership. This whole thing is inciting mass hysteria and gaining some equally psychotic and power-hungry allies. My team of shifters is comprised of the best the military offers, but our numbers are pathetic comparatively. I can't send my men into a losing battle. We need more shifters. More supernaturals. Diversity is what's going to give us the advantage if we can get enough soldiers."

"You have the vampires' support," Cristian assured the general, standing tall. "I will do whatever it takes to make sure Alpha Jones pays for what he's done. He killed my father, and I'll be damned if I let him get away with it. We will see justice served." His voice was full of determination, a fire burning bright in his eyes as he promised retribution against the man responsible for causing so much pain and anguish.

It was strange watching Cristian transform from a carefree frat boy to a literal king overnight, but I knew that was what I was witnessing. He may not have wanted the job like this, but he certainly seemed to have been made for it.

"Thank you." My mate nodded, looking Cristian directly in the eye. "When this is all over... when I gain control of my pack, I will owe you a significant debt."

The two men seemed to have some sort of silent conversation, a mutual respect and understanding, if I was reading them correctly.

Cristian nodded once in reply.

"But we will still need more numbers," General Minifred replied.

I chewed on my lip. "More wolves?" I asked.

"That would be ideal, but no pack is going to ally themselves with Alexei. They're too afraid of Alpha Jones right now. We can't expect children to go to war."

"Maybe we don't have to find a new pack," I mused, an idea coming to me. "We just need to create our own."

"What are you saying, Nicole?" Bee asked.

I rolled my shoulders back. "I can make more wolves, right? I'll need my uncle's help, but I think if I learn how to use my powers, we can have an entire army of shifters." And with the suggestion of power, a pulse of magic thudded in my veins. This was how we would take down Alpha Jones.

"You're sure you can do this?" General Minifred cocked his head to the side, his expression unsure but hopeful.

"I am." I totally wasn't, but we didn't need

doubts right now. I was a demigoddess, right? I had to act like it.

"If we can do this…" Alexei breathed. "If we can grow in numbers, then maybe we have a real chance."

General Minifred nodded. "I'll start interviewing soldiers to find suitable candidates."

I let out a deep exhale. "And I'll get to work on learning how to harness my powers."

My mate smiled and took my hand, giving me a reassuring squeeze. "Then let's get to work. We have a pack to build, and it starts with us, baby."

CHAPTER

TWENTY

Nicole

I sᴀᴛ with my legs crossed and my eyes squeezed shut. I could feel Alexei staring at me with his warm look as I steadied my breathing and focused on the task at hand.

"Do you need anything?" he asked.

I scrunched my nose up. "Just some silence. I'm going to reach for Corbin. Don't tell me where he is."

Alexei didn't respond.

Taking a deep breath, I let my thoughts drift as I sought Corbin's presence. My body relaxed, and the room faded away in its entirety. The darkness that surrounded me was almost tangible; it filled every nook and crevice of the space and seemed to crawl over me like a comforting blanket. I stayed still, keeping my mind focused on one thought: Corbin.

The surrounding darkness became less dense, and suddenly I could feel a strange sensation of weightlessness spreading throughout my body. It felt as if gravity had vanished, carrying me up into the sky in an effortless ascent. I watched in awe as the stars twinkled brightly against the ink-black night sky above me. As I gazed up at them, they seemed to pulse with life—guiding me in their own unique way toward whatever destination lay ahead of me.

A faint, eerie light flickered in the distance, and I was pulled toward it. I was in a weird ghostly state in an unfamiliar room, but I knew it had to be located inside the witches' headquarters. The stone walls were inscribed with strange symbols and patterns, hinting at some ancient secrets. Candles of various sizes levitated in the room, emitting an ethereal glow and illuminating the surrounding space.

As my eyes adjusted to the dim lighting, I could make out various pieces of furniture. They seemed out of place in such a grand space but somehow added to its charm, nonetheless. Intricately detailed bookcases lined one wall while larger-than-life paintings adorned another; it was like wandering through a museum filled with relics from another time. Jarred herbs and strange tools lay strewn about.

I was about to search for Corbin when I heard a loud moan.

Turning around, I saw Juniper and a man tangled together on a bed in the corner of the room. They were naked, bodies glistening with sweat and their faces contorted with pleasure. As they moved against one another, I could see sparks of magic radiating brightly to mingle and form a vivid spectrum of colors that danced along their skin like tiny fireflies.

Juniper let out a low growl as he thrusted deep within her, her back arching as she reached for his lips before letting out a ragged moan that seemed to echo throughout the room. Their movements became faster and more frenzied, intensifying with each passionate cry until finally they both collapsed onto the bed in rapturous ecstasy.

Juniper looked around the room, laughing as she caught my stare, a mischievous twinkle in her eye. "I didn't know you were a voyeur, Nicole. You're welcome to indulge whenever you'd like, but I think your mate would prefer that you stop watching us fuck."

I gasped and pulled out of my trance, suddenly

back in the room with Alexei. My cheeks were burning with embarrassment as I realized what I had just witnessed.

"What's wrong?" he asked.

"I... um..."

Alexei narrowed his eyes. "What did you see?"

"I saw Juniper and... Ivan? I *think* it was Ivan. I haven't actually met him yet." I shook my head in disbelief. "But what's really weird is that she *saw me, too*?"

He frowned. "That could be dangerous if you were spying on the wrong person."

"But that didn't happen when I projected to you," I told him. "I dunno... maybe it's because it's a witch thing."

He took a moment to consider that. "Well, it's definitely something we need to verify. Why are you so flushed? Are you dizzy?"

"Uh... nope. I feel perfectly fine. I just wasn't prepared to see what I saw."

Alexei cocked his head to the side. "What did you see?"

"They were... er... kinda, sorta, having..." I struggled to spit it out. "Sex."

Alexei's expression hardened, and he crossed his arms over his chest. "Perhaps you should try again, but this time, don't think about Juniper."

"I *wasn't* thinking about Juniper," I insisted.

At least I didn't think so.

"Well, *really* make sure this time. I don't exactly like the thought of you in the same room with another dude's dick hanging out."

I rolled my eyes but didn't bother saying anything else. I could tell he was jealous, but I didn't have time to worry about my mate's Neanderthal-ish attributes right now.

I took a deep breath and closed my eyes, using all of my energy to find Corbin once more. I tried to focus, pushing past the embarrassment. But no matter how hard I tried, my mind kept wandering back to the image of Juniper and Ivan locked in a feverish embrace. The way their bodies moved together—the passion and energy that seemed to crackle between them—it was undeniably beautiful, and it was almost impossible for me to not think about it.

Once again, I was back in that damn room with Juniper and Ivan. They lay in bed catching their breath, both of their bodies glistening with sweat. Suddenly, Ivan rolled over and started licking Juniper's cum-covered pussy.

"Oh, yes," she purred. "That's perfect..."

Her golden eyes wandered around the room before falling on me. Another wave of embarrassment washed over me as I realized she knew I was watching—again. Instead of feeling shocked or mad, though, she actually looked rather pleased they had an audience.

"I love how Ivan eats me out." She winked. "He's got a great tongue and really puts his all into it. You can always tell when someone loves eating pussy or if they're just doing it because they feel obligated. But I bet the latter isn't a problem with you and your mate, is it?"

"How can you see me right now?" my ghostly form asked, completely mortified, but I had to know why she could see me. "Is this normal?"

June's perky breasts pointed to the ceiling as she writhed beneath Ivan's tongue. I was about to get the hell out of there, but then she turned back to me. "No, it's not normal, Nicole. The privacy ward we have in place here at headquarters can't prevent astral projection, but it *does* magically alert the guard whenever someone does it, by making the astral body visible. I'm the one who placed the ward, so I'm the guard."

"Okay. Good to know. I'll let you get back to your..." I waved my hand at them. "You know."

I blushed as Juniper giggled, and opened my eyes.

Alexei's gaze met mine. "Went right back there, didn't you?"

"Yes," I admitted. "But I did get to ask June why she could see me, and it's totally just her. It has something to do with the wards they have here at headquarters."

My mate thought about that for a moment. "Well, that's reassuring. Now, do you want to tell me why your cheeks are red, my mate? And you're breathing so hard?"

He stepped forward and grabbed my wrists, pulling me close. His voice was soft, but it held the promise of punishment if I didn't stop watching another couple screw their brains out.

"If you go back there again, I'll make you crave me so intensely you won't ever be able to think of anything else. Understand?" His voice was low, dripping with dominance and a promise of pleasure that made his words even more tantalizingly real.

I nodded quickly, feeling both fear and excitement course through me at his words. He released my wrists.

"The more I think about not watching them, the more my brain goes back there..."

Alexei smirked. "Well, then maybe I should do something about that, hmm?"

Before I could react, Alexei grabbed me and

pushed me onto the ground. He lifted my skirt, tearing my underwear off with a devilish glint in his eye. "I think it's time to teach you a lesson."

An icy chill ran down the back of my neck. "What kind of lesson?" My core clenched, growing hot and wet. The sight of my mate towering over me and baring his teeth was captivating and absolutely irresistible.

"I don't want your eyes to feast on anyone's naked flesh but mine." He reached down and started playing with my clit. "You're mine and mine alone. Understand?"

I nodded quickly. "I understand..."

Without warning, he shoved his finger deep inside of me. I let out a loud moan as my back arched and a wave of pleasure consumed me. My mind faded away into a sea of bliss. All I could feel or think about was the heat of Alexei's touch.

He worked his finger in and out of my dripping wet pussy, gradually increasing the speed and intensity. His other hand stroked my clit in a soft, circular motion. My orgasm built up inside me like a pressure cooker about to explode.

Alexei brought me to the brink of unadulterated bliss, teasing me with each movement, every touch. My body quivered with anticipation as he expertly tested my thresholds, each touch pushing me closer and closer to release. My body trembled from the sheer intensity of it all, but Alexei didn't relent until I was catapulted over the edge into pure ecstasy.

My heart pounded as he kissed my inner thigh. "Forget about them." His words were like liquid fire injected straight into my veins. "Focus on me. What I'm doing to you."

His tongue circled my clit, and I could feel myself growing wetter by the second. Alexei sucked on me, swirling the tip of his tongue on my flesh until I squirmed, a hot flush of pleasure rising through my body in pulsing waves. I tore at his hair and bucked against his mouth. His hands gripped my waist, steadying me as he licked and sucked my aching pussy.

Tiny explosions erupted throughout my body, leaving me feeling almost painfully sensitive. His tongue moved ever faster until finally, my orgasm barreled through me like an unstoppable force. Every muscle in my body was tense as I rode it out.

When it finally passed, Alexei kissed my inner thigh one last time before sitting up. "That should keep your mind off of them for a while." He looked down at me with a satisfied smirk. "But maybe one more for good measure." He bent lower, tongue circling around my clit, sending me spiraling into ecstasy as I screamed out his name. I came within seconds, my body shaking as wave after wave consumed me. Alexei licked away all traces of my pleasure before pulling away with a satisfied expression.

"See? Now you won't be thinking of them, will you?" He brushed my hair away from my face and kissed me deeply before pulling away and helping me up.

I shook my head, feeling both embarrassed and ravished all at the same time. "Nope. That should do it."

Alexei smiled and pulled me close to him once more. "Good," he said possessively. "Would you like to try again?"

"I'm not sure I can. Now all I can think about is you." I laughed as he gave me a smug smirk.

"Try. But don't go to Juniper again, or I'll lose my shit. I mean it, Nicole."

I nodded and closed my eyes, taking a deep breath and letting my mind wander. I thought of Corbin, feeling my body relax as the surrounding room slowly disappeared. In its place was a much larger space, filled with ancient-looking artifacts.

Suddenly, catchy music blared out of nowhere, and Corbin leapt onto a large obsidian table in the center of the room. He shook his hips and limbs in a wild disco, as if he were possessed by the beats. He was totally carefree as he gyrated his body, his eyes tightly closed in bliss. His laughter carried throughout the room as he twirled around in dizzying circles.

It was comforting to witness someone living their life so unapologetically, embracing every moment with an unwavering authenticity that made me want to do the same.

Before I knew it, Bee had joined in and was now dancing alongside Corbin. Her movements were graceful and full of life, her skirt swirling around her as she spun around the room.

I couldn't help but smile as I watched them dance together, lost in this moment. Together, they were nothing short of breathtaking, both with huge grins on their faces that only seemed to get wider with each passing second.

I felt Alexei's hand squeeze mine, and I opened my eyes, breaking the trance. He pulled me close to him, a satisfied smirk on his face. "Did you do it?"

I smiled triumphantly. "I did! Also, I did not know Corbin was such a wonderful dancer."

Alexei laughed as he nodded in agreement. "He's always been like that—dancing up a storm everywhere he goes."

I laughed as I shook my head. "Well, he's

certainly got a lot of energy to burn off. I kind of want to go dancing with him."

Alexei's eyes suddenly flashed dangerously. "Not fucking happening."

"So possessive, Alexei," I teased.

"Damn right, I am," he said sternly, his grip tightening around my waist. "You are mine and no one else's." He kissed me passionately on the lips before pulling away and grinning. "Do you want to try some more?"

My heart raced in my chest as anxiety creeped up on me. "Yes, I think I'm ready to find your father now."

Alexei's face grew serious. "Are you sure? I don't want you to push it too far." He brushed my hair away from my face, looking deep into my eyes as if searching for any signs of trepidation. "I just want to make sure that you're safe before we do anything else."

I nodded, my heart swelling with confidence as I looked back at him. "I'm ready, Alexei—I can handle it." With that, I closed my eyes once again and began to meditate. My mind went deep within itself as I imagined the old brick of Redwood University. I thought about Alpha Jones's anger—the sense of danger his presence emitted. I felt myself slip away until the air was heavy with a strange, menacing terror.

When I opened my eyes, I was standing in the middle of a large office. Alpha Jones was seated behind a desk, talking to someone on the phone. He had an air of control around him that made me want to hide, but I was determined to help our team.

"I knew the Greenwood pack would reach out. They can't deny our power," he said with a smirk. "With their numbers, we'll be unbeatable."

I looked around as he continued to speak, taking in every detail from the rich mahogany furniture to the scattered art pieces displayed throughout the room. I thought he was in the administration building on campus, but I couldn't be certain.

"I'm going to love watching them swear allegiance to me." His tone was triumphant, dripping with malice. He then growled at something the person said on the other line. "What do you mean people are rebelling? Use the fucking serum on them if you have to!"

I gasped, and his eyes flickered to where I was levitating. My heart stalled as he looked right through me. He couldn't see me, but it was still unnerving.

"Yes," he replied distractedly to whomever was on the phone. "I don't care. They follow me, or they lose their wolf. I am not interested in negotiating a third option."

His words hit me hard, and I quickly opened my lids, feeling tears well up in my eyes. Alexei's father was so cruel, and it scared me to think of what he was capable of doing if he ever got the chance.

Alexei immediately enveloped me in his arms, whispering soothing words into my ear as he rocked me back and forth. "It's okay, Nicole. It's okay."

"He's hurting them, Alexei. I just heard him say he's removing people's wolves if they refuse to join his army. All those poor shifters..."

Alexei stiffened in my arms. "We'll stop him, Nicole. I promise."

I nodded, nuzzling closer to him as I tried to push away the fear that had just crept over me. I reminded myself over and over that as long as we had each other, nothing could stop us from getting through this.

CHAPTER
TWENTY-ONE

General Minifred

"Please be careful," Anya said.

I clutched the phone as we drove in the armored town car toward the meeting spot Alpha Jones picked.

"I will," I promised.

Anya didn't seem convinced. "He's crazy, August. I just don't want him to steal another person I care about. Can't you find another way? I don't like the thought of you being anywhere near him, especially not on his turf."

The vulnerability in her tone broke me. When Anya had reached out a few months ago, I hadn't expected to once again open my heart to another.

But we were bonded by the loss of our fated mates and determination to bring down her evil husband. Once everything was settled, I fully intended on showing her how she deserved to be treated. She'd spent too long in that psychotic man's clutches. She served dutifully as his luna, as a mother, for over two decades, yet he treated her like garbage. It was reprehensible in so many ways.

"I promise I'll be okay," I said. "I'm wearing the mask, so he won't even know it's me. I'll come home to you. Just stay where you are. He can't get to you at the safe house."

"I feel so useless here." She sighed loudly through the phone. "It's bad enough I couldn't protect Alexei from his father when he was just a pup. What kind of mother just stands by and allows that kind of abuse? I should've taken Alexei and ran the first time he laid a hand on my baby."

"If you had, neither one of you would be alive right now," I gritted out. "You know that, Anya. You did the best you could for the situation."

"Maybe we *both* would've been better off that way." My heart clenched when she sobbed at the end of her sentence.

This wasn't the first time we'd had this conversation. Anya Koenig led her pack with an immense amount of pride and grace, while secretly suffering her husband's wrath in silence. She was willing to live a double life for the greater good—to paint a smile on her face for her pack regardless of how miserable she was on the inside—but when Alpha Jones started beating Alexei under the guise of alpha training, her spirit broke more and more every day. She knew her husband's training methods were barbaric and unnecessary, but she felt powerless to put an end to it. The one time she tried, he'd nearly beaten her to death for interfering. The guilt she carried from not being able to shield her son from his father's abuse was immense.

"That's not true. Alexei was meant for greatness. And you... we wouldn't be as close as we are to ending this if it weren't for you. Your intel was far more valuable than any other. *You* are valuable as a luna, a mother, and a woman. Your son needs you. *I* need you. When this is over, I have every intention of showing you just how much. You deserve to be cherished, Anya. I'm going to fucking prove that to you if it's the last thing I do."

"August," she breathed out. "I did not know you felt this way. Why didn't you say anything before now?"

I pinched the bridge of my nose. "I admit, my timing could be better. I didn't mean to just blurt it out like that, but I don't regret what I said. I meant every word, Anya. I never thought I could find another after losing my mate... but you make me feel like I've been given a second chance. I don't even know if that's possible, but I'd be a fool not to explore this. If you're willing, that is."

"I am," she whispered. "Promise me we'll make it out of this safely. Promise me Jones won't win."

"He won't," I vowed. "I'll make sure you never have to worry about him again."

"I hate that you're going into this alone," she whimpered.

I glanced at my driver, his aura a blend of blue and red. He was scared about going into this meeting, but his mask was steel. I picked a driver that was good with a gun. I didn't plan on killing Alpha Jones today—I absolutely refused to become alpha —but I had every intention of surviving this meeting.

"My driver is the best. We will both get out of here alive, and he won't know what hit him. I promise, Anya. I'll be safe. I'll come home to you."

"Thank you, August. I..." Her voice trailed off and I could practically hear the declaration in her soul. She wasn't ready to tell me she loved me, and that was okay. I was a patient man, and I wanted her to work through her trauma.

"Save that thought for when this is over. You

don't have to say it yet, but just know I feel the same way."

"Be safe," she croaked. "Oh, and don't forget Jack Graham isn't chatty. His left hand twitches when he's nervous, and the only time he does talk is to brag about his yacht."

"I remember." Anya had been observing people for years while Alpha Jones kept her submissive and quiet. Little did he know, she was one of the best assets I had in this war. "I'll see you soon."

I hung up the phone and felt a deep sense of peace, but also, the weight of responsibility was like an anvil on my chest. Anya deserved better, and I knew it was my job to make this work. I had to convince Alpha Jones I was his old friend—Alpha Jack.

"We're here, sir," my driver said.

I looked around the abandoned, seedy motel parking lot and frowned. Alpha Jones was a prideful man who liked to showboat in front of other packs. If he wanted us to meet here, then that meant he wasn't as concerned about appearances, which was unusual for him.

"Leave the car running and be ready to run," I told the driver before getting out of the vehicle.

It was strange not wearing my service uniform with all my medals and accolades. Instead, I wore an

Armani suit that cost more than my monthly salary. My mask of blond hair was styled to the side, and my wolf resented the fact that I was posing as a much shorter, slimmer man. Jack Graham might have been an alpha, but if this mask was anything to go by, then he didn't work out much. He probably used his money and pretty boy smile to get what he wanted.

I was significantly stronger than any member of the Greenwood pack. My alpha wolf was like a beacon, and I had to rein it in if I didn't want to tip off Alpha Jones. It would be hard, but I'd been keeping my wolf contained for a lifetime.

Alpha Jones pulled up in a car far too expensive for this motel parking lot and got out. His eyes landed on me, and my alpha nature buzzed with anticipation. Jones was the worst kind of man, one who overcompensated with cruelty to hide the fact that he wasn't as strong as he proclaimed. I knew Alexei was more than capable of taking him down. He just needed to get past his mental blocks first.

"Alpha Jack," he greeted. He surged forward and clapped me on the back, and I had to force my wolf not to growl in protest. I hated pretending to be buddy-buddy with the guy, but this was a job. My magic eye cataloged his aura, and I was almost sick by the display of swirling colors, with red being the predominant one. He was angry but... all over the place.

"Hello, Alpha Jones." Jack Graham wasn't chatty, which suited me just fine. I had every intention of keeping this interaction as short as possible.

Jones smiled, but there was something off about the way his eyes narrowed, something manic in his broad grin. "I'll admit, I was very surprised that you called. I thought the Greenwood pack wanted to stay neutral. When we last spoke, you seemed adamant about keeping out of the fight."

"A lot of things have changed since Summit. You put on a powerful show with your new serum. I'd be a fool not to align our packs. What's this I hear about you having a new luna? Have you and Anya parted ways?"

I was baiting him, trying to see how important Mara was to him. It wasn't in the plan, but I was trying to figure out how deep she was. She was Corbin's sister and the mother of Alexei's sibling, which meant she needed protecting. I didn't particularly like Corbin, and I would not be wearing that damn friendship bracelet he made anytime soon, but I cared about the damn kid. And she was his sister.

"Luna?" Alpha Jones scoffed. "No. Mara likes to think she's luna material, but she's merely a warm body to sink my dick into for breeding. Nothing more. Anya is still very much my luna, but her bleeding heart is too soft for pack wars. I sent her away to be safe. I will tell her you said hello."

In my research, I learned that the Greenwood pack was quite fond of Anya. Whenever they did deals, they primarily spoke with her. It made sense that Alpha Jones didn't want to admit she was missing.

I grinned. "Well, that's a relief on all accounts. Once this is all done, we should go sailing. I know she loves the ocean."

Alpha Jones's aura turned orange with annoyance. Alpha Jack must have bored him with his yacht too many times to count.

"Sure. I'm sure she would love to see you. How's Rebecca doing?"

"She's well," I replied, remembering what Anya had told me about the Greenwood pack's luna. "Hounding me for another pup."

"You can never have too many backup plans. It's why I bred Mara. Alexei has been such a disappointment."

I forced a sympathetic frown. "It's unfortunate that Alexei has been so... resistant. I was appalled when I heard he had given up his claim on the pack."

Alpha Jones's aura turned black. "I'll deal with

him soon enough. He's not strong enough to lead *any* pack, so it's really no loss on my end."

"Still... such a shame. A waste of perfectly good genetics." I was sick to my stomach as he nodded in agreement.

"Well," Alpha Jones began. "I suppose we should get down to business."

I was relieved to get to the meat of the conversation. The more personal talk we did, the more opportunities he had to figure out I wasn't Jack Graham.

I squared my shoulders. "The Greenwood pack would love to open trade negotiations with you again, Alpha Jones. We have a history of working well together, and I'd like to discuss the serum you debuted at Summit."

Jones narrowed his eyes. "And what purpose do you have for the serum? You wanted to stay out of the fighting." He laughed mockingly.

"My pack is itching to put the witches in their place. We've been chained to their whims for too long." That part wasn't entirely untrue. In my research, I learned the witches had been increasing costs for spells for Greenwood these last few years. "We have a containment spell in town, and they keep increasing their rates to maintain it. Those magical bitches are bleeding us dry."

Jones raised his brows. "Yes, the witches think they have all the power. My goal is to put a stop to all of them and finally bring shifters to the top once again."

"Speaking of being on top... what would you say if I told you I wanted to use the serum on the high priestess?"

His greenish-gold gaze never left mine as he absorbed my question. "It would benefit me greatly if you took down that conniving slut. But how would you get close enough? Her protection detail is impenetrable."

I forced myself not to snarl. "Greenwood has been invited to a meeting with the witches to discuss your rise to power. You're not the only one trying to build an army. We both know I have a large enough pack to tip the scales. If I had the serum when I attended this meeting, I'd be in the perfect position to dismantle one of your enemies from the inside out."

Alpha Jones paused for a moment and stared at me. I wondered if he was catching on. My aura eye didn't pick up on any changes, but then again, his was a swirling mess of emotions. "Alpha Jack! I've always liked you!" Jones patted me on the shoulder and let out a booming laugh. "I *love* that idea. It pissed me off Eve survived the attack on the council.

I'd like to neuter the bitch, and this sounds like a great way to do it."

I forced myself to remain aloof when he pulled out a vial of the serum. Jones waved it in the air a little, letting the liquid slosh around. "How about this," he began. "I'll give you this, and once you've eliminated the witch, I'll give you more."

That was fucking fine with me. I just needed a little bit.

I nodded. "Sounds fair."

Alpha Jones grinned. "I'm a benevolent alpha." Yeah. Whatever. I held my hand out for the vial, but he paused to look at me. "Ah…" He clucked his tongue. "You know how we handle deals. We always shake on it and give our word before we make a trade." His brow arched, and I saw a flash of green in his aura, signaling distrust.

Shit.

"Right. Sorry. I got excited. I really want to take this bitch down." I laughed conspiratorially.

Alpha Jones cocked his head to the side but smiled again. "I know the feeling. Hey, do you remember the deal we made two years ago? For the…" He looked up as if he was trying to remember.

My heart raced. I didn't know what fucking deal he was talking about, but Alexei said they usually traded lumber, so it was my best shot. "The lumber?"

Alpha Jones eyes widened and his aura flared an even brighter green. "No. I was referring to our *personal* deal. Don't you remember? I said you could fuck my wife if you let me have Rebecca for a night." My stomach dropped, and rage burned through my veins. "God, that was fun," he continued while lifting on his toes to bounce like a preening peacock. "Rebecca was wild in the sack. You never told me if you enjoyed Anya. She's got a tight little cunt but can be pretty boring."

I could barely contain my inner alpha. My wolf wanted to rip this asshole's face off. Jones must've felt my rush of power, because he flinched slightly.

"Anya was a blast," I said through clenched teeth, not liking the idea of talking about her in such a way.

His face twisted into fury, and his aura turned blackish red. "You're not Jack. Who are you?"

I tilted my chin up and frowned. "What are you talking about?"

Jones surged forward and grabbed my collar, and I would have torn his head clean off his neck if he wasn't clutching the vial. "Alpha Jack would *never* share his wife. I tried plenty of times to get Rebecca into my bed, and that was one deal he refused to make. *Who are you?"*

I let out a low growl, barely containing my wolf. "Wouldn't you like to know, Jones?" I refused to give him the courtesy of his alpha title. "You've caused quite a stir."

I lunged for his neck, my fingers wrapping around it and squeezing as tightly as I could while he sputtered. I was worried he'd drop the serum and it would shatter on the concrete if he shifted. Suffocating a shifter was one surefire way to keep them from turning because our muscles needed oxygen for their transformation.

He thrashed against me as I used my free hand to rip the vial from his grip. He was strong but not strong enough. His face turned pale, and he reached out to kick me, landing his designer shoes against my shin.

I didn't even flinch.

Jones's fists landed against my chest. His body shook and flailed and fought.

But it wasn't enough.

I could see the flickering of his aura and the life drain from his eyes. I wanted nothing more than to watch him die in this motel parking lot. I wanted to make him suffer for hurting Anya, for torturing his son, for hurting all those kids.

And if I wanted to, it would have been easy to snap his neck.

He didn't deserve to be alpha.

I was the superior wolf. There was no one stronger than me. My instincts were begging me to finish this.

But I refused to kill him. I had no desire to lead a pack. I was damn good at my job with the military, and I had no intention of limiting my skills like that. Plus, Alexei had earned the right to formally challenge his father. He'd earned the right to be the alpha of this pack, and I had every confidence that he could do it. I wanted to avoid a war, but cutting off the head of the snake wasn't enough. We had to rebuild with trust, and we couldn't do that unless Alexei formally challenged his father and the pack kneeled before him.

I looked at the serum in my free hand until Jones's eyes rolled back, and then with a shudder, I dropped him on the pavement, watching as his lungs expanded. He gasped as I spun on my heels, making my way back to the waiting car.

"Anya is too good for you," I said over my shoulder, my wolf howling with revenge. "And the only reason I didn't kill you is because I think *that* pleasure should belong to Alexei. Your pack deserves a powerful alpha—*a good alpha*—and we both know he's the right wolf for the job."

Jones reached for me with angry eyes while pulling himself off the ground. I knew his shifter healing capabilities would kick in soon, but I liked the bruises I left around his neck. I should have ripped out his fangs and broken his jaw.

"Stop searching for Anya. I won't hesitate to end your life if you even *think* about her."

I got into the car and slammed the door shut.

The hair on the back of my neck stood on edge.

"Go!" I said to my driver the moment I sat down. "Take the long way back to the portal. We can't risk being followed."

"Yes, sir," he dutifully replied.

I knew what I'd just done put an even bigger target on our backs. Jones Koenig was not a man who liked to lose.

But for today, I was calling it a win. Once Alexei became alpha, my family would be safe. Bee, Nicole, and even fucking Corbin could have a good life.

That's all I wanted.

We now had the serum, which meant there was hope. And hope had a tendency to strengthen one's resolve like nothing else.

Goddess knew, we could use every ounce of faith we could muster.

TWENTY-TWO

Alexei

"Dad!" My mate ran to her father the second he stepped through the portal from Faerie.

Cristian's contact had come through, allowing us to pass messages between here and Faerie. It turned out that they had already heard about Alpha Jones's new serum—evidently, Nicole's uncle could somehow communicate with Macey, who heard us talking about it—so they were planning to come anyway to strategize.

"Hey, sweetheart." Dr. Fairweather embraced Nicole, closing his eyes as he squeezed her tight.

A throat cleared. "As charming as this is, would

you mind stepping aside so the rest of us can get by?"

My hackles rose at the disembodied masculine voice.

Nicole giggled as she tugged her dad to the side. "Oops! Sorry."

In the next moment, a tall man with golden hair and flawless skin popped into existence through the shimmery green disturbance in the air.

"Whoa," Corbin muttered beside me. "That may very well be the most beautiful yet ruggedly handsome man I've ever seen in my life. No offense, bro."

I was secure enough in my masculinity to agree with my beta. I knew immediately this was Nicole's uncle, Cyrus. If I had to describe this being in one word, the only one that came to mind was *godly*.

"Yeah, he is," Juniper agreed with a sigh. "Uncle Sexypants is one giant piece of eye candy, for sure."

The god's ethereal blue eyes tracked June's voice. "Juniper, how many times do I have to tell you not to call me that? It's... disconcerting."

Corbin's witchy ex twirled a purple curl around her finger. "My bad. Maybe you should spank me? I'm sure I'll remember, eventually." She flashed him a megawatt smile. "Ivan is around here somewhere. I know he'd *love* to watch a sexy spanking session."

I would've never thought a literal god would be afraid of a petite witch, but I could swear Nicole's uncle looked terrified at that thought. Not that I could blame the guy. Juniper had been a great help to us recently, but her cray cray, as Corbin called it, was an acquired taste.

I stifled a laugh just as Cammie walked through the portal, her designer heels clicking on the tile the moment she arrived. Her hair was pulled back into a bun, and she looked fierce.

Dr. Fairweather blushed before walking over to her and holding out his arm.

"Thank you, darling," she said with a smile.

Nicole stared at them with her mouth open. "Are the two of you...?"

Dr. Fairweather spoke nervously. "Well, honey. I wanted to talk to you about things, but with everything going on..."

"It's okay, Dad. I approve. I just want you to be happy," Nicole said, saving the poor man from fumbling through more words.

I opened my mouth to greet them, but a snarky tone echoed throughout the hallway.

"Is that worthless asshole god here yet?" Jade screamed.

Nicole pinched the bridge of her nose in frustration before speaking. "Oh goodness. Cyrus, prepare yourself. My aunt is lovely, I promise. Just has some anger issues."

The god smirked and bounced on his feet, as if excited.

"That motherfucker owes me a manicure!" Jade roared while wagging her fingers.

Hannah ran after her with an apologetic look on her face.

The moment Jade arrived, she gave Dr. Fairweather a smile. "You look good, David. Missed you bunches." She blew him a kiss before turning to the god in question. "Are you the asshole that sent us on a wild chase for some fucking horn in the woods? Do you realize how many holes I dug?"

"Jade, maybe let's not piss off the god, hmm?" Hannah suggested.

Cyrus dragged his eyes over Jade like she was a delectable treat, then smirked. "I sincerely apologize for all the trouble you've been through." If you asked me, he didn't sound all that sincere.

Jade seemed startled for a moment but quickly recovered. "Don't you try to charm me, mister. You may be a sun god, but the sun does not shine out of your ass!"

Cyrus raised a regal brow. "Are you sure about that? Maybe an inspection is in order."

"Yes!" Juniper whispered excitedly, rubbing her

hands together. "It looks like Uncle Sexypants has met his match. When those two finally do the deed, it's gonna be so freaking hot. I wonder if they'd let me watch."

"Jade." The god's gaze briefly sliced to June, clearly unimpressed, before stepping closer to Jade, lifting her hand. "Truly, you have my deepest apologies." He kissed the tip of her fingers, one by one. "I would never dream of harming these beautiful hands."

Jade sputtered. The guy definitely had moves. She looked at him in a daze before snapping her hand back and sneering at him. "Nope. Not good enough, asshole. Do you know how exhausting it is to dig holes?"

"Perhaps you need a massage to loosen up those sore muscles?" Cyrus asked with a wink.

"You're smooth, I'll give you that," Hannah said, drawing the attention to her. "But if I were you, I'd protect my balls since you're within kneeing distance."

Cyrus didn't seem worried in the least. In fact, he seemed almost... excited at the possibility of Jade assaulting him. Or maybe it was the prospect of the hate-fucking that got him worked up. I didn't need a seer to know that particular activity was in their near future. "I'll take the risk."

"This is so awkward," my mate said with a cringe. "Stop flirting with my aunt, Cyrus. Or, like, do it somewhere else."

I was pretty sure every single person in the room was watching with rapt attention, waiting to see Jade's reaction. It had taken almost a full week before Cristian's contact could open the lines of communication for us. While most of us were waiting on David's arrival so we could get started on the antidote, I was fairly certain Jade was just waiting to rip the god a new asshole.

Jade's dark lashes blinked slowly as she considered her next move. "I'll deal with you later."

"I look forward to it." Cyrus chuckled as she huffed and walked away. He then turned his attention to my mate. "Darling niece. It's good to see you again."

A loud bark preceded the black ball of fur barreling toward Nicole. She didn't even have time to brace herself before Macey tackled her to the floor, dousing her face in wolfy kisses. That damn dog had barely left her side since they'd been reunited. I knew I should be grateful my mate's familiar was so protective, but I was tiring of being on the receiving end of her stink eye.

"Macey!" Nicole squealed excitedly. "Did you

have a pleasant walk? I have someone that wants to see you! You know Cyrus, right?”

The wolf yelped excitedly and licked her face before turning to Cyrus.

“Watch your shoes, dude,” Corbin grumbled. I guess he hadn’t gotten over Mace peeing on his suit and my Jordans when they first met.

Mace huffed at him, then slowly walked over to Cyrus. He patted her on the head. “Such a good girl. You’ve done well, Macey.” The wolf preened, and I wondered if Cyrus would teach me how to get her to like me, too.

While Nicole was busy catching up with her family, I straightened my tie and went to speak with Dr. Fairweather. We hadn’t met under the best of circumstances, and I knew that since Nicole and I were mated, I needed to make a good impression. Her father was important to her, and I wanted to do my best to get to know him.

“Hello, sir. We’re very thankful to have you here.” I knew I sounded oddly formal, but we were just getting to know one another.

He looked me up and down as if I were a bug he wanted to squash. “Yes, well, I’m here for my daughter. I’ll always be there for my daughter.” He took a step up to me, and even though I was much taller than him, he somehow made me feel like he was looking down at me. "And if you ever hurt her again, I'll make you suffer."

We both knew he wasn't capable of beating me up, but his disapproval hurt as much as a punch would. "I wouldn't dream of hurting her, sir."

"Right," he replied in disbelief.

Corbin, who was standing behind me, let out a low whistle. "Oh man, I'm so excited that it's Alexei's turn to woo his future father-in-law." I rolled my eyes. "Let me show you how it's done," he added before walking up to Dr. Fairweather and holding out his hand to shake.

Dr. Fairweather looked down at his hand, then back up at Corbin. "And you are?"

"Corbin Sullivan. Also known as Nicole's best friend, sir."

"Bee Minifred is her best friend," David challenged.

Corbin waved him off. "I'm the *other* best friend. And, even better, Bee's mate. Plus, I'm Alexei's beta and bosom friend."

"Bosom friend?" I asked incredulously. "Have you been reading those regency romance books again?"

"Anyway," Corbin said, cutting me off. "I'm so happy you're here. I've heard a lot about you. Bee mentioned you like comic books? I might have had a few special editions delivered today if you're up to taking a look after all your hard work in the lab. I like to unwind with a good book and thought maybe you would, too."

Dr. Fairweather's eyes widened with excitement. "Really? Wow, how thoughtful of you."

Corbin winked at me. Ass-kissing motherfucker. He was jealous that General Minifred and I were getting along, so he wanted to be Dr. Fairweather's favorite.

"I like comic books, too!" I rushed out.

Dr. Fairweather turned to face me. "Oh? Which ones do you read?"

My face bloomed with embarrassment. I'd never seen a damn comic book in my life. I was too busy training to be alpha or dealing with our pack. "Oh, um," I stumbled.

Corbin beamed. "Yeah, Alexei, which comic?"

"The one where he flies?" Dammit. I didn't mean for that to come out as a question.

Dr. Fairweather's eyes narrowed. "Right."

"David," Cammie interrupted this shit show, placing her hand on his forearm. "Perhaps we should check out the lab the witches have set up for us? Finding the antidote needs to be our top priority."

Dr. Fairweather smiled at the fae as if she were

the sun, the moon, and the sky all wrapped into one. "Right. Good idea, Cammie."

Nicole beamed, clearly pleased her dad had a romantic interest.

"I'll do it!" Juniper raised her hand. "While I'm taking the brilliant scientists to do science-y stuff, why doesn't someone show Uncle Sexy to his quarters?" She turned to Jade and Hannah, giving the women a cheeky wink. "Any volunteers?"

"Yeah, yeah, whatever," Jade huffed. "C'mon, asshole. I'll show you to your room."

Cyrus smiled. "Lead the way."

"Alexei?" Nicole grabbed my hand. "You coming? I want to help my dad get set up."

I didn't miss the way Dr. Fairweather's eyes narrowed as he looked down at our joined hands. "Of course." Macey's bushy tail wagged as she nudged her snout against Nicole's leg. "Hey, Corbin. Why don't you hang out with Macey? A lab isn't the best place for a wild animal."

Macey growled at my jab. I knew she wasn't a wild animal—hell, she had better house manners than most of my former frat brothers—but I was feeling touchy from the pointed hostility radiating off Nicole's father.

"Sorry, bro." Corbin held his palms out. "Bee's

waiting for me back in our room. Gotta take advantage of the general's absence."

I rolled my eyes as he ran off. General Minifred was at the capitol, meeting with his team. Ever since he left, I swore Corbin and Bee had barely paused their banging long enough to take care of their basic needs. Meanwhile, I'd barely had a moment alone with my mate, thanks to her overbearing aunts and her familiar. Now, I had her father and uncle to contend with as well.

I grunted in disapproval, causing Nicole to give me a knowing smile.

"Soon," she mouthed.

I squeezed her hand as we all started walking toward the wing where the lab was located. *Soon* couldn't come fast enough. I wasn't the most patient man on a good day. With all the added stress from everything we were dealing with, I needed a physical connection with my mate more than ever. Our brief stolen moments weren't enough anymore.

I just wanted to get all of this over with so we could get started with our *happily ever after*.

I just had to successfully murder my damn father first.

TWENTY-THREE

Alexei

"You're doing this all wrong, man. I told you it's a ten-step program," Corbin said as I paced the room.

My feet slapped against the slick marble floor as my jaw tightened. Corbin was really beginning to irritate me, and I nearly howled with the urge to run free as a wolf.

"I'm not using your ten-step program to get my father-in-law to like me, Corbin," I snapped.

"Come on! It worked for me. General Minifred smiled at me yesterday. That's totally an improvement."

I rolled my eyes. "He smiled because you tripped and fell on your face."

He pressed his lips into a thin line. "I didn't *trip*. Macey was running to the kitchen to get a steak. She knocked me over." He scratched his jaw. "But maybe... Do you think I should do shit like that on purpose? If it makes him smile, I could work it into the plan. Maybe spill some hot soup in my lap."

I stopped pacing to give him an incredulous look. "Are you serious right now?"

Corbin shrugged. "You gotta be willing to do the impossible. I think by Christmas, we'll be wearing matching ugly sweaters for the family card. I ordered personalized ones with our faces on them from a lady online. We're hugging. It's epic."

I knew without a doubt that General Minifred wouldn't don a sweater with a photo of him embracing Corbin. My best friend was bound to be disappointed on that front.

"Look," Corbin said. "I know you've been on edge. It's impossible being cooped up like we have been. I know your wolf wants to run, but you've gotta chill."

"It's not just that," I insisted. "I barely have any alone time with Nicole, and it's hard. We never got the normal start to a mate bond, and the less... intimacy between us, the crazier I feel."

"I understand," Corbin said with a sigh. "I

haven't licked Bee's pussy in six hours, and I'm feeling hangry."

I growled in frustration. "Corbin, you're not helping. Not even a little."

"Man, big cities have their advantages, but the lack of nature is a real bummer. How do any shifters live here? It's not like you can casually stroll through Central Park as a wolf. Nobody wants to get tranqued by animal control. Remember when Uri Lassen took that trip to Chicago with his girl? Damn, I really hope the freaky sex made it all worth it."

Corbin and I both winced. Uri was one of our frat brothers at Alpha Nu. I didn't exactly ask for the details, but I suspected he and his girl had a femdom thing going on. One day while on vacation, she took him on a walk through the streets of Chicago in his wolf form, which any self-respecting shifter would *never* allow, but that was an entirely different can of worms. Not too long into their stroll, Uri got the urge to run, and he ran off. Animal control tagged him and brought him back to the pound. Got Fish and Wildlife involved, too. Mara had her work cut out for her, convincing all those humans they didn't see Uri transform back into a human, right there in his kennel. It was a freaking mess. My father kicked Uri and his girlfriend out of the pack for putting us all at risk like that.

I couldn't get booted from a pack I no longer belonged to, but it was a stark reminder why Corbin and I couldn't just shift and run free, no matter how badly we needed to.

I exhaled. "I really need to freaking run. Maybe we can ask June to magically transport us somewhere upstate."

"Oh!" Corbin's eyes rounded in excitement. "That sounds like an excellent plan, my friend. I'll go find her."

"Find who?" the purple-haired witch asked, strolling into my room hand in hand with some guy. He was a wiry thing… black hair, bronzed skin, wide-set eyes. He was a shifter of some kind, but I couldn't get a read on which. All I knew for sure was he was *not* a wolf.

"Juniper!" Corbin shouted. "Just the woman we were looking for!" His eyes sliced to the man beside her. "Who's this?"

June raised an eyebrow. "Really, Corbin?"

"What?" Corbin looked as clueless as I was.

Mystery Guy rolled his eyes. "You never were the brightest bulb, were you?"

"Hey!" Corbin glared. "If you're going to insult me, at least tell me your name beforehand so I know whose ass I'm kicking."

The guy snorted. "I'd like to see you try."

Juniper barred her arm across his chest. "Ivan. Chill. Corbin is a mated man now. His mind is elsewhere."

"Ivan?" Corbin questioned. "*This* is Ivan? As in your one and only? Well... the only dude in your life with long-term potential?"

"Yes, Corbin." June gave him a *be nice* look. "This is my fiancé, Ivan. I don't know why it's so hard to grasp, considering you two have met *many* times."

Corbin blinked a few times before saying, "Huh. Guess I didn't recognize you without all the feathers and squawking. Nice of you to finally make an appearance, I guess. I'm sure after all this time off page in our story, my boy Alexei probably thought you were made up."

Truthfully, I didn't give it *any* thought. I was a pro at tuning out Corbin's constant sexual over-shares. Well, mostly. I remembered him telling me that whenever he and June were fucking, Ivan would watch them while in his raven form, but I hadn't realized he'd *never* shifted back into his human form. I had so many questions, but I didn't think I wanted the answers, so I kept my mouth shut.

"June has been keeping me... busy," Ivan said with a smirk.

I tried not to growl, thinking of Nicole's little astral Peeping Tom incident.

Ivan turned to greet me, thrusting out his hand with a smile. "And you're Alexei?"

"Yes," I grunted. His brow cocked, as if he was confused why I was being so hostile. I still didn't like that my mate got turned on by him.

"Oh, Alexei." Juniper sighed. "Are you still peeved Nicole was watching us bang? You can't blame her. We're quite acrobatic in the bedroom, naturally drawing one's eye. We love having an audience. She's welcome to pop in on us anytime."

My wolf—who was already agitated—growled threateningly. "She will *not* be watching you again. Don't get any ideas."

Ivan smirked. "If you ever change your mind, we'd be happy to have you both join us in person."

I was going to kill this guy.

"Sheesh, Alexei. You're on edge. When was the last time you let your wolf run?" Juniper asked.

"That's why we were looking for you, Junie," Corbin told her. "Alexei and I need to run. Our wolves are very... sensitive right now." He held his hand over one side of his mouth and stage-whispered the next part. "Side note, I probably wouldn't talk about Nicole and sex in any capacity. Bruh has major blue balls right now."

Fucking Corbin.

"Anyhoo..." he continued. "We were hoping you

could magically send us somewhere upstate so we can run? Preferably some place heavily wooded."

"Why don't you just use the Enchanted Woods?" Juniper asked, giving us a *duh* look.

"*The what?*" Corbin and I asked simultaneously.

She arched her brow. "The Enchanted Woods. It's a beautiful place. I lost my virginity in the—"

"Yeah, I don't want to know," I gritted. Talking about sex made me think about how I wasn't having any sex, and my wolf was already testy enough as it was. "Where is it, and can I run freely?"

She rolled her eyes. "Shifters are so emotional. Follow me. My mom had it made for our familiars. I'm surprised you don't know about it already. Macey has spent practically every day there." Well, considering I was avoiding the bratty familiar because she liked to growl at me incessantly, I hadn't noticed. "It's magically manufactured, so it's a totally controlled environment, a few hundred acres in size. You can run, swim, play in the dirt. All the things you silly, sweet little wolfy puppies like to do. Ooh! Can we play fetch?"

Ivan chuckled as she walked down the hallway.

I resisted the urge to yell.

"We don't play fetch, Junie. I've told you this a million times," Corbin said while blowing out a puff of air.

"Such a waste," she mused playfully before turning a corner. We stopped in front of a towering wooden door with ornate carvings dug into it. She beamed at us. "I thought the reason Alexei was so grumpy was because he hasn't fucked Nicole in a while. But you should have said you needed to run, silly."

Ivan looked me up and down. "Oh no, babe. This is a man that *definitely* needs to fuck. If you'd like an audience, when you finally get some action, let me know. I think it's only fair since Nicole got a show from us." He arched his brow, and it took everything within me not to slam my fist into his face. The idea of anyone seeing my mate while she was naked and wrapped around my body pissed me right the fuck off.

"I don't think Alexei is into that, babe," Juniper said with a laugh. "Okay, so here's the deal with the door. You need to offer a blood sample so it'll recognize your essence from the other side."

"What happens if we don't give a sample?" I asked.

"You won't be able to get past the wards to get back in here. But don't worry, it's a one-time donation. You just prick your finger on this"—she pointed to what appeared to be a tack on the wall, followed by a rectangular pad—"and press the droplet on this right below it. It's spelled to instantly sanitize everything, so nobody needs to worry about accidental blood bonds or anything."

"How reassuring," I said wryly.

Juniper ignored my sarcasm. "Have fun, boys. And watch out for the bears."

She grabbed her mate's hand and sauntered away. Corbin and I exchanged a look before frantically doing the blood thing and ripping open the door. A warm breeze hit me the moment we stepped over the threshold. The bed of decaying leaves crunched under my feet, and birds sang from the trees. The tall, slender trunks proudly shaded the green grass, and beams of light filtered through the canopy, carving out shapes in the ground.

I inhaled, my wolf excited to run. The air smelled like pine and fresh earth.

"Oh man, this is just what I needed." Corbin practically fell over in his haste to get undressed.

I looked around and vaguely wondered if Nicole would mind sneaking off here for an hour or two. The idea of crushing her body with mine and pounding her into the dirt was making me hard.

"No boners while we're naked, dude. That's the rule *you* made, remember?" Corbin's hands sat proudly on his hips as his flaccid dick dangled between his thighs. God, I was glad his horse-sized dick was no longer hanging around. Not that I'd spent much time looking at Corbin's cock, but his constant complaining about lugging that thing around all the time made it really hard to ignore. I scowled at Corbin and turned around to take off my pants, feeling the pain of arousal deep in my core.

I needed time with Nicole soon.

But first, I wanted to run.

The second I was undressed, I called upon my wolf, while my best friend did the same. Within seconds, our skin and bones shifted and lengthened. My olive skin was coated in white fur, while my beta's took on several shades of brown. I playfully snapped at Corbin with my elongated teeth, prompting him to yip and bounce on his paws in response. We growled and snarled for a bit as we danced around, the freedom of assuming our wolf forms after much too long without them briefly distracting us from our objective. I barked, commanding him to put an end to the play-fighting before I dug my paws into the dirt and pushed off with my powerful legs. My pointed ears twitched as they absorbed the myriad of sounds, cataloging the rustling of leaves, flapping wings, and miscellaneous creatures stirring. I ran my snout along the brush, inhaling the trace scent of a small animal that wandered through here not too long ago. A rabbit, I guessed, but I had to remind myself that any animal, no matter how tempting in this form, was off limits for hunting. I was certain the witches wouldn't be impressed if one of us murdered their familiar.

My paws dug in deep as I ran, stretching my muscles and relishing the burn in my bones. I panted, my tail wagging as I ran out all the frustrations I'd been feeling. My worry about Dr. Fairweather. My fear about my father. My stress about the pack.

It all melted away.

But there was one thing I couldn't shake. A lingering hunger. A damning desire thudding through my pulse.

I wanted Nicole.

Badly.

Corbin disappeared through the maze of trees, giving me space to run without an audience. I dodged low-hanging branches and leapt over a log, stopping at a magic stream flowing through the woods. Crouching low, I drank from it, the cool water traveling down my throat but doing nothing to stop the burning heat in my stomach.

The sound of a branch breaking made my ear twitch, and I twisted to see who was approaching. A sweet scent mingled with the pine, washing over me in waves.

Nicole was here.

I followed her scent as fast as I could.

"Alexei? Juniper said you were looking for me?" She swatted at a bug and then pushed her way through the branches until she was standing beside me. She gave me a beaming smile and reached out to run her hand through my fur. My wolf melted at her touch.

"You're so soft," she said with awe. "Are you okay?"

I missed you, I told her, using our telepathic connection.

I missed you, too, she replied in the same manner, smiling at me.

I took a deep breath and called my wolf back within my soul, slowly shifting until I was towering over her, stark naked with my hard cock aimed right at her stomach. Her mouth popped open in surprise, and I watched with hunger as she chewed on her lip.

"I need you," I growled. "I can't fucking wait anymore, Nicole."

She took a step closer, placing her palm on my bare chest. "I need you, too."

Relief rushed through me as our mouths fused together. Mindful that Corbin was around here somewhere, I dragged my mate behind a large boulder and stripped Nicole bare, kissing every inch of skin I'd exposed. If Corbin got close enough to hear us, he knew to run in the opposite direction, giving us privacy. I couldn't bear the thought of wasting this rare opportunity to connect with her. My fingers slid through her folds, my cock jerking as I found her wet and wanting.

"Alexei," she panted. "We can spend extra time on foreplay later. I need you inside of me now."

She didn't need to tell me twice.

I gently lowered the other half of my soul to the ground, and in the next moment, I was inside of her, right where I was meant to be. Our lovemaking was desperate, primitive, but at the same time, perfectly us. As Nicole came with my name on her lips, I followed right behind her, finally feeling the peace I'd been longing for. And at that moment, I knew that whatever we were about to face, we were going to triumph.

TWENTY-FOUR

Nicole

My uncle's sharp words jolted me awake. "Are you meditating or just taking a nap?"

I shot him an icy glare. "I'm trying."

"Focus is half the battle. Controlling your mind will help you control your powers."

"I thought when you offered to teach me about my powers, we'd actually be doing something," I muttered, my annoyance growing by the second. "Not just sitting here and meditating for hours on end."

I rose to my feet and let out a cynical scoff. "I don't have time to sit around and meditate, Cyrus. I have to work on my abilities!"

"We *are* working on your abilities," he grunted, rolling his eyes. "Meditating is a big part of that. Now sit down."

I huffed and begrudgingly lowered myself back onto the beanbag, crossing my arms. Cyrus grumbled something under his breath.

"What was that?"

Cyrus glared at me with a steely gaze. "I said you're just as stubborn as your mother was."

"Oh," I choked out, my eyes filling with tears.

I didn't know why I was getting so emotional suddenly. It wasn't like I couldn't talk about my mother. My dad and aunts talked about her all the time as I was growing up. They went out of their way to share what they knew about her so I'd feel like I knew her. As much as possible, anyway. Except that part about her being a goddess, which would've been quite helpful to know before now.

A tear fell down my cheek, and I swatted at it, frustrated with myself. I was so overwhelmed lately. Nervous about Alpha Jones. Worried for Alexei.

"I know this is..." He frowned as he seemingly searched for the right word. "Difficult. I think having heightened emotions is perfectly natural under the circumstances."

"How do you know I'm not normally like this?" I

challenged. "You don't know me at all. You left me for nineteen years, Cyrus." I was still bitter about that, even though I knew he had a good reason for staying away.

My uncle gave me a sad smile. "I didn't want to stay away, Nicole. And I know what you're like because you're your mother's daughter. I see so much of Celena in you."

"Yeah, I know. I'm practically her little Mini Me." Everyone had been telling me that for years. I couldn't say it wasn't freaky sometimes, seeing an old picture—or as of lately, a vision—of my mother, thinking anyone could mistake her for me. Even my own reflection agreed.

"I'm not just speaking about your physical traits, although the resemblance is striking. I was referring to your personality. Your strength. It's almost as if her soul transferred to you when her powers did."

I couldn't help but feel comforted by his words. For so long, I'd felt distant from the woman who created me. I'd spent a lifetime trying to feel closer to her. Hell, it was why I was so adamant about rushing. Fighting to be a member of the sorority she was in now seemed like a distant memory.

"Can you tell me about her?"

He stared at the ground, as if reminiscing was

painful for him. "Your mother loved doing mating ceremonies. She loved the idea of love."

I smiled at that. Catching glimpses of her relationship with my father was proof enough of that.

"What else?"

He looked up at me and gave a little shrug. "Everyone always flocked to her. She had this bright smile that was infectious. For the mating ceremonies, she didn't just give her blessing and go about her day. She took time to get to know the couple. She chatted with them. Wished them well. Practically glowed with happiness for them, actually. I've never been so... sentimental. Usually those events annoyed me. But not your mother. She was patient and kind. Perfect for the job, if I'm being honest."

"How does the blessing part work, anyway? Like, are there certain words that need to be said, or can I just wave my hand and nod?" I did a poor imitation of a royal wave to demonstrate.

My uncle chuckled. "You know, the best way to learn how to bless a mating bond is through hands-on experience. Do you want to see if your friends would be interested?"

My jaw dropped. "You mean Bee and Corbin?"

"Is there another fated pair roaming this

compound who are still waiting to complete their bond?”

“I don’t know.” I shrugged.

“You *would* know,” he insisted. “Instinctively. At least if one part of the couple was a wolf shifter.”

His statement reminded me of a question I’d been meaning to ask for a while now, but I always got sidetracked.

“So, how does the whole fated mates, moon goddess thing work? Am I responsible for all fated pairings in existence? Because that sounds exhausting.”

“No,” he replied with a smile. “Only wolf shifters. Each faction has their own gods or goddesses.”

“But a lion shifter is just as much of a shifter as a wolf shifter,” I argued. “It’s the same faction.”

“I think any wolf shifter would beg to differ.” We both laughed at that, because let’s face it, wolf shifters and giant egos seemed to go hand in hand.

“Can you show me how to perform a mating ceremony? I know the logistics of it from my studies, but—”

“It’s a very emotional process,” Cyrus finished for me. “But probably the easiest of your skills to master. The core of that ability is love, and you have an abundance of that." He stroked his chin. "Actually, that's a great idea. You're close to Corbin and Bee, and having a sense of who the mated pair can help you with the ceremony. Go get them."

I blanched. "You want to do a mating ceremony right now?"

"Yes." He crossed his arms over his chest. "Is that a problem? You were just saying that you wanted to practice working with your powers."

I rubbed the back of my neck nervously. "But isn't it like a wedding? Shouldn't we make it special?"

He checked his watch. "Is an hour enough time to make it special?"

I gaped at him. Gods truly were out of touch. "I mean…"

"We have to do it under a full moon. You're in luck because there's one tonight. Go tell the happy couple."

I stared at him for a moment longer before fleeing the room. Bee would probably be happy with a simple ceremony, but Corbin was going to have a fit.

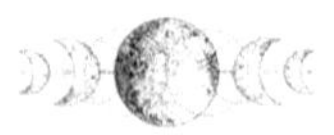

"But I have nothing to wear!" Corbin whined while tossing clothes onto the ground. "What about my bouquet?"

"I thought the bride gets a bouquet," Alexei said while staring helplessly at his best friend.

Corbin frowned. "That is incredibly sexist, Alexei. I deserve pretty flowers, too."

Bee patted his cheek condescendingly. "You can have *all* the pretty flowers, baby. I don't even need a bouquet."

"God, you really are the perfect woman for me," he growled against her mouth. "Come with me and I'll show you."

My best friend laughed as he tugged on her arm. "Later, Romeo. Ceremony first, then you can show me all your fancy tricks."

"So we're really doing this?" Alexei asked. "We're throwing a mating ceremony in the middle of preparing for a war?"

"Yep." Bee smiled. "June's mom is going to pick my dad up in D.C. He's been busy selecting team members for Nicole to change. He said he found a few contenders but needs a little more time to narrow it down. June will send him back to finish up after the ceremony."

"Probably for the best." Bee squealed when

Corbin grabbed her butt, making no attempt whatsoever to be discreet. "With the things I'll be doing to you later, General Daddy needs to be far, far away. I doubt he wants to hear your enthusiastic praise as I'm railing you six ways from Sunday."

"*Nobody* wants to hear that," Alexei insisted. "I mean it, Corbin."

Juniper chuckled. "Relax, Grumpy McGrumperson. Some of the girls and I are getting a special honeymoon suite all set up as our gift to the happy couple. It'll be fully equipped with every prop imaginable and, more importantly, a soundproofing spell."

Alexei nodded. "Thank God."

"Ooh." Corbin rubbed his hands together excitedly. "Tell me more about these props."

Juniper led him by the elbow. "C'mon, handsome. Let's get you to your groom's suite, and I'll fill you in on the way." She winked at Bee over her shoulder. "Don't worry, I'll make sure he cleans up well, and your groom will meet you under the moonlight in the Enchanted Woods."

"Thanks, June." Bee blew Corbin a kiss.

I grabbed Alexei's hand, giving it a firm squeeze. "You should probably keep an eye on him. Make sure he doesn't get distracted by all those props."

A crease formed between his brows. "Do I have to?"

I pressed up on my toes, placing a soft kiss against his lips. "I need to help Bee get ready and consult with my uncle to make sure I don't screw this up. Go with Corbin. We both know that boy needs a keeper. After tonight, that'll officially be my bestie's job."

He grabbed the back of my neck as I tried to pull away, kissing me breathless before releasing me. "I love you."

I sighed, resting my head on his chest. "I love you too, Alexei."

Once he was gone, I started putting Bee's curls up in a loose updo. "I can't believe I'm getting married. At eighteen. That's crazy, right? This is crazy. But I love him. We're soul mates, right?"

I squeezed her shoulders. "You're meant to be."

She sighed at her reflection. "I always thought I'd get married when I was in my late forties to a billionaire sugar daddy."

"I mean, Corbin *is* a finance guy. I'm sure you could still have a billionaire sugar daddy in the future."

She giggled. "I took a peek at the reports he made for my father. Did you know he has savings accounts set up for our nonexistent children already?"

I laughed. That sounded like something Corbin would do. "He's a planner," I replied with a shrug. "Which is perfect for you since you barely have the next five minutes figured out, let alone the rest of your life."

"I'm a free spirit," Bee replied. "Corbin… grounds me. He's playful and kind and… gosh, I love him so much, Nicole. I just never imagined that this would be our life."

I beamed at her. "I'm happy for you."

"And we're going to have great sex for the rest of our lives. I was worried when I saw his giant dick, but man, Corbin wasn't kidding when he said he was perfectly average. It's definitely boyfriend dick."

I let out a snort just as my uncle appeared. "Are you almost ready? We need to get set up." He seriously needed to work on his people skills.

"Weddings take time, Cyrus. Give us a break," I snapped at him before continuing to get Bee ready. I pinned one last curl in place, and Bee turned to face me. "Love is scary, Bee. It doesn't always happen when you expect it to. Or even *how* you expect it to. But fate brought you together. You're literally perfect for one another in every way. It's going to be great."

She beamed at me. "I better put my dress on. Speaking of, why did Juniper have a wedding dress just hanging in her closet?"

I winced. Bee definitely didn't need to know that Ivan and Juniper liked to role play runaway bride scenarios.

"I don't know," I lied before giving her a smile.

"I feel like you *do* know but you're saving me from something that'll gross me out, so thank you."

My uncle cleared his throat. "We need to hurry, Nicole."

I rolled my eyes and gave Bee one more hug before getting out of there.

While Cyrus and I walked to the Enchanted Woods, he spoke. "The most important part of the ceremony is giving your blessing. And it's not just a verbal command. It's an outpouring of love for their union. Your mother said it felt like overwhelming joy."

I loved Corbin and Bee, so that should be easy enough.

"Do I have to say anything special?" I asked as we got to the ornate door leading to the woods.

"I bless this union," he replied. "Short and sweet. Your mother would close her eyes and allow herself to feel the love they shared. The fated mate bond is a limitless, universal experience. I think having your own fated mate will help you tap into those feelings." He paused as the dirt crunched under my feet. "In the beginning, your mother struggled to understand that love. She'd never experienced it before."

I nodded. The mate bond was unique and overwhelming. Something impossible to recreate. "So, will I have to be at *every* mating ceremony? There are a lot of shifters."

My uncle shook his head. "Many of them will ask for your blessing, and you'll feel the request. Almost like a prayer. You can bless them from anywhere. But the first few times, you should be present. It helps you learn how to draw from your well of power."

"Anything else you can think of?" I asked as we entered the clearing.

"Just open yourself up to the experience. You'll feel the love and give the blessing. But since these are your friends, you might want to say something sentimental."

The clearing was sparkling with magic. Fairy lights dangled from the trees, and flowers coated the ground. Alexei and Corbin were already gathered in front of a gorgeous arbor decorated with ribbons, flowers and lights.

"Wow," I said as I approached.

Alexei smiled at me while Corbin tugged on his bow tie.

"June better come through with releasing the doves. I wanted fireworks, too," the anxious beta shifter said.

Alexei wrapped me in a hug and pressed his lips against the shell of my ear. "You look beautiful, mate."

When we pulled away, I looked at his suit and grinned. "You look pretty good, too."

"Hello?!" Corbin spat. "What about me?"

I sighed before giving him a hug as well. "You look great, Corbin. Everything is going to be perfect, I promise."

When we pulled away, he spotted a witch and started chasing her down. "Hey, you! Can you conjure an ice sculpture?"

"He's a mess," I said softly to Alexei and my uncle.

"I'll go see if I can help." The corner of Cyrus's mouth twitched in amusement. "Spend some time with Alexei to get in a peaceful, loving state of mind. It'll help you bless the union." He spun to leave but stopped. "Oh, and be careful."

I gave him a confused look. "Careful? Of what?"

"It's a full moon," he replied, as if that explained everything.

"And..."

Alexei looked between us, also confused.

Cyrus furrowed his brow. "And it's the one night of the month that you draw on the power of the moon. Now that you've reached magical maturity, you'll get about ten times stronger than you normally are. The longer you're under the full moon, the more powerful you get. Just don't hug anyone too tightly or pat anyone on the back. You'll be fine."

"Cyrus!" I exclaimed. "Don't you think that's something you should have told me sooner? What if I accidentally hurt someone?"

I looked up at the moon, as if I could see the power flowing into me, as he said, "You'll be fine."

I took Alexei's hand, needing the physical contact to ground me.

"Damn, he wasn't kidding," Alexei chuckled.

I jumped back. "Shit! Did I hurt you?"

His lips curved into a sexy grin as he wrapped an arm around my back, pulling me into his embrace. "No, Nicole. But I can definitely feel a difference."

My eyes widened. "Seriously?!"

"Yeah." He nodded, assessing me thoughtfully.

"What's that look for?"

"I was already looking forward to spending some time alone with you after this ceremony, but now I find myself even more excited."

It didn't take a genius to figure out what he wanted to do with me during that alone time, but I couldn't figure out what my increased strength had to do with it.

"Why's that?"

His brown eyes were filled with heat as he took a moment to form words. "Extra strength means you're less breakable. Less breakable means we can be more... enthusiastic."

My face flushed. "I don't think we've ever been *un*enthusiastic during sexy times, Alexei."

"You're right." He leaned into my ear to whisper his next words. "I didn't realize it until much later, but I should've known you weren't human after the first time we made love. It's common knowledge to any supe that you'd have to mute yourself during sex with a human because you could do some serious damage otherwise. But with you... I didn't hold back. I didn't have to. You may not have had the extra strength like you do right now, but you're a demigoddess by blood. Maybe our mate bond was guiding my actions even then. It knew you could take it."

I was practically squirming as I remembered our first time together. "So why would tonight be any different?"

He pulled back with a Cheshire grin. "Because,

my beautiful mate, with your extra strength, we have some new positions at our disposal."

I gasped as he winked. "Alexei! My uncle said I'm supposed to get into *a peaceful, loving frame of mind*. You can't get me all hot and bothered right before I'm supposed to do this whole blessing thing! I can't focus when I'm flipping through my mental list of sex positions!"

Alexei released a hearty laugh, my admonishment clearly not having any impact. "How extensive is this catalog of yours?"

My jaw dropped as I swatted him. "Go find Corbin! You're not helping my focus at all."

He held his palms out in surrender as he backed away. "I'd say I'm sorry, but I'm really not."

"Go!" My eyes narrowed as he laughed again before walking away to find the groom.

"Damn, girl." Juniper fanned herself as she sidled up to me. "I can feel your desire from a mile away. Maybe I should reinforce the soundproofing spell in your room, huh?"

Now that she mentioned it, that probably wasn't a bad idea. But before I had time to agree, my uncle, Corbin, and Alexei were back, taking their places at the front of the makeshift aisle June had formed.

"Didn't have to go far to find him," Alexei

explained with a wink, earning another dirty look from me.

My uncle motioned for me to join him under the arch. "Are you ready to begin?"

I nodded. "Let's do this."

TWENTY-FIVE

Nicole

I GLANCED around at the crowd that had gathered for the wedding. There was a fair amount of people that I had gotten to know better over the last month. The witches were kind and very open, and overall good people. I liked that we were bonding; it gave me hope for a unified future.

My father and Cammie walked into the clearing, and he came forward to wrap me up in a hug. I breathed in his warm scent as he pulled away. "You look so beautiful, sweetheart. I'm so proud of you."

Cammie gave me a kind smile. "You look like your mother. She loved these ceremonies. She was always so giddy to bless a union. It was such a joy to watch her perform them, and I'm so thankful I get to be here for your first one."

My father's eyes filled with tears as he looked at me, and Cammie laced her fingers through his.

"I'm just so proud of you. You're going to do amazing, Nicole," he said. "Don't be nervous. Cammie said this is all about love, and that is one thing you have in spades. Such a beautiful heart."

I cleared my throat, trying not to sob at the sentimental moment.

Cyrus approached and smiled at them. "If you'll both find your seats, we can get started."

My father gave me one last smile before leading Cammie to a space near the front.

Cyrus turned to me. "Since you are here, we are going to perform a full ceremony. It is an honor to have a demigoddess at your mating ritual; the blessing that you give them will ensure a happy union. I already asked Juniper to prepare some cleansing moon water for this special occasion. It's not required for *every* mating ceremony, but it will add extra significance to this one."

We hadn't discussed this, but what better way to learn than through practice, right?

"Okay, I guess," I sighed. "What do I need to do?"

As I stepped forward, Juniper handed me a small bottle.

"Put some around your head like a halo," she said with a smile.

I poured some into my palm, and I used it to trace a circle around the crown of my head. June took the bottle back and poured some into a circle surrounding the arch of flowers.

June and I locked eyes, and she smiled encouragingly. I trusted her implicitly, so I took a deep breath and went with it as she traced a new circle in the surrounding air. The sensation of magic sinking into me made me gasp as she finished. It was a strange feeling, but it didn't hurt. I hadn't even noticed when I started to glow, but when June's eyes widened, I glanced down to see a gentle white light enveloping my entire body.

"Wow," I whispered.

"Beautiful," Alexei murmured, making me beam.

"It's time for Bee to walk down the aisle," Cyrus said, motioning for the trio of violin-wielding witches to begin.

As a delicate melody rang through the forest, I took a deep breath, inhaling the pine aroma laced with the sweet scent from the flowers Juniper had conjured.

Corbin turned to look at the canopy of trees, and

his mouth dropped open when he saw Bee walking toward him, linking arms with General Minifred, who had tears in his eyes.

"Oh my God, I've never seen her look more beautiful." Corbin's voice was filled with awe.

Wow.

She really was stunning. Her olive complexion contrasted beautifully with the off-white of her flowing gown. The bodice had lacy floral appliques woven into it, which complemented the crown of lush green leaves sprinkled with gardenias she wore around her head. The fashion major in me had always dreamed of designing my best friend's wedding dress one day, but I had to admit, everything about this was perfect. It was understated yet elegant, which couldn't suit Bee any better.

The beautiful bride marched toward us as her father whispered something in her ear. The moment she got to the end of the aisle, Corbin leaped forward to hug General Minifred. "I promise to take care of her, sir." Corbin's words were choked and full of emotion.

"I'll kill you if you don't," the general grumbled.

Corbin paled.

Bee laughed.

General Minifred rolled his eyes and wrapped his arms around Corbin. "You're not a terrible mate for my girl, Corbin. I almost kind of like you. *Almost*."

Corbin pulled away with tears in his eyes and whispered excitedly to Bee, "Do you hear that? *He loves me!*"

Bee grinned and reached out to grab Corbin's hand.

Cyrus cleared his throat as they got into position and faced me. "We've come here today to celebrate the union of this mated pair."

Damn. I wished I had a notepad so I could write down what he's saying. Was this part of the ceremony?

"First, if the two of you would like to exchange your vows..."

Bee's eyes widened with fear, as if she wasn't prepared to say anything, but naturally, Corbin pulled out two sheets of paper and discreetly handed her one.

"I wrote yours just in case," he whispered. "I know public speaking makes you nervous."

He was truly prepared for everything. I beamed, and the glow filling me seemed to brighten as I thought about their love.

Oh.

Evidently, the light was an indicator of how I felt. At least now I knew which emotions to tap into.

"Bee?" my uncle asked. "Would you like to go first?"

"Uh... sure." Bee unfolded the paper and giggled as her eyes looked it over. "Corbin, you are the best thing to ever happen to me." She looked up at him and shook her head playfully. "I have never known what it's like to be truly happy until I met you. I never expected to have a mate who I respected and admired. You are selfless and strong, and you are more than I could've ever asked for. Whenever I'm afraid, all I need to do is look at you and know every-thing will be okay. I promise to stand by your side through thick and thin, in sickness and in health, until death do us part. I love you with all of my heart, Corbin." She refolded the paper and waited for him to recite his vows.

Corbin's eyes were glossy as he took her hands in his. "You're my entire world, Bee. If I didn't have you in my life, I don't know who I would be. I love you with all my heart, and there's nothing I wouldn't do for you." He laughed and swiped his thumb over her cheek where a tear escaped. "Even wipe away the tears you cry because you're so happy." He winked at her. "I swear to give my heart and soul to you, to always be there for you, to love you for all eternity." He opened his mouth to continue, but Bee beat him to it.

"I love you, Corbin."

"Forever," he murmured, gazing into her eyes.

"Forever," she replied with a smile.

Cyrus cleared his throat. "The joining of two hearts as fated mates is a remarkable thing. Corbin and Bee, do you now present yourselves to be joined? To accept the gift the goddess has bestowed upon you?"

"We do," they said, their voices in unison.

As they gazed into one another's eyes, tears welled up in mine in response. I was flooded with thoughts of how much I cared for them both and wanted them to have a life full of love and joy. I thought about Corbin's unwavering presence. Bee knew no bounds when it came to loyalty. I thought about how giving, loving and compassionate they both were. Corbin's commitment to the people he loved was so strong, and Bee was so gentle and understanding.

My skin shimmered as I inhaled deeply, feeling my love for them expand. My thoughts drifted toward their future, the children they may one day have, and the life they could share together.

They held my hands as they passed through the arch, and they turned to face the crowd. The magic flooded into me, and I used it to invoke their mate magic. It mixed with mine, and the surrounding glow intensified, my light drowning out their magic for the barest moment.

"Wow," Cyrus mouthed.

My powers swirled together with theirs, and I used it to speak for the first time. "Corbin and Bee, I give you my blessing on this joyous occasion. I bless this union, and I promise you will achieve all of your wildest dreams as long as you're together. I bless your future, your children, and I bless your life together." I paused and took a deep breath. "I bless my two best friends."

A surge of power ran through me and poured into them, amplifying the magic that already surrounded them. I sensed their hearts beating with delight. His love for her was obvious and strong. I saw Bee surrender her last guarded piece to him, allowing their mutual love to flood her being. The emotions were overwhelming. If I weren't careful, I thought I could have melted into a puddle on the floor. Instead, my cheeks ached from the magnitude of my grin.

Cyrus put his hands in the air, his eyes seeming to glow for a moment. "The magic has connected you. Your bond is now complete, and you are mated for life. Congratulations."

Corbin grabbed Bee and held her tightly, their heads close together as tears filled their eyes. When they let go, he dipped her and planted a kiss on her lips that started out innocent but quickly intensified. With so many people around, it was becoming less and less suitable for public display.

”Don't maul her face in front of the general,” I whispered jokingly at Corbin, who seemed like he couldn't care less.

When Bee playfully swatted his shoulder, he pulled away, and they both laughed. As a feeling of contentment washed over me, the surrounding light slowly dimmed before fading completely.

Everyone put their hands in the air and cheered. Alexei grabbed my hand and tugged me into his arms, a look of wonder on his face.

"You're incredible, my mate."

I wrapped my arms around him and kissed his lips. "I've never felt closer to my mom," I admitted. "She got to do this. It's... beautiful."

He looked lovingly at me. "Yes," he whispered tenderly. "You are."

CHAPTER
TWENTY-SIX

Alexei

I took Nicole's hand and, without a word, dragged her to our bedroom. After I slammed the door shut, I fumbled with her clothing, desperate to feel her skin on mine. That mating ceremony had stirred a wildness inside me that needed to be sated.

"Do you think they'll notice we left the party early?" Nicole asked between kisses.

I bit back a groan as her nails dug into my chest. "I don't particularly care if they do."

"I feel... different. The full moon..." she rasped while sinking her teeth into my neck. "I feel so... so... animalistic..."

My wolf howled in approval. This wasn't tender or sweet. This was craving. Aching. A feral fuck.

She laughed and hiked her leg up, curling it around my body. She was strong. Very strong. The moon power coursing through her veins was heady and intense. I could almost taste the potency of it on her tongue. My wolf was thrilled not to have to hold back.

The delicate fabric of her dress tore as I dove to my knees, clasping her ass with both hands and pressing my face into her. She let out a gasp of pleasure, her soft fingers entwining through my hair. I inhaled deeply, smelling how turned on she was for me. My stomach clenched in anticipation as I ripped the fabric away and tossed it aside. My mouth watered hungrily as I spread her wide open and ran my tongue up her slit, mercilessly parting her sensitive lips. I groaned in pure ecstasy as I caressed every inch of her opening with the tip of my tongue, and she quivered against me. She was a trembling ball of need. Her pink nub pulsated against my tongue, hard and swollen. I sucked and nibbled on it, eliciting a moan from deep within her chest and watching as her body convulsed against me.

I clasped my hands onto her hips, my fingers digging into her flesh as I slammed my mouth onto her clit. She screamed out, her knees going weak and her fingernails scraping my back. "Alexei, this is…"

"I know, baby. I know."

The remaining fabric of her dress fell as I ravished her, the feral part of me howling and clawing my insides, desperately wanting to break free and claim her as mine. Nicole clutched the back of my head, her fingers playing in my hair as she rose against me with each breath, moaning and crying out in pleasure.

"I need you," she gasped, pulling me closer. "Now."

"Here I am," I growled in response.

She grabbed my shoulders and kissed me with a fiery passion, her tongue exploring mine and her hands tugging me toward the bed. I landed on the mattress beneath her weight, feeling her body press against mine. She detached from the kiss, breathing heavily and with a devilish smirk on her lips.

"I wanna try something new," she murmured before she locked lips with me again.

Passion flooded my veins, the beast within me roaring for release. I merely nodded, too overwhelmed to speak. She wrapped her limbs around me and clung to me, my hardness throbbing against her entrance, begging to plunge into her and possess her.

She shook her head, her lips curling up into a cruel, seductive smile. "No, Alexei. This time, I'm in charge."

It went against every instinct I had, but I surrendered to my mate, eyes wide with anticipation as I watched her rise above me, dark hair cascading around her beautiful face. She kissed me again and pulled away, her lips curling into a wicked smirk as she peered down at me with those intense blue eyes.

"I want you to watch," she whispered throatily. "I want you to watch as I take you."

My heart was pounding like a war drum in my chest as I stretched toward her. A desperate need for our connection was filling me up like a wildfire, yet she danced away from me, a playful chuckle echoing around us. Her eyes had filled with a mischievous, predatory gleam as she shifted her hips forward and dropped her ass down, trapping my cock between her smooth thighs.

"Nicole," I grunted, the tips of my fingers curling into the sheets.

"You're such a good boy," she whispered, her fingers trailing along my chest and her hips popping up and down against my length. I felt the very tip of me take her as she slid down, a sharp stab of pain mixed with an intense pleasure that nearly dragged me into ecstasy.

"Do you want me?" Nicole purred seductively, her voice husky and dripping with lust.

I nodded, barely able to speak. I was completely under her spell. She rose up, slow and torturous, pausing briefly before slamming back down. We both moaned loudly, the pleasure and pain mingling together. She pulled away, and I groaned in agony, desperate to bring her back against me.

"Beg, Alexei," she teased, winking at me.

"Please," I begged.

She shook her head, a sly smirk growing on her lips.

"Please, what?"

"Please, Nicole. Fuck me. Please."

She nodded and slammed against me, drawing a curse from my lips. She pounded away with heavy strokes, her hips coated in sweat and her eyes filled with raw lust. Her walls gripped me tighter, and my body tensed as she let out a moan of pleasure. My eyes rolled back in euphoria as her body quaked.

"Oh, Alexei... that's it, baby. Fuck me, baby." She moaned, her nails digging into my chest as she rode me harder.

We were both nearing our limits, our bodies glistening with sweat and dripping with want and desire. She leaned closer, our noses brushing together as she started tightening around me.

"Now," I gasped, my voice straining.

"No," she whispered, pulling away and shaking her head.

"No?" I repeated, my cock pulsing to the rhythm of her breaths.

"Not yet," she said, popping up and slamming down, impaling herself on me.

My body went rigid and I could feel the explosion building up within me. I grabbed her hips and hammered into her, desperate to feel the release that was slowly creeping up on me. She had taken me so high and so hard that I felt like I was going to implode. My head was spinning and her scent was nearly driving me insane. One last thrust. Two last thrusts. Three last thrusts and she was there, falling over the edge with me. She screamed in pleasure, her fingernails digging into my skin as she clawed and scratched at me. I let out a guttural cry of my own, my cock twitching inside her as I pumped her full of my cum.

"Alexei," she cooed in sweet serenity between gentle kisses. With a content sigh, she nestled closer into my embrace, and I wrapped my arms around her. We both breathed in unison, her heart thudding against my chest. Gratitude and admiration swelled within me while I looked at her.

After a few moments, she finally smiled and

glanced up at me, her eyes shining with adoration. "We need a nap before round two, don't you think?"

I merely nodded, already fading into a blissful state of relaxation.

Damn. I'd always loved the full moon, but I had an even greater appreciation of it now.

"ARE YOU SURE THIS WILL WORK?" I asked, looking nervously at my mate's father.

I would never apologize for pleasing my mate, but it was still awkward being stuck in this tiny lab with her father mere hours after I last finished defiling her body. David Fairweather was much smaller in stature, but the guy was a master with the *don't even think about touching my daughter* glare.

"I'm positive the additional serum we made is an exact match." He flicked the vial in his hand, watching as the milky substance sloshed around a bit. "As for the antidote... I'm almost certain it will perform as planned, but there's no way to know for sure without test subjects. Ideally more than one."

"And that's the problem," Dr. Viden added. "Who's going to volunteer to have their power stripped from them in the hope that this antidote can reverse it? It's a big ask for any supernatural being."

"What about that elemental my father used for his demonstration at the Summit?" I proposed. "Could we get him here?"

Cammie considered that for a moment. "We could. But then we risk exposing the fact that we're working on an antidote. It's best to keep this as low-key as possible. Who's to say that elemental isn't working with your father?"

"Everyone at the Summit saw his powers being stripped. Any supe could smell the genuine fear flooding from him."

"Yes, but that man consented to it, regardless of his fear. Your father would've never gotten past the anti-violence spell otherwise. He probably rewarded him handsomely behind the scenes." She raised a delicate brow. "Or... more likely, blackmailed him, perhaps threatening his loved ones."

Fuck.

That was something my father would do without question.

"So what do we do?" Nicole asked, her brow furrowing.

"I'll do it," a familiar voice called.

My mate gasped as she whipped around, facing

the woman standing in the doorway to the lab. "Hannah! No way! Why would you volunteer for something like that?"

Hannah shrugged. "Why not? I'm a half-breed. If something goes awry, it's not like I'd have anything to miss. I can't shift and I can't perform any kind of fae magic without going to Faerie. But I *would* be able to feel the magic drain from my body, so I should be able to feel it return if the antidote works. Right? When you think about it, I'm the perfect candidate."

Nicole shook her head furiously, her blue eyes brightening with unshed tears. "No. No way. I'm not putting you at risk like that."

"Honey..." Dr. Fairweather started. "I think maybe we should consider Hannah's offer. She makes a valid point."

Hannah turned to my mate. "Everyone else's abilities are too important. I want to feel like I'm helping in some way." She looked around the room, her eyes finally falling back on Nicole. "I'm willing to take that risk for you if it means keeping you safe."

The silence around us was thick as Nicole's eyes darted back and forth between Hannah, Dr. Fairweather, and me. I could feel her anxiety and indecision, her panic and hope.

"Nicole," I whispered, taking her hand. "Hannah can handle it."

"And I'll be taking it with her," Jade said while stomping into the room, her designer heels clicking on the floor. "We can take shots like finals week in college. Thirsty Thursday, bitches."

Nicole shook her head. "No. Not you too."

Jade gave my mate a hard look. "I love you, kid. But this isn't your decision to make. We can do it." Nicole opened her mouth to argue, but Jade cut her off. "I know this is hard to accept. It sucks. But you have to let us handle this."

Nicole looked back at me. "I don't like this."

I squeezed my mate's hand tighter as I spoke. "You have to trust your father and Dr. Viden, baby. They'll be fine."

Nicole shook her head. "How can you be so sure?"

"We just have to have faith."

Nicole nodded and Dr. Viden got out two vials of what I assumed was the serum, handing them to both Hannah and Jade. "Step one."

"Do you have a chaser?" Jade joked.

The two women both nodded, uncapping their vials and downing the contents. Both immediately began to gag and cough, their skin turning ashen. Hannah fell to her knees, her eyes rolling into the back of her head, her body shaking. Jade panted, her eyes nearly rolling up into her head as well, but she managed to hold herself up, her eyes never leaving my mate's. I respected her greatly at that moment, trying to be strong for Nicole.

Jade's entire body shook as she spoke, the words sounding forced. "I can feel it... I can feel my powers leaving me."

Hannah groaned. "Shit, Doc. That's a fucking doozy of a drink."

Dr. Viden's lip quirked. "How do you feel?"

"Like I got hit by a truck," Hannah replied.

"Like I attended an orgy for giants without stretching first," Jade added.

Nicole's lip twitched in amusement.

Her father coughed awkwardly.

Dr. Viden checked both of their vitals, looking for any signs of a reaction. "It seems to have worked. This is very good. Do you both want to try the anti-dote now?"

Jade licked her lips. "Does it taste and feel like the last thing? Because that was straight up nasty. Like licking the inside of a belly button."

"Or drinking spoiled mayonnaise," Hannah added.

Dr. Viden handed them another vial—the liquid inside blue this time—and the two women were much less enthusiastic about throwing this one back.

"Bottoms up?" Jade asked her best friend.

"Fucking hell," Hannah replied. "Let's do it."

They both drank the potion and again, they began to gag. Hannah's eyes rolled back into her head, her body becoming limp. Jade swayed back and forth as she coughed. Nicole gripped my hand so tightly that my bones were starting to feel crushed.

"They're going to be okay," I whispered to my mate.

Nicole nodded, her eyes bright with unshed tears.

"Hannah! Jade! Come on, girls. Come back to us," Dr. Viden urged, slapping Jade's face.

Jade's eyes popped open, meeting Dr. Viden's. "Yuck. So fucking gross."

"Ew, so fucking gross," Hannah echoed as she came back to herself as well.

A few more seconds passed before Jade found her voice again. "Oh, shit. It's... it's back, Doc."

Dr. Viden replaced her stethoscope around her neck. "Can you feel it?"

"Definitely," Hannah replied. "Kind of feels like..." She eyed her best friend.

"Free falling. It's... incredible."

"Better than an orgasm," Hannah added. "Whoa, that's quite the rush, getting an influx of power all at once."

"This is wonderful!" David grinned, clapping his hands together. "We'll need to keep a close eye on you for any side effects over the next forty-eight hours or so, but if all goes well, I'd say we have a winner."

Nicole's full breasts pressed into my chest as she threw herself into my arms. "It worked!"

I wrapped my arms around her slim torso, resisting the urge to play grab ass in front of her father. "This is good, baby. Really fucking good."

I held my mate tight, reveling in the spark of hope thrumming through my chest. My father's serum may have given him a temporary advantage in this war, but we now had the ability to disable his greatest weapon.

And I couldn't fucking wait to see the look on his face when we revealed our ace in the hole.

TWENTY-SEVEN

Nicole

"You want me to do *what*?!" I could feel my eyebrows knitting together while Cyrus and General Minifred glanced at each other, their expressions hardening.

"We want you to turn these men into shifters," the general repeated, gesturing to the dozens of military men standing at attention before me. I slowly looked from one man to the next, trying to comprehend the task that lay ahead of me.

I was sure turning a human into a shifter was arduous work, even for a demigoddess. "But... how would I do that exactly?" I had basic knowledge of the process thanks to the texts Cammie gave me, but as with most magical things, theory and practice could be miles apart.

Cyrus let out a sigh. "I'll guide you through it, Nicole. The power rests inside of you. Your intention, combined with the summoning horn, will activate it."

I thought about my first encounter with the wolf spirit in Faerie. "Well, now I know why you asked me to meet in the Enchanted Woods. I highly doubt High Priestess Hale would appreciate a bunch of wild wolves running through the witches' headquarters. My intention is to call upon the Wolfy Powers That Be, right?"

My uncle's blond hair stuck on end as he ran a hand over the top of his head in exasperation. I didn't know why he was so easily agitated whenever I asked simple questions. I thought it was perfectly natural under the circumstances. Although, I supposed most people in a god's life wouldn't challenge everything they said.

"Technically, there won't be any *wild* wolves," Cyrus corrected.

I held my arms out, gesturing to the untamed woodland. "What's stopping every wolf in the vicinity from coming here when I call upon the mother wolf? Look what happened in Faerie with the spirit pack."

"I'll field this one," Dr. Viden—or Cammie, as I'd taken to calling her now—piped in, likely sensing my uncle's irritation. "You didn't call upon any spirits then. She sought you out. Fáel likely inhabited those wolves because she sensed your power and wanted to investigate. She has no need to send scouts this time. She will recognize your power being amplified by the summoning horn. She will understand your intent."

"How could she sense my power in Faerie if I wasn't using the horn?"

"The veil between the spiritual realm and Faerie is much thinner than it is here," Cammie answered.

"But when I turn these men into shifters—*if* I manage to accomplish it—we'll still have a bunch of rowdy animals on our hands."

Alexei chuckled under his breath, earning a pointed glare from me. "Nicole, when a shifter is in their animal form, they are quite cognizant of their actions. Their baser instincts may be harder to resist, but they think very much like they do in their human forms. Do you remember that day you hurt your leg at the river float? We carried on a perfectly normal conversation as if I weren't a giant wolf at the time."

He had a point, but I couldn't help but roll my eyes. "Besides the whole telepathy thing."

"Besides that." My mate winked, the *touché* implied in his tone.

My uncle frowned, clearly approaching his patience threshold. "You are correct in a way, though. I asked you to meet me in the Enchanted Woods because when these men do shift for the first time, they will feel the urge to run, to test the physical limits of their wolves. The forest allows them the space to do that and to connect with nature as it's meant to be."

"Plus, it'll give me a chance to see if we need to have any changes in hierarchy," General Minifred added. "The sooner I can identify any obvious strengths or weaknesses, the better. I know who my most competent men are *now*. But even the strongest or most skilled soldier isn't always as adept when they're in animal form."

"Speaking of skill..." I pulled the scrunchie off my wrist, gathering my long hair into a bun. "How confident are you that this is going to work? I feel like something as big as changing someone's *species* would be a skill one develops through practice. *Lots and lots* of practice."

"Nonsense," General Minifred growled in a deep, thunderous voice, his eyes narrowing with hostility. "You're fully capable. You were literally born for this purpose. But you won't be able to do *anything* with that negative attitude."

Sheesh. I'd always known General Minifred as a kind father-figure, but now, he was giving me the full war-general stare down, which made me cringe.

He must've seen my discomfort with his magic aura eye, because in the next moment, his face softened a fraction. Emphasis on the *fraction*. "Nicole, the fact of the matter is, we need the numbers if we're going to have any chance of defeating Jones. Alexei needs an army of soldiers who've been trained for combat."

The mention of my mate being at a disadvantage against his father made my stomach clench. I knew he was right. Alexei needed his own skilled fighters to join him, because the one thing I knew for sure was that Alpha Jones had no qualms about playing dirty.

"We'll be able to take them down faster with more shifters," the general added, his eyes boring into mine.

I gave the gathered soldiers another once over. Their faces remained stoic, shoulders squared. They may have been dressed casually in their PT uniforms, but there was nothing easygoing about these men.

"And everyone here volunteered for the job?"

I didn't care how many soldiers we needed. I refused to alter someone's entire identity without their consent. That would make me no better than Alpha Jones.

Bee's father narrowed his eyes at me, but I told myself to ignore the compulsion to cower. "*Of course* they did. Do you honestly think so little of me?"

"No!" I insisted, feeling like a jerk for doubting him. The general may have been a hardass, but I knew his moral compass was pointed north at all times. "I'm sorry. This is... a lot. I'm nervous."

"Breathe, baby." Alexei rubbed my back soothingly.

I took a few deep breaths, honing my focus as I leaned into his touch. "There's so much riding on my ability to do this."

"I know you have your doubts, but I'm certain the power will rise naturally within you," Cyrus assured me. "You'll inherently know how to direct the magic, just like you did when you gave Bee and Corbin your blessing during their mating ceremony."

I nibbled nervously on my lower lip. "Part of me still thinks it was dumb luck that my blessing worked."

My uncle smiled indulgently. "It wasn't, but I

appreciate your humility. Yet another thing you got from Celena.”

“Agreed,” Cammie said, nodding her head.

At the mention of my mother’s name, a warm breeze blew across my cheek, but there weren’t any visible signs of wind running through the forest.

Weird.

I shook off the strange sensation, shifting my focus to the task at hand. I needed this to work. We *all* needed this to work to take Alexei’s father down. It wasn’t just a matter of helping my mate take his rightful place as alpha of the strongest pack in North America. Alpha Jones’s sinister intentions went far beyond a single pack. They went far beyond the entire shifter population. That man was a tyrant in every sense of the word. I knew in my gut that he would stop at nothing until he reigned over all supernaturals. And if that happened, the entire human population would be screwed as well.

“I’m not trying to push before you’re ready, but we don’t have much time to spare,” Cyrus added, the lines on his face growing deeper. He knew what kind of toll the process would take on me, and he wasn’t wrong. It would be hard on my body to change so many men at once. I might not have tried it yet, but of that, I had no doubt. “These soldiers need time to acclimate to their wolves and train in their animal forms."

Frenetic energy pulsed through my veins as I thought about the dire consequences of waging war against Alpha Jones without a sufficient army. If I supposedly had the ability to help, I had to try. There was no other choice.

A bead of sweat trickled down my temple as I looked over at General Minifred. "Ok." I took another deep breath, feeling my body beginning to tremble with anxiety. "I'll do it."

The general's shoulders relaxed, and he spun on his heel. I blinked rapidly as he marched toward the door that led to the witches' headquarters. No matter how much time I spent in this forest, I didn't think I'd ever get used to seeing a wooden door suspended in thin air like that.

General Minifred turned the knob, revealing Juniper standing just inside, holding a familiar box. "Here you go, General Hotpants."

Was the big, scary general blushing?!

He coughed into his fist. "How many times do I have to ask you not to call me that?"

June extended her arms, transferring the box to him. "I'll stop when your reactions stop being so entertaining. I've gotta warn you, though. Your odds aren't looking too great."

He tucked the box under his arm and started to close the door.

"Hold up." June held her arm out, preventing him from shutting it entirely. "Are you sure I can't stay? It's not every day someone turns a human into a shifter."

Bee's dad sighed. "I've already explained this. It's in Nicole's best interest to limit the number of people present."

"But—" Juniper began.

"Wait! Why is that?" I asked, just now noticing how most of our team was missing. Besides the human guinea pigs, it was just me, Alexei, my uncle, Cammie, and the general. Cristian was still away dealing with whatever was involved in becoming a vampire king, but Corbin, Bee, June, my father, and my aunts had been closely involved in every little decision, so their absence was especially odd.

"Goodbye, Juniper," the general said pointedly. "We'll return as soon as we're done here."

This time, my witchy friend allowed him to close the door in her pouty face.

My uncle took the case from General Minifred and began walking toward me. "Nicole, are you ready?"

"Wait." I held my hand up. "Will someone answer my question please? Why is it in my best interest to limit the number of people present? I know you're hiding something."

A wave of peace washed over me as Alexei took my hand. "I'd like to know as well."

I knew Alexei would never hurt the general or my uncle, but his tone was dripping with alpha vibes. I half expected him to start grunting and pounding his chest.

The general and my uncle wore matching expressions filled with exasperation. They might as well have been bracing their hands on their hips like that one GIF gritting out, "Youths!"

"Calm down, Nicole," General Minifred said.

My brows rose. "You do realize telling any woman to calm down is going to have the exact opposite reaction, right?"

His lips twitched, seemingly unbothered by my rising irritation. "Oh, trust me, my daughter made me well aware of that fact many moons ago."

Despite my annoyance about being left in the dark, I laughed. My bestie definitely wasn't afraid to speak her mind. "Can we fast forward to an explanation please so we can move on?"

Cyrus shrugged. "Simply put, the fewer distractions you have, the easier it will be for you to focus. Plus, the fewer people we have present, the lower the odds of you accidentally changing one of your friends into a squirrel or something equally embarrassing."

"WHAT?!" My eyes felt like they were bulging out of my head.

Cyrus's grin widened as he said, "Kidding. That's not possible."

I turned to my mate. "It would be wrong to strangle him, right?"

Alexei's full lips curved. "Probably."

"Dammit," I muttered under my breath.

My uncle held his hands up. "In my defense, I *wasn't* kidding about the focus part. If you haven't noticed, your friends—and your aunts for that matter—tend to be a bit... disruptive. August and I thought it would be best to include only those who were essential to the process. The general and I need to be here for obvious reasons. Camelia is here because she's witnessed your mother do this more than anyone else. She's my... backup, so to speak."

"Then why am I here?" Alexei asked.

General Minifred rolled his eyes. "Two reasons. One, I knew you would be insufferable if I asked you to stand on the sidelines while your mate was doing something so monumental. It was easier to include you than to try keeping you away."

Alexei and I both nodded in agreement.

"And secondly?" my mate prompted, looking far too proud of his caveman reputation.

"Secondly," the general continued, "your mate bond could lend Nicole strength if the process becomes too taxing. In a nutshell, you're our Plan B."

I searched my mental encyclopedia, trying to decode his words, but I was coming up empty.

Alexei scoffed. "Power sharing is a myth."

"Is it now?" my uncle challenged. "Are you positive about that?"

Alexei's brow furrowed. "Well, I *was*."

"Power sharing?" I asked. "Like we can blend our powers together? That little piece of info seems to be missing from my mind-fuck database."

"That's because it's virtually unheard of these days," General Minifred explained. "Each time you share power, your life forces are strung together. If you do it enough times, that tether becomes unbreakable. If a fated pair decides to bind themselves in that manner, it's not usually something they'd advertise."

"Why not?" I asked.

"Because if one dies, so does the other," Cyrus answered, a grave look on his face. "If you had enemies... your mate could be targeted. There have been accounts of mates being kidnapped and tortured, drained of life over an extended period of time. Meanwhile, their other half would feel their mate dying. They would know they were suffering. Some were driven mad being away from their mate for too long, unable to find them. Death became their only viable option for peace. Many took matters into their own hands."

Oh.

Alexei's hand clenched around mine. As we looked into each other's eyes, I knew he was thinking about the times we were apart. That painful longing that dug into your marrow. It was so tangible I could swear it became its own entity. Even when I was trying to resist our mating bond, I ached for Alexei. I couldn't imagine how strong that pain would be if we were forcefully separated. If I could feel him being slowly tortured to death.

"God, those poor people," I choked out. But I still had more questions. "What if one of the mates had a significantly longer natural lifespan than the other? If they died of natural causes, would it be at the shorter or the longer lifespan?"

Cyrus was the one to answer. "It's... complicated. There's not enough history of such an occurrence for me to give you a definitive answer. But... if I were to make an educated guess, I'd say that timeframe would probably meet somewhere in the middle of the two. If your inquiry is directly related to you and *your* mate, which I suspect it is, I'd remind you that while you're powerful, you're still half human, which means killing you is not impossible."

"But my power *could* make Alexei stronger, and it would very likely extend his lifespan?"

"In theory, yes," Cyrus said, but his tone hinted that he wasn't exactly fond of the idea.

"I'd hate to break up this delightfully cheery conversation," the general interrupted, "but can we table this for later? We really need to get started."

I blew out a breath. "Of course."

Cyrus opened the wooden box, the jewels embedded into the golden horn winking back at me. "Good. Now, let's turn these men into shifters."

TWENTY-EIGHT

Nicole

"Are you ready for this, Nicole?" My uncle's blue eyes were filled with hope and encouragement.

I nodded and took a seat on the oversized log he had gestured to. "What now?"

Cyrus handed me the box. "Pull the horn out. You might feel some of the magic flow through you at first."

I nodded and took a deep breath. I carefully lifted the horn from its velvet bed, the gold metal heavy in my hands. My skin tingled as I closed my eyes, images of the dozens of men standing before me filling my mind. Unbridled power coursed through me, causing me to nearly drop the summoning tool in shock, but a firm hand clasped over mine and held it up, pulling me back into the present moment. My eyelids fluttered open to find Cyrus standing beside me, holding the horn for me.

"It's alright, Nicole. It's just the power. You'll be fine."

I curled my fingers around the horn, feeling the warmth spread up my arms and fill my chest with a powerful energy. I focused on taking slow, even breaths, allowing the buzz to flow through every inch of me.

"Soldiers, prepare for your transformation," General Minifred commanded.

Huh? Weren't they already prepared for—

My jaw dropped open when they began to strip, one by one, freakishly in sync with the other members of their unit. First, they lost their shirts. Then their sneakers and socks. Their dark-colored shorts went last, leaving each one in nothing but a pair of briefs that did nothing to hide their impressive... builds.

"Don't make me haul your ass out of here to remind you who you belong to," Alexei growled under his breath.

Oops. Was I staring?

"Sheesh, give me a break," I whisper-snapped. "I wasn't exactly prepared for the impromptu show."

"*It's not a show,*" he snapped right back, matching my low volume. "Undressing before shifting is required if you want something to wear when you shift back."

"I know that!" Now I was whisper-shouting. "I was just stunned for a few seconds because I wasn't expecting them to strip down to their skivvies! Hell, why not just take it all off? Let those peens fly free and—"

Alexei growled even louder this time.

"Captain Mayes," General Minifred barked, putting an abrupt end to our argument. "Step forward."

The captain stood tall and proud, his jaw set and eyes straight ahead. His buzz-cut hair emphasized his sharp edges and rigid posture. His gaze never wavered as he complied with the command, but his body was tense and poised for quick action—a pretty impressive feat in your undies, if you asked me.

"Yes, sir."

Cyrus stood by the man and looked him up and down with a critical eye before speaking in a low, authoritative voice.

"Stand still and close your eyes."

The man's face softened into a mask of concentration as he complied, his posture so rigid and controlled it appeared as if he were carved from marble.

"Do I have to blow into the horn?" My brow creased.

"No, you don't need to blow into it," Cyrus said, gently taking the golden instrument from my hands. He wrapped his fingers around the smooth surface, almost like a prayer. "It's more of a talisman. Hold it up and connect with the magic."

I scrunched my nose in confusion at his words. "How?"

Cyrus handed it back to me and stroked his chin. "Reach out to it with your mind."

Well, that was totally not helpful.

I tried to do what he said, and after a few moments, the warmth of the magic emanated from my chest and flowed over my fingertips. I raised my arms and began to mentally draw small swirls in the air in front of the man. A small silver wolf's head appeared in the swirls and then winked out of existence. I focused with greater intensity, concentrating on the loops and curves, and the wolf's head grew more and more distinct.

I let the steady warmth of the magic emanating from my chest course through my body, like a river of energy. I let it build until it overflowed from my fingertips, creating a sparkling halo in the air. I focused my mental energy, feeling it pulse through my arms, and in front of me, a wolf's body took shape, shimmering in its outline. I pushed harder, imagining the swirls around the soldier, and the magic transformed into a bright red light that quickly blanketed his chest and abdomen in a protective cocoon.

The magic continued to flow out in the same pattern as I concentrated on the image of the wolf, willing the magic to take it to its last form. The swirls around the man's body exploded in a burst of red light, and a second later, a full-grown wolf stood in the center of the swirls, releasing a deep howl.

The air rippled with excitement. The wolf shook his head a few times, his ears twitching in all directions. He looked down at his body, and a low growl escaped his lips. He lifted his head toward Cyrus and let out another howl.

"Nicole, you did it. You were amazing," Alexei said from beside me. I turned to look at him and found his face glowing with pride, all signs of tension from our mini fight had disappeared.

I wanted to celebrate, but my triumphant excitement was overshadowed by exhaustion. My body felt like it weighed a thousand pounds. I blinked rapidly as my head began to spin.

The general gestured toward the wolf. "You're free to run, soldier."

The wolf bowed to me and turned his newly furry body away, only to trip and fall on his face.

"Did I break him?" I shrieked, wincing as the poor guy sneezed dirt out of his snout.

"It's a complicated process," Cyrus chuckled, "He has to get used to his new body."

I nodded as the wolf stood, shaking himself off and scurrying away. I didn't think it was possible before now, but I could swear the animal looked embarrassed by his baby deer impression.

One down and only a couple dozen to go.

I was glad I was sitting down, because I was wiped out.

"Officer Thomas," General Minifred said. "Step forward."

"Already?" I whined.

Man, I could really use a few minutes to take a breather.

The general looked me over with concern as Thomas's eyes swung toward me. He quickly fixed his gaze on the ground when he saw Alexei glaring at him.

Cyrus smiled softly. "I know it's a lot, but we really need to keep moving. Go ahead, Nicole."

"Okay," I answered my uncle before turning to Officer Thomas, tightening my grip on the horn.

Once again, the swirls converged around the man. I closed my eyes, reached out with my mind, and let the magic flow. Within seconds, I knew something wasn't right. My chest ached. My head throbbed. I was pretty sure I was on the verge of fainting.

It was almost as if the wolf spirit was resisting the pull of my power, but why would she do that?

"Soldier?" Cyrus asked.

The worry in my uncle's tone prompted me to open my eyes.

An angry vein popped in the officer's neck right as he fell to his knees.

"Why does this fucking hurt?" he gritted.

Thomas collapsed flat on the ground, his eyes wide and panicked.

"Is he..." I asked, my voice wobbly. "Is he okay?"

That's when Thomas let out a howl that rivaled the wolf's from before, but his came from a human mouth, so it was especially disconcerting. I cringed, wishing I were wearing earplugs. Blood poured from his eyes as he writhed, making me shriek.

"It can't be," Cyrus murmured, confusion clear in his tone.

"Take this man to a medic STAT," the general

commanded.

Two of the soldiers cautiously approached their fallen peer, picked him up, and carried him away as he screamed in agony.

"What happened?" I asked. "What did I do wrong?!"

Cyrus shook his head "I don't know... I don't think you did anything that would've caused that. I think... I think the wolf spirit rejected him."

"Why would she do that?"

"It's quite rare but not entirely unheard of. The last time this occurred was..."

"With David," Cammie supplied.

My head swung to her. "I'm sorry, but *what*?! David? As in my father? *That* David?"

"Yes." Cammie nodded.

I stood, crossing my arms over my chest. "I'm going to need you to explain that."

Alexei placed his hands on my shoulders as he stood like a sentinel behind me.

Cammie looked at me with soft eyes. "General, I know we're pressed for time, but may I have a few moments with Nicole?"

"Please make it quick," he replied.

"Let's talk, Nicole," Cammie suggested, taking her own seat on the log and patting the spot beside her.

Alexei guided me toward the log, silently taking his place beside me. When I felt dozens of eyes on me, I looked up, tensing when I found every single soldier staring at us. Sensing my discomfort, my mate stood back up and barked, "Go find something else to do for a bit."

Half the soldiers looked like they were about to piss themselves, while the other half looked to General Minifred, waiting for his command.

"You heard the man. Go!" the general yelled.

They all took off then, running in three different directions, their only purpose being to get the hell away from here.

The general stood to his full height. "Somebody had better start talking."

Cyrus and Cammie looked to one another, seemingly having some sort of silent communication. Upon my uncle's nod, Cammie spoke.

"Nicole, do you remember when you first arrived in Faerie and learned about your heritage?"

I gave her an *are you kidding?* look. "Finding out you're half goddess isn't exactly something one could just forget."

"Not that part," she said. "The part about your mom being raised on Faerie. About the promise I made to her."

Now that she mentioned it, I had completely

forgotten to address that promise part. The only explanation I could think of was my brain was over-loaded at the time and I glossed over it.

"And?"

"Well... the thing is, your mom was my best friend. I never had the chance to meet her loved ones on earth, because I was still living in Faerie then, but we remained in touch by sending letters through a mini portal disguised as a keepsake box. When she met your father... when they fell in love, she was *so* happy. But she was also incredibly distraught."

My brow furrowed. "Why?"

Cammie looked lost in thought. "Because, your father's lifespan was a blip in time compared to a goddess's. She was afraid she would blink and his life would be over. She didn't want to lose him."

I rubbed at the sudden ache in my chest. "But that doesn't make sense. Why would she intention-ally get pregnant then, knowing she would die in childbirth? She could've had decades with him. That's gotta be better than nothing."

"Celena's secrecy pact prevented her from telling your father she was a goddess, but she told him as much as she could. He knew she was immortal. He knew she somehow had the ability to transform humans into shifters. Your mother was convinced she and your dad were fated, but since mate bonds are exclusive to the supernatural community, she thought she'd have to turn him into a shifter before her goddess powers would kick in and make it official. And once that happened, she planned to bind their life forces together. Your father was fully onboard with that plan."

What happened next wasn't hard to piece together. "So she attempted to turn him into a shifter, but it didn't work?"

"Right." Cammie nodded.

"Did she ever figure out why?"

"She said Fáel came to her in a vision after her attempt to transform your father had failed. The wolf spirit assured your mom that she and your dad *were* fated, but evidently, David's existence had a greater purpose beyond being the love of Celena's life."

"What purpose?" Alexei asked, just as invested in the answer as I was.

"To sire Nicole," my uncle explained. "Because you, my dear niece, have an even greater purpose. The wolf spirit didn't explain what that purpose was, but Cammie and I suspect it has something to do with your role in stopping this war that Alpha Jones is waging."

My eyes rounded. "Say what now?"

Alexei took my hand, placing a kiss over my knuckles. "It makes perfect sense, Nicole."

"It does," General Minifred agreed.

"Whoa," I breathed out.

I didn't know what to think or how to feel about their theory. The pressure was suffocating to say the least.

"Are you okay?" my mate asked. "If you need time to process, I'll make it happen. We can work on transforming the soldiers another day."

"I really wouldn't advise that," General Minifred argued. "But if you need time, I can make it happen."

Alexei and the general stared each other down so hard it would be comical if we didn't have so many heavy issues at play. Bee's dad was a lone wolf by choice, but he was all alpha, all the time, just like my mate.

"But what about that Thomas guy? Is he going to be okay? Is that going to happen again? I don't want to hurt anyone."

"Obviously, David is fine, so I would expect Thomas should also be," Cammie said, comforting me. "Only the wolf spirit knows what Thomas's purpose is, or any other soldier's. We shall let what is meant to be take its course. Okay?"

I nodded slowly, feeling the weight of my responsibility settle.

"Nicole?" my uncle prompted. "Are you okay to continue, or would you like to rest for a bit first?"

I was freaking exhausted, more exhausted than I ever thought possible. But I was also hell-bent on making this happen, and there were few things in the world that could rival a determined woman's strength.

"Call 'em back." I straightened my spine. "Let's do this."

General Minifred and my uncle beamed at me with pride. Alexei gave my shoulder a little squeeze, telling me he felt the same. At that moment, I knew, no matter how difficult or tiring changing these men into shifters would be, I was going to be just fine.

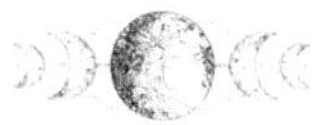

He scooted closer to me, tucking some hair behind my ear. "You need to *rest*. We can talk later."

"I've been resting for over twelve hours."

I sighed as he combed his fingers through my scalp, massaging gently. Mere seconds after I had successfully transformed the last soldier into a shifter, I lost consciousness. Alexei had carried me back to our shared bedroom at the witches' headquarters, which is where we'd been ever since. I'd woken here and there, even had a light meal, but I was feeling too restless to sleep anymore. I couldn't stop thinking about what I'd learned about binding your life sources together. With all the chaos we'd been surrounded in lately, Alexei and I hadn't had the chance to discuss the one thing that had been weighing most heavily on me since learning about my heritage. It was even more prevalent after learning my mother had tried doing so with my dad.

It seemed almost cruel for the fates to match two people who had such an alarming gap between their natural lifespans, but considering my mom was the one who blessed my bond with Alexei, I had to trust she had faith in the spirit. She knew first-hand what it was like to love someone who was supposed to live a much shorter life than her own.

"What's on your mind?" he asked while stroking my cheek. I leaned into the touch, relishing in the feel of his warm skin on mine.

"I can't stop thinking about my parents. What would have happened if she didn't have me? Dad would have grown older, and she would have stayed the same. I don't want that to happen to us."

He smiled tenderly. "We have plenty of time to

worry about that. How about we focus on one problem at a time."

I shook my head. "I can't stop worrying about it. I don't want you to go into battle with no safeguards. I know you've been training to fight your father, but what if—"

"I will not fail, Nicole," he gritted.

I stared deeply into his eyes. "Alexei, I know how strong you are. I know that when you go up against him, your chance of winning is greater than it's ever been. But why shouldn't we use every defense we have available to us? I can't stand thinking that you'll be in danger. And I want to know when you go off to fight that you'll be safe. If we power shared enough times before then to bind our life forces together, it'll make you a little less... vulnerable."

I made a mental note to ask my uncle how many times we'd have to do it to complete the process.

"And what if he successfully kills me, Nicole? What if he somehow finds a way? If we're bound together, that would mean you'd die too. I can't handle knowing you'd be at risk."

His concern was touching, but I had to be selfish about this. "I want to be with you for as long as I can. If there's even a chance that binding our life forces would give me a little more time with you, I want to do it. Please."

His eyes flickered between mine, and he was silent for several moments. "I have conditions."

My brow furrowed. "What *kind* of conditions?"

Alexei's dark eyes softened when my voice caught on the last word. "The thought of you outliving me for possibly hundreds of years *does* concern me, Nicole. I know how you're feeling. When I thought you were human, I was facing the same future, though not nearly as long. But I remember how badly the thought of your human fragility gnawed at me, so I get it. Okay?"

"Why do I feel like there's a *but* coming?"

"*But...*" He smirked when I pinched him. "I don't think this is a decision that should be made without looking at it from all angles. I won't put you at risk on a whim. And the fact of the matter is, we simply don't have enough time before I need to challenge my father. He needs to be stopped before he gains any more allies. He's a liability to the entire supernatural community."

"I know that, which is why—"

Alexei placed his index finger over my lips. "I'm standing firm on this, Nicole. I am absolutely willing to explore bonding our life forces—*after* I take down my father."

My chest rose on a shaky inhale. "Alexei, if you—"

"Have a little faith, baby. I won't lose." He gave me a cocky wink. "Quite frankly, your concern is a little emasculating. I'm a big, bad alpha, remember?"

I rolled my eyes. "You're a big, bad *something*, alright."

A deep chuckle rumbled from his chest before his expression sobered. "I love you, Nicole. More than anything."

"I love you, too, Alexei." I smiled and leaned closer to him, pressing my lips to his.

He deepened the kiss, his lips warm and insistent, caressing mine with a heat that seeped into my bones. I melted against him, losing myself until we both gasped for air. He smiled at me, his eyelids half closed and his voice husky.

"I want you." His words were thick like a sultry purr. "But you need to rest. Your uncle said it could be another couple of days until you're feeling top shape. And I need to go check on the new shifters."

"I'll be fine," I said. "But maybe another nap couldn't hurt."

He laughed and pulled me back against his chest. "I'll make sure to give you something to dream about until I return."

"Oh?" I said. "And what might that be?"

"Take a guess."

I smiled coyly. "Hmmm…"

He kissed me again, his mouth pressing roughly against mine, taking my breath away. I moaned softly as his lips trailed down my throat, making my skin tingle as he kissed me. His soft lips and gentle touch were a stark contrast to his fierce hands and raking fingertips, which made me gasp as he lifted my shirt. He trailed his fingertips along the line of my bra, and I sighed, my breath coming in staggered gasps.

His lips found my ear, and he grinned, his breath sending a shiver down my spine.

"I love you."

I smiled back at him, wiggling to get free of my shirt, but he grabbed my hand, stopping me. "No, I have to go check on the new shifters. You get some rest."

I sighed. "That's no fun." He smiled and kissed me, lingering for a moment. "Gotta run. See you for dinner."

"If I wake up on time," I teased. "You promise to revisit this conversation after you challenge your father for alpha?"

He looked at me, his eyes flickering with an emotion I couldn't place. "I promise."

Alexei

"MY SOLDIERS WILL LAUNCH an offensive on the western flank," General Minifred declared, his steely gaze scanning the conference room, or the *war room* as he'd dubbed it.

Evidently, after my father had booted all the students off the Redwood University campus, he converted it into a makeshift military base. It made perfect sense, seeing as he had access to housing and state-of-the-art lab equipment to manufacture his serum.

Cristian, who had arrived the night prior with his small regiment of vampires, nodded. "Where will we be deployed?"

"You'll be attacking from the east," the general replied. "You'll be at a disadvantage since you have fewer numbers, but we've obtained intel that the base has increased security along the perimeter closest to the laboratory on the west side."

June eyed General Minifred with a determined look, rubbing her hands together in anticipation. "And what about us?"

"You'll be at the center of campus so you'll have a better vantage point over everyone. As we discussed earlier, we'll need you to keep an invisibility cloak over our troops until Alpha Jones has been located and Alexei is in place to formally challenge his father. From there, we will need you and your mother to focus on maintaining and protecting the portals."

"Consider it done." June nodded. "That's gonna take a shit ton of power, though. I'll need more pubes."

Eve smiled proudly at her daughter. High Priestess Hale agreed to be present since her power would certainly benefit our cause, but she appointed her daughter to take the lead in representing their coven. I had a feeling Nicole's quirky purple-haired friend would take the reins from her mother sooner rather than later. When I first met Juniper, I thought she was just Corbin's sex-crazed hookup. But the more I got to know her and saw what she was capable of, the greater my respect grew. We really were lucky to have her coven on our side.

"Good thing we've got plenty to spare," I said with a laugh.

I couldn't wait to see the look on the soldiers' faces when Juniper brought out the clippers and asked them to manscape for the cause. If Corbin's goofy grin was any indication, he was looking forward to that moment just as much as I was.

Cristian's eyes met Nicole's, his voice heavy with apprehension. "And what about Alpha Jones's serum? Are you sure the antidote works?"

She steeled herself. "My father and Cammie have assured us the antidote, it *will* work. They made plenty to go around if anyone from our team gets dosed with serum."

Cristian nodded, seemingly satisfied.

"Remember, we need to draw out my father as quickly as possible so I can formally challenge him," I added. "Once a challenge is issued in front of the pack, he'll have to either fight or forfeit. I don't think anyone is under the delusion that my father will choose the latter. Correct?"

Murmured sounds of agreement echoed throughout the room.

"Good." I nodded. "The sooner I take him down,

the sooner I'll gain control over the pack, so that's the goal. I don't want anyone to die needlessly."

"You're sure they'll pledge allegiance to you? All of them?" Cristian had a worried look on his face. The guy looked fucking exhausted, but I supposed assuming leadership of an entire kingdom of North American vampires was stressful without adding my father's bullshit to the mix.

"I've known that pack my whole life. I believe the majority will be eager to accept me as their new leader and stand down. They're family-oriented people. They don't want a war."

"How can you be certain?" Cristian pressed.

"Wolf hierarchy is complex," General Minifred answered. "Lower-ranking wolves are compelled to follow their alpha. The higher-ranking ones *could* resist if they wanted to, but that would require a challenge of their own for power, which I don't see happening. Leading the Ridgeview pack is Alexei's birthright. That alone garners great respect within the shifter community. Alpha Jones has tried to tarnish Alexei's reputation these last few months, but any shifter can easily recognize the alpha power that resides within him. When he officially inherits the role, that power will grow exponentially and will be instantly felt among the pack. Speaking of..." The general turned toward me. "Alexei, it'll be jarring once you step into your new position. I'll guide you through the process of sending out your will to your pack before we launch our attack."

I nodded in acknowledgement.

Nicole cleared her throat. "What about me? What am I going to do?"

Cyrus spoke up. "You'll be with me."

I instantly tensed, which didn't go unnoticed by my mate. I didn't want her going anywhere near the battle. If I had my way, she'd stay safely at the witches' headquarters, away from danger. But I knew it would be impossible to convince her of that. Plus, we really did need all hands on deck. It went against my nature to allow her on the front lines, but as I constantly reminded myself these days, Nicole was a demigoddess. Now that she had magically matured, she was naturally hard to kill. Maybe even more so than me. And she was stubborn as fuck. If I tried stopping her from helping, she'd no doubt hand me my ass on a silver platter. My mate was a determined badass, which drove me crazy yet also wild with desire.

Nicole looked at me questioningly as I chuckled under my breath. "And how will we fight? Will we join the vampires? Or will we be with Alexei and the shifters?"

Cyrus shook his head. "Neither. We're going to

astral project and pinpoint Alpha Jones's exact location. General Minifred decided it's best if you were somewhere on campus so the moment you locate him, Alexei can hunt him down. But the tricky part was finding a place that was also far enough removed from any danger. Alexei suggested a small man-made cave in the forest, which we believe will work well, so the witches will open a portal that will take us there. The general's contact has already installed mini surveillance cams in and around the cave, so we'll have plenty of warning to escape if anything goes awry. Once you've secured Alpha Jones's location, you and I will head back here to the witches' headquarters through the portal."

Nicole twisted her face, obviously disappointed by this. "I don't want to stand on the sidelines while my mate and best friends fight."

General Minifred frowned. "Nicole, the faster Alexei can find his father, the fewer lives will be lost. Your role in this is incredibly valuable."

"You have to stay safe, Nicole. I won't be able to focus if you're in danger," I insisted. "Macey can't protect you like I can." My mate's familiar growled, baring her teeth at me.

Nicole patted Macey's head to soothe her, or perhaps convince her not to attack me. Although, the glare my mate was shooting my way made me question the latter.

The general cleared his throat. "Maybe we should get back on track. To recap, Nicole will use astral projection to locate Alpha Jones. Once we've secured his exact location, we attack en masse. The vampires will enter through the portal on the east side of the campus, shifters from the west, and the witches will take the center. Is everyone clear on that?"

He glanced around the table, waiting for everyone's acknowledgement.

"I want to do more," Nicole said.

"Baby," I began. "I told you—"

"I know you want to keep me safe, Alexei, but I'm part goddess, right? I should be able to do something else. And Cyrus is a full-fledged god of the freaking sun! We can help!"

I clenched my jaw. I understood why Nicole was so adamant. She was my mate and wanted to make sure I won. But I couldn't bear the thought of her getting hurt.

Cyrus cleared his throat, obviously trying to diffuse the tension. "Nicole is right. Technically, we're the most powerful beings in this room. There's no reason we can't use that to our advantage."

"Nicole is untrained," I pointed out, earning another death glare and another threatening growl, but I didn't care. I had to get this out. "She barely knows what she's capable of. She certainly hasn't had time to practice most of it. It doesn't matter how much power she has if she doesn't know how to channel it properly! How can I be expected to focus on my father if I'm worried about her?"

How could they ask this of me? Why was everyone ignoring Nicole's obvious lack of practice in controlling her magic?

My mate gasped, tears threatening to spill as she scooted her chair away from me.

"Baby—" I reached for her, but she scooted back further.

Nicole held her hand up. "Nuh-uh. This is not solely your decision, Alexei! I can do more than serve as a freaking locator device!" She thumped her clenched fist over her heart. "I may not have had a lifetime to get used to my abilities like everyone else, but I can *feel* my power like I can feel my lungs expanding each time I inhale. It's always buzzing beneath my skin, calling out to me. Begging me to summon it. To mold it, shape it to my will." She stood, chin high and shoulders squared. "How many humans did I successfully transform into shifters? Who else is capable of something like that? *No one!*

Plus, I am directly linked to the moon! You know that thing in the sky that affects the earth's gravitational pull? The ocean? The seasons? Without it, this entire planet would be fucked! *I am powered by that, Alexei!*"

I stood as well. "Nicole. Calm down. I know—"

"I wasn't finished!" she shouted.

"You tell him, Nicky!" Corbin cheered, earning a dirty look from me.

"Shut up, Corbin!" Nicole and I both yelled at the same time.

"Nic—" I began.

"*You shut up, too!*" she screamed. "I wasn't done!"

It wasn't easy, but I resisted the overwhelming urge to take control of this conversation. But I could feel her pain, and I had already caused Nicole enough pain to last a lifetime. The least I could do was keep my mouth shut for a few minutes.

I nodded in acquiescence as I took my seat, giving her the floor.

"*As I was saying...* I think I can do more to help give us the advantage. I can do your little locator thingy, but I can also orchestrate a distraction before we attack, confuse them as to where the real threat lies."

General Minifred smiled proudly. "What do you mean?"

"The wolf spirit," my mate answered. "When I was in Faerie... Fáel sent a bunch of wolfy ghosts to scope me out, right? Well, what if I can summon the spirit pack to Redwood? They couldn't do any physical damage since they're... you know, *spirits*, but it sure as shit would be confusing, don't you think? And while Alpha Jones's army is trying to figure out how to battle apparitions, we can attack."

The general rubbed his chin thoughtfully. "How exactly would you summon these ghosts? The summoning horn calls the mother spirit to create shifters; it doesn't round up her pack."

Nicole nodded to Cammie. "Cammie said the veil between Faerie and the spiritual plane is thin. So, what if Cammie opened a portal to Faerie, and I summoned them from there? On the earth side, I mean. I wouldn't want to risk traveling to Faerie with the whole *time passing differently* thing."

"It could work," Cyrus mused. "What do you think, General?"

He turned toward Cammie. "Dr. Viden, do you think Nicole's plan has potential?"

"I do." She nodded. "I think it's quite brilliant, actually."

Fucking hell, I hated being proven wrong, but I thought so, too.

"I agree." I smiled at my mate. "I'm sorry I doubted you."

"Thank you," she whispered, taking her seat once again. When she grabbed my hand, I breathed a sigh of relief. "One more thing. I think Macey should stay here with Jade and Hannah." The wolf whimpered at that, prompting Nicole to pet her behind the ear. "I'm sorry, girl, but I think you're better off here with the children. They've already been through a lot, and you make them feel safe."

Nicole's familiar barked in reply before settling on the floor down by her feet.

"She doesn't like it," Juniper said, obviously using her animal telepathy, "but she understands."

My mate smiled lovingly at the wolf.

"Okay, then. So it's settled." General Minifred looked around the room. "Is everyone clear on the plan?"

Murmured agreements coursed through the room.

"I never thought I'd say this, but being human is dumb." Bee crossed her arms with an exaggerated pout. "I feel useless."

"Not true, baby." Corbin hooked his arm around the chair she was sitting in, pulling her closer.

"You're the most important person I know. Plus, you and Nicole's aunts are going to be helping the witches in the infirmary, remember?"

The witches planned to open a portal that dropped directly into their medical ward. I hoped they wouldn't see too many patients, but it was better to be prepared. It didn't hurt to have a little magical medical intervention in your pocket, especially if any member of our team was struck with my father's serum.

"You'd better make it out of this, Corbin. I'll resurrect you from the dead and kill you myself if you don't." The apples of her cheeks flushed as Corbin nuzzled into her neck.

"Save the kinky ideas for later, baby," Corbin whispered, though I was sure everyone in the room heard him just fine. "After we beat Pack Daddy's ass, I'm gonna need some *extra special attention* from my mate, if you catch my drift."

"People in fucking Siberia catch your drift," General Minifred barked. "How many times do I have to tell you, boy? Quit trying to feel my daughter up!"

"But she *likes it* when I feel her up!" Corbin whined, quickly backtracking when Bee's dad practically glared a hole through his forehead. "Uh... I mean—"

The general stood, slamming his open palm on the conference table. "I know *exactly* what you meant!" He pointed to his magical aura-seeing eye. "I can see your emotions, remember? Don't make me maim you right before we head to the university! You drive me batshit sometimes, but you have proven you're a valuable beta. Alexei needs you."

Corbin sat up straight, beaming. "Awwww, is that General Daddy speak for, 'I love you, Corbin. I'm so glad you're my son-in-law because life wouldn't be the same without you'? It's cool, Pops. I feel the same." To punctuate his statement, he curved his fingers until they formed a heart in the center.

General Minifred's jaw clenched so severely I was surprised he didn't fracture something. "Stop addressing me by those stupid names!"

Corbin turned toward Bee. "See? I told you he'd warm up to me, eventually."

Bee giggled before whispering, "Maybe you should stop talking now, babe. That vein on my dad's forehead looks like it's going to burst."

Every single head in the room snapped toward the general.

Damn. It really did look like it was about to explode right out of his skin.

I could see Nicole fighting a smirk in my periphery. Leave it to Corbin to turn our final strategy session into comedy hour. But as I looked around the room, I could tell the brief levity was exactly what everyone needed at that moment.

He really was the best fucking beta.

THIRTY

Alexei

THE DARK CAVE seemed to swallow us whole as our small group crept inside, illuminated only by the soft twinkle of the ethereal lights that hovered in front of us like mini fireflies. Juniper had magically transported us to the cave's entrance, only pausing for a few seconds to cast the glowing little particles into existence before hopping back onto the Witchy Express to meet her mother at the center of the campus to help her maintain the invisibility spell. It was important the powerful duo was in place before the rest of our troops crossed into enemy territory, so they could keep them hidden with a cloaking spell until it was time to attack. The element of surprise was crucial to our success, so we couldn't take any chances.

The smooth rock walls curved to the left as the dirt path descended downward, prompting us to do the same. The ceiling in this narrow section was lower than I remembered from the last time I was here, forcing me to bend my knees at an awkward angle so that I didn't strike my head. Nicole and Cammie could get by with only a slight hunch, but the general and my mate's uncle looked just as ridiculous as I did, practically in a duck walk at one point. Thankfully, it didn't take too long before we were in a wide open space toward the back, which was... well, cavernous, despite the fact that we were actually underground now. This place wasn't suitable for the claustrophobic, that was for certain.

I shook my head as I recalled the last time I was here, thinking about my best friend's ridiculous antics.

"What?" Nicole asked.

"Nothing," I replied. "I was just remembering the last time I was in here."

"When was that?" she questioned. "This thing is so well hidden I would've never known it existed if I were just passing through the forest."

It was true; the cave was well hidden. The mouth was naturally camouflaged by large ferns and moss draped long and low to the ground. Above the rocky dome sat a thick layer of soil and grass to provide even further concealment. Anyone walking by would likely see nothing more than a small hill unless they took the time to look carefully around the earth goddesses' natural smokescreen. It reminded me of one of those ancient passage tombs they had throughout Ireland and Scotland. I had never seen one in person, but any history book about the fae contained plenty of photos or illustrations to identify several noticeable similarities.

"Alexei?" Nicole touched my forearm to get my attention. "Are you going to answer my question?"

"It was the middle of my sophomore year when Corbin went off the grid for a few days. At first, I thought little of it because there was a new girl he had been seeing. I'm sure you can remember what he was like before he met Bee, since it wasn't that long ago."

The general growled at the mention of his new son-in-law, though I knew he was more bark than bite where Corbin was concerned. I also knew I wasn't doing my best friend any favors by telling this story in front of his mate's father, but it was a little too late now. In my defense, it wasn't exactly a secret. Corbin tended to overshare more often than not, especially when it came to sex. And with the general's connections, he probably already knew about the incident from running a background check on Corbin or something.

The lighting was dim, but I could easily see the whites of Nicole's eyes as they rolled back. "Yep, no need to elaborate on that one. So he was holed up in this cave?"

"Literally." I smirked. "The girl he was seeing... she was an earth elemental. And she caught him screwing another girl, so she taught him a lesson. By burying his dick in the dirt. The thing was stuck in the ground like it was encased in cement for three damn days. Evidently, she lured him here with some bullshit about connecting with nature and how it fed her elemental magic, which would serve as an aphrodisiac. The moment Corbin was naked, the ground trembled, and the next thing he knew, he was being deep-throated by the dirt. The only thing he had to keep him company was the jug of water she left for him and the fear that his dick would get eaten by worms or something."

General Minifred barked in laughter. "Too bad the worms didn't succeed."

"Imbecile," Cyrus muttered. "How dumb would you have to be to find yourself in that situation?"

"Not dumb necessarily," Nicole corrected. "Exceptionally horny, which is pretty on brand for

Corbin. Which... now that I think about it, that affliction has probably resulted in a lot of human and supernatural regret over the years. *Especially* during the college years." She looked toward the general nervously. "Uh... not that I would know anything about that. Neither would Bee."

Now, the general rolled his eyes. "Damn kids are going to be the death of me one day."

The sun god sighed. "I can't believe I'm entertaining this topic, but how did the idiot get free?"

I laughed. "That's the best part. Juniper crafted a counter spell. Evidently, she and the elemental chick were friends. They went out for drinks where Alessia —that's her name—was boasting about it. Juniper showed up later that night and rescued him. She reported the incident, and Alessia got expelled. Corbin was enamored with June from that first night they met for saving his favorite appendage, although he was on a self-imposed dry spell for a while. Said he couldn't handle the thought of *anything* hugging his dick."

"Oh, Corbin," my mate giggled. "He's so freakin' lovable but such a hot mess sometimes. He really is the perfect mate for Bee."

"Yeah, those two seem to fit, don't they?" I agreed.

"Fucking hell. Somebody make it make sense," the general muttered, causing Nicole to snort.

"I'm lost as to where *you* come into this story though," Nicole mused. "You said '*the last time I was here*,' but if June rescued Corbin, that doesn't make sense."

I shrugged. "Corbin insisted on bringing me here to show me the spot where his cock almost died. I played along out of morbid curiosity, I guess." I toed a spot a few inches away from my foot. "It's filled in now, but it was right about there."

Nicole, General Minifred, Cyrus, and Cammie all took a few steps back. I couldn't exactly say I blamed them.

The fae professor cleared her throat. "As... lovely as that story was, we really should get started, don't you think?"

My hands were instantly clammy, and my heart thudded in anticipation. It wasn't like I had forgotten why we'd come here, but that little anecdote had sufficiently distracted me for a few. The thing was, I couldn't afford to be distracted right now. This was the moment I had been waiting for my entire life. My father's reign of terror was ending, and it was up to me to take my place as alpha.

Fear raced through my body, yet I could not

allow it to stop me, not with my pack counting on me.

Not with Nicole counting on me.

Cammie stepped to the side, her arms swirling in a graceful dance as she cast a spell to open the portal. She warned us we had two hours before it would close, sufficient time for the spirits to distract Alpha Jones's army, but also enough time for them to return home.

I swallowed harshly as I sensed Nicole's eyes on me.

"Are you ready?" she asked.

No, I wanted to scream out loud, but I knew I had no choice. I had to be brave and prove myself worthy of being alpha of the pack.

My gaze met hers, and taking a deep breath, I gave a confident nod. "Yes."

I closed my eyes, and I felt her warm hand on my cheek. When I opened them, Nicole's smile lit up the dark space, radiating like the morning sun and dissolving my fear. "You can do this, Alexei. You are the strongest and bravest man I know."

General Minifred straightened his shoulders. "Do not be afraid. Do not let him get inside your head. Use his ego against him. You are the rightful alpha of the Ridgeview pack. Use it to your advantage."

I took a deep breath and nodded, thinking about what Corbin said to me before he took his position outside the portal that led to the west end of campus where the shifters would soon attack.

"Don't die on me, man. Who else would I annoy the shit out of every day?"

I laughed at the accuracy of that statement.

"I promise," I said, though part of me wondered if it was a promise I could keep.

I shook my head, pushing that negative thought aside. The general was right. I *was* the rightful alpha. My father was a tyrant who needed to be put down, and I was the man for the job.

Cammie's chanting echoed throughout the chamber, the walls trembling with the force of her words. "Fifteen seconds until the portal opens. Nicole, get ready."

My mate looked up at me, her icy blue eyes blazing with anticipation. "I love you, Alexei. Come home to me."

I hesitated for the briefest moment before pressing my forehead to hers. "I promise."

"Five... four... three... two..." My heart started to race as a ripple sent a blast of air toward us as the veil between Faerie and our world opened. Nicole breathed in deeply, and a grin spread across her cheeks that sent shivers up my spine.

"Now for the fun part," she said before raising her hands up and closing her eyes in concentration.

I watched as her brown hair flew around her face, whipping at her cheeks as she summoned her power. A brilliant light radiated from her chest as it coursed through her veins and toward the portal. With a powerful pulse, a beam of pure awe-inspiring magic burst through, calling forth a storm of glowing embers that lit up the entire space. We couldn't have possibly chosen a better place to pull this off. Being underground like this was the only place on campus that I could think of where Nicole could summon the spirit pack and avoid notice.

"They're coming," she uttered breathlessly, her voice quivering.

In the next moment, brilliant auras of moonlight flooded the confined space, illuminating the glowing silhouettes of the wolf spirits as they surged through the portal toward my mate. Tears stung my eyes as I beheld their magnificent splendor, and my chest filled with anticipation as my wolf roared in triumph at the sight of his dynasty. The power of their family, of their pack, crashed down upon me and consumed me in a wave of raw energy and primal emotion.

I stepped closer to my mate, taking her hand. The walls glowed, tinting the atmosphere with an eerie blue light that sent chills down my spine. I watched in awe as one ghostly wolf after another flew through the air, howling with excitement.

"They're so beautiful," Nicole whispered in reverence.

"They know you," I replied as they swirled around our heads in a flurry of glimmering bluish-white.

One spirit approached my mate, its partially transparent body hovering in the air. "I'm with you, sister," an ethereal voice boomed. "We are *all* with you."

Nicole gasped, her eyes widening as she sucked in a breath. "Did I just imagine that?"

I looked around in question, seeing matching expressions of disbelief. Nope, that definitely just happened.

A single tear trickled down Nicole's cheek as she gave the spirit an acknowledging nod. "Thank you."

I felt a deep sense of love and respect for her at that moment. *I* may have been uncertain of what Nicole was capable of, yet she seemed to suffer no such fate. This was a woman confident in her abilities, a fucking goddess in action. I couldn't have possibly been any prouder.

Slowly, Nicole exhaled, and the spirits took action. They circled around her once more and then moved with speed and purpose toward the narrow passageway that led to the open forest.

Nicole clung to me, trembling from the exertion of summoning such powerful apparitions. She looked up at me with a tired yet content smile, her voice barely a whisper as she said, "They feel like home, Alexei."

Cyrus stepped forward, his own eyes glistening with pride. His voice was gentle yet determined as he asked, "Are you ready to find Alpha Jones?"

A swell of fear blossomed in my chest as the mention of finding my father stirred up tussling emotions within me. I took a breath and nodded, steadying Nicole as we both braced ourselves for the fight to come.

My mate's expression hardened with determination. "Yes," she snarled, her voice deep and reverberating like the echoes of a great wolf spirit.

Cyrus stepped toward us and took Nicole's hands in his. "Let's do this."

Nicole closed her eyes, her forehead creasing in concentration.

"Remember," Cyrus urged. "You must direct your focus calmly and completely. Visualize Alpha Jones in your mind, connect to him through the tether of his soul."

Nicole nodded, and we all stared in wonder as a

bright white light began to emanate from her body, illuminating the vast cave even more. Her radiance pulsed with energy, and my wolf inside me answered with a howl. I had known some pretty powerful beings over the years, but I had never seen anything like the magic Nicole was wielding tonight. I was humbled and honored to be at her side.

Though I was afraid, I was also ready to confront the demons of my past and move on with my life. With *our* life. A secure future with my mate was the ultimate motivation.

Nicole's face twisted up in disgust. "I'm connected with him. He feels so... angry."

"Hold on to that tether," Cyrus insisted. "Do you recognize the area? Can you get a lock on his location?"

Nicole shook her head and sunk into a deeper state of concentration. After a few moments, the light gradually dimmed and my mate exhaled deeply before opening her eyes, her voice softened by the enormity of the moment. "I got him. I know where he is. I know where Alexei needs to attack."

I looked directly into her eyes. "Then it's time for him to die."

THIRTY-ONE

Alexei

MY WOLF RACED through the woods, propelled by a burning rage that had been locked away for far too long. The spirits' howls echoed in my ears; I could feel their power growing with every step, fueled by their connection to my mate. My fur bristled with electric energy as the ground seemed to pulse with anticipation the closer I got. I leapt over fallen branches and dodged the snarling ghosts as we headed toward the quad, where Nicole had seen my father, barking orders at his henchmen. I was invigorated, ready to launch myself into battle with strength and agility that only a true alpha could possess.

Right before I reached the end of the forest, my claws dug into the dirt as I came to a grinding halt. The wolf spirits continued their trek, and within seconds, distant shouting and growling rang through the air as they reached their destination. My ears perked up at the sounds of chaos rippling across campus, but my true focus was trained on the blonde curled into a fetal position against the base of a large evergreen. The layer of reflective cells behind my canine retinas allowed me to see the mottled marks all over her exposed limbs, even though the moon hardly shone through the canopy of trees in this part of the forest. She was black and blue, baring the evidence on her skin of recent repeated blows. The pungent smell of blood trickling from various wounds tickled my nose as I crept closer, taking care not to spook her. Dried leaves clung to her tangled hair as she noticed me.

"A... Alexei?" she croaked, lifting her chin slightly. "Is... is that you? You can't be here. He'll kill you."

I chuffed, nudging her gently with my snout.

"I'm so sorry," she whimpered, her voice shaking. "I'm so sorry for hurting you." Mara struggled to get up, but the obvious pain she felt made her quickly rethink that decision. Both of her eyes were so swollen she could barely open them. "You have to leave, Alexei. He's gone mad. This is what he did to me. He doesn't even care about his heir anymore. All he cares about is power. Your father is an evil man."

I nudged her again, pressing my face into the crook of her neck as I let out a low, guttural growl. I didn't like or trust this woman one bit, but I could hear the truth in her words. And the fact of the matter was Mara Sullivan was pregnant with my little brother or sister. I vowed not to let an innocent child suffer my father's wrath, and I meant it. I rubbed my furry cheek against the slight bump on her torso. She was warmer to the touch than normal, a sure sign a baby was growing inside of her. At least for now. Who knew what internal damage my father had done to Mara's body? Her exterior was pretty banged up.

Screams and roars and a cacophony of other-worldly noises reminded me I needed to get a move on. I lifted my snout, looking Mara right in the eye, trying to convey the message that I'd come back to check on her.

"It's okay," she whispered, nodding once in understanding as she rubbed an open palm over her belly. "Go."

I turned back and took off running again. The pads of my paws pressed into the thick undergrowth as I reached the tree line, moving with caution to avoid notice. I picked up my pace when the sounds of fighting drew closer, taking care to stay out of sight before jumping out of the shadows and fearlessly hurtling my body into the fray. My jaws locked onto one of my father's enforcers, sinking my teeth deep into the flesh of his throat. He cried out in pain, clawing at my face to get me to stop, but I wasn't having it. I snapped his carotid, vindication thrumming through my soul, knowing these moments were his last. From Nicole's description of the night her father was kidnapped, I was pretty sure this was one of the guys directly involved. I tossed the meathead aside like a rag doll, spitting out a mouthful of his putrid blood as I leapt toward my next target.

The second man was a little smarter than the first. He knew to keep his distance as he swung a knife at my head, but I was in top form. I could smell his fear in the air, like sour sweat in the sweltering heat. Why wasn't he shifting? Wolf shifters were stronger in their animal forms. More agile. The decision to shift when attacked was as natural as breathing, but as I briefly glanced around, I could see that easily half of my father's known loyalists were fur-free and no match for my new army. What the hell was going on?

"Get back!" the guy yelled, wildly swinging the blade toward me.

I dodged to the left, growling as he attempted to stab me again. He screamed as my fangs latched onto his forearm, clamping down until they met bone, forcing him to drop his weapon. He swung his free arm at me, delivering a solid blow to my temple, successfully dislodging my fangs from his forearm. I shook off the ringing in my ears and snarled. The man's eyes widened in fear as my hind legs kicked off the ground, propelling me forward. My huge paws slammed into his shoulders, shoving him backwards. I wasted no time finishing him off, ripping his throat out as he collapsed to the ground. Blood gurgled from his demolished larynx as life drained from his eyes. I howled as his jaw fell slack and he took his final breath.

Out of the corner of my eye, I spotted Cristian and his team of vampires fighting hard against a group of wolves. It seemed as if everyone had converged in this one area, which was surprising considering Redwood had such a sizable campus. Blood dripped off the vamps' sharp fangs as they attacked with a savage fury. Corbin was up ahead, yipping excitedly as he faced down two wolves, his brown fur doused in red as he severed their arteries. My beta was quick on his feet, dodging and weaving in a way I'd never seen before, delivering a final blow that took both wolves out at once. I supposed now that he was a mated man, he had much more at stake.

I marveled at the fact that this group of unlikely allies stuck together under such dire circumstances, persevering despite our disadvantage in numbers. Satisfied they didn't need my assistance, I wove through the battle with a single target in mind. It didn't take long to find him right where Nicole said he'd be. I wasn't surprised to see him positioned on a newly erected dais in the middle of the quad, sitting on a literal throne as he watched the pack battle for their lives while his enforcers forged a shield around him. They were the biggest wolves in the pack behind me and my father, a wall of raised hackles and snapping jaws that could crush bones with little effort. But the menacing wolves were of no concern to me. My father may have been unstable, but his ego made him predictable at times like these. My vision became clouded by rage as I charged toward him, ready to finally show him my true strength. When he spotted me among the pandemonium, his face twisted with fury.

"You!" he yelled, gesturing toward the menacing horde of spirits surrounding him, their eyes burning red with rage. "You're responsible for this?! How did a pathetic pup like you manage to pull this off?"

My heart pounded against my chest as his insult

triggered a barrage of memories from my childhood. Hundreds of beatings I'd endured throughout my life at his hand, never able to fight back. Countless doubts racing through my mind as I suffered his abuse year after year after year. This man made me question my strength. My goddamn sanity. But now I saw his abuse for what it was with startling clarity. My father had beaten me down—his only heir—because he was threatened. He knew I would grow into a formidable alpha. He knew one day I would be capable of overpowering him and forcibly taking his place as leader of this pack. Jones Koenig was *afraid* of me.

Well, now it was time to give him something to really fear.

I bared my teeth, growling in warning.

My father's eyes narrowed as he pushed through his wall of muscle. "Well, look at you. Finally growing a set of balls, I see." His guards, wisely sensing the threat at hand, began to move toward me as one until my father said, "Stand down. I've been waiting for this moment for a long time. Alexei is *mine*."

The wolves lowered their heads in submission, whimpering as they heeded his command and scampered away with their tails tucked between their legs. A crowd of shifters gathered around us, in their human and wolf forms, but I was confident they wouldn't interfere. They knew what was happening here, even before the words were spoken. Every shifter, even the shadiest motherfuckers I'd ever met, lived by an infrangible code that if a challenge was issued against the current alpha, you must stand by and let it play out. Whoever the victor was, would immediately become the pack's alpha. The only way to overturn that, was by issuing a challenge of your own and winning the battle. Shifter law always had and always would operate on a *survival of the fittest* mentality. No pack wanted a frail leader, because a weak alpha would put them all at risk.

My paws moved forward without thought, striding confidently toward my father. The wolf spirits howled with approval and moved closer around us as I marched toward him until I was mere inches away.

The sudden silence that followed felt strange and heavy—like time itself held its breath for that moment, waiting for me to make a move. Looking into my father's cruel gaze, I waited for him to speak. I knew he had some long-winded diatribe begging to be set free.

"You were always unworthy of being my heir,"

my father spat, anger bleeding through his tone. It was something he'd said to me many times.

My claws dug into the grass beneath me as I braced myself to make my move.

"Worthless," he hissed with venom in his voice. "Just like your mother. You know, the traitorous bitch who will regret the day she ever met me once I get my hands on her?"

I growled again, salivating at the thought of ripping into him with my teeth.

He laughed. "So, this is it, huh? Are you formally challenging me, boy? Are you ready to *die* for your pathetic cause?"

My ears were pinned back as I snarled in confirmation.

He stepped out of his Italian loafers, removing his slacks as if he didn't have a care in the world. He even took the time to fold the woolen pants and carefully place them on his throne. I recognized his lackadaisical attitude for the slight it was, but I allowed him to think he had the advantage.

"You know what? I *accept* your challenge, you worthless mutt. And I'm going to *really* enjoy destroying your mate after I'm done destroying you." His mouth curved into a vicious smirk. "But I think I'll enjoy her fit little body a bit first. I bet her screams are absolutely delicious." He made a show of licking his lips and grabbing his brief-covered crotch suggestively. "I can't wait to see how she takes a real man's dick. Nicole will be begging for death by the time I'm done bloodying every one of her tight little holes."

I knew he was goading me, but it didn't stop the horrific images from forming in my head the moment he uttered my mate's name. My base instincts were in control now. My wolf was prepared to protect his mate at all costs and claim his alpha status once and for all.

I lunged as he shifted, a giant black wolf tearing through the remainder of his clothing as it broke free. A feral howl ripped from my mouth and echoed across the quad as I leapt at him, my long claws ready to tear into his flesh and claim my vengeance.

My father's eyes momentarily widened in fear, but it was quickly replaced by the same rage that made my blood boil with a fury unlike anything I'd ever known. The fur on my back bristled as our teeth gnashed against each other, and our claws ripped through the air, trying to gain purchase. His eyes were wild with desperation as he realized I wasn't going to back down this time. The spirits barked excitedly, calling out in encouragement as they watched the battle.

A sharp pain exploded through my paw as I

slashed at my father and missed, but I didn't dare stop to check the damage. My lips pulled back as my teeth connected with his shoulder, tearing into the meat of his flesh, but he didn't seem to notice. He launched himself over the top of me, landing on my back and sinking his teeth into my shoulder. The pain was excruciating, like a thousand needles being shoved beneath my skin at once. The spirits bellowed a mournful howl when I yelped. I swiped a paw at my father, this time connecting with one of his haunches. His razor-sharp claws dug into my left side, shredding my skin as I stumbled forward, stunned. I whimpered as my body struggled to heal itself, but the damage wasn't severe enough to stop me. I shook off the pain and snapped at the air, still intent on my father's throat.

I felt a surge of satisfaction and power as we tumbled to the ground, rolling across the grass as we grappled for the upper hand. The spirits zipped through the air, their ghostly bodies stirring the chaos as we broke apart and engaged in a stare down. The apparitions began furiously barking, seemingly trying to warn me about something, but I couldn't afford to take my eyes off my father long enough to see what they were fussing about. My father growled, his body tensing as he prepared to pounce on me. I growled right back, digging my claws into the ground to steady myself. A blur of movement passed through my periphery as I launched into action, grunting as a sharp pain pierced my side. I looked down in confusion, spotting something sticking out of my fur. Was that... *a dart?* I didn't have time to figure it out, because in the next moment, I was forced to change back into my human form. I screamed in agony as my bones ground together, haphazardly trying to find their rightful place. I writhed as my body transformed, trying to figure out what was happening to me. This wasn't my will. This was...

No.

I reached down, plucking the sharp object out of my skin. I held it in front of me with shaky hands, inspecting the empty chamber between the needle and the stabilizer. This wasn't an ordinary dart. It was a fucking tranquilizing dart. Or, more accurately, *a serum-injecting dart.*

I was so stunned by the overwhelming void inside of me that I wasn't prepared for what happened next.

My father's teeth closed around my neck, his sharp bite piercing my flesh.

The pain was blinding, and for a moment, I was a pup at the mercy of his abuser. A child beaten within an inch of his life. A bleeding, innocent son who just wanted his father to fucking love him for once in his goddamn life.

I whimpered in agony as he tightened his grip, the blood loss making me dizzy and weak. I fell limp, screaming inside my head but utterly paralyzed as my body fell victim to this fight. I tried to telepathically communicate with Nicole, but the serum made it impossible. I mentally apologized to my mate for failing her, telling her how much I loved her one last time, hoping that somehow, she would get the message.

I reached for our mate bond, desperately wanting to feel her comforting embrace. I thought of her smile, her tender touch, her heart that beat only for me. I thought of every regret I'd ever had and the life I wanted so badly to share with her. I braced myself for my father's final blow, waiting for the darkness that would follow.

But much to my surprise... that moment never came.

Instead, a soothing warmth radiated around me. My father jumped back as if he had been shocked with a cattle prod, whimpering as infallible love flooded through me like a river of energy. With each second that passed, I became stronger. I rose from the ground as my broken skin slowly started knitting itself back together. I was sure we were a ridiculous sight to behold. Me, naked as the day I was born, towering over a large wolf, my muscles bunched with fury and anticipation. And despite the serum flowing through my veins from my father's clearly premeditated and cowardly attack, my inner wolf had returned, ready to finish this.

I smiled as I figured out what had just happened. My mate had come to my aid, restoring my wolf and lending me her power in my moment of need. With that one action, she proved to me without a doubt that as long as we worked together, nothing could stand in our way. Not even the sadistic son of a bitch before me.

I reveled in my father's obvious shock as I called upon my wolf with newly found confidence, the power of my mate bond flowing through me like a surge of electricity as I shifted. Blood still leaked from various wounds. Every bone in my body ached. But I was determined to show the pack who their real alpha was. I summoned every ounce of strength I could muster as I charged my father, going straight for his throat with my teeth, determined to end this now. It all happened so fast he never stood a chance. I shook his body with my powerful jaws and felt the tough cartilage give way until his neck snapped with a loud crack. Jones Koenig's last breath, an anguished gasp, echoed throughout the quad. His furry black body slumped to the ground, all signs of life quickly fading from his eyes.

The deathly quiet that followed seemed like an eternity. Dozens of pairs of eyes stared at the scene before them. I stepped back, the fear and anger replaced with a sense of relief. It was finally over. My father could no longer control me. I was the alpha of this pack now.

In perfect synchrony, the spirit pack ran off toward the forest, and every shifter surrounding us lowered their heads in submission, recognizing their new leader. I didn't know if it was Nicole's power or my seriously enhanced alpha energy, or maybe a combination of both, but there was no denying I was the strongest shifter present. My chest expanded as I looked my pack over, breathing through the buzz caused by the wild current running through my veins. It was disorienting and a bit dizzying, if I was being honest, but it also felt... right. As if this was how it was meant to be all along.

"Alexei!" Nicole screamed.

I whipped around as I heard her voice, finding her speeding toward me, her uncle, Cammie, and General Minifred right behind her. As much as the general wanted to be involved in the attack against my father, we all agreed it wasn't a smart move. With his alpha energy, if a pack member spotted him in battle, they could have potentially assumed he was challenging my father. It was important there was zero confusion in the matter, so he reluctantly stayed back in the cave.

I instantly shifted into my human form, so by the time Nicole reached me, I was able to pull my mate into my arms where she belonged.

"I thought I was going to lose you," she sobbed into my chest. "I've never been more scared of anything in my life."

I pulled back just enough to look into her crystal blue eyes. "How did you know I was in trouble?"

"Fáel," she explained. "The spirits told me you were in danger. Then, I did the whole astral projection thingy and saw you on the ground with your father on top of you, and... I don't know. I'm not sure how I did it, really. I just knew you needed my help and I had to give it to you somehow."

"It's as if you haven't listened to a single word I've said," Cyrus huffed. "The power is *within* you. All you need to do to call upon it is focus on your intention. Kids, I swear."

Nicole side-eyed her uncle. "Do ya think we might save the verbal lashing for later?"

The sun god smirked, holding his palms up. "Of course."

I knew our audience was curious; their intrigue

was nearly tangible. The last they'd heard, I had mated a human. But now that Nicole had reached magical maturity, it was obvious that wasn't entirely accurate. Plus, Cyrus wasn't exactly subtle. The dude oozed otherworldly beauty and power. But as gods and goddesses didn't give off the same vibes as any other supe, the crowd's confusion was understandable. I intended on keeping Nicole's true heritage a secret from the general public to keep her off any collectors' radar, but as my luna, our pack deserved to know how special she was and how very lucky we were to have her. But that revelation would have to wait until I ensured their loyalty.

I pressed my forehead against my mate's, breathing in her sweet lilac scent. "You're magnificent, Nicole. I love you so fucking much."

"I love you." She sighed.

A scuffle toward the right drew our attention. When Nicole and I pulled apart, Corbin and Cristian were pushing their way through the crowd. When they made it to the front, my beta tossed a velvet bag onto the ground.

"What's that?" I asked.

"A bunch of darts filled with what I'm guessing is the serum. We caught Jorah Kline up in a tree with this bag and a blowgun. Dude might as well have painted his hands red."

Jorah Kline was my father's beta. It made sense he'd be appointed to take action if my father was in danger of losing.

"Where is he?"

Cristian smiled, flashing his bloody fangs. "I got hungry. Probably took it a little too far." He buffed his nails on his collared shirt. His *suspiciously clean and perfectly pressed* collared shirt. Did the guy bring a change of clothes or something? "Oops."

I rolled my eyes and Nicole chuckled as Corbin high-fived the vampire. I supposed that meant my father's beta was no longer a problem. I certainly couldn't say I was torn up about it, seeing as the slimy bastard had tried to kill me and all.

General Minifred cleared his throat. "Alexei, congratulations. I'm proud of you, son."

I stepped forward to shake the hand he was offering. "Thank you, sir."

"Son?!" Corbin balked. "Uh... General Daddy, I think you may be a little confused. If anyone around here deserves the honor of being your son, it ain't Alexei." My idiot best friend winced as I glared. "No offense, dude."

The general folded his thickly muscled arms over his chest. "You wanna rephrase that statement, boy, before I surgically implant my foot up your ass?"

"Uh…" Corbin paled. "What I meant to say was… *please-love-me-you're-the-best-daddy-ever-and-if-you-kill-me-your-daughter-will-be-very-very-sad-so-you-probably-shouldn't-do-that-mmkay-thanks-bye.*"

I pinched the bridge of my nose, muttering, "Jesus. Is he for real right now?"

Nicole patted my chest. "Do you really need an answer to that?"

No, I really didn't. But despite his occasional theatrics, Corbin Sullivan was the most loyal and capable beta I knew. With him and Nicole by my side, I knew the future of our pack was secure. The coming months wouldn't be easy. Not everyone would like the changes I planned on implementing. But I was certain we were the perfect team for the job.

THIRTY-TWO

Nicole

GAZING OUT AT THE PACK, I noticed how frail and exhausted they all seemed. They had deep dark circles under their eyes, as if they had been awake for days, and their skin had a sickly pallor to it.

"Everyone, up on your feet. If anyone has questions, now is the time to ask." Alexei puffed out his chest and lifted his chin. "If anyone here is loyal to my father and wants to challenge me, step forward."

The pack slowly lifted themselves from their kneeling positions.

One man with a damaged leg pulled himself forward, dragging his foot along the ground. "I have no intention of doing the latter. But you should know, over half of us couldn't issue a formal challenge anyway."

Alexei's brow furrowed in confusion. "Why not?"

Another man with dark black hair and empty, soulless eyes spoke up. "Your father tested his new serum on us. Tried making an antidote and failed." He looked at the ground and spat. "We're practically human. Don't even know if we belong to a pack anymore. Don't even know if we *want* to. I've served your father for twenty years, and this is how he repays me? I'm wolfless. Beaten down. I don't know if I want to trust another alpha, especially not one with his DNA."

Why would Alpha Jones test his weapon on his own people?

"I am *not* my father," Alexei growled, gesturing to the fallen wolf at his feet. "Think about it, Liam. Do you really believe I would've challenged him had I agreed with his agenda?"

"H-how do we know you won't hurt us like he did?" a woman with dull brown-blonde hair asked in a nervous stutter.

Alexei released a staggering sigh. "I guarantee the pack's protection would be a high priority for me as your alpha, at all times. I would *never* take your wolves. I have been a part of this pack my entire life, and I have every intention of leading it. But I will *not* force you to follow me. I will not make any attempt to stop someone from walking away."

A few of the shifters gasped. Some scoffed. I supposed they weren't used to an alpha that genuinely wanted to take care of his people.

"Yeah, right," the dark-haired man who spoke earlier said. "You expect us to believe that you'd just let us leave without any consequences?"

I grabbed Alexei's hand, offering him support. "Alexei is not cruel or unfair. He worked hard to protect you all."

"He renounced his rights to this pack!" a woman in the back shouted. "He left us to deal with his father!"

"I renounced my alpha rights as my father's heir. I *always* planned on challenging him for the position. I just needed a little time away to prepare for that. I know you're wary, and I get it. As a gesture of good faith, I will help you restore your missing wolves. And if you still choose to leave this pack afterward, so be it. But if you choose to stay, then I will offer you my protection."

"How can you restore our missing wolves?" Liam asked.

"As you know, my mate's father is a brilliant

scientist. He has successfully created an antidote to my father's serum. I will happily give it to you—"

"In exchange for what?" Liam snapped.

"I give you the cure with no pretenses. I am not like my father. I am not like the cruel alpha who tortured you and abused his position of power. I came here to *help* you. I came to end his tyranny."

"I don't believe you, boy," Liam growled angrily. His face twitched, and his whole body shook with anger. "I don't believe that my wolf can be restored. I don't believe that you could be as benevolent as you claim. I know your type. You're no different than him."

"I am *not* the man that raised me. I want to help—"

Liam lunged forward, his fist flying toward Alexei's jaw, causing me to jump back. My mate easily caught the man's fist, looking almost bored as he twisted Liam's arm behind his back. Everyone gasped as Alexei pinned the other shifter to the ground, his foot on Liam's back.

"I could kill you right now if I wanted to," Alexei hissed. "But I'm here to help. Someone bring me the serum."

"On it!" Juniper called out. "Be back in a few."

She disappeared through her witchy portal, then popped back into existence a few seconds later, right next to us, holding up a vial of blue liquid. She winked as she handed it to me.

Liam struggled to get out from underneath Alexei's foot, but Alexei tightened his grip.

Alexei looked at me over his shoulder. "Nicole? Care to assist?"

"What's this?" Liam snarled. "A trick? How do I know you're not about to kill me?"

He sounded so lost. So helpless. I couldn't help but pity him. I also couldn't help but feel pity for every other shifter that stood around us, wondering what to do next.

I shoved the antidote in Liam's face, holding it to his lips. "I don't care if you take it or not, but Alexei has always had your best interest at heart. He was willing to choose this pack over everything. You have the freedom to decide what you want to do."

Liam raised his head and looked at Alexei, who was still holding him down. His eyes darted to the vial, then back up to Alexei. "Is this really the cure?"

Alexei nodded. "Drink it and see for yourself."

Liam hesitantly opened his mouth, allowing me to tip the contents onto his tongue. Alexei removed his foot as the man cautiously drank the disgusting liquid. Immediately he contorted in pain, his body shaking as if trying to reject it. The crowd watched in horror, but soon Liam's tremors eased and he began to calm. Slowly but surely, his face softened and he sat up, then moved into a standing position.

The surrounding shifters looked on in disbelief as Liam shifted into a magnificent gray wolf before our eyes. He shook himself off and ran through the crowd before heading off into the woods with a joyous howl.

The other shifters were visibly awed by what they'd just witnessed.

"You see," Alexei said, finally breaking the silence that had befallen them all. "I will give you the cure. You can choose if you want to be a member of our pack, but we will have rules—"

"What *kind* of rules?" a woman asked, her voice soft and tender.

Alexei took my hand. "We will no longer be segregated from the rest of the supernatural factions. As alpha, I will reward ranks to those loyal to the pack—loyal to making this place a better home for all of us. We will not fight amongst ourselves unless threatened. We will band together and work as a team."

"What will happen to those that disobey you?" the same lady asked.

"I am not afraid to mete out a punishment to fit the crime if need be, but I do not want anyone else to needlessly die. Ideally, we'll never get to that point. It's all up to you."

"How do we know you'll keep your word?" someone else asked.

"You don't," Alexei said. "But I swear on my life that I will not be like my father. I'll earn your loyalty and respect every damn day."

The pack sat in silence, staring at each other, each of them thinking over Alexei's words.

"I want my wolf back. It feels... wrong... not having it," a man finally said, bowing his head. "I'll follow you, Alpha Alexei."

One by one, the other shifters began to lower their heads again, and Alexei smiled.

"I'm so proud of you," I whispered, squeezing his hand.

"I couldn't have done it without you," he said, kissing my forehead. "I'm proud of you, too."

He turned to face the pack and raised our joined hands. "I'd like to formally introduce you to my mate, Nicole. Our new luna. I wouldn't be standing here before you without her help."

I watched as the shifters looked at me with a newfound respect and obvious curiosity. But they held their questions at bay, choosing to have faith in their new alpha. I had never been prouder than I was at that moment.

"We have a lot of work to do," Alexei announced. "But I think we can do it together."

I couldn't agree more.

"Almost all the shifters have been cured," Corbin said before plopping down in a seat.

We were exhausted. I'd spent all day in the Literature Auditorium. We'd set up a resource center in the Fine Arts building and had been busy all day handing out supplies.

The first round of shifters was easy enough—those that were willing to get the cure—but the second and third rounds were a little more difficult. They were hesitant, and some even left the pack, but Alexei was determined to give them the freedom his father had denied everyone.

"They're all cured? No issues?" I asked.

"A couple had broken bones that needed to be set before they could take the cure. Your father and Cammie are working with them," Corbin replied. "The others are still a bit unsettled, but I think they just need a few days for this to sink in, and they'll be back to normal. Some of them went weeks without their wolves and have a lot of traumas to deal with."

"Well, I'm glad we were able to help them," I said.

I knew it was hard for Alexei to see all of his old pack mates suffering. It was a lot for me to take in, too, but we'd been through so many ups and downs that I knew we would survive it.

"Where is Alexei?" I asked.

He'd left with a group of men a couple of hours ago, but I didn't have time to check on him.

Corbin sighed. "He's cleaning up some of the wreckage on campus. Should be back soon. He'd want you to rest, Nicole."

I looked down at my hands and sighed. "I need to call June to portal in one more shipment of food."

Bee and I had spent most of the day getting food for the pack. Since Alpha Jones cut them off from the rest of the world, their supplies were running low. Everyone was starving.

Corbin got up and placed a hand on my shoulder. "I can do that. You and Bee need to rest." He nodded at his mate, who had just handed a carton of supplies to a crying shifter woman before walking toward us.

Bee was just as eager to help as I was, but we were both exhausted. We had a lot to learn about pack life, though, and I believed this was an important step in making that happen.

"I'll be back," Corbin said before leaving to search for June.

I leaned back in my chair and sighed. "It's going to be crazy here now, Bee. Are you sure you want to stay? You don't have to, you know. Alexei loves Corbin, but he'd be okay if the two of you decided this wasn't the life you envisioned. You're human—"

"Nicole, I know Alexei would understand, but I *do* want to stay," Bee interrupted. "I mean, I've seen what the shifters can do, and I know it's dangerous. I was raised by an alpha, remember? But I love Corbin and I love you. You're my best friend, and I want to be a member of this pack. I've been wanting to talk to you about helping me become a *real* member of this pack."

My eyes widened in surprise. "You want to become a shifter?"

Bee nodded. "Yes, if that's okay with you and Alexei. And... if, you know, the mother wolf is cool with it."

My jaw dropped. I was speechless. She wanted to become a shifter? It was hard enough to adjust to the wolf pack, but this would be even harder.

"Bee, are you sure?" I didn't want her to make any rash decisions. "It would be a *huge* change."

"I know," she said, her voice soft and determined. "But I think it's something I need to do—for Corbin and for myself. I want us to be tethered. I want to live my life fully with him. I love him, Nicole. He's the best thing that ever happened to me."

I nodded with understanding. Bee had been through so much in the past few weeks that she deserved a long life with her mate, and if being a part of the wolf pack gave her that, then I was all for it.

"Okay," I said finally. "If you really want to become a shifter, then I'll do it."

She sat up and grinned. "Really?"

"Bee, I would do anything for you. If I have this ability, then of course I'll do it. I just want you to be happy."

Just then, the door swung open and Alexei stepped in. He was exhausted, his face smudged with soot, but he immediately stood up straight when he saw me.

"Nicole," he said, crossing the room to pull me into a hug. "You've been working all day. You should rest." He pulled back to look at me and Bee, his expression softening as he eyed us both. "What's going on?"

I quickly filled him in on our conversation, and he listened intently before nodding slowly.

"I understand," he said finally. "If it's what Bee wants, then we'll make it happen." He smiled warmly and placed a reassuring hand on Bee's shoulder. "I would be proud to have you in our pack, Bee. Corbin will be thrilled."

Bee beamed at him gratefully.

"Thank you, Alexei," I said softly.

"Come, let's take a break," he suggested.

He grabbed my hand and led the way down the hall, eventually stopping at a storage room. He opened the door and pulled me in before locking it behind us.

The musty scent of old books filled my nose as I looked around the dimly lit room. All of a sudden, Alexei's lips were on mine, his powerful arms holding me tight as we kissed more passionately. My heart pounded as he drew me close to him, and I was lost in the moment as our embrace went on until eventually we parted, both of us breathless.

He smiled before leaning in to press our foreheads together. "I love you, Nicole. But you've gotta stop distracting me. I watched you helping those people today, and I was so fucking proud.

Completely awed by how effortless assuming this new role seems for you. You're the perfect luna."

"Thank you." I smiled back, overwhelmed by his words and the emotion in them. "But how is that a distraction?"

"Because..." He slowly started to kiss my neck, gently grazing my skin with his teeth as he pulled me closer. "I couldn't stop thinking about throwing you over my shoulder, dragging you away, and rewarding you for being such an excellent luna."

"Oh," I panted. "Sorry, not sorry?"

A deep chuckle reverberated in his chest as he pressed closer, slipping his hands beneath my shirt, exploring my curves before pulling the shirt over my head. Alexei continued to strip away my clothes until I was standing there completely naked in front of him. His gaze swept over every part of my body before he leaned in for another kiss. His tongue and lips moved expertly over mine as we shared sensual kisses that soon grew rougher and more animalistic with each passing moment.

"All day I thought about your pretty pussy squeezing around my cock. How I wanted to thank you for being such a good mate."

My heart raced in my chest as we clung to each other.

Alexei's hands roamed over every inch of me

before finally finding their way between my legs. He slid a finger inside me, and I let out a husky groan. My mate's experienced hand moved and caressed my intimate parts as his lips ravished mine, his other hand grasping my breasts and pinching my nipples with masterful skill. He thrust his finger harder and faster in his desire to bring me to ecstatic bliss.

I wrapped my arms around his neck, pulling him closer as my release built up inside of me.

"Mine," Alexei whispered against my lips as he moved his fingers faster. Suddenly he stopped and stepped back, a look of awe on his face as he admired my body. "God, you are the sexiest fucking woman I've ever seen."

He dropped to his knees and slowly licked my inner thighs. He leaned in to whisper against my pussy, his voice deep and commanding as he told me to wrap my legs around his neck. I followed his directions and soon his tongue penetrated me, circling before he pressed his face into the apex of my thighs. The sensation of his mouth against my delicate skin caused waves of delight to ripple through my body, and I whimpered audibly as Alexei ate me.

He worked his lips and tongue in sync, his teeth lightly grazing my skin as I shuddered, feeling the pleasure wash over me. I clung tighter to him with my legs as a second wave began to swell within seconds.

Alexei looked up at me with a wicked smile on his face as he watched me squirm under the intensity of his touch. With one last flick of his tongue against my sensitive clit, my body shook as I was engulfed in one of the most intense orgasms I had ever experienced. I curved my spine and moaned as he kept licking me until I was filled with blissful delight.

I gasped for air as my orgasm subsided, and I watched Alexei stand up again. He wiped his mouth on his sleeve and pulled me closer to him.

"You're so sexy when you come," he growled in my ear. "I can't wait to feel you do that on my cock."

I swallowed hard at the thought of him inside of me. He leaned in to kiss me, his heady scent filling my nose. He pulled away and slowly removed his clothes.

My gaze moved hungrily over his muscular frame. His chest was wide and his hips were narrow, and his ripped abs drew my eye. His biceps seemed like steel, and his thighs were powerful, prompting me to take a step closer. We ended up close enough that our skin touched, the connection sending heat through me with every movement he made, leaving me weak in the knees.

Alexei leaned in to kiss me once more before lifting me up in his arms. I wrapped my legs around his hips, and he teased me with his cock.

"I'm going to fuck you hard, Nicole," he whispered. "I'm going to claim you in every way possible."

"Yes, please."

His hand slid down my back, resting on my ass and hitching me higher. I gasped as the head of his cock pressed firmly against my opening. I was on the brink of begging him to fuck me as Alexei slowly teased me with his cock, running the head up and down the slits of my pussy. I sighed in relief as he finally pressed forward, slowly burying himself inside me.

My mouth dropped open as his cock filled me to the brim. Needing to move, I rocked my hips against him, urging him on.

"Fuck, Nicole," Alexei groaned as I increased the pace of my movements until I was bouncing against him in a frenzied rhythm, racing closer to the edge.

I moaned as every inch of me was consumed by his stiff, throbbing dick. He gripped my ass firmly with his hands as he took control, his cock sliding in and out of me with a deep, determined energy.

I leaned in to kiss him, and our bodies began to move together in perfect rhythm, our moans growing louder as the pleasure built up inside of us.

"Damn, Nicole, you're so tight." Alexei squeezed my flesh as he increased the pace. "I could live inside this pussy."

The euphoria was almost too much. Every nerve ending in my body was tingling, my climax on the brink of explosion.

Alexei growled in my ear as I started to spasm around him, "That's it, baby. Come all over my cock."

With that, my entire body was overtaken by ecstasy that left me shaking. I groaned as my release finally came and my pussy clenched around him.

"Oh, fuck, Nicole," he bit out through clenched teeth as my walls contracted around his cock.

Alexei slowly set me down on the ground, bending his knees so he was still buried deep inside of me. I was panting and exhausted from my orgasm, but Alexei was determined to take me over the edge again. He kissed me fiercely, his tongue penetrating my mouth as he started thrusting into me. His moans became deeper and louder with each passing moment, signaling that he was close to his own release.

We continued to kiss as our bodies finally

released their pent up passion, our orgasms washing over us simultaneously. Alexei groaned as he filled me with his cum, his body shaking against mine.

"Fuck," he murmured into my mouth before he collapsed against me, and we both sunk down to the ground.

The moonlight shining in through the window cast a glow over his body, and I couldn't help but stare at his muscled, sweaty torso as he slid out of me. He turned to look at me, a soft smile on his lips as we both slowly caught our breath.

"You're the perfect mate," he whispered softly. "Promise me you'll always stay by my side?"

"Always," I whispered back.

His dark eyes glowed in the moonlight as he smiled. "For better or worse, the rest of our lives."

I nodded, never feeling more sure about anything than I did at that moment. "For better or worse, the rest of our lives."

EPILOGUE

5 YEARS LATER

Nicole

THE FULL MOON was shining overhead, casting a beam of light on the thriving couple, who were glowing with happiness. A soft breeze was blowing, carrying the sweet scent of pine and jasmine through the summer air. Anyone lucky enough to know these two could see how perfect they were for each other. Their destiny was written in the stars, but it certainly wasn't an easy journey. They each had to overcome decades of trauma and loneliness to reach this monumental point in their lives. It was a colossal point in *all* of our lives, really.

And I was deeply honored to be a part of it.

"As you all know, this isn't your typical mating ceremony."

I looked around the small audience, smiling as my loved ones' gazes met mine. First, there was my father and Cammie, who'd been committed to each other for quite some time, but they never mentioned marriage or anything like that. It was nice to see an end to his loneliness though. He and the beautiful fae weren't fated, but they undoubtedly loved each other. And they had both loved my mother dearly, which I believed bonded them closer. It may have seemed odd, but I believed my mother would've wanted them to be happy, regardless of who they found that joy with.

Next, there was Hannah and Jade, followed by my uncle. Jade and Cyrus had been not-so-secretly hooking up whenever he visited this dimension, but neither of them were willing to admit their relation-ship went beyond anything physical. I didn't buy it, but I also knew better than to meddle. The one time I tried to pry, I was firmly reminded that my job as a lunar demigoddess involved *wolf shifter* pairings, not any other beings.

In the second row sat Juniper and her husbands, Ivan and Hunter—*yes, she had two husbands*—and their daughter, Rosalie. After the dust settled with taking over the pack from Alexei's father and getting classes at Redwood University back up and running, I couldn't stop thinking about how forlorn Hunter had been about his missing wolf. As a member of the pack, he knew I was a demigoddess and what I was capable of, so offering him a chance to claim his inner wolf bore no risk. I'd never forget the first time he'd shifted into a stunning silver wolf. He was so visibly elated, so free, I cried buckets of joyful tears.

Evidently, Hunter had already been June and Ivan's secret third for months, and that night, while they were celebrating his new wolf, Hunter had gotten June pregnant. The baby may have encouraged them to make things legal, but I was convinced they'd be a throuple with or without little Rosa in the picture. The best part was that Hunter wasn't ousted from the pack for cross-breeding as he would've been under the prior alpha's leadership. Alexei and I had a firm policy that you could love—and breed—with whomever you wanted, regardless of their species. June and Ivan were members of our pack just as much as Hunter was. And in turn, June, now the High Priestess, considered Alexei and me to be honorary members of her coven.

Moving along the line of our found family... the vampire king flashed a little fang as he smiled adoringly at the beauty by his side. Their story was too complex to get into at the moment, but those two certainly earned their happily ever after. It was pretty dicey for a while, but I was glad they found their way.

There were a lot of happy endings these days, and I was here for it.

"Nicole," Bee whispered at my side. "You okay?"

I startled for a moment, shaking myself out of my musings. Bee gave me a knowing look as she rubbed her heavily pregnant belly, clearly catching me spacing out in the middle of performing a mating ceremony.

Oops.

I cleared my throat. "Sorry. Where was I? Ummm... oh yeah. *Not your typical mating ceremony.* Got it." The audience chuckled teasingly. "As I was saying, when you're gifted by the fates with a mate, they are yours, and you are theirs, until the end of time. Your heart and soul are so consumed by each other there is no room for any other."

My own mate smiled back at me from his position as best man, an honor bestowed upon him much to the annoyance of his beta.

"But that isn't exactly true anymore, is it?" I turned my attention toward my mother-in-law.

She looked radiant in the light blue gown I had designed as she smiled adoringly at the man in front of her. "No. It's not."

General Minifred took her hand, placing a gentle kiss on her knuckles. "To be fair, I never did like to half-ass anything. Right, sweetheart?"

The crowd chuckled.

Anya blushed as her groom winked suggestively.

Alexei groaned, making me giggle. You'd think he'd be used to their over-the-top affection after dealing with it for several years, but as he'd often reminded me, he'd be perfectly happy pretending his mother was a nun and not a hot-blooded woman with perfectly normal desires.

I cleared my throat. "Right. Well... maybe we should keep going before my mate has an aneurysm, yeah?" The audience laughed again. "As I was saying, you are witnessing a moment that'll undoubtedly be in shifter history books for a long time to come. Anya and August are the first known pair to *ever* be blessed with a second chance at a fated pairing. And they are here tonight to solidify that bond. As August and Anya have already recited their vows, our next step is the rings."

A round of quiet *awwwws* sounded from the crowd as four-year-old Ryder, wearing an itty bitty tux, proudly carried a pair of rings to the altar on a satin pillow. He looked so much like his big brother it took my breath away sometimes. Alexei nodded to his sibling, encouraging him to present the rings.

"Here ya go!" his little voice shouted, right before he threw the pillow and ran off to jump on his mommy's lap.

"Whoa!" General Minifred exclaimed. "Good thing my reflexes are still sharp, kid." He untied the gold bands from the pillow, handing one to his bride.

Ryder blushed, tucking his face into his mom's neck. Mara ran her hand over his brown hair, hugging him closely. I would've never thought it was possible, but being a mother had really changed Mara. Jones's betrayal and her subsequent need to move back in with her parents and ask for help was humbling, for sure, but *kind* wasn't a word I'd *ever* use to describe her back then. But the moment Ryder was born, it was as if she'd had a personality transplant. That little boy became her reason for living, and she was an amazing mom. Alexei was convinced his little brother was a future alpha from the day he was born, but when he talked to Mara about it, she was surprisingly reluctant to allow Alexei to train him as such. But one day about six months ago, there was no denying the alpha energy that lived within her son. He was also showing great promise as an influencer, like her. She knew she'd need our help to guide her son on the right path, and we wholeheartedly agreed.

"Please place the rings on each other's fingers," I instructed. August went first, then Anya. After they both wore symbols of their union, I continued. "So, for this ceremony, we obviously don't need to ask the goddess to bless this union." I winked. "But I *will* ask, do you both accept this blessing? Do you understand how special it is and agree to treat each other accordingly?"

"We do," the couple said in unison.

My powers awakened as they agreed, swirling inside of me. I closed my eyes to call them to the surface as I said, "Well, then I officially bless this union. I wish you many years of love and happiness together. Congratulations." When I opened my eyes, August and Anya were sealing their union with a kiss, haloed by the white light that was emitting from me as I absorbed their love for one another.

Alexei joined me as the newlyweds walked away, pulling me into his embrace. "I don't think I'll ever get over how amazing it is watching you do that."

I placed a soft kiss on his lips. "I don't think I'll ever get over watching you lead our pack." I sighed contentedly as he kissed me again. "You were meant to be their alpha."

"Like you were meant to be their luna."

"Like you were meant to be my mate," I added.

We liked to play this little game of one-upping

every once in a while. Had to keep the spark going, right? Not that Alexei and I had *any* trouble igniting some serious heat. Plus, let's face it, my cocky alpha needed his ego checked every once in a while, and I was more than happy to fill that role.

"Like you were meant to be the mother of our future children," he countered.

"Like you were meant to be the father of our future children," I sassed.

Alexei and I had decided we'd adopt one day. Lord knew there were plenty of children in the world who needed a loving home. But the pack and growing my new apparel brand was our priority right now, and we were both perfectly okay with waiting until the time was right.

Alexei leaned into my ear. "Like you were meant to be my forever."

I smiled, conceding defeat on this round. Forever with this man sounded pretty damn good. There was no way I was going to top that because, to me, there was no greater prize.

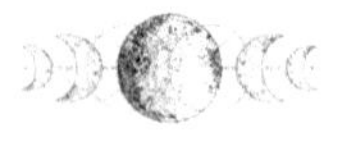